RATTLESNAKE ROAD

A SMALL TOWN MYSTERY ROMANCE

AMANDA MCKINNEY

HH TISEVICH

Paperback ISBN 978-1-7358681-2-7
eBook ISBN 978-1-7358681-1-0

Editor(s):
Pam Berehulke, Bulletproof Editing
Nancy Brown, Redline Proofreading
Cover Design:
Steamy Reads Designs

Amanda McKinney
AUTHOR OF SEXY MURDER MYSTERIES

https://www.amandamckinneyauthor.com

DEDICATION

This is it, Mama. For you, once again. For you, always.

ALSO BY AMANDA MCKINNEY

Lethal Legacy

The Woods (A Berry Springs Novel)

The Lake (A Berry Springs Novel)

The Storm (A Berry Springs Novel)

The Fog (A Berry Springs Novel)

The Creek (A Berry Springs Novel)

The Shadow (A Berry Springs Novel)

The Cave (A Berry Springs Novel)

Devil's Gold (A Black Rose Mystery, Book 1)

Hatchet Hollow (A Black Rose Mystery, Book 2)

Tomb's Tale (A Black Rose Mystery Book 3)

Evil Eye (A Black Rose Mystery Book 4)

Sinister Secrets (A Black Rose Mystery Book 5)

BESTSELLING SERIES:

Cabin 1 (Steele Shadows Security)

Cabin 2 (Steele Shadows Security)

Cabin 3 (Steele Shadows Security)

Phoenix (Steele Shadows Rising)

Jagger (Steele Shadows Investigations)

Ryder (Steele Shadows Investigations)

Rattlesnake Road

★*Redemption Road, coming Summer 2021*★

And many more to come...

AWARDS AND RECOGNITION

THE STORM

Winner of the 2018 Golden Leaf for Romantic Suspense
2018 Maggie Award for Excellence Finalist
2018 Silver Falchion Finalist
2018 Beverley Finalist
2018 Passionate Plume Honorable Mention Recipient

THE FOG

Winner of the 2019 Golden Quill for Romantic Suspense
Winner of the 2019 I Heart Indie Award for Romantic Suspense
2019 Maggie Award of Excellence Finalist
2019 Stiletto Award Finalist

CABIN 1 (STEELE SHADOWS SECURITY)

2020 National Readers Choice Award Finalist
2020 HOLT Medallion Finalist

THE CAVE

2020 Book Buyers Best Finalist
2020 Carla Crown Jewel Finalist

DIRTY BLONDE

2017 2nd Place Winner for It's a Mystery Contest

~

Praise for the #1 Bestselling Steele Shadows Series:

"Holy crap! What a book!" -5 STAR Goodreads Review

"Riveting mystery romance." -5 STAR Amazon Review

"A page-turning blend of suspense, steam, and heartbreaking angst." -5 STAR Amazon Review

"My mind is BLOWN." -Book Blogger, Books and Beauty by Cassie

"A brilliant, raw, breathtaking story. This book should be read by every romantic suspense lover." -5 STAR Goodreads Review

"Wonderful, amusing, absolutely addictive." -5 STAR Amazon Review

"Scorching." -5 STAR Bookbub Review

"My mouth literally hung open when I finished this book. You do not want to miss this one." -5 STAR NetGalley Review

Praise for the Berry Springs Series:

"One of my favorite novels of 2018." -Confessions of an Avid Reader, **The Fog**

"**The Woods** is a sexy, small-town murder mystery that's guaranteed to resonate with fans of Nora Roberts and Karin Slaughter." -Best Thrillers

"Danger, mystery, and sizzling-hot romance right down to the last page." -Amazon Review, **The Creek**

"A dark, ominous thrilling tale spiked with a dash of romance and mystery that captivated me from start to finish..." -The Coffeeholic Bookworm, **The Lake**

"**The Storm** is a beautifully written whodunnit, packed with suspense, danger, and hot romance. Kept me guessing who the murderer was. I couldn't put it down!" -Amazon Review

"I devoured **The Cave** in one sitting. Best one yet." -Amazon Review

"**The Shadow** is a suspense-filled, sexy as hell book." -Bookbub Review

LET'S CONNECT!

Text **AMANDABOOKS to 66866** to sign up for Amanda's Newsletter and get the latest on new releases, promos, and freebies! (Don't worry, I have no access to your phone number after you sign up.) Or, you can sign up below.

Amanda
MCKINNEY
AUTHOR OF SEXY MURDER MYSTERIES

https://www.amandamckinneyauthor.com

RATTLESNAKE ROAD

Everyone hits rock bottom, only the brave escape.

Welcome to 1314 Rattlesnake Road.

A quaint two-bedroom log cabin nestled deep in the woods of the small, southern town of Berry Springs—the perfect hideaway to escape your past.

Tucked inside thick, mahogany walls lay mysterious letters, forgotten and untouched for decades. Floor-to-ceiling windows frame breathtaking views of jagged cliffs, deep valleys, and endless lies. Mature oak trees, tall enough to touch the clouds, carry the whispers of the haunted, of stories untold.

Inside sits Grey Dalton, emotionally battered and bruised, her only wish to pick up the broken pieces of her life. But outside, await two men, one a tattooed cowboy, the other a dashing businessman.

One will steal her heart, the other, her soul.

Rattlesnake Road is a standalone mystery romance about love, loss, hitting rock bottom, and clawing your way to the other side.

Your escape awaits...

Praise for Rattlesnake Road:

★ "A dark, **edge-gripping emotional read**." - *Obsessive Reads*

★ "Strong characterization bolsters this **profound, romantic tale**." - *Kirkus Review*

★ "One of those books where you keep telling yourself 'just one more chapter.'" – *Life According to Jaime*

★ "**Raw. Real. Absolutely enthralling.** Hand's down, one of the best books I've read." – *Goodreads Review*

★ "You know sometimes the **best romances** are the ones that rip your heart out, tear it up, and patch it back together even better than before. This is one of those. - *Bookbub Review*

★ "I devoured Grey and Declan's emotional story. A truly **captivating must-read**." - *Mum Reader Dreamer*

★ "Makes your gut clinch and your **heart sing**." – *BookBub Review*

★ "Intense, emotional, hot sexy characters, and an **ending that leaves you breathless**." - *Goodreads Review*

★ "A **brilliant read**." - *Crazy Kalm*

★ "No sugarcoating. **No bullshit.** Real life. Real people. Real conversations." - *Kikke Reads*

★ "The **most intense book I've ever read.** Superb storyline, real characters." - *Bookbub Review*

★ "**I did not see that ending coming.** A shocking, five-star read." - *Goodreads Review*

Fair Warning: Due to serious subject matter and mature content, please be aware that this book might be an emotional trigger for some readers.

1

My hands trembled as I took the pills. Two doses of four pills, taken four hours apart.

Eight hours, and this nightmare would be over. This completely unexpected, slap-you-in-the-face nightmare.

I often look back on that day, thinking that if things hadn't happened the way they did, how different my life would have been.

It wouldn't have been a lie when I promised "for better or for worse." It wouldn't have been a lie when I told myself I had everything under control.

I might have become a PTA mom, the mother of two strapping young boys, whose greatest worry in life was snagging her eight-karat diamond ring on her cashmere sweater. A trophy wife, a gracious hostess, a homemaker in our many homes across the world.

My life would be easy. Secure. Simple.

Until it wasn't.

Before the day that changed all that, I foolishly considered my life to be stable and controlled. *My* life. But the assumption that my life was my own was the biggest misconception of all.

The reality is that our lives are not our own.

Instead, our lives are a culmination of events, most of which are out of our control, governed by the ripple effect of our reactions to those events. We fight that knowledge, deny it, numb it with drugs and alcohol, but at the end of the day, we're all merely the point of a pendulum slowly being pulled back, waiting until the day we're released to our fate.

This was my day.

The day the universe let go. The beginning of a journey that took me to the deepest depths of hell.

I remember the hyper-awareness of that morning. The way the single bead of sweat trickled down my back as I paced back and forth. My heart, a pounding staccato, in sync with that stupid instrumental jazz music my husband demanded play through the speakers of our Upper East Side penthouse suite. Every day—every *single* day—starting at six a.m. The kitchen stank like old, burned coffee from the pot I'd started an hour earlier but had yet to drink.

My palms were cold and clammy as I wrung my hands, staring at the city beyond the window, still concealed in shadows although the sun had risen not long ago.

"You took them?"

Startled at the deep voice behind me, I turned.

Tucking his navy dress shirt into his Tom Ford slacks, William stepped into the kitchen, his dark hair wet from a shower and combed flawlessly to the side, as usual.

Disdain brewed in my churning stomach as I took in the perfection of my husband. While William had been enjoying a shower, I'd been fighting off a panic attack, clutching a prescription bottle in my hand.

Words weren't able to penetrate the haze of my

emotions, so I simply nodded in response. The last fake response in a house built on lies.

"Okay." William returned my nod while he adjusted his shirt to his liking. "It will all be over soon."

Blinking, I stilled. *It will all be over soon.* His unfeeling response to my suffering was like a knife through my heart.

Satisfied with his shirt, William refocused on me. He crossed the kitchen and opened his arms. My movements were as stiff as a wooden doll as I enclosed them around him, the bottom half of our bodies not even touching. He smelled like exotic fruit, a new cologne, and I wondered which of his whores had gifted it to him after he'd spent an hour between her legs.

It smelled like passion fruit, the scent loud, obnoxious, stinging, arrogant. I hated it. I hated him for going about his normal morning routine while I was experiencing the worst agony of my life. Of our life. It should be *our* life, not just mine.

Despite the shower, he was cold. Or maybe *we* were cold.

William stroked the back of my tangled hair and kissed my forehead in mindless habit, the brief touch like poison on my skin. I pulled back, suddenly suffocating, welcoming the space between us like a breath of fresh air.

Having done his husbandly duty of checking on me, William turned and left the room. Numb, I stared at the empty space where he'd stood until he returned a minute later in his matching suit jacket, looking like a million bucks. Or ten million, if you considered his bank account.

I, on the other hand, was still wearing my wrinkled pajama T-shirt under a robe draped haphazardly over my shoulders. I was barefoot, having kicked off my slippers when the sweat started.

Unlike William, my normal routine was the last thing on my mind.

He eyed me warily as he breezed past, like one might a new patient at a psychiatric ward. He plucked his keys from their designated spot on the console table in the entryway by the front door.

A moment passed as we stared at each other from across the room. He broke first.

"Call me if you need anything."

I nodded, cursing the flood of tears building behind my eyes. Another tense moment passed as we simply looked at each other—another moment of pretending I was okay before my husband disappeared out the door.

After all, he had places to go.

A rush of air escaped my lungs as I heard the lock slide into place behind him. I was alone.

Alone.

My heart rate tripled, and I wondered if I was having a reaction to the pills—which spun me into an entirely new level of anxiety. I took a deep breath, and another, then another.

Call me if you need anything.

That's what I got from my husband before he left, and that's all I got from him all morning. Not a phone call or a text message. Not even flowers.

Looking back, that day was the nail in the coffin of our marriage.

It was the one day—the one *freaking* day—that I, the stubborn, fiercely independent Grey Dalton, *needed* my husband. Was it too much to ask for him to be sympathetic, to console me? To care?

But I didn't ask him to stay, to be there for me, and maybe that was the problem.

The thing is, I didn't want to have to say the words, "I need you." I wanted my husband to just know. To *want* to be there for me, if only from the other side of the bathroom door. I wouldn't have asked him to hold my hand, to wait on me hand and foot, to cry with me. I simply wanted someone there.

But William didn't show up for me that day.

The last day.

I took another deep breath and reminded myself—or tried to convince myself, rather—that I was strong.

"I can handle this," I whispered, sniffling back the tears.

I can make peace with this.

I'm better alone.

Always have been.

I began pacing again, my sole focus on my stomach—every cramp, every twinge, magnified by a thousand percent.

For a few minutes, I thought I might have a heart attack. I'd never in my life felt such emotion as on that day.

Is it happening? I obsessed with every sensation in my body, the nerves, the anxiety like a tornado shredding my insides.

Ironic.

Thirty minutes ticked by with agonizing slowness, and I realized it wasn't going to happen immediately, as I'd hoped. The doctor told me it could take a full twenty-four hours, and in some cases, would require another dose of medicine.

I also realized I couldn't go through the entire day pacing the kitchen in crazed anticipation, so I began busying myself with chores. Dishes, dusting, laundry. Crying in between.

William texted sometime around lunch asking if it "had happened yet."

No.

Ironically, the cramps and bleeding started five minutes later. I ran to the bathroom, my heart pounding as I sat on the toilet. Waiting.

Nothing.

Confused and distraught, I forced myself to stand up again and stumbled out of the bathroom.

More laundry, organizing cabinets. Tears. Waiting.

After four hours, I took four more pills. More busy work, although this work included taking breaks to double over in pain. Excruciating pain. I wondered if that was what birth felt like.

What a mind fuck.

After nine hours—a full day—instinct had me retreating to the bathroom. I took my place on the ice-cold toilet seat and locked eyes with the ratty teddy bear I'd placed on the bathroom floor in front of me so I wouldn't feel so alone.

I settled in and began to cry.

We stared at each other, the bear and me, my expression riddled with fear, his steady. Strong.

You're not alone, he seemed to whisper.

I wept as it started to happen, but kept my focus on the bear. He was my strength that day.

You're not alone.

I screamed out in pain, in pleading sobs as I felt it—he or she, I didn't even know what to call it—slip out of me.

A loneliness, dark and heavy, invaded my soul like a virus, slowly consuming my spirit. My light.

I physically felt a shift inside me that day—the day I aborted the two-month-old baby that had died in my belly weeks earlier. A missed miscarriage, the doctor had called it.

After removing the fetus from the bottom of the toilet, I wrapped it in paper towels and frantically looked around our penthouse suite, not knowing what to do, where to put it. My gaze landed on the lavender plant that I kept next to the window in our bedroom.

William hated the plant, constantly complaining that it resembled an ugly weed when it wasn't blooming. But, oh, when it bloomed, it was glorious. Lavender represented calm and healing. Something about that plant drew me.

It represented my baby, I decided that day.

With tears streaming down my face and blood running down my legs, I buried her in the soil of the plant. My baby was a girl, I somehow knew then. I named her Violet.

In that moment, I sensed that my life had taken a turn and would never be the same again. The pendulum had been released, and I'd started my free fall.

I fell to the floor in a mess of heaving sobs, my strength gone. I pulled my knees to my chest and closed my eyes.

Help me, I begged. *If you're there, please help me.*

I need you.

I need someone.

My eyes fluttered open, my teary gaze focusing on the stuffed bear that had been with me through the journey. I squinted, reading the small stitching on the bottom of his left foot that I'd never noticed before. It read SERENITY.

"Serenity," I whispered, my voice weak and lifeless. I closed my eyes again as tears overtook me and my mind wandered.

To accept the things I cannot change, courage to change the things I can, and the wisdom to know the difference.

If you're there, help me.

Help me. I'm listening.

I could really use some help right now.

A cool breeze floated in from the open window, sweeping over my heated skin like silk.

I took a deep breath.

The seasons were changing. I could feel it in the air, in my soul.

Yes, things were changing.

Little did I know I had to hit rock bottom first.

2

Two months later...

It was an evening of glitz, glamour, and endless champagne. Harp Magazines spared no expense at its annual employee recognition banquet. The black-tie event was held on the heels of the annual meeting that brought in top-level management from all over the world.

Men mingled, postured, hunted in their tuxedos and bow ties, with little white tan lines on their ring fingers where their wedding bands had curiously escaped them for the evening.

Women gossiped, teased, winked from behind their mink eyelashes. Up-and-coming New York designers socialized among them, interjecting their perfectly rehearsed sales pitches. Half of them I'd invited myself, all of whom were waiting for me to join them in the ballroom.

The thing was, I couldn't feel my lips, let alone carry on a coherent conversation.

I wasn't quite sure when I'd crossed that thin line between being "pleasantly buzzed" to "knee-walking drunk," but assumed it was somewhere between the words "vodka," and "make this one a double."

I checked over my shoulder for the tenth time, my gaze sweeping the bottom of the stalls behind me to ensure I was alone in the hotel restroom.

I pulled the flask from my perfectly organized Fendi purse, clumsily opening it before tipping it to my lips, and blinked with confusion when nothing came out. I didn't remember emptying it. With an exaggerated sigh that could have lit the building on fire had there been a candle burning nearby, I screwed on the lid and tucked the flask back into its secret spot.

As I stood there a minute, I tried to wrangle my incoherent thoughts into a plan. I decided I needed more lip gloss.

Squinting for focus, I leaned over the gold-plated sink until my nose was inches from the mirror, willing the two heads on my shoulders to merge back into one. The beachy waves I'd given my long dark hair had fallen limp, now clumped together in stringy strands and frizzed at the ends, much like Medusa, the dreadful and fearsome beast. Ironic, and definitely not good for the year's hottest fashion event.

The navy eyeliner I'd applied earlier to my blue eyes was smudged at the bottom, a smoky look I hadn't intended. My blush was somehow gone. I looked pale. Worn. Older than my thirty-one years.

Does my dress look okay?

The full-length mirror at the end of the restroom didn't lie. I wrinkled my nose at the ten extra pounds I'd gained in the last few months. Although I had to admit, they were hidden well on my five-foot-nine-inch frame under a pair of Spanx.

I'd learned how to hide many things well over the last few months. Emotions, wine bottles, vibrators.

Turning back to the counter, I reached into the neckline of my gray Gucci cocktail dress and repositioned my barely B-cup breasts, giving myself temporary cleavage. Impressed, I leaned in for a shimmy.

The movement set off the sensor on the faucet, causing water to blast into the sink and splash onto the front of my dress. I yelped and jumped back, dropping my lip gloss, and then desperately grabbed the sink for stability.

"Shit." I wanted to laugh, but it was an expensive dress.

Not that I'd paid for it.

Designer garments were given to me weekly in hopes I'd feature the designer in an article, or better yet, on the front page of the online magazine I ran. I hadn't paid for clothes in years, but that certainly didn't make them any less special to me. When you grew up the way I did, material things become far more than simple necessities. Each was coveted, guarded, hung on to with bloody fingernails.

My first designer piece was a monogrammed Louis Vuitton canvas purse. I paid for it myself, in cash. The moment meant so much more than simply getting a new purse. It meant my circumstances were changing.

I still had that purse. It was wrapped in a silk bag, tucked safely in the section labeled handbags in my obnoxiously large closet.

I lived for fashion. Respected it. Respected what it took to make it, to design it. To obtain it. Every step of the process of making a luxury garment fascinated me, from the fabric choices to the color palette, the design, the cut, the accessories, the presentation.

Nothing made me feel more capable than slipping into a couture suit. Powerful. A woman with the world at her fingertips. In control. Happy.

Everything I wasn't.

And everything my Gucci dress wasn't at that moment.

I began madly wiping down the front of it, the light gray fabric darkening to black as water seeped through the fibers. The black splotch spread across my torso, a few dots of it circling my nipple like a bull's-eye.

Paper towels rained down around me as I aggressively plucked what I needed from the dispenser. One fluttered over my forehead, startling me. I wobbled, but caught my balance and recovered. Over the last eight weeks, I'd become almost as good at wobbling on heels as walking on eggshells.

I was wiping—shredding—a paper towel against my stomach when my phone beeped. Checking it, I found I had fourteen missed texts.

Fourteen. How long have I been gone?

I needed another drink, but knew I couldn't go to the three bars I'd already been to in the massive hotel. People might notice.

I clicked open my internet browser to google bars near me, and frowned at my last search.

Where to hire a penis investigator

Damn autocorrect. More accurate searches followed—

Private investigator fee
Best private investigator
Private investigator near me
Henry Cavill no shirt

And for the grand finale:

Where to buy the rabbit

I startled when the restroom door swung open to admit two giggling blondes in matching black cocktail dresses and six-inch stripper heels. A cloud of cheap vanilla-scented perfume assaulted my nose as the door closed behind them. Barely twenty-one, if I had to guess. Still young and hopeful, not yet jaded by the real world.

I recognized one girl instantly. Disdain brewed like fire in my stomach, the security footage my buddy had shown only me flashing behind my eyes. Kat was her name. Of course it was Kat. The new stylist—or assistant stylist, I wasn't sure which—was the latest in a long line of the boss's mistresses.

The other girl was the barista at the in-house coffee shop. Based on the bauble on her left ring finger, making coffee wasn't her only talent.

Quite a duo.

They'd done themselves up for the banquet, a thinly veiled attempt to posture for future promotions, as I'd done many years earlier, fresh out of college. Although, back then, my baubles were purchased from a cloaked man in the alley outside my studio apartment, and my Prada was a Prado, purchased along with a Diet Coke from a hot peanut stand.

Look at me now.

The girls went silent when they saw me, their eyes rounding as if they were a pair of third graders passing the principal alone in the hallway. They jerked their shoulders back, and I imagined them chanting in their heads, *Act sober, act sober, act sober.*

"Mrs. Dalton," one said, greeting me with a mature dip of her chin.

I inwardly cringed at the sound of my last name, but forced a smile. "Good evening, ladies." I hated the tone of my voice, so practiced. Polished.

"You look beautiful," the other said.

"Yeah, I *love* your dress."

My lips twisted into a smile. "So does the water faucet."

They laughed at this.

Yes, I'm very, very funny. All the time.

I waited until the girls went into their respective stalls before dropping the facade and hurrying over to the dryer. Paper towels weren't cutting it, and I needed to get out of there fast. The dryer clicked on at tornadic speed.

Bending like a pretzel, I froze in position under the dryer, willing it to hurry the hell up.

Toilets flushed and I quickly straightened, my back popping like a twenty-one-gun salute as I quickly shuffled back to the sink. My dress was still damp, but not as noticeably, and I decided it would have to do.

The girls washed their hands in unison, side-eyeing me as I put the makeup I didn't remember laying out on the counter back into my purse.

"I haven't seen your husband tonight, Mrs. Dalton."

"No, you wouldn't have. He's out of town this week."

"That's a shame."

"Is it?" I snapped, my voice suddenly ice cold. The mention of his name set off a bomb inside me, inciting the anger I'd tried so hard to contain. Infidelity had a way of throwing even the most composed woman off-kilter.

Turning, I grabbed my purse and nodded to the red silk string peeking out of the side of Kat's Prada handbag.

"Might wanna tuck that thong into a side pocket, Kat.

God forbid someone recognize it from the security footage of you sucking off Mr. Devlin in the concierge lounge last week."

Dropping the metaphorical microphone, I turned and made my exit, instantly regretting the barb.

Shit, shit, shit.

My damn mouth.

The door slapped shut behind me as I ground my teeth, wanting to punch a hole in the wall. I'd lost my cool—again.

"Grey!" a voice called out from the distance.

Dammit, dammit, dammit.

I quickly turned a corner, hoping it would go away. It didn't.

"Grey! Hey, Grey. Stop."

Inhaling and forcing a smile, I stopped and turned to see Chance, the art director of *Catwalk Magazine*, striding my way in a maroon paisley jacquard jacket and eyeliner to match. His patent leather wingtips snapped like tap shoes against the marble of the hotel foyer.

A wave of nausea washed over me, the last two shots of vodka beginning to take their final hold. I reveled in it.

My hand was unsteady as I pulled a breath mint from my clutch. I popped it in my mouth and drew in a breath.

"What the hell are you doing, girl?" He gasped. "And what *the hell* happened to your Gucci?"

"Water."

"Oh God." Chance began frantically wiping down my dress, his hands sweeping over my breasts drawing attention from bystanders. If not for the fact he preferred male companionship, I might have slapped him.

"Oh dear. Well." He stepped back and cocked his head. "It kinda looks like it's supposed to be there. Abstract design, you know. Come on. You're needed at the banquet."

"Needed?"

"Yep." He winked, looping his arm through mine. "Come on."

Before I could protest, I was pulled across the lobby. My sole focus became not why I was needed, but instead staying upright in my heels.

Left, right, left, right, left, right. I clomped like a Clydesdale across the marble, avoiding eye contact with the curious glances cast in my direction.

The scent of Chanel mingled with chicken marsala as I was pulled into the ballroom. The crystal chandeliers had dimmed since I'd last been in the room—*thank God*—and the music had been replaced by a monotone male voice over a speaker, which was almost as excruciating as the lights.

I recognized the voice as belonging to the president of Harp's North American magazines. Otherwise known internally as Golden Dick Devlin, father to three teenage misfits, and husband to a wife who turned her cheek to everything other than her bible.

Cheating bastard.

The room was dead quiet, so I assumed he was saying something of great importance. I concentrated to listen.

"*. . . after graduating magna cum laude with a dual degree in business and communications and a minor in journalism, this tenacious woman began her career with us as an intern, where she worked her way up to editorial assistant within thirteen months. Two years later, she turned her pet project,* Catwalk Magazine, *into the number-three online magazine for young adults in the United States. She's also responsible for launching the career of one of the hottest new designers, Miss Abby Ross, who now remains loyal to our magazines, giving us exclusives and first-looks. Her grit, determination, willingness to get her hands dirty, and unprecedented work ethic is why we are naming*

Catwalk Magazine's *editor-in-chief, Grey Dalton, this year's recipient of the Harp Heart Award for Excellence."*

I stumbled, trying to piece together what was happening.

Chance caught me while releasing a loud squeal of excitement. "You got it! You got it, girl!"

A glass of champagne was shoved into my hand. All eyes turned to me, the roar of applause not nearly as loud as my racing heartbeat.

"Get up onstage. Go! Get your award!"

Holy. Shit.

A speech? I had to deliver a freaking speech.

My mouth went dry—like cotton-ball-between-the-cheeks dry—and I frantically searched for a glass of water. But before I could quench my thirst, I was pushed onto the first step of the stage.

What felt like a nuclear blast of heat washed over my skin as the spotlight captured me. Sweat beaded on my forehead and under my arms, and I suddenly felt like I was on a sailboat in the middle of a hurricane. My pulse was roaring, my stomach swirling. I swallowed the knot in my throat and blinked a few times.

As I took the next step, I stumbled. *Act sober, act sober, act sober.* By the grace of God, I made it onto the stage.

Golden Dick Devlin reached out his hand, soft as a baby's butt from time spent behind a desk, avoiding manual labor almost as much as he avoided his wife. All I could see was the grainy surveillance footage of him sitting in a chair with his head tilted back, his hands gripping Kat's head, guiding her lips over his cock as he saw fit. Then dismissing her with a dip of his chin after he blew his wad all over her face and throat.

An all-too-familiar image at that moment.

I thought of my dear husband as I accepted the award statuette from my boss, wondering if anyone had ever called William "Golden Dick Dalton."

The light was blinding as I stepped up to the lectern. I took a moment to let my eyes adjust to the crowd with their fake smiles, fake teeth, fake tits, fake marriages. The image began to waver. I took a step back, then forward again, using my elbows to steady myself as I resumed my position behind the lectern.

I. Am. Wasted. I finally had to acknowledge that fact. *Focus on one spot,* I told myself through the haze.

I picked a chair, any chair to focus on—and saw her.

Her. In a blood-red, low-cut, knock-off Zac Posen number emphasizing a pair of hot-air balloons below her chin.

Bitch.

I set my godawful obnoxious golden statue award on the lectern with a thud. Next to it went my half-spilled flute of champagne.

The crowd went silent.

"Well . . ." A fake smile cracked my face as I looked down on the crowd. "This is almost as unexpected as finding out your baby doesn't have a heartbeat at your two-month ultrasound."

Correction—*now* the crowd was silent.

Despite my better judgment, I continued. Because *wow, that felt good.* I cocked my hip, settling in behind the microphone.

"But the silver lining there is that when you're employed with a company as stellar as Harp Magazines, you're given all the time off you need, as long as it includes answering emails and phone calls from nine to five while you recuperate, and making late-night visits to the twenty-third-floor concierge lounge." I looked over my shoulder. "So, thank you for that, Mr. Devlin, whose generosity extends far beyond paid time off, to the pearl necklaces he so graciously gifts our new hires."

I turned back to the crowd with a chuckle. "Seriously, though."

I paused to take a sip of my champagne.

"Devlin here mentioned the eight years I worked as an editorial assistant—an editorial assistant with more education and experience than both my male and female counterparts combined. Competency aside, I was blessed to work with exceptional talent during those years as an assistant living barely above the poverty line."

Smiling, I said, "So, on that note, I'd like to thank Leslie Monroe, fellow editorial assistant, who was promoted after only eight months into her position after bending over Carl Hunt's desk during the office Christmas party, giving an entirely new meaning to icing the cake. And to the incomparable Kylie Conner, promoted only ten months after being hired, who spent more time in Cecil Davie's closet than his wife. And finally, dear Marylin Peachtree, the faithful assistant whose daily Caesar salad wasn't the only thing she tossed inside of Sir Walter Harrison's office."

Ignoring the shocked faces in the crowd, I plowed on.

"Yet, after watching these ambitious women get promoted ahead of me for their *hard work*—and I use the term *hard* loosely—here I stand, accepting an award of excellence that has nothing to do with my ability to fake an orgasm. Which, by the way, is gold-medal worthy. I am accepting this award on behalf of those women here at Harp Magazines unwilling to sacrifice their dignity for a promotion. You know, all two of you—Bella, the company labradoodle, and Dolce, the aggressively large rat that lives in my office."

Unsteady, I raised my glass, spilling more champagne, and focused my fury on the blond bitch in the front row, otherwise known as my husband's mistress.

"And last, but certainly not least, I'd like to thank my loving husband who, despite having a masters from Harvard, was unaware that his cell phone automatically connected to his new iPad, thereby receiving copies of all his text messages."

I stepped out from behind the podium. "And to Paula, right there in the front row, whose ability to find a selfie angle that doesn't highlight her crooked dollar-store titties is only outdone by the number of fingers she can cram in her own asshole."

The last thing I saw was my left Louboutin spinning toward my face as I tumbled off the stage.

3

After waking up in the back seat of an Uber with my head in Chance's lap and one foot out the window, I was carried up to my penthouse suite, given two aspirin and a bottle of water, and tucked into bed.

Five hours later, I woke up with a sunbeam scorching my retinas and a machete piercing my temples. I lay there, quiet and unmoving, as I tried to piece together the events from the banquet the night before.

Not that I really needed to, because my phone had been ringing nonstop with dozens of calls and text messages asking what the hell I was doing, and what was wrong with me. A few even sent laughing emojis accompanied with pictures of pearl necklaces.

But it was the text moments after I awoke that really got my blood pumping. It was a message (I'd missed the call) from my boss, Golden Dick Devlin, requesting to meet me for coffee. *Meet for coffee.* I knew exactly what that meant.

So I pulled myself together the best I could, thanking my lucky stars that William was still overseas on his business trip. He hadn't texted or called, as usual, so I wasn't sure if the gossip from New York City had crossed the Atlantic yet. I had no doubt it would, and soon.

With a jackhammer pounding inside my skull, I sat stoically across from my boss, who was dressed to the nines in his five-thousand-dollar suit, as I was fired from the only thing I'd ever loved. Effective immediately.

I was informed that my assistant would gather my things and have them delivered to my home by the end of the day. I wasn't allowed back into the building—something about bringing down the company morale. As if I hadn't obliterated it enough the night before.

Not bothering to argue, I didn't defend myself or my actions. I simply picked up my purse, held my shoulders back, and walked to the first bar I saw. By noon, I was passed out on my bathroom floor in a puddle of my own vomit.

I remember waking up, wiping chunks of vomit from my mouth, and wondering what life would be . . . without it.

And that was it. The moment I knew I needed to make a change. Nothing good would come from the path I was barreling down with reckless abandon.

I needed to leave my cheating husband, the one who I was certain I'd never been in love with in the first place.

I needed to leave the city, the chaos, the speed, the noise.

And I needed to quit drinking.

So, in the haze of PMS and a red-wine hangover, I packed five suitcases with only the necessities and a few sentimental possessions, then left a note for William on the bed, telling him I was leaving and I wanted a divorce. Short, sweet, to the point. Because that was all I had in me at the moment.

The last thing I did in my beautiful penthouse suite was brew a mug of coffee. And for the first time in sixty-four days, I skipped the Baileys.

With my hair twisted into a messy knot on top of my head, bags hanging from my shoulders and tears in my eyes, I took the first step out of the life I'd spent the last ten years building.

The first step into the past that I promised myself I'd never return to again.

4

Buckeye's Motel was like something out of a nightmare, a long, decrepit one-story brick building in the middle of nowhere. Lights flickered from behind curtains drawn tightly against cracked windows. On the roof, a large flashing sign simply read OTEL. Apparently, the M was silent.

Flexing my gloved fingers as I pulled into the parking lot, I sighed because a groan would have taken too much energy. It had been a full day of driving, fighting nerves that crept up with every mile, it seemed, and a headache that had grown to migraine levels.

Somewhere between New Jersey and Pennsylvania, I'd taken down the top of my BMW to fight the random sweats my body would break out into, shedding a layer of clothes, only to pull them back on an hour later. Eventually, I settled on a wool peacoat, a cashmere scarf, and a fuzzy beanie that I could rip off at a moment's notice. Although spring was in full bloom, the temperatures had dropped to the mid-fifties when the sun went down. I was weak and tired—everything that told me I needed to pull over and get some sleep.

Three run-down pickup trucks were parked in front of thin motel doors painted a deep evergreen. Noticing a Buckeyes bumper sticker on one, I realized I must have crossed over into Ohio at some point. Under a flickering streetlight sat two 18-wheelers, one glowing with running lights.

I parked my BMW in front of a blinking office light, secured the top, and after a wary glance over my shoulder, got out. The asphalt parking lot was cracked, warped from years of in-and-out guests who probably paid by the hour.

A bell jangled on the office's glass door as I pulled it open and walked inside, greeted by the odors of stale cigarette smoke and burned coffee. Large fluorescent ceiling lights—the kind that reminded me of my elementary school cafeteria—cast a blinding glow over once-white walls now stained yellow from years of cigarette smoke.

Behind a counter was a door, cracked open enough that I could hear the murmur of the evening news reporting on a local drive-by shooting. To my left, two mismatched plastic chairs flanked an end table with a dish of faded potpourri in the center. A few crumpled Reese's cups wrappers littered the floor.

"Just a minute," a low, raspy voice called out from behind the cracked door.

A chair scraped across tile, and it sounded like something fell to the floor, followed by quick shuffles. To my surprise, the door opened to a woman pushing eighty, I assumed, based on her thinning gray hair and widow's hump. She wore a brown sweater under a striped wool coat, and thick glasses on the tip of her nose.

"Need a room?" she croaked.

"Yes, please."

She eyed me a moment, then turned her focus to the computer, her acrylic nails clicking on the keys. "All night?"

I bit back a gag. "Yes."

"How many?"

"One."

"How many nights?"

"One."

"That'll be sixty-nine even."

Was the fee ironic? Too tired to overthink it, I handed her my credit card. The woman didn't even ask for my name. Just returned my credit card after swiping it, along with a key card for my room.

"Room seven. Coffee in here in the mornings, if you need it. Bar at the far end of the motel. Got snack food if you're hungry."

She said something else about parking, but I was still hung up on the word *bar.*

"Thank you."

The woman grunted before turning to disappear back into her den.

My motel room was exactly as I'd expected. A pair of double beds with obnoxious paper-thin brown comforters dominated a room with stained brown carpet. A small TV sat on a chest of drawers, next to a single window covered with a black curtain. A round seventies-era chair was tucked into the corner next to the bathroom, which had a small shower, a toilet, and a cracked mirror over a single sink. Inside the nightstand was a Bible, its spine yet to be cracked.

I set my Prada purse on the bed and stood in the silence a minute with one word pummeling my thoughts.

Bar.

Bar.

Bar.

No, no, no.

Gritting my teeth, I grabbed the remote and sank onto

the end of the bed, clicking on the TV. I shifted, then shifted again, one foot nervously tapping the carpet. After ten minutes of HGTV, I decided I needed to do something with my hands. Drink something.

I grabbed a dollar, walked to the drink machine outside, and bought a Sprite. Returned to my room and chugged it.

Checked my email, for no reason at all. Checked my Nordstrom app, found a cute coat, then remembered that I didn't have a job.

More HGTV.

I checked my map app again, tracing the path I'd chosen. Eleven hours to go. Nerves rippled through my stomach. I set the phone aside.

Another visit to the drink machine, this time for a Coke.

More HGTV, although this episode was impossible to hear due to the sound of squeaking mattress springs from the next room, accompanied by groans, slaps, and words I hadn't heard since I caught my husband watching BDSM in the middle of the night. The distinctive smell of pot wafted through the vents. Annoyed, I turned my head toward the paper-thin wall behind me that was vibrating with each thrust.

Cursing silently, I pushed off the edge of the bed, weighing my options. Confront the stoned porn stars and report them to the front desk—in which case, they'd know it was me—or leave the room. I contemplated this last option with an angel on my shoulder. If I left the room, there was only one place I was going, and it involved copious amounts of alcohol.

"Dammit," I spat out.

Unsure what to do, I stared at the room that was my home for the evening, taking in its stained walls, ripped carpet, and cracked windows. My pulse kick-started with anxiety. Fear. Regret.

What. The hell. Did I do?

Panic at the realization that I'd left my entire life behind burst through my veins, the headache between my temples roaring now.

My thoughts spinning, I began pacing.

Should I go back? *Could* I go back? Rip up the note I'd left for my husband and simply pretend it never happened?

I checked my phone. Still nothing from William.

Shit, shit, shit.

Pitched screams and gasps vibrated through the wall, startling me and making the hair on the back of my neck stand on end.

I closed my eyes and took a deep breath. Then another, and another.

Nothing helped.

I was on the verge of a panic attack and needed to calm down.

More screams, more slaps against bare skin.

Grabbing the remote, I sank onto the end of the bed, turned up the volume, and tried to block everything out. The sounds on the other side of the wall, the sounds in my head, the need for more booze.

The rest of the night went something like this . . .

10:38 p.m.: Began pacing. Sweating. Freaking the F out.

11:14 p.m.: Hands began to shake. Headache worsened. Ran to toilet, dry heaved.

12:14 a.m.: Popped two more aspirin and wondered how to fashion a shiv from a ballpoint pen.

12:44 a.m.: Cried myself to sleep on the floor with the Bible clutched to my chest.

5

Two days and seven hundred miles later . . .

Two days with no booze. Two days of aspirin every six hours. Two days of incessantly checking my cell phone, looking for a call or text from my husband, shamelessly begging me to come back.

It never came.

I had no doubt William had heard the gossip by that time. If not from his mistress, then from any of the hundreds of people at the banquet where I fell off the stage after roasting my boss.

My husband's lack of response or communication was typical of how we addressed problems in our marriage—we didn't. His lack of communication was meant to tell me that he was so mad at me, so embarrassed, that he couldn't even stomach talking to me. William knew he was torturing me, and he reveled in it.

According to the itinerary he'd emailed me before he

left, William wasn't due back from his business trip until late that evening, which meant he hadn't yet found my letter demanding a divorce. The letter that half of me wished he'd never find. The letter that half of me regretted.

It had been two days of wanting to call him but forcing myself not to, then berating myself for being so weak. Two days of analyzing every single moment in our relationship, which was doomed from the start, really.

My husband and I were from very different backgrounds.

William was born with a silver spoon, the son of a prominent New York lawyer who owned a prestigious law firm that raked in millions a year, this income on top of old, inherited family money. William not only appreciated luxury, he demanded it.

I, on the other hand, grew up with my single mother in the sticks of upstate New York with no central air and heat, and less than that on the dinner table. I didn't know my father. He left my mom and me when I was two years old. I knew lots of men, though, none of whom were my father, if you catch my drift. I was always third in my mother's priorities. First was alcohol. Second was men. And in a distant last place was me.

I spent my childhood learning how to become a woman from reading *Teen* magazine and *Are You There God? It's Me, Margaret.* Unfortunately, neither delved into how to deal with hormones or how to freshen clothes that hadn't been washed in a week.

I was the poor girl in school. I didn't realize it at first because, to me, living "less than" was simply life. But I remember the exact moment that I came to realize my life was different from everyone else's.

It was the sixth grade. School had just started, and my

little town was in the middle of a record heat wave. I was waiting in line at the school bus when a pair of junior high girls behind me started giggling. I knew it was about me, but I couldn't make out the whispers. Until I sat down on the hot pleather seat—until I smelled myself. To this day, I'd never felt such humiliation in my life. I, Grey Dalton, was the stinky kid in class.

That very day, I made a vow to myself that I was going to have a lot of money someday. "Boatloads of it," according to the diary I'd kept beneath my mattress, and that I would "never end up like my mother." Two decades later, I'd followed through on that promise. But what I realized driving all those hundreds of miles was that I hadn't done it on my own. I didn't live in a penthouse suite on the Upper East Side because of *my* checking account.

I wondered if I subconsciously married William because of his money. If I'd been more drawn to his lifestyle than to him.

When I found out I was pregnant, I was elated. Not because William was the father, or that we were going to become a family together, but because I was finally going to get the chance to be the mom I'd always wanted to be.

And this was where stuff got really screwed up.

When I learned the baby inside me wasn't alive and I would have to force the miscarriage, it was the worst grief I'd ever felt. But this heartache was soon followed by a weird sense of relief.

I began to think about all the things I could do again now that I was no longer pregnant. The things I didn't have to worry about anymore—like a miscarriage, because, well, that already happened—and what I couldn't eat and drink, lotions and skincare that I couldn't use, being careful to avoid getting overheated, sick, stressed, making sure to sleep on my right side. And last, but certainly not least, I could release the worry about having a baby with a man I knew I wasn't madly in love with.

Pretty messed up, right?

Then my thoughts switched to why it happened. Was the miscarriage my fault? Was it something I did that killed the baby? Was I not strong enough to carry a baby?

More importantly, was I unworthy of being a parent?

I'd read it isn't uncommon to get postpartum depression after a miscarriage, exactly as a woman might after a full pregnancy. I still wasn't sure if that's what happened to me. All I knew was that I couldn't get out of bed. For days.

Two days after the miscarriage, William had left on one of his business trips. This was when I found the naked pictures on his iPad.

And *that's* when I really started drinking.

The day I found the clit shot of another woman—because there's no other way to refer to it—I popped open a bottle of red and never looked back. I drank, I cried, drank, cried, drank, cried. Two bottles made me feel like myself again. Three bottles numbed the pain.

I decided numb was good. Optimal.

Then I started shuffling money around.

When William and I married, we agreed to separate bank accounts. I didn't realize at the time this was more to his benefit than mine. I also didn't realize until years into our marriage that his father paid for our rent and our bills. My husband had led me to believe he was paying for our extravagant lifestyle—taking care of his wife, he told me. I still didn't know what William did with the money he made.

As for me, I put every penny in savings, which I transferred to a new account the day after uncovering his latest indiscretion. I emptied a Roth IRA account I'd started at age twenty-one, and added that to my new savings account, creating a hell of a nest egg for myself. All those years of penny pinching was finally paying off.

I still didn't know why I didn't confront William when I found the pictures. I think because deep inside, I knew there was no going back. It was the third time he'd cheated on me, and if history is doomed to repeat itself, I'd get the same empty promise that it would never happen again.

It was my fault. I should have left him the first time.

I blamed myself. For him cheating on me, for the miscarriage, for losing my identity in a man I didn't love.

So I drank.

I drank when I woke. I drank at lunch. I drank during my mid-afternoon snack of twelve almonds and a handful of grapes. I learned how to hide my drinking. Although wine and tequila were my drinks of choice, the scent carried, so I switched to vodka during the day. I drank at dinner, I drank in the bathtub, I drank myself to sleep. For two months, there was not a single waking hour that I was sober.

I thought I had it under control . . . until I lost my job.

And now here I was, my entire life packed in the back of my car, barreling down a rutted dirt road on my way to my new home—a house I'd purchased on the internet.

6

With one hand gripping the steering wheel, I tapped two aspirin from the bottle directly into my mouth and washed them down with a swig of Coke. A *real* Coke, not that diet, zero, caffeine-free bullshit. The full-blown, delicious, ice-cold, billion-calorie Coca-Cola. For whatever reason, caffeine and sugar helped curb the headache that I was now certain was from alcohol withdrawal.

I was two days sober.

I pulled the cashmere scarf from my lap that I'd been using as a blanket and tossed it in the back seat. When I'd left my motel in northeast Missouri at the ass-crack of dawn, it was cold enough to see your breath. Eight hours driving south later, the temperature had climbed to a humid seventy degrees. I was thankful for this, considering I'd taken the top down for the drive. Something about the fresh air made me feel free, or maybe just less suffocated.

The morning sun had disappeared behind thick cloud cover, leaving a bleak, overcast afternoon that hinted at rain.

And that was the last thing I needed while navigating roads as thin as toothpicks.

The last hour had been hair-raising at best, giving an entirely new meaning to the term white-knuckle drive. Steep ravines and cliffs hugged roads riddled with hairpin curves shadowed by soaring mountainsides. It had been years since I'd been that deep in the woods, where concrete didn't replace the grass. Where trees grew strong and tall, untrimmed and scraggly as nature had intended.

It smelled different from the city I'd grown accustomed to. Clean, crisp air scented with honeysuckle and budding flowers. Dirt. Nature. I'd passed a man on a tractor, and not far beyond him, two others on horseback. It was like going back in time. All the way to my childhood.

It made me squirm.

My nose tingled, causing my eyes to water for the hundredth time since crossing into the mountains. Along with blooming dogwoods and budding daffodils came an itchy throat and more snot than a two-hundred pound Saint Bernard. Allergies, I assumed. I grabbed a tissue from the box I'd purchased from the local Git 'N Split. Three vicious sneezes later, I tucked it into the bag I was using for trash, next to a dozen other used tissues.

Springtime in the South—all new to me.

A strand of hair escaped the baseball cap I'd pulled on, whipping around my face as I checked the time.

"All right, guys." I glanced at my road-trip buddies—the lavender plant I'd named Violet, and the bear named Serenity—strapped into the passenger seat. "Four hours is eleven o'clock. I can take two more aspirin at eleven o'clock. Got it? Got it."

"*In one hundred feet, take the next right*," the robotic voice from my map app informed me.

I slowed, braking next to a rusty sign, barely visible through the brush that had grown around it.

RATTLESNAKE ROAD

Nerves fluttered in my stomach as I turned onto the dirt road, this one narrower than the one before. Trees closed in around me, creating a tunnel that blocked the waning light. A rusted barbwire fence lined the ditches, doing a poor job of containing the underbrush. Vibrant patches of green ran down the center of the dirt, an electric green I'd only seen in paintings.

I looked in my rearview mirror, watching the crooked, rusty sign shrink behind me.

Rattlesnake Road.

What a terrible name for a road, I thought, seconds before my car bottomed out in a pothole, bouncing me out of my seat. I cringed at the sound of metal on rock, and then wondered if that was why I'd passed people on tractors and horses, instead of in cars.

Up ahead, the road split into a *Y*.

To the right was a gray brick building with a tin roof under soaring pine trees. An auto shop, I assumed, based on the three large garage doors. Rows of old tires stacked haphazardly against the building, next to a red door with a window on the end. A few rusted cars sagged near the woods that surrounded the building, windows cracked, parts missing. Multiple woodpiles were tucked carelessly among the trees. A blacked-out Chevy was parked behind an old dumpster.

To the left of the *Y*, the dirt road continued, disappearing around a bend lined with thick trees.

I slowed to check my phone, surprised when the map didn't show the *Y* or the building. Based on the location of the little blinking blue dot that marked my destination, I should hang a right. After taking one last look at the building that, I wasn't sure why but felt totally out of place, I veered to the right.

"*One mile*," the GPS warned me in a deadpan robotic voice, breaking the silence.

Those nerves in my stomach turned to a flock of seagulls.

My pulse rate increased as the distance between me and the little blue dot began to close in.

"*Destination, next left . . .*"

My heart pounded as I leaned forward, squinting, looking for a driveway.

It wasn't until, "*You've arrived at your destination*," that I noticed a break in the tree line, giving way to a rocky dirt driveway. A rusty mailbox lay haphazardly to the side, dented, covered in dead leaves. Faded numbers read 1314.

There was no way I could turn into the driveway without my car getting scratched to hell from the bushes at the base, so I reversed and repositioned, adding the first thing on my "new house to-do list."

I eased in, slow with anticipation. The driveway was long and narrow, and much like the road leading to it, totally enclosed in trees. I was driving uphill, I noticed.

Two bottom-outs and one scratch down the side of my car later, I laid eyes on the dilapidated old cabin I'd purchased online.

Two words went through my head. *Holy. Shit.*

My phone rang. Struck dumb, I reached over to answer it without speaking.

"Mrs. Dalton, this is Nancy. I'm just checking to make sure you arrived all right, and that you found the key?"

I rolled to a stop at the top of the drive, gaping at the house in front of me, then cleared my throat. "Ah, your timing's impeccable. I just pulled up."

It was my seventh phone conversation over the last forty-eight hours with Nancy, owner of Pendleton Real Estate, to iron out the details and discuss the paperwork I'd pulled over at three separate coffee shops to sign and email back during the drive. It was alarmingly easy to buy a house online. What came next, I wasn't so sure.

"Oh, that's fantastic," Nancy drawled in a thick Southern accent. "How was the drive? I worried about you traveling all that way alone."

Her statement surprised me, considering the woman didn't even know me.

"I had good weather today, so I can't complain."

"Good. Glad to hear it, dear."

Dear?

"I'm sure you've got a mess of things to do," she said, "so I'll let you get on it, but the key is under the welcome mat. Bought that brand-new for you yesterday. Also, I worked with Carl to make sure your electricity, internet, and water got turned on this mornin' as you requested. And you'll be by first thing in the morning to sign the final paperwork, correct? Utilities'll need you to come by. Bank too."

"Thank you, and yes, that's the plan."

"Shouldn't take long on my end since I already got your down payment."

I grimaced, remembering the dent that down payment had put in my savings account.

"Oh, and don't worry, dear. I haven't told Cassidy or

anyone else you're here. As you asked. She'll be so excited. She's such a sweet thing."

My grip tightened around the phone. "All right, well, thank you, Nancy, for everything. I'll see you in the morning."

"Call me if you need anything, hon. Welcome to Berry Springs."

7

I slammed the car door, the sound seeming to echo through the woods for miles.

God, it was so quiet. Where were the horns, the shouts, the sirens? I never realized how jarring silence could be. Or was it the total solitude that was jarring?

Another sneeze doubled me over. A duo of birds swooped out of a nearby maple, annoyed by the disturbance. A leaf drifted past my face as I pulled a tissue from my pocket, blew my nose, then stuffed it back in.

Huffing out a breath, I perched my hands on my hips and gazed at the house that was starkly different from what I'd seen online. The pictures on the website showed an "aged"—as they'd called it—wood-shingled home resembling a quaint cottage. A place you'd picture fairies and little gnomes nesting inside. In the pictures, potted plants filled with blooming flowers lined the pebbled walkway that led to a wraparound porch. Warm and cozy.

Nope.

Apparently, the photo used for the listing had been decades old.

The only thing true to the website was that the house was rock and log with a wraparound porch. It was far beyond aged with weathered logs, stained rock, and a crooked porch with several planks missing. The "pebbled walkway" was a path of dirt. Dead, scraggly bushes and tall grass had overtaken the small yard, trees closing in around the roof like witches' fingers about to strike. The roof was littered with dead limbs, twigs, and leaves. Half the wood shingles were missing.

In the overcast afternoon, the property resembled a scene from a horror flick.

Nice.

Dollar signs flashed through my head as I gaped at my new home. My plan had been to renovate it while I "found myself again," then sell it and move on to wherever I chose to settle for good. I hadn't planned on this much work.

But I was in too deep now. I sucked in a breath and popped my neck from side to side like a boxer before a fight.

Good thing I don't mind getting my hands dirty. And with that thought, I forced one foot in front of the other and shifted my focus from shock to visualizing what I could turn the place into.

Look at the positives, not the negatives.

I noticed a small dogwood tree with beautiful white buds. Another, this one pink, on the far side of the house. *Pretty*. A peek of blazing yellow caught my eye at the back of the house. I crossed the yard carefully so I didn't twist an ankle on the fallen twigs that littered it. Forsythias in full bloom lined the wooden legs of a back porch, their long, thin arms of sunshine yellow stretching wildly at all angles.

I smiled. *Very pretty*. I imagined many mornings sipping coffee on that porch.

The backyard was small, but had potential. A garden, maybe.

Since when did I garden?

I made my way back to the car and unbuckled Violet and my serenity bear from the front seat.

"*This* is fresh air," I whispered as I carefully set them on a flat spot next to a dogwood. "What do you think?"

I scratched my chin, turning back to the house.

"Yeah, I know. Me neither." I shrugged. "Well, I'm going to go check out the inside. Enjoy the beautiful outdoors. I'll be back."

Dead leaves tumbled across the porch as I stepped onto it. An old rocking chair sat to the side, creaking back and forth in the breeze. Arranged by Nancy for show, I imagined. But in an ironic twist, it only made the house look creepier. I kicked aside a branch, then flipped over a welcome mat adorned with watermelons and picked up a shiny gold key.

The key to my new house.

The front door was thick and heavy, with intricate carvings framing a beveled-glass window in the center. Very *Lord of the Rings.* It opened with a slow, haunting creak.

Cool air smelling of must and mothballs greeted me as I stepped over the threshold and into a large living room. Ahead of me, muted sunlight pooled onto the faded hardwood floors through a wall of cracked, smudged oversized windows. The windows looked out onto a back porch, and a small yard bordered by woods. I found the light switch, flicking it on and off to confirm it worked.

The floor was scuffed, stained, and covered in dust bunnies and a few leaves that had snuck in from outside. Wood paneling lined the bottom half of the walls, undoubtedly beautiful once, now stained and nicked. Dust covered the windowsills and the old seventies-era fan in the center of the ceiling. Spiderwebs clung to the corners.

Scanning the room again, I began to itch.

Clean, was the first word that materialized in my head. Nothing less than a top-to-bottom scrub down would do.

To the right of the windows, a half wall of cabinets with a granite countertop separated the living room from a small kitchen with an island in the middle. It was tiny, which was fine with me, a woman who considered Red Baron's gourmet pizza.

The master bedroom was to my direct right. I stepped inside and stifled a scream. Not because of the spiderweb the size of a satellite dish clinging to one corner of the ceiling, or because of the cracked windows, but at the sight of the two side-by-side closets the size of crackerjack boxes. *Horrifying*.

I couldn't understand in what scenario a man—because it had to be a man—would think closets that size were acceptable. And why *two separate* closets?

Slack-jawed, I ran my fingertips along one closet's door frame as one might inspect the doorway to another dimension. And for me, it was.

"Well, that's simply not going to work," I said, already mentally mapping out my demolition.

Thank God I was pleased with the bathroom. It was dingy and dirty but featured a claw-foot soaking tub that gave me major princess vibes.

I strolled back to the living room and decided the best part of the house was unquestionably the sweeping windows that overlooked the woods. But the amenity I was drawn to the most was the massive stone fireplace with a thick wooden mantel that split the other end of the house. To one side was a small bedroom and bathroom that would probably never get used. The other was a den of sorts with walls of built-in shelving and a bay window that overlooked more forsythias.

In the far corner of the den was a staircase that led to a large room upstairs with more sweeping windows, more dust and grime. The room appeared to be newer than the rest of the house, possibly added on sometime over the last decade. My mind started racing with what to do with it. There was no bathroom or closet, only hardwood floors, windows, and a rock wall that was the back of the chimney. I wondered what the former resident had used it for.

I stepped over to the windows, so dirty I couldn't see outside, and scanned the floor for something to wipe them with. Not surprisingly, I came up short. I started to use the sleeve of my coat but remembered its price tag, so I slipped out of my boot, yanked off my sock, spit on the window, and began scrubbing.

Slowly, the view revealed itself.

Below the hill and past the woods, emerald fields glowed in the waning light, sectioned off by rows of white wood fencing. A dozen cows grazed the fresh grass. A bird swooped along a large pond sparkling in the breeze.

In the distance, a man rode on horseback. My fingertips lifted to the window as I leaned forward, squinting to get a better view of the dark silhouette. A cowboy hat sat over broad shoulders. The man was tall, massive, not dwarfed by the large horse.

My brow arched.

A real Southern cowboy.

His head turned in my direction, his face shadowed, blurred with distance. I dropped my hand from the glass. He stared a moment—at the house, I assumed—then refocused on his business.

I watched the man for a moment as he rode the horse along the fence line and eventually faded out of view. A surprising sense of relief came over me. I wasn't totally alone on Rattlesnake Road.

Turning, I refocused my attention to the second-floor room, and what the heck I was going to do with the space.

According to Nancy, the cabin had been empty for eight years—with not a single offer—after the former resident passed away. This surprised me because, although the house was in desperate need of a renovation, its bones were good, plus it had the wood paneling, fancy tub, and built-in bookcases going for it. At one time, the house must have been beautiful, but that wasn't what sold me on it. No, it was the thirty acres of mountainside that came with it. For someone who'd lived in the city all her adult life, the thought of being surrounded by nature made me feel free.

When I asked Nancy why it hadn't sold before, she suggested the remote location and the fact that someone could buy a house twice as nice for the same price in town. Little did I know at the time that she was leaving out one very unsettling reason.

I stepped over to the chimney and placed a hand on the cool rock, my head spinning with ideas of what I could do with the room, when the door slammed shut behind me. I spun around, a zing of fear shooting up my spine.

I squinted at the closed door. The room was still and silent, making me question my sanity.

Ice-cold fingertips danced along the back of my neck, making the hair on my nape stand on end. The room suddenly felt ten degrees cooler.

I looked around, then back at the door. When nothing happened and no bogeyman appeared, I decided a breeze from downstairs was to blame.

My eyes narrowed, I crossed the room and jerked open the door.

Nothing.

Heaving out a breath, I shook my head and descended the staircase, deciding it was a good time for some fresh air. Maybe walk around the land I'd just purchased. As I stepped out the front door, a flash of black darted across the porch, followed by a bone-chilling hiss. I jumped back, slapping my hand over my heart.

"Holy sh—"

Three kittens followed, although their little hisses were less menacing than their mother's. The pint-sized balls of fur joined a pair of golden eyes glaring at me from behind a bush.

"Well, I'm *sorry.*" I sneezed and wiped my nose with a tissue. "I wasn't informed the house was already taken."

The kittens disappeared into the brush, making me wonder what other scares the home had in store for me. As the cats stared back at me, waiting for my next move, I scanned the porch for something I could use for water or food, or whatever the hell cats ate, then added the items to my growing list of things to buy. Maybe a few chew toys.

"Well," I said with a sigh. "Don't mind me. We'll figure something out. Okay? *Mi casa, su casa.*"

The mama cat darted into the woods, her kittens scurrying behind. No dad was anywhere to be seen—of course.

"Men." I scowled with a shake of my head as I stepped off the porch. "We don't need them." I hollered over my shoulder, "We'll do just fine without them. You and me. You, me, and your gaggle of hissing kittens."

I rounded the corner of the house to the backyard and found a faded footpath that led through the pines. The sun had dropped behind the mountains, taking its warmth with it. A cool breeze swept over my skin, and I caught myself smiling as I stepped out of the tree line and onto the large cliff—otherwise known as the selling point of the house.

Yards from my little, boring backyard was a single cliff jutting out from the woods above a steep ravine that faded into fields of green. It was the only thing as beautiful as the pictures suggested.

I stopped, inhaling slowly as I scanned the mountains in the distance, miles of thick gray clouds resting on the peaks. My gaze shifted to the fields I'd seen from the second-floor room. The cowboy was gone.

Closing my eyes, I took a deep breath, noting the twinge of a headache beginning to squeeze behind my temples.

Two days.

Two days sober.

Anxiety rolled through me, heating me from the inside out. My heart started to pound.

Opening my eyes again, I focused on the view that was postcard perfect, but now seemed disconcerting. Because I was completely out of my element, I realized.

No city.

No job.

No husband, no baby.

A breeze lifted my hair, and a few strands tickled my nose.

It was time to get my shit together.

I was here to find myself again, find who I'd always wanted to be. Or maybe to get to know a woman I'd never met before. Peel back the layers and find the real me.

And as I gazed at the mountains in the distance, I shivered, fearing what I might uncover.

8

Twilight fell with a blue glow that settled between the trees as I dragged my last suitcase into the master bedroom.

Five. My entire life fit into five suitcases. That was it.

In my emotional haste to escape the life that had gone to shit, I'd grossly miscalculated the impact of not having any furniture. I hadn't even tossed in a blanket—although I had taken the time to meticulously fold and stack my clothes. Because that was what mattered.

My to-buy list was growing by the second. I ran the calculations again, ensuring I had enough left in my savings to purchase the bare minimum of what I needed, and to pay the mortgage until I found a job and figured out what the hell I was going to do with my life. At that point, I'd get a loan and begin the big renovations. Then flip the cabin for profit.

Hopefully.

The prospect was terrifying and exhilarating all at once.

After sweeping away the dust bunnies, I knelt on the dirty hardwood floor and unzipped the suitcase closest to me, although my thoughts were miles away. Twelve hundred miles, to be exact.

I tapped the screen on my phone and checked the time —7:47 p.m. William's plane should have landed fifteen minutes ago. In under an hour, he'd discover that I'd left him.

Guilt crept up, along with more anxiety. I closed my eyes and massaged my temples.

Gritting my teeth, I pushed off the floor and grabbed a Coke from the fridge. Chugged half, then went back to the suitcases.

Focus on what's in front of you, Grey.

I slid the phone across the room so it wouldn't be in my line of sight and flipped open my suitcase. And blinked. Underneath dozens of plastic hangers were suits. Power suits. Diane Von Furstenberg, Ralph Lauren, Dolce & Gabanna. The red heel of a Louboutin stuck out from the corner.

City clothes. Rich-girl clothes. Pricey pieces that were useless to me now.

My lungs deflated like a popped balloon. I sat back on my haunches as I stared at the life I'd left, then at the house I'd so hastily purchased. I looked around the bedroom at the faded walls, cracked windows. No bed, no chair, no pictures.

Nothing.

Tears burned my eyes, flashbacks of my childhood making my gut twist. It was as if I'd gone back in time—despite my efforts to do the complete opposite. And that thought hit me hard.

I was back in the childhood that I'd vowed never to return to again. In an old, dilapidated house with limited funds. I was back *there.*

Four days ago, I was an editor-in-chief making six figures

a year. Four days ago, I was married to a man who'd guaranteed me a stable future.

And I'd walked away from it all.

No. I'd lost it all.

Wanting a drink more than my next breath, I brushed a tear from my cheek, along with a trail of snot. The walls of the dirty bedroom started to feel like they were closing in on me.

Shit, shit, shit.

Focus, focus, focus.

Sniffing, I refocused on the suitcase and clothes that I wondered if I'd ever wear again. And then I wondered if there were jobs in Berry Springs that even required suits.

My stomach rolled.

What the hell was I going to do for work in this Podunk town? I pictured myself wearing a hairnet and a blue poly-blend uniform in the local chicken processing factory.

No.

Then, in gloves and a construction hat, maybe doing stucco work?

No.

A black-and-white waitress uniform?

No.

Lastly, I pictured myself in a cowboy hat—or was it cowgirl?—and a pair of starched denim overalls as I shoveled cow shit at a ranch, or maybe oats at the feed store.

Hell no.

Deep in thought, I fingered the collar of my suit. *What do I want to do?*

Create something. Build something. That much I knew.

Ever since I was a little girl running through the woods of upstate New York, I was either inventing something or building something out of sticks and mud. As I got older, I'd taken up knitting and churned out pot holders, coasters, scarfs, shirts for dogs. I'd also tried my hand at painting, beading jewelry, making pottery, weaving baskets, and the grand finale, making paper lanterns that I tried to sell to my neighbors for three dollars apiece. Then I'd grown up and built one of the most successful online fashion magazines in the country.

What now?

House first, I reminded myself, *then work*.

I grabbed a jacket from the suitcase and slid it onto a hanger, then pushed off the floor and hung it in the world's smallest closet. I hung another, and another, forcing myself to focus only on the present moment. What I could control.

I was one suitcase down and starting on another when a knock sounded at the front door. Surprised, I jumped, sending my Fendi purse tumbling onto the floor.

Who the hell would be visiting me?

I knew it wasn't the real estate agent because we'd planned to meet in the morning. Aside from Nancy, I only knew one other person in Berry Springs, and I'd yet to make that call.

Frozen, I stood in the closet, wishing the unannounced visitor would go away. Then I remembered the top was still down on my BMW, and I was pretty sure the trunk was still open. Every single light was on in the house, and I hadn't even thought to lock the front door.

I searched my suitcases for a weapon, settling on a letter opener that apparently was more important to pack than a blanket. Tiptoeing across the room, I cringed at how the floor creaked with each step, noting to myself that going undetected wasn't an option in my new house.

I crept into the living room, immediately exposed by the bare windows that flanked the front door.

Shit. A dark figure stood on my porch, silhouetted by the even darker night.

I squared my shoulders, tightened my grip around the letter opener, and cautiously pulled open the door.

"Hi, there, neighbor!"

I blinked at the petite elderly woman smiling up at me behind a pair of red-framed Coke-bottle glasses. Clouds of fluffy silver hair framed a small, wrinkled pixie face with rosy cheeks and fire-engine-red lipstick. A dozen gold necklaces dangled over an orange tracksuit, with joggers to match. Next to my BMW sat a four-wheeler.

I liked her instantly.

A loud hiss broke the silence between us as I studied the cartoon character standing on my front porch.

The woman scowled. "Ugh. Goddamn cats. Feral. Hundreds around here, and they keep populating. I can help you git rid of them, if you want."

"Uh . . . no, that's okay. Hi." I gave her a tentative smile, then noticed the platter in her hand, covered in plastic wrap.

"Hope I'm not intrudin' . . ."

Her Southern accent was almost as thick as the musky rose-scented perfume she wore. She lifted the platter, a tattoo on her wrist peeking out from beneath the sleeve of her tracksuit.

"My name is Etta May. I wanted to come by and introduce myself, and welcome you. I live down the road. Well, not down the road. You know that *Y* a ways back? I live on the left side. Alone. Husband died twelve years ago. God rest his soul," she said with a frown. "Anyway, I couldn't believe my ears when I heard this old house finally sold, and when I found out it sold to a single woman, well, I figured you'd need these cookies to make it through the first few nights."

"If they make it past tonight." I took the plate from her hands, inhaling the scent of warm sugar. "I'm Grey Dalton. Pleasure to meet you, Ms. Etta."

"Grey," Etta said, repeating my name with the same thoughtful expression I'd seen more than once when I introduced myself. "Beautiful name."

"Beautiful" was better than the usual "interesting."

"Where're you from?" she asked.

"New York."

"New *York*?"

"Yep."

"Wowie. Talk about far from home. Quite a change down here, ain't it?"

"Understatement of the decade," I said, my attention drawn back to the platter in my hands.

Etta smiled widely. "They're oatmeal raisin, but don't go bitchin' about it until you try mine. I don't know why oatmeal cookies get such a bad rap. They've got all that protein, and I even added some flaxseed for extra energy. Figured you'd need it."

"I love oatmeal raisin, and at this moment, I'll eat anything that promises to give me more energy."

"Just wait until you get my age. And to seal the deal . . ." Etta bent down to lift a carton of milk from the woven basket resting at her feet, and winked.

I smiled widely. "Ms. Etta from the left of the *Y*, I believe you just became my best friend."

"Then put away that letter opener you've got clutched in your palm like the Hope diamond."

I laughed and set it on the windowsill, which was so crooked, the letter opener slid off. Shaking my head at it, I said, "Come on in."

A sneeze surprised me as I stepped back to let her in, several dramatic short inhales before the explosion.

Etta took a subtle step back. "Goodness. A few more of those and these walls might come down."

"Wouldn't take much." I sniffed, then opened the door wider so she could come inside. "You're clear. That one should last me about thirty minutes."

"Give a gal a heads-up next time, will ya?" Etta stepped inside and looked around. "Oh my." Her eyes widened as she gaped at me.

I sighed. "Just say it."

"Oh, honey. Maybe I should have brought over two dozen." Etta sucked in a breath and walked to the sweeping windows I'd yet to clean.

I set the milk and cookies on the counter that divided the living room from the kitchen.

Etta slowly spun, taking in the mess, her wrinkled expression frozen in disbelief.

"I know," I muttered.

She waved her hands in the air, as if to wave away the bad energy. "Cookies and milk first. Good Lord in heaven, cookies first."

"I think I've got some cups in my car. Hang on." I jogged to my car and began searching through the trunk, cursing myself for everything I hadn't packed. "Cups, cups, cups. Come *on,* cups."

A rustle of leaves made my head snap up. Night had fallen, and the woods were a solid black mass against the darkness. I looked back at the house, yellow pools of light spilling onto the front porch. Another light glowed from the second-floor room that I didn't remember turning on.

"Ow." I yanked my hand back and felt the warm trickle of blood down my finger. *Guess I found the knife*. "Shit."

I sucked the blood. *Gross.*

Waved my hand. *Ouch.*

A hiss pulled my attention to a pair of narrowed electric-yellow eyes staring back at me.

"Ah. There you are. Professional spooktress."

Another hiss came, this one followed by a twig popping.

"Well, I didn't expect company either. Sorry."

The cat stepped forward, her back arching, ready to attack.

"What? You don't like her? Her name's Etta. She brought cookies."

A kitten meowed from behind the bush.

"See? Your babies want some."

The cat scowled at me, two alpha females feeling each other out.

"Okay, Miss Moonshine, let's get one thing straight. I'm here now. The sooner you accept that fact, the sooner we can learn to live together."

With a long hiss, the cat turned and darted into the woods. Shaking my hand, I grabbed the bag and slammed the trunk.

"Oh dear, what happened?" Etta rushed over as I stepped inside. She grabbed my elbow and took the bag from my hand. Blood was running down my wrist.

"Nicked it on a knife."

"Come here, child."

I fought a grin as she rushed me to the kitchen. My finger was shoved under running water, then examined. I protested, but she wasn't having it. Etta then wrapped the wound in a handkerchief that magically appeared from one of her many tracksuit pockets.

"Don't worry, it's clean." Etta winked. "Now hold it tight.

You don't need stitches. What you do need is someone to help you carry in your bags."

"What I need is a bag of kibbles to feed the family I unintentionally evicted."

"Damn cats. I don't know how they survive with all the coyotes around here."

My eyes rounded. "Coyotes?"

"Oh yeah. Hundreds of them. Packs. Don't ever leave food out. Draws them, and the bears."

I groaned.

"Don't worry, honey. They're as scared of you as you are of them. Unlike the cats around here. Is she all black, with three kittens?"

"Yep. That's the one."

"She comes sniffing around my house every so often. Hate to tell ya, but I think you're right. This is her home base."

"Well, Miss Moonshine is going to have to learn how to share."

"Moonshine?"

"Dark-colored and kinda creeps up on you."

Etta threw her head back with a laugh. "Ain't that the truth. Never had a worse hangover in my life than from moonshine. How's your finger?"

"Hungry."

She grinned. "I was hoping you'd say that. Cookies make everything better. And they're still warm."

As we stood at the island in the kitchen, Etta unwrapped the platter, its floral print identical to the flowers printed on the clear wrap. I topped two coffee cups with milk, one a handmade stone mug. The other, white ceramic with the words bitch, please printed on it.

"I'll take the Bitch, Please."

I grinned and handed her the cup.

We bit into the cookies, groaning simultaneously.

"Oh my God," I muttered as a crumble escaped my lips. "These are delicious."

"Told ya. And they'll fill you up too. Now, eat up—you look like you could gain a few pounds—and tell me who the hell you've got lined up to renovate this place. Assuming you are because of the fancy BMW you got out front."

"You're looking at her." I wiped a trail of milk from my chin.

Etta cocked a brow. "*You're* going to renovate this house?"

"Yes, ma'am. In half the time, if you keep bringing me these cookies."

"Oh, I'll keep bringing 'em. I'll also bring Tad, from Tad's Tool Shop, who can help repair the cracks in the walls, and Joanne's boy to help paint. Carl, at the flooring place, can redo these floors, and dear God in heaven, please don't tell me you're going to bake in that oven."

"I'm not. You are."

"In that case, better get Cameron out here to measure for new appliances. He'll give you half off if you don't mind the dents. How are the bathrooms?"

"As acceptable as the closets."

Etta sighed as she nodded. "Thought so. All right, give me the tour, young lady."

9

I led Etta through each room, visualizing my money flying out the window with the long list of renovations she "suggested" for each. After a quick cookie break, we made our way to the second floor.

"This room is a mystery to me."

"Yeah, I see that." Etta tilted her head to the side, taking it in. "I wonder why ol' Bonnie had this added on."

"Who's Bonnie?"

"The woman who owned the house before you."

"Bonnie," I said thoughtfully. "The real estate agent never gave me the name. You knew her?"

"Honey, I know everyone. Especially my neighbors." She jabbed her finger into the air. "*Love thy neighbor as you love yourself.* Don't forget it."

"Noted. Did Bonnie live here alone?"

"Mostly. Her husband left her not long after moving in. Moved up north somewhere. Another woman. Left Bonnie all alone out here, middle of the woods. Poor thing."

"Men." I scowled.

"Tell me about it. Everyone talked about it. That's something you'll learn about small towns. Gossip is traded like gold."

"Doubly noted. How long did she live here?"

Etta scratched her chin. "Well, let's see. I've lived in my house about twenty years. She was in this one ten before that."

"Wow."

"Yeah. She was born and raised around here. Never left."

"Did she like to garden? I noticed the raised beds outside, and the forsythias."

"Not a day went by that Bonnie wasn't in her garden. Until . . ." Etta's face fell.

"Until what?"

"Until she . . . kinda got lost."

"In the closet?" I said, joking.

Etta laughed. "No dear, her mind. Went a little nuts. Which was ironic because the woman was as smart as a whip. Witty too. Had her doctorate in psychology, spent her days as the high school counselor. Could have worked at any clinic she wanted, making triple the money, but her passion was helping kids. Troubled teens, specifically. But I think all those years alone got to her. She and her husband never had kids, so she had no one."

"That's so sad."

Etta glanced over her shoulder at me. I blinked, the implication of her subtle look hitting me like a Mack truck. I, too, was alone, in the same home where Bonnie had been alone, in the middle of nowhere, with no one—no husband, no kids.

"Anyway," Etta said quickly, breaking the silence. "She worked in the flower shop and at the farmers' market on the weekends, selling her flowers. Didn't have much. I worried about her, financially, you know."

"Did she date?" I asked. "Have boyfriends?" *Please say yes.*

"Nope. Not a single date after they divorced. Got the feelin' he took her heart with him. Not a single man in her life after her husband, all those years. Ain't that somethin'?"

I turned my head, unable to ignore the similarities between Bonnie and myself, and I didn't like it. "Were you two friendly?"

"Oh yes. Bonnie walked every day, a loop around the *Y* and back. She'd always stop by to chat with me. We were friendly, bonded over her love of flowers and mine of baking. But about five years before she died, she quit walking. It was like something changed in her. I started checking on her regularly, but she'd lost that sparkle. The desire to chat, be friendly. So I decided to give her space. She'd lost weight too. Kind of slipped away."

"What did she die from?"

"Never found out. Next thing I knew, her things were being auctioned off, you know, because she didn't have kids or anyone else to pass them on to."

"Who discovered her?"

"Her body?"

"Yeah."

"The mailman at that time, Bob Hammonds, got suspicious when her mail began piling up. Called the cops for a welfare check. They found her dead."

I cringed.

Etta stared at a spot on the wall a moment, as if choosing her next words carefully. "I've driven by the house over the last few years on my way into town, just to make sure it was still standing. Sometimes, lights have been on." Her gaze cut to me, a shadow crossing her dark eyes.

"What do you mean, the lights have been on?"

"Exactly what I said. I called the electric company, and they told me there's been no electricity on in the place for years."

"What are you saying? I've got a ghost here?"

She shrugged as if she hadn't just dropped a nuclear bomb at my feet. "Maybe. But don't let that bother you. We all die. Nothin' morbid about it. Some of us go on to heaven, hell, whatever. And some of us have unfinished business to take care of."

"You think Bonnie has unfinished business?"

"You're assuming she's the ghost."

I threw my hands in the air. "You think someone else is haunting these walls?"

"Don't know. You bought a very old house. No telling how many people have crossed its threshold. You're bound to have a few spirits lingering around. Hell, I got one. Two, actually, in my house. Ignore them, talk to them, try to help them, totally up to you. But enough of that." She turned fully toward me and put her hands on her hips. "Now that you've taken me through your house, and we've got the small talk out of the way and sized each other up, I've decided I like you, Miss Grey."

"Yeah?" I grinned. "Why's that?"

"Despite the fancy car—that you undoubtedly overpaid for—and fancier clothes in your closet, you've got calluses on your hands and fire in your soul that I can see in your eyes. The fact that you plan to fix this place up all by yourself tells me you've got grit. But," she said as she held up a finger.

"There's always a but."

"Yes, ma'am. Always. The fact that you purchased the thirty acres that surrounds it tells me you've got secrets."

I cocked a brow. "The fact that you drive a Can-Am and

have a barbwire tattoo on your wrist tells me you've got the balls to ask about them."

"Yes. And you're observant, young lady." She raised the sleeve of her tracksuit, revealing a vine of flowers around her wrist. "Got this decades ago to cover a few scars I got when I tried to befriend a stray dog in the woods. I'm telling you, watch out for the strays around here. There's your tip of the day."

She lowered her sleeve. "Now. My question for you, Miss Grey, is what are the secrets that have got you running to the middle of nowhere, and more importantly, why don't you have a man to chase out those ghosts?"

I wasn't prepared to talk about William, or why I'd moved. "Let's just say Bonnie and I have the same taste in men."

"He cheated on you?"

I nodded.

Etta spat, then shook her head. "You poor thing. I'll never get it. I was lucky, and believe me, I count my lucky stars every day for my late husband, but I know I'm one of the few. Men think of women like public transportation. There'll always be another around the corner. Cheaper—and full of viruses."

I laughed.

"Hear me, child." Etta closed the inches between us. "Someone who looks like you, coming to this boring small town, is going to have their pick of the litter. Mark my words. Seriously, honey, do you realize how beautiful you are?"

Of all the things Etta had said that night, those words rendered me speechless. Did I?

I'd always been a confident woman, although I had no idea where this belief in myself came from. Certainly not from my mother. There was a time in my life that I appreciated my reflection in the mirror, but when was the last time?

Had I lost that confidence?

As if reading my thoughts, Etta continued. "You've got that stunning, classy look that women try for years to achieve, only to realize they can't. You're either born with it or you're not. And, honey, you are. You look like the second coming of Shania Twain. Pre-Botox."

I laughed. "I'll take that."

"Good. Leave your asshole husband in the past and find yourself a strapping Southern gentleman to take care of you. Words of wisdom. Listen to me. All right, enough about men. Now, where's all your furniture?"

"The furniture store."

"You didn't bring any?"

"Didn't want all the viruses."

She laughed. Hard. "Good thinking. What are you sleeping on tonight?"

"I bought a blow-up mattress on the way into town."

"Did you get the electric pump to go with it?"

I opened my mouth, my eyes wide, then clamped it shut. "Shit."

Etta shook her head with pity. "Good grief, child, you can't—"

"Don't worry. I'll make it work. I'm planning to go into town tomorrow. This town has a furniture store, right?"

"Nonsense." Etta waved my plan away with a flick of her tattooed wrist. "I've got an entire shed of old furniture you can sift through. Nice stuff too. But I outgrew it. I save everything."

"No, no, I couldn't—"

"I insist. Rummage through my things first, then you can go buy your fancy pieces from Abe in town. His store is off

Main Street. Overpriced, but you didn't hear that from me. Actually, fine, you did. I've told him a hundred times. But you'll look at what I have to offer first. I've refinished a lot of it myself. I'll cut you a good deal."

"Does this deal involve more oatmeal raisin cookies?"

"Depends on how much you take." She winked.

"Miss Etta, you've got a deal."

We shook hands on it.

"Good," she said. "Now, let's go back downstairs because I've got something to talk to you about."

My brow cocked. "Ah. Suddenly this visit and the homemade cookies don't seem so random."

Etta laughed, then led the way down the stairs as if she'd been here a hundred times. Maybe she had. We returned to the kitchen and huddled around the cookies, a habit already forming.

Etta clasped her hands together. "Okay. Serious stuff now. I—"

"Wait." I bit into my fourth cookie and chewed. Once I'd swallowed, I said, "Okay. Now I'm ready for serious talk."

"All right, listen up. You've got exactly twenty-nine point seven acres that came with your property. It backs up to mine. I own fifteen acres, bought one by one over the years with hard-earned money, proud to say. I want to leave the property to my daughter, currently living in Texas, but she'll move back. Between me, you, and a few others that live around here, we've got a combined three hundred acres of woods, pastures, and a river that runs into Otter Lake. Beautiful land."

"Where are you going with all this, Etta?"

"Beautiful land, and apparently we're not the only ones who think so. There's a fancy-pants big-dick hotel company in town right now—probably from New York."

She rolled her eyes, and I grinned.

"They're wanting to buy this land to develop some gaudy monstrosity of a resort to compete with another in the area, Shadow Creek Resort, that's done very well for itself. This might be a small town, but tourist season is huge here. People seek refuge from the nearby cities, needing a break from the people, the cars, the goddamn sidewalks. People *need* nature. They need to escape to more simple roots. Folks here in Berry Springs still live off the land, like old times. We respect the land. We like it this way, and we intend to keep it this way."

I washed the cookie down with a swig of milk. "Okay, I don't disagree with this, but what's your point here?"

"The hotel people have already been to my house. Twice. Trying to buy me out."

"They're offering to buy your house? So they can bulldoze it and build?"

"Exactly." She scoffed. "The first time, I politely told them no. I was in the middle of making a sponge cake. Dammit, those things take attention, so I wasn't in the mood to get pulled away into a fight, but they wouldn't back down. Told the son of a bitch he'd have better luck trying to sell birth control to the Joachim family down the road. Ain't happening. God bless that woman's soul. Nine kids. I imagine they shoot out like a ride at the water park by now. Anyway, the second time they came around, I answered the door with my sawed-off shotgun."

"And what did the fancy-pants New Yorkers say to that?"

"Not much. Which is exactly what I intended. My point to all this, dear, is that they're going to come knocking on your door. Offer you a lot of money to sell out. If you do that, you devalue the entire side of this mountain and ruin what all of us have worked so hard to keep. Our land. *Ours.* And as I look around at this place," she scanned the kitchen, "I worry they might make you an offer you can't refuse. You know, like furniture and food." She ended with a wink.

"Miss Etta, I might be a lot of things—trust me on this—but I ain't no easy mark. Did I use that word correctly?"

One corner of Etta's lips curled into a smirk. "Good job, New York. A couple more of those, and you'll be trading in those Louie Bootins for a pair of shitkickers."

My brow arched. "You *kind of* know your designer brands."

"I watch that entertainment show after the local news." Etta reached for another cookie but pulled back. "I better get going before I eat what I baked for you." She lifted my wrist, checking my finger. "Looks like you'll live. Keep that cut bandaged up through tomorrow. If it doesn't close up, come on over and I'll stitch it up for you."

Etta patted my ass before sauntering across the living room. "Enjoy the cookies. Left of the *Y*, that's where I'll be if you need me. Tomorrow, I'll bring over some allergy medicine that'll dry you out quicker than menopause. I'll see you soon, dear."

I smiled as my Southern guardian angel walked out the door.

Then the phone rang.

10

The conversation with my husband went as expected.

William hit me with a barrage of questions, and I returned fire with multiple accusations. We argued, cursed, poking at each other's soft spots that we knew so well. During the entire call, my stomach felt like I'd swallowed a ball of barbwire.

As with most of our arguments, the conversation revolved around facts and figures, and very little emotion.

I recited the evidence I had of his three indiscretions, and how he hadn't been there for me during the miscarriage. He threw my drinking in my face, telling me he'd found a few bottles I'd hidden around the penthouse. He argued that the real love of my life was my job, and that he was in a distant second place. William emphasized this point by reminding me that I never cooked for him, never did his laundry, never asked about his day or rubbed his feet after a long day's work—like a "real" wife should. As if those shortcomings were equal to his multiple indiscretions, or even worse, the cause of them.

Sounds ridiculous, right? Not as ridiculous as the fact that I felt guilty.

Yes, it was true that William had cheated on me, but he'd also given me an extraordinary life. Free of financial stress. Free of worry. Free of love. And it was also true that I didn't provide him home-cooked meals, or do his laundry, or ask about his day, or rub the bunions on his feet.

Maybe if I had . . .

Maybe if I'd worked a bit harder at our relationship, things would have been different. Maybe if he'd give me a second chance . . . and maybe I assumed he would.

Maybe I subconsciously thought my move to Berry Springs was temporary, and William was going to sweep me up, sell the house I'd bought, and whisk me back to our penthouse suite, where he'd shower me in diamonds and hundred-dollar bills.

It was then, though, that William went for the kill. He brought up my childhood and terrible upbringing, implying I'd be nothing without him. And for the grand finale, he brought up my mother—my roots, the train wreck of a woman who made me.

Bastard.

When we ran out of ammunition, William asked what address he should send the divorce paperwork to. It was like a punch in the gut. During the entire forty-three-minute conversation, he never once begged me to stay. Not a single time.

And that was it, the moment I knew that I could move on—eventually. Why? Because I wanted a man who couldn't bear the thought of a life without me. A man who would walk to the ends of the earth just to keep me close.

William had never been truly in love with me, as I never was with him. It was a facade. While that should have provided a sort of relief regarding the death of our marriage, instead I felt immense sadness. Anger. Defeat.

And the damn guilt.

William had accepted the end of our relationship, just like my boss. I was easily tossed out, cast aside, soon to be forgotten and ultimately to be replaced.

When we hung up, I realized William and I were truly done, a ten-year marriage down the tubes. I, Grey Dalton, was officially going to be a divorcée.

As I took in the home I'd so hastily purchased, falling apart at the seams, I began to question my judgment. I'd married a man that I wasn't in love with because I'd wanted a family and the security he provided. I'd worked my ass off to ensure I had a life that would never lead me back to my childhood. I'd gotten pregnant to fill a hole inside me.

And then I'd lost all three. I now had no job, no family, no plan—and worse, no direction.

With that daunting thought, I couldn't fight the tears any longer. Phone in hand, I slid down the wall, collapsed onto my nasty, dirty floor, and cried.

11

Six oatmeal cookies, four aspirin, and two glasses of milk later, I peeled myself off the floor with a mental kick in the ass and got to work. I turned off my cell phone, turned up *Today's Hits Radio*, and reset my focus from the death of my marriage to the to-do list I'd begun the moment Etta left.

It was divided into four sections. The first was titled "House Stuff." This included everything the house needed to function again, such as new windows, new roof, new appliances, new HVAC system, new door locks, new mailbox, refinished floors, new planks to replace the rotted ones in the porch. Things like that.

The second column was "Aesthetics." This was by far the longest list, and included everything I needed to make the house feel like a home, such as paint, replace crown molding, replace wood paneling where needed, add window treatments, pressure wash the fireplace, refinish the mantel, new ceiling fans, new light fixtures, new bathroom mirror. The list went on and on.

The third was titled "Furniture to Buy." This was the

shortest list with just the bare minimum, since I'd decided renovations would come before comfort.

The final column I'd titled "Outside Stuff To Do." At the moment, that list seemed too daunting to even begin, so I left it blank.

At the very top of the list, the number-one priority was bolded, accessorized with crooked little stars at each end. It read:

★ *REDO CLOSET* ★

Staring at the two separate little closets in my master bedroom, I cursed the man who'd built them for the hundredth time. I thought again of Bonnie, the previous house owner, and wondered what she'd been thinking to allow them to remain.

Or if she'd been thinking.

Hands on my hips, I studied the closets. The issue had to be dealt with, I decided, right that second. Two needed to become one.

I squeezed inside the closet nearest me, the one with no clothes hanging in it yet, and examined its walls and structure like I knew what I was doing. Then I did the same in the other, rapping on the wall between with my knuckles.

The separating wall was thin, as best I could tell, but what the hell did I know about construction? About as much as cooking, my husband would say.

After chugging the rest of my milk, I swiped the foam from my upper lip and grabbed the hammer I'd bought along with my blow-up mattress. After popping my neck from side to side, I squeezed back into the empty closet, said a Hail Mary, and took a swing. Dust and chunks of drywall blasted into the air as the hammer penetrated the wall that separated the two closets. I stumbled out, spitting, wiping the dust from my eyes.

Once I'd donned a baseball cap that read YOU HAD ME AT MIMOSA, a pair of Fendi sunglasses, and a bandanna secured around my nose and mouth, I returned for another go at it.

I pounded at the wall again and again, each blow—each explosion—releasing loads of pent-up anger I didn't realize I'd been carrying. I imagined the wall as William's face, as his whore's face, my mother's face, my father's (what I imagined his face to look like), and lastly, my stupid uterus that couldn't hold a baby. Tears streamed down my cheeks as the hole grew bigger and bigger.

My chest heaving, I moved away until my back hit the opposite wall of the closet. I slid down it, sniffling, my heart pounding.

"Goddammit." I ripped the bandanna from my mouth and swiped away the tears. "Dammit," I snapped again. I hated crying, and I'd done more of it the last few days than in my entire life.

I huffed out a breath, studying the mess I'd made.

Past the jagged hole were a couple of two-by-fours that stretched from floor to ceiling. Behind those was a layer of fuzzy, ripped insulation that I guessed had once been home to a colony of mice. Perhaps still was. I also guessed it was at least ninety percent asbestos.

I estimated the distance between the two closets to be around three feet. Not a ton of extra room, but when it came to closet space, three feet might as well be three hundred.

I crawled forward, gripped the bottom of the drywall, and yanked. It didn't give. I blasted it with my hammer a few more times, then yanked again. This time, a huge piece broke off. I repositioned myself and slammed my boot into the remaining wall, again and again, until most of the bottom half was destroyed.

Sweat beaded my forehead, my head beginning to feel like a balloon in high altitude. Too much dust, too tired, too sober.

I checked the time—11:47 p.m.—then glanced at the bare windows framing the inky darkness outside. It was time to give it a rest for the evening.

I was stacking the broken pieces of drywall when my gaze was drawn to a patch of dingy white between the closets, peeking through the debris. Whatever it was, it was out of my reach, so I maneuvered myself into the small space and pulled an envelope from the rubble.

Frowning, I blew the dirt from the top of it and turned it over in my hands. The edges were worn and stained, one corner chewed to shreds by a mouse or a rat, or maybe Moonshine herself. The flap was sealed. There was no address, no stamp, no indication of what was inside it.

My stomach tightened as I dug my nail into the top corner of the envelope and ripped away the seal on the flap. Inside was a folded piece of notebook paper. Once white and crisp, it was now dingy and limp.

A shattering noise came from the other room, startling me.

I dropped the letter and padded across the bedroom, peering into the dark living room. When I was sure no one was in the house, I peeked into the kitchen. The coffee cup Etta had drunk from—my favorite BITCH, PLEASE mug—lay in shards on the floor.

I spun toward the sound of a young girl's giggle coming from the den, or the room on the second floor, maybe. Goose bumps rose on my arms, and I blinked, staring at the arched doorway.

"Hello?"

My heart hammered as I forced one foot in front of the other, crossing the living room and peering into the den.

No one was there.

I turned toward the windows, black with night, then stared at the shadowy corner where the staircase led to the second floor. My heart pounding, I checked upstairs.

No one.

My knees a little shaky, I walked back downstairs and returned to the closet, convincing myself I was simply hearing things.

I grabbed the mystery envelope and sat cross-legged in the center of the bedroom. My hands trembled as I unfolded the letter, as if my body knew what was coming before I did.

The writing was faded, scribbled in ink with mad slashes and slants across the letters, as if written in haste or anger. The words were barely legible. The letter was old, written maybe twenty or so years ago, although that was just a guess.

That tightening in my stomach was joined by the racing of my heart as I took a deep breath and began.

12

Letter #1

I stopped taking the pills. I hate them. They make me feel dizzy and confused. No one knows I stopped. I flush them down the toilet after pretending to take them.

Idiots.

I feel like a fucking idiot writing this.

I've started a journal because the new psychologist Dad takes me to suggested I do it. Find a quiet place, sit down, and write about anything that comes to mind, she said in her stupid tweed suit. She reminds me of the women that starred in those stupid shows my mom watched when I was young.. She also suggested a bunch of other bullshit.

I'm not doing those things but thought I'd try this because I'm bored in my room where Dad has sent me away. Again. Where he thinks I'll be safe. He should put better locks on the windows.

This is so stupid. I don't even know what to say.

I guess I could talk about when it all started. Not that you would understand. Because no one understands.

I'm different. I've known it since I was really young. I've always felt different. Mom and Dad didn't notice until fifth grade, and even then, they avoided it like they avoid sleeping in the same bed. They think I don't notice. Hard not to notice when I walk downstairs in the middle of the night to find my dad jacking off while watching the Late Show. Which is an entirely separate subject, maybe more disturbing, that I don't care to go into here.

Things started really getting bad when I was in seventh grade. There was this girl that would always take my stuff. My notebook and pens. She'd laugh, then give them back, teasing me in front of everyone. Every single day.

One day, she took the candy bar I was eating and called me Fat Pants. I lunged at her with my pencil, sending chairs and desks flying, and jabbed it into her neck. I missed, barely nicking the side of her throat. I'd aimed for the center, although I didn't tell anyone that.

The idiot teacher, Mrs. Green—God, I hate her—ran over and tried to hold me back. I started crying like a little bitch. I don't know why. I was confused and so embarrassed. I remember all the kids were staring at me, wide-eyed with shock. Laughter would have been better. But they didn't laugh, they just looked at me like I was crazy.

Crazy.

That was the first time I acknowledged it. Yes, I was crazy. At age twelve, I knew I was crazy.

They were scared of me. And the truth is, so was I. I remember being shocked at my own behavior and wondering, later that day while sitting in the counselor's office, if I really meant to hurt the girl. Kill her.

Yeah, I did.

After the pencil incident, the outbursts, as my mom calls them, started happening more and more. Everyone kept asking why I was so angry all the time. My mom and dad, the counselor, the teachers. I couldn't explain it, and that only made me angrier. I hate when they ask. It makes me feel even more different. I can't fucking explain it! It's just me. I'm fucking crazy.

There was a break in the letter here as if the writer had walked away. The forthcoming script appeared more controlled, less angry.

Anyway, after that, no one picked on me anymore at school. They still don't. They avoid me like the freak I am.

On most days, I eat lunch in the bathroom. I cry like a stupid little baby. Like the fucked-up person I am. I hate myself. I hate them. I hate my fat body. Everything. I hate it.

I started drinking around the time of the pencil incident. I stole some wine from my mom, vomited it up an hour later. Then I tried coconut rum and mixed it with a Coke. I like to drink. Alcohol helps even me out.

I remember the first time I got in trouble. Real trouble. I stole my dad's truck after one of our arguments. Mom was screaming from the front porch as I took off into the night. It felt good. I felt free. I sped through town, ran over a few trash cans and a few construction cones.

When I heard sirens in the distance, I hid in the same alley where I bought my first bag of weed. An hour later, I set the truck on fire. The cops were called. I was put in handcuffs. I'd been arrested before for stealing but never put in cuffs.

I remember people watching from the windows and the cops telling me I was lucky the surrounding apartment buildings didn't catch fire and I didn't hurt anyone. That was the second time I wondered what it would be like to really hurt someone. A little kid was watching from a window. I wanted him to fall and catch on fire. I wanted to watch him burn.

After that, my reputation got worse. I started skipping school. Drinking before class.

Last summer, I pushed Katie off a cliff at the lake. I was just playing around. She wouldn't jump and it annoyed me. She was fine, but broke a few bones. I was grounded for a month for that.

I had sex for the first time the night I got ungrounded. With two people, a boy and a girl. We were drunk and high. Jason found some porn, and we played it at his house while his parents were at work. It felt dirty at first and then good. My heart felt like it was going to explode out of my chest. We did it again the next day too, and the next. That time, we used dildos he found in his mom's room. It was such a rush. I guess this makes me a whore. And gay. Add those to the list of things pills can't cure.

God, I hate it here.

There's this stupid girl I always see jogging by the house. The neighbor, I guess. I tried to talk to her once. Thought maybe we could be friends. Pass the time while I'm in this hellhole. She's a year younger than me, I think. I thought I could talk her into stealing some alcohol from her parents. I know they drink because I've seen them outside with beers. She said she'd get in trouble and told me she didn't want to be friends. I hate her. She plays the cello, and I guess she's won some contests. She's really skinny too. I guess she runs track. Yeah, let's run around in a circle a hundred times, that sounds fun. She even suggested I'd lose weight if I ran. What a cunt. I told her if she fingered something other than the strings on her cello, she might get a date every now and then. I think she told her dad because he glares at me every time I see him. Fucker.

God, I hate her. She's so perfect.

I hate it here.
I hate my life.
My hand hurts.
And this is stupid.
I hate you so much.

13

I awoke on my blow-up mattress with my body curled into the fetal position, my arms wrapped around my knees. The room was ice cold, but I was drenched in sweat from nightmares of burning toddlers and sharpened pencils.

Horrible nightmares on the first night of my new home. Not a good sign.

Shivering, I unfolded myself and quickly slammed the window shut. Dawn was just beginning to light the woods. A thin fog danced through the trees. Apparently, the warmth of a Southern spring only reached the daytime. I mentally added a space heater to my "Furniture to Buy" list.

I grabbed a pair of sweats from the suitcase on the floor and pulled them on, my thoughts returning to the place they'd been when I'd fallen asleep the night before.

The letter.

Almost as disturbing as the letter itself was the fact that I'd reread it seven times before going to bed.

Seven.

Eventually, the words began to blur together except for

the sentence, "Alcohol helps even me out." The admission had resonated with me deeply. The entire letter had, for reasons that I didn't realize at the time. All I knew was I felt some sort of weird connection with the writer.

I looked at the closet where I'd tucked the letter back in its place, under the dirt and between the slats. I wasn't sure why I put it back, maybe a subconscious desire to leave the haunting words undisturbed. To close, seal, and hide the Pandora's box I'd just ripped open.

The letter itself gave no indication of who the writer was, but I assumed it had been written by Bonnie—the previous homeowner who'd "lost it," according to Etta. Although, the writer appeared to be a teenager. Maybe it was a letter from Bonnie's childhood? But the odds of a teenager with obvious mental issues going on to obtain a doctorate in psychology, as Bonnie had done, seemed slim. That part didn't make sense. Or maybe the letter was from Bonnie's husband, written during his troubled youth and hidden away before he left her.

My second assumption was the letter could have belonged to one of the occupants before Bonnie and her husband—whoever that was. My final, and most unnerving assumption was that the letter had been written by the spirit that I was sure now, more than ever, haunted my house.

One thing was for certain. I wanted to know more about the writer, about the tormented soul who no one understood. More about the person who was a bit different from everyone else.

But first, coffee.

As I walked into the kitchen, I noticed the echo of my footsteps on the hardwood floor, and wondered how long it would take to get used to the silence. I glanced out the sweeping windows of the living room. Through the woods, past the cliff, the mountains' edges glowed in the early light, a splash of colors peeking out from behind.

Breathtaking.

A bird swooped past the kitchen window as I pulled the coffee and condiments from a grocery sack on the counter. Yawning, I plugged in the coffeemaker, poured the water, inserted a filter and the grounds, and set it to brew. With nowhere else to sit, I pulled myself onto the counter and stared blankly at the room in front of me while the pot gurgled and hissed.

So much to do today, including reconnecting with my roots.

Sweat broke out on the nape of my neck at the thought.

What would she be like? The same? Different? Would she be happy to see me? Or would seeing me only dredge up memories that we'd both spent years trying to forget? Memories of pain. Of death.

Would she remember my promise? Our pact from so long ago?

I was in the middle of pouring my first cup when tires crunched over the gravel driveway. I finished filling the travel mug, then pushed off the counter, sloshing coffee onto my bare feet. It wasn't even seven in the morning. I knew it wasn't Etta on her cherry-red Can-Am because the engine of this vehicle wasn't nearly as loud.

A car door slammed, followed by boots on the gravel and a knock at the door.

I grabbed my weapon—the letter opener, which was ironic—and stepped out of the kitchen, catching my own reflection in the window. My hair was in a knotted mess on the top of my head, and a baggy sleep shirt hung to my knees over even baggier sweatpants. Shania Twain? Nope. Try Amy Winehouse circa 2007, which was ironic as well.

A large silhouette loomed outside the door. Definitely not Etta. And definitely a man.

And I was *definitely* getting window curtains ASAP.

The figure shifted impatiently. I peeked out the side window at the blacked-out Range Rover sitting on twenty-twos.

Hmph.

As the man raised his hand to knock again, I opened the door, coffee in one hand and letter opener in the other. Something resembling a shot of espresso burst through my veins.

Of all the people to show up at my door, I hadn't expected Clark Kent. He was an Adonis, a chiseled statue of perfection with jet-black hair combed perfectly to the side, a nose almost as sharp as his jawline, that I assumed could pop a thong with one nip. And those eyes, his eyes, as black as sin with a mischievous sparkle to match.

His gaze swept me from head to toe. The corner of a pair of thin but strong lips curled up in both amusement and approval.

My brow cocked, and I gave him a once-over of my own.

He was put together to perfection, not a single wrinkle or speck of dirt on his designer suit. He reminded me of the models we'd use for fashion shoots at *Catwalk Magazine*. Every piece of the man matched, everything planned, everything had a purpose. From his air of cockiness—which clung to him like a French cologne—to his monogrammed gold cuff links, the man was totally, one hundred percent my type.

He raised a large lidded to-go cup and flashed a smile seen only in Colgate commercials. "Coffee?"

Without a word, I tilted my head with one brow raised and lifted my own cup.

He held up a brown bag in his other hand. "Doughnuts then?"

I leaned against the door frame. "Does everyone around here assume sugar validates unannounced drop-ins?"

"Probably."

He was a bit smug with an unmistakable air of wealth and privilege. I could spot it a mile away. Hell, I'd married it.

"Then I guess I'll have to add a gym membership to my list of things to get."

"Not necessary." He scanned my body again to punctuate his point. "And I'm not just anyone. There's also a ham-and-cheese croissant, a sausage-egg-and-cheese biscuit that, according to the waitress, is the best in the entire world. And in the event that you might be vegetarian, a spinach-and-cheese fold-over thing that looks like a pile of dog shit."

"What if I was vegan?"

"No one's vegan in the South. Oh, and there's a cheese Danish too."

"Sold." I set my coffee on the windowsill, praying it would stay. Still clutching my letter opener, I took the bag from his hand, missing the vein on his wrist by a half inch.

His brows arched questioningly as he lifted the coffee.

"Sure." With my free hand, I took it too. "Now, what's got you standing on my doorstep before seven in the morning, Mister . . ."

"Covington."

Of course. Covington.

"Lucas Covington. And please accept my apologies for my early visit. I always get a jump on the day. Will you speak with me for a moment?"

I sipped at the coffee. Vanilla latte perfection. "Yes, now I will."

"Thank you. Miss Dalton, I've come here today to offer you a deal you can't refuse."

"Ah." I nodded. "You must be from the big-dick hotel company."

"My reputation precedes me," he said, not missing an excuse for a sexual innuendo.

"I've been warned."

"Of course you have." He winked. "Good thing I kick ass at first impressions."

I nodded to the SUV behind him. "First question. Who's the guy sitting in your Range Rover, staring at me?"

"Ah, that's Edward Schultz. My partner. Too early for him. Second question?"

"How do you know my name?"

"I never visit a lady's house unannounced unless I know her name."

"Creepy."

"I won't consider myself creepy until I start showing up with a letter opener clenched in my fist. Would you mind?" he asked as he reached for it.

I jerked it back. "How about you tell me exactly why you're here, and then we'll see where the opener ends up."

"Miss Dalton, my company and I would like to offer you the appraised amount of your property, plus an extra fifteen thousand for your swift move out of the premises."

"That's more than a few zeros."

"Is that a yes?"

"No."

"No?"

"No."

"How about dinner?"

"Sure, I'll let you take me to dinner for the appraised value of my property."

He grinned. "Expensive dinner."

"But you get all this." I swept a hand over the train wreck of my appearance.

"Worth every penny."

"You're one smooth talker, Mr. Covington."

"I have to be."

"I imagine so."

"So?"

"I'll have to think about it."

"Dinner or the money?"

"Both."

"I'm afraid I can't give you much time, Miss Dalton. I'm in town only for a short time, just long enough to close on your house and two others by the end of the week."

"You move fast."

"When I know what I want, yes." His gaze dropped to my lips as a buzz of attraction built between us.

"Well, Mr. Covington, as much as I appreciate the Danish and coffee—"

"And an extra fifteen thousand dollars for your inconvenience."

"Right. As much as I appreciate it all, as you can see," I nodded behind me, "I've got a big day ahead of me."

"I can see that."

He peered over my shoulder, and I felt a twinge of embarrassment. I didn't like that.

"I'll be on my way then." Lucas pulled a card from his pocket, black with gold foil letters, and handed it to me.

Lucas R. Covington
Covington Hotels and Resorts

On the back was a list of numbers, including his cell phone number.

"Nice to meet you, Lucas R. Covington."

"Nice to meet you, Grey Dalton."

As the Range Rover disappeared down the driveway, I had a feeling it wasn't the last time I was going to see Mr. Covington.

14

On my way into civilization, I passed five churches, four horses, three tractors—is that even legal?—and two groups of cyclists. A narrow two-lane road with the unimaginative name of Main Street led to the town square, the hub of all things Berry Springs and the location of the only stoplight in the entire town. The kind that hung over the street on wires.

Despite it being before eight in the morning, the square was buzzing with activity. Last night's coolness had already faded, transformed into a mild morning with a sapphire-blue sky and bright sunshine. A mixture of fresh morning dew, budding flowers, and horse manure scented the air.

While I waited for the light to turn green, I looked around at the modern-day Mayberry in both shock and awe that this was my new home.

Temporarily, I was now more certain than ever.

Colorful pots of impatiens and begonias lined the storefronts, where the citizens—most in cowboy hats and boots—went about their business. I noticed Tad's Tool Shop that Etta had mentioned the day before. Next to it was Bonnie's

Bouffant, where two men with matching canes sat comfortably in rocking chairs outside, waiting on their wives to finish their styling. Gino's Pizzeria was catty-corner to it in a brick building with a bright red door. The post office, a bank, and the courthouse shored up the other side of the square.

But without question, the main attraction was Donny's Diner, a stereotypical small-town eatery with a line out the front door. Blue-and-white checkered curtains hung from windows that announced the daily specials in colorful paint on the glass.

When the light turned green, I drove ahead slowly, searching for a place to park. After ten minutes of circling the block, I was forced to settle for a spot on a side street between two duallies, one with a snarling Rottweiler chained in the truck bed.

I cut off the engine and took a second to gather myself, nerves and memories already starting to get the better of me. With a heavy exhale, I grabbed my purse and got out. The snarling monster snapped at me as I locked the doors. I grinned, imagining he was no match for Moonshine.

A few whistles followed as I made my way up the sidewalk, causing multiple heads to turn in my direction. Stares lingered, and I began to question the fitted mint-green sundress and sky-high wedges I'd chosen for my breakfast date.

I dipped my chin as I passed a duo of stay-at-home moms pushing double strollers, both wearing matching hot-pink spandex. Behind them walked another pair of women, these two in freshly pressed mom jeans and T-shirts that read SUPPORT THE BOBCAT BOOSTER CLUB.

Clutching my Louis Vuitton purse, I stepped to the end of the line outside of Donny's Diner. More heads turned, more lingering gazes, this time accompanied with whispers.

Definitely should have rethought the sundress.

I cleared my throat and squared my shoulders. It wasn't the first time I'd been whispered about, and probably wouldn't be the last.

"Grey!"

The crowd parted, the sunlight catching the bleached-blond hair of my breakfast date—my cousin, who I hadn't seen since that godawful day.

A blast of butterflies in my belly made for a crooked smile as my cousin, Cassidy, pushed through the crowd, and two vanilla-scented arms enveloped me in a bear hug.

"Oh my God, you look amazing." Cassidy pulled back, examining me from head to toe.

Time had been kind to her. Although she was five years younger than me, my cousin barely looked twenty-one.

"You do too," I said. "And I'm so glad to see you."

"Oh, don't worry about them." Cassidy shifted her attention to the whispering women behind me. "It's a Louis Vuitton, Sharon. She's from the city."

A grunt sounded behind me before Cassidy pulled me past the line.

"I've already got our booth. I couldn't believe it when you texted me last night. You're *here.* I can't believe it." Cassidy slipped her hand into mine and squeezed, sending a warm feeling through me.

My cousin's demeanor was exactly as I remembered, a bubbling ball of happiness and zest for life, despite her past. Her hot-rolled curls danced on pointy shoulders above a vintage Waylon Jennings T-shirt. Frayed cut-offs and flip-flops completed the look. *Note to self on Southern fashion.*

Although it had been a decade since I'd seen her,

Cassidy was still long and lean and had that familiar playful sparkle about her.

A wall of air-conditioned air perfumed with coffee and grease greeted us as I was pulled through the front door of Donny's Diner.

The restaurant was packed. A group of wary hunters lingered by the door, waiting for a booth. Multiple conversations about the latest sales tax increase, the upcoming high school baseball game, and something about the mayor's mistress carried over the shouts from the kitchen and the hum of classic country through the jukebox.

A packed countertop lined the back of the diner, a busy kitchen with a cut-out window directly behind it. To the right, rows of red leather booths hugged the windows. The floor was covered with gleaming black-and-white checkerboard tiles. An old soda fountain sat next to the antique jukebox whining something about cheating lovers. Heads turned as we slid into the only open booth, in the back corner.

"Okay, seriously, do I have something in my teeth?" I flashed a toothy smile.

"No. We're just not used to city folk around here. Or anyone new, other than tourists, which we don't mind."

"They don't mind tourists but don't like city folk?"

"Tourism is half the town's yearly revenue stream."

"Well, why don't they assume I'm a tourist?"

She waved a hand at my body with a grin. "You don't exactly scream nature-lover."

"Thanks."

Cassidy laughed, then glanced at the cartoon-cat clock on the wall. "How long do you have?"

"My appointment with the realtor is at eight thirty."

"Okay." Her smile widened as she took me in. "Damn,

Grey, it's been seventeen years since I've seen you. You know that?"

My heartbeat pounded in my ears as we stared at each other for a minute with the weight of a thousand words. The past that bonded us, a sisterhood borne of pain and tragedy.

"Okay." She waved a hand in the air, dismissing the negative energy that had settled around us. Leaning forward on her elbows with puppy-like enthusiasm, she said, "Tell me everything."

I released a breath, grateful we weren't addressing the elephant in the room. *Yet.*

"Howdy, ladies. Cassie, good to see you."

A silver-haired waitress stepped up to the table, pulling a yellow number-two pencil from behind her ear. From my vantage point, she had three more threaded through the silver bun on the top of her head. Wide-rimmed glasses sat at the tip of her nose, a black-and-white apron over wide hips and a paisley dress.

"Morning, Ms. Booth," Cassidy said as the waitress eyed me with curiosity. "This is my long-lost cousin, Grey Dalton."

"Pleasure to meet you," I said.

"You too. My, what a dress. Where're you from?"

"New York."

"'Splains it."

I didn't bother to tell her that New York didn't necessarily mean the city.

"What brings you to little ol' Berry Springs?" she asked.

"I bought a house here." My attempt to sound upbeat failed miserably.

"Did you now?" Ms. Booth's eyes rounded. "Whereabouts?"

"Rattlesnake Road."

"You're kidding. You're not talking about that old cabin down from Etta's, are you?"

"Yes, ma'am."

The waitress blew out a breath, shaking her head in disbelief, which did nothing to ease my worries about the house. "Well, welcome to Berry Springs. Your first breakfast here at Donny's is on the house."

"Thank you."

"My pleasure. Happy to see someone fixin' that place up again. Beautiful weather for it. Nancy sell it to you?"

"Yes. She's been wonderful." And apparently the only real estate agent in town.

"Better be. She's my third cousin. Anyways, what can I git for y'all?"

Cassidy ordered a ham-and-cheese omelet with a side of grits and sweet tea, and I ordered scrambled eggs, toast, and a Coke.

"When did you get in?" Cassidy asked as Ms. Booth moved on to the next table.

I noticed the waitress addressed everyone by name. Small town, indeed.

"Late yesterday afternoon."

"You drove?"

I nodded. "Twenty *hours,* Cassie."

"Holy smokes. Straight through?"

"No way. Stopped overnight twice." To vomit, cry, and question every decision I'd ever made in my life, but she didn't need to know that.

"How's the house?" Cassidy asked with a wrinkled nose. Apparently everyone, with the exception of myself, knew about the condition of the cabin down Rattlesnake Road.

"It needs work."

"I don't doubt that. It's been a while since I've been down

Rattlesnake Road. Used to be a shortcut to the lake, but that road has overgrown now. I've been to that house at least a dozen times, you know that?"

"No. Really? When?"

"When the lady before you lived there. Bonnie. This was a while ago, when I used to deliver Sunday dinners from the church to single women, widowed, whatever. I'd just got my license. It was my first job." Cassidy laughed before her face dropped with pity. "The house needed work then, so I can't imagine what it looks like now. I'm here to help. And I mean that."

"Thanks. I might need it. So, you knew Bonnie?"

"Everyone did."

I thought of the letter but decided not to bring it up. Lord knew there was a dark enough cloud lingering above my cousin and me. No need to add to it.

"What was she like?" I asked.

"Smart as a whip. Witty too. Gardened a lot. Kept herself busy, despite being all the way out there by herself. Then she just got old. I heard she got dementia or something." Cassidy's brow furrowed. "I worry about you being out there alone, you know."

"Don't, really. I'll be fine. I've lived in the city for years. I can handle this. Did Bonnie ever talk to you about her problems or anything like that while you were there?"

"No. Only polite small talk. She'd give me some tasks to do while I was there. Even had me paint a few rooms for a few bucks one time. Why do you ask?"

"I'd just like to know the roots of the place."

Ms. Booth delivered our drinks, along with a basket of biscuits with butter and jelly.

"Well, that place has got plenty of overgrown roots, I'm sure of it. Again, I'm here to help." Cassidy paused, taking a short breath. "I still can't believe you're here. That you really went through with the pact. Our pact."

"I made a promise to you that if I ever left New York, I'd come here." A promise made from the binds of guilt, I knew now.

"And here you are. You know you could have stayed with me."

"No, no. Thank you, though." *Way too much baggage*, I thought but didn't say.

"Okay, I get it. I'm just so glad you're here." Tears glistened in her brown eyes, but she blinked them away. "Okay. Enough of that. Now that we've got our drinks, spill the tea." She frowned deeply. "Tell me what happened with you and your husband."

I sipped my Coke. "Well, Cassie, it's a story as old as time. Bastard cheated on me."

She shook her head in disgust.

"Three times."

"Bastard." Cassidy shook a Splenda packet, ripped the top, and dumped its contents into her drink. Stirring, she said, "I'm so sorry. I know it's hard. I've been cheated on once, but wasn't married. I'm sure that makes it harder."

I decided against telling her about the miscarriage, being fired, or my struggles with alcohol. Too soon, too personal, and too raw. All Cassidy knew was that I'd left my husband and lost my job. And that was enough for me.

"I'm glad you left him," she said. "A lot of women stay and accept a loveless, mundane life. I don't get it. You're better than that, Grey. You've always been better than that, despite your upbringing."

I swallowed hard, then took a sip of Coke to wash down the knot in my throat.

"How long were y'all married? I forget."

"Ten years, and we still are. Separated now—I guess that's the technical term. His dad's a lawyer, though, golf buddies with the judge. He'll have the divorce pushed through in days, I'll bet. I have no doubt about it."

"Have you two worked out the division of assets?"

I nodded. "We had a prenup. He's keeping what's his. I'm keeping what's mine."

"Good for you. What does he do again? You told me in one of our emails, but I forgot."

"He's a financial consultant."

"Fancy."

I snorted. "He was never home. Traveled constantly."

"Where?"

"All over. Companies hired him to assess their P&Ls, or something like that. He evaluates their operational costs, staff, vendors, negotiated better pricing on their behalf."

"Sounds boring."

"Not when you're getting head under your desk by your secretary on a regular basis."

She wrinkled her nose. "Gross. I'm so sorry."

I flicked a hand in the air. "It is what it is. Men are assholes."

Cassidy lifted her tea. "Cheers to that. So, you left him and came down here. What are you going to do now?"

"Renovate this damn house . . . and figure it out as I go, I guess."

She mirrored my sad smile. "Listen, I can get you a hundred jobs around here, if you need help finding one. Might not be as glamorous as working in fashion, or pay as much, for that matter. But it'll keep you afloat until you figure stuff out."

"Thank you. Really. I've got some money saved up, but yeah, I'll have to figure out something soon. I've got a neighbor . . ." I laughed, thinking of Etta with her foul mouth and tracksuits. "She's offered to give me a bunch of her old furniture."

"You talking about Etta May? She already came over?"

"Yep."

Cassidy laughed. "I shouldn't be surprised. She's like everyone's stand-in grandmother. I bet she's been watching over that place like a hawk. Woman's got her nose in everyone's business. A huge gossip. But people accept it because she's the best baker in town."

"I can personally attest to that. Anyway, I'll still have to get the big stuff like beds and couches. According to Etta, I only have one option here in town, right?"

"Abe's?"

"That's the one."

"I know his son. They're good people."

"That'll lessen the blow of the check I'm about to cut him."

"New furniture, new beginnings. All worth it."

I smiled, but it didn't reach my eyes. These new beginnings were sure feeling like the past.

Ms. Booth slid our breakfast plates onto the table. Cassidy dove into her omelet like a starving POW.

"Anyway, enough about that," I said, biting into my toast. "Tell me about your love life. How're the pickings around here?"

"Girl, you haven't seen cowboys until you've been in these parts." She swiped a string of cheese from her chin. "You're in for a treat, my dear friend. The men down here are every bit as yummy as you Yankees imagine."

I grinned, although her assessment was incorrect. For me, anyway. While I'd certainly ogled a few corn-fed cowboys in my day, I'd always been more attracted to the ones in three-piece suits. The ones with the devil's twinkle in their eye, an ace up their sleeve, and lips as cunning as their bank account. The kind of guys who were trouble.

Guys like Lucas Covington.

"My last cowboy was named Jeremy," Cassidy said.

"Yeah . . ." I thought back. "I remember that name from our emails. But then you stopped talking about him."

"For good reason. He was one of the first people who befriended me after I moved here. We dated on and off during and after high school. Broke up for a few years, then got back together. Three years ago, he popped the question. I said yes." She looked down, heartbreak shadowing her face. "Bastard broke up with me six months later. Said it was all too much. Felt like he needed to 'see more of the world,' whatever the hell that means."

"Ouch."

"Yeah. Last I heard, he was living in Oklahoma City, working for an oil company. Still single, according to his Instagram feed that I stalk daily. Pitcatso_countrycutie, here. One of his hundred female followers." She rolled her eyes.

"They're probably bots. Paid for." I tilted my head to the side. "Pitcatso country cutie?"

"It's my cat's name, Pitcatso. And I like to think of myself as a country cutie." Cassidy winked. "She's a tortoiseshell cat. Black, yellow, white, tan, brown. I swear she's got a little blue under her neck too. Plus, her eyes are kind of crooked. One's higher than the other." She shrugged. "Reminded me of a Picasso painting. Did you know tortoiseshell cats are almost exclusively female? Males are usually sterile."

"Lucky cats."

She laughed. "Tell me about it."

"Okay, so you still stalk your ex. Anyone else in the picture?"

Cassidy shook her head. "No. I've dated a few guys here and there, but that's it. You know I'm on the slippery side of thirty."

"It creeps up on you. You're twenty-six, right?"

"Yep. Clock's ticking. All my friends have at least one baby."

My stomach dipped at the thought of the baby that had been in my belly. "Don't rush it, Cassie. We're still young. And hell, I'm single again."

"Your luck's about to turn. I'm sure of it. All the guys will be after you once word gets out about a new girl in town. You'll be the shiny new toy for about a year, until the next girl running from something moves to town."

I tapped the clock on my phone. "A year before I'm forgotten and labeled a pathetic Berry Springs spinster. Good to know."

She laughed. "Yep, they'll . . ." Her words trailed off as her eyes rounded, focusing on something at the front of the restaurant. The fork dropped from her hand. "Holy . . . speaking of a shiny new toy . . ."

I glanced over my shoulder, and our eyes met instantly.

Lucas Covington was wearing the same three-piece suit as when he'd been on my doorstep an hour earlier. I got a better look at it under the harsh fluorescent lights of the diner. Navy. Brioni, based on the slim-tailored perfection.

His lips curved as he saw me, and I couldn't help but grin back. Nor could any woman in the diner. The lingering gazes I'd received when I walked in had nothing on Lucas Covington. The next table over, a man snapped his fingers at his gawking wife.

I broke our stare and turned back to Cassidy, who was still gaping as if staring at the second coming of Christ.

"That is quite possibly the most gorgeous specimen of

man I've ever seen in my life. He looks like he was made in a test tube," she whispered.

"He wants to buy my house."

Her gaze snapped back to mine, and her jaw dropped. "What? You met him?"

This, apparently, being a more important thing to address.

I nodded. "He—his name's Lucas Covington—came to my house this morning. Offered to buy my property."

"Dear Lord in heaven, please tell me you had sex with him."

"Yep. That's right, Cassie. Right there on my rotted front porch at seven in the morning. With my morning breath and four-day leg stubble."

She closed her eyes, swallowed, and sighed. "Would be nice, wouldn't it?"

An image of a naked Lucas Covington flashed through my head. It would be nice, I imagined.

"Who's the guy with him?" she asked.

I glanced back at the large man standing in Lucas's shadow, recognizing him instantly as the man sitting in the Range Rover while Lucas and I flirted on my porch.

Gray hair and deep-set wrinkles suggested he was at least a decade older than Lucas. A dark tailored suit suggested he had about the same amount of money. Although his expression was relaxed, bored even, he wore a scowl on his face comfortably, as if habitually. Like Lucas, the man was put together like a million bucks. Unlike Lucas, he was invisible to everyone in the room. He didn't speak, simply patiently waited for Lucas to lead him to a table.

"I think that's his partner."

"He's *gay*?"

"No." I laughed. "His work partner."

"Oh. He looks mean. Anyway, I've heard about—Lucas, you said his name is?"

I nodded.

"I heard there was a hot guy in town but hadn't had the pleasure of seeing him. According to the gossip, he's been in town for the last three days." Cassidy swirled the cheese from her omelet around her fork. "Everyone's talking about him. Every woman, anyway. The men hate him. He's trying to get to know the locals, schmoozing, all that stuff. Wants to build some big-dick resort on the lake."

"That name has really caught on."

"Well, people don't like it. I mean, they like looking at him, but they don't like the idea of an outsider owning a hundred acres of the mountainside."

"But the resort would bring in more tourism, right? Didn't you say that's a huge part of the local economy?"

"We've already got a big resort that brings in plenty. You see, from the outside, Berry Springs might appear to be a run-down one-horse town, but people from all over come to visit—spring, summer, fall. We're known for our camping, hiking, fishing, caves, hunting. If we keep building, clearing the forests, we're going to lose everything that makes Berry Springs special."

As Lucas mingled with the small-town folk in his five-thousand-dollar suit, I sneaked another peek. Unfazed by the stuttering women and scoffing men, he owned the room, sauntering from table to table, hell-bent on making them like him.

In that moment, I realized how similar we were. Two fish out of water, doing what we needed to do to get the job done. His job focused on dollar signs, and mine focused on healing.

Lucas Covington was the walking poster boy for the

kind of men I used to date. Smart, charismatic, attractive, successful, and cocky. He was the type of man I fell hard for, as did most women. Something that wasn't lost on him, I was sure.

And on that note, I refocused on Cassidy.

"So, you're saying if I sell out to him, the one year I have as the shiny new toy in town would be erased."

"Exactly. You'll be hated almost as much as Rat."

"What's Rat?"

"You mean who's Rat? We've got one homeless person in town, and they call him Rat. He's usually harmless, but the last few weeks he's gone around spray-painting penises on every brick wall within a five-mile radius. Big, gangly penises with hairy ball sacs." She laughed. "You should have seen ol' Opal when he did her wall. Chased him down the street with a straw broom. It was on the news. Went viral. Anyway, you'll be banished from town. But you'll always have—"

"Miss Dalton." A low voice interrupted us, as smooth as Donny's fountain Coke.

"Lucas." I looked up into pitch-black eyes. "Are you stalking me?"

"Would this offend you?"

"Depends on how many more Danishes you've got in your pocket."

"I have a few other things in my pocket that might interest you."

Cassidy choked on her tea.

"This is Cassidy, my single friend. Cassidy, this is Lucas Covington, fan of sexual innuendos and owner—I'm assuming—of Covington Big-Dick Hotels and Resorts."

Lucas grinned as he offered his hand to Cassidy. "Single by choice, I'm assuming. It's a pleasure to meet you."

"You too." She blushed like a schoolgirl as she shook his hand.

He turned back to me. "Have you made a decision about what we discussed this morning?"

"Which offer are you referring to?"

"Both."

"No."

"Sounds like I wasn't convincing enough. Shame on me. Dinner, tomorrow, seven o'clock. We'll talk numbers and Danishes. I'll pick you up. Will that work for you?"

"Yes," Cassidy blurted. "Yes, it works great for her."

Frowning, I sliced a look her way.

"Great," Lucas said, his gaze never leaving mine. "I'll see you tomorrow at seven o'clock, Miss Dalton. By the way, nice dress."

15

After breakfast, I met with Nancy to sign papers, crossing the t's and dotting the i's. Later, I met with the utility companies and the bank, doing the same. The afternoon was spent running errands as I dodged intermittent rain showers that had moved in not long after breakfast.

First stop, the post office to submit a change of address. Then I cringed for an hour at the DMV while waiting to get an updated driver's license, avoiding all surfaces, door knobs, and hand rests.

Once those tasks were done, I visited Abe at the furniture store. Although I'd given the man half my remaining savings, I was told he wouldn't be able to deliver at once everything I bought, and not until at least the next day. Something about a mother-in-law's broken hip.

Next up, the tool shop and the grocery store. Then I followed the signs for a flea market and bought a few things there, and when I left, got lost for thirty minutes. Shocking, considering the size of the town and that all roads led to Main Street. At that point, I decided to head home for the day.

As promised, Etta had left a care package at my front door. More oatmeal cookies, a six-pack of Coke and a bottle of allergy pills. Yep, the woman was, without question, my Southern guardian angel. I took her offerings inside, then unloaded my car.

Five o'clock—previously known as happy hour—came and went without much agony. I considered that a huge success. Sobriety sucked, but I was getting better at it. The headaches were easing, the night sweats abating.

Cassidy texted me eleven times after our breakfast together. *Eleven.* Half were giving me advice or tips pertaining to navigating small-town life, and the other half were images of Lucas she'd found on the internet.

I'd refrained from googling him, but according to Cassidy, Lucas had been born in Dallas where his grandfather built the first Covington hotel. Four decades later, the family's net worth had grown to five hundred million bucks. Lucas was forty-five years old, had never been married and had no kids. I thought this was weird at first—and then I looked in the mirror.

After berating myself for looking at his pictures for the tenth time, I grabbed a Coke and returned to the master bedroom, the epicenter of my life. I clicked on the harsh ceiling light, which was another thing I needed to update.

The rainy afternoon turned into a cool, damp evening, so I opened the window, enjoying the scent of rain thick in the air. The light from the house pooled onto the small backyard, illuminating the edge of the woods, dark with night.

I wondered where Moonshine was, and if she and her kittens had found refuge from the rain.

As my gaze shifted to the fields in the distance, my thoughts moved to the cowboy on horseback. I wondered if he was sitting in his kitchen at that moment, having dinner with his large Southern family. Something filling like spaghetti, meatballs, and homemade garlic bread probably filled the table, all made by his loving wife. I envisioned kids washing their hands in the sink, and a baby asleep in its bassinet in the next room.

The total antithesis of my life.

Turning away from the window, I shifted my focus back to work. Open suitcases littered the floor, clothes strewn about. I'd leaned a mirror against the wall next to the blow-up mattress where mounds of my toiletries were scattered over a towel on the floor. A makeshift vanity. A poor girl's vanity.

It was a mess.

I was a mess.

With a sigh, I lowered myself to the floor in front of a suitcase, tucking my legs under me. I pulled a cashmere sweater from the heap of clothes, wrapped it around my shoulders, then began sifting through my clothes and folding them.

A few minutes had passed when the faintest creak pulled my attention to the doorway. Followed by another creak, like tiny footsteps on the uneven hardwood floors.

My pulse rate picked up. I tossed the sweater to the side, pushing myself off the floor, and tripped over the suitcase as I took the first step too quickly. Clothes tumbled out of it, but I didn't care. I stumbled to the doorway, waiting to hear that same giggle I'd heard the night before.

But like then, there was no one. No ghost, no little girl.

When I returned to the bedroom, I was surprised to see a small plastic storage box had fallen out of the suitcase I'd tripped over. I picked it up, my stomach sinking with recognition. I didn't remember packing it. *Must have been drunk.*

I popped open the lid and stared down at the handful of memories I'd shoved inside. My first thought, as I looked at the photos, was how few there were. There weren't many memories of my past that I wanted to hang on to.

The first was an image of my wedding day, complete with the expected white dress, white roses, and fake smiles, along with empty promises and vows that would be destroyed years later. I set it aside, then picked up another picture, this one of myself centered in a line of giggling girls. Behind us were the blinking lights of Vegas. College friends —*old* college friends.

I studied each face, wondering what each girl had done with their lives, and then wondered why I didn't know. When had I lost touch? When was it that my entire life revolved around a paycheck, around money?

Inhaling deeply, I tossed it back into the plastic box. But before I could secure the lid, the pictures shifted.

I froze, blinking at the corner of a photo I hadn't seen in decades.

Slowly, I set aside the lid again and lifted the picture. She looked so much like Cassidy. That same sparkle for life in her eyes. The same blond hair and long, lean frame.

Tears welled in my eyes and my breath caught, my lungs suddenly constricting with memories from that night.

"Oh my God," I whispered as tears began to fall.

I remembered it like it was yesterday.

We were as thick as thieves, Brianna and me. Cassidy tried to keep up, but having the title of Brianna's "little sister" made her as welcome as a bad rash. My aunt and uncle lived two neighborhoods down from my mom and me in New York.

Brianna and I did everything together. We got ready for school together in the mornings, rode the bus together, ate lunch together, played outside together until the sun went down. We'd play make-believe—princesses, fairies, pop stars. We'd called each other sisters, deciding it was a better fit than cousins.

It happened the day after her tenth birthday. Brianna had come over with her loot of nail polish and hair ribbons. My mom had stayed home from work that day. I didn't know why then, but I do now.

Sometime after sundown, Mom decided she was hungry but didn't want to cook. As she grabbed her keys, we begged for ice cream, a late birthday celebration.

She said okay.

The roads were wet from rain that refused to go away. I remember thunder rumbling as Brianna and I piled into the back seat, so excited. Bursts of lightning lit our smiles as we descended the driveway.

We were less than two miles from home when Mom fishtailed around a corner, slid off the road going forty miles an hour, and slammed into a tree.

The next thing I remember was waking up in her arms to the sound of sirens wailing in the distance. Her face was bloodied, her eyes wild. I'll never forget that look.

There was so much commotion around me. Strangers had pulled over, and one woman was screaming for help. I remember wondering why everyone wasn't fussing over me. Then I saw Brianna's frail little body on the asphalt, her eyes closed, her face covered in blood. An image that still haunts me to this day.

I screamed, fighting like a rabid dog to get out of my mom's grasp, but couldn't. She was crying so hard. Uncontrollably. Her tears wet the side of my face, and I remember wiping them away and yelling at her to calm down.

Why wasn't she helping Brianna?

A few minutes later, my cousin was taken away in an ambulance to a hospital, where she remained for two days under observation. I didn't leave her side. Brianna was eventually released and told everything was going to be okay.

Mom was arrested for drunk driving and endangering the welfare of a minor. She spent the next month in jail. While she was away, I lived with one of my mom's friends because she and my aunt—my mom's sister, mother of Brianna—weren't speaking. Rightly so. I wasn't allowed to see Brianna or Cassidy.

Family rift.

Again, rightly so.

Four months after the accident, Brianna started having seizures. Her parents blamed the accident, but doctors couldn't link it. They said it was an underlying health condition that she'd likely had since birth, and puberty kicked it into drive.

After that, I only saw Brianna at school. She was different. I knew she was medicated, but it was more than that.

Cassidy and I became close during that time. Our friendship was never the same as Brianna's and mine, but I think it helped fill a hole for both of us.

Brianna died at age fifteen while suffering a seizure in the bathtub. The next year, her family moved from upstate New York to the small Southern town of Berry Springs to restart their life.

To escape their past.

To escape my drunk mother, who they never spoke to again.

Before they left town, Cassidy and I cried together. She didn't want to move. We exchanged email addresses because we were worried about using the phone too much. I promised her on that day that if I ever left New York, I'd go to Berry Springs.

I hated my mother. Blamed her. I wanted them to be able to link Brianna's death to the accident so that the family would have closure. I wanted my mom to pay for the horrible decision she made that night.

You see, by that point, my mother was no longer my mom. She was an alcoholic. An addict. My aunt told me that my mom drank morning, noon, and night, ever since suffering postpartum depression after I was born—although she drank heavily before then as well. It only got worse as the years dragged on. My aunt said that between the addiction and the constant struggle to make ends meet, Mom couldn't handle the day-to-day pressure.

Depression. Addiction. Money.

Damn the money. I promised myself I'd never become my mother and I'd never be poor again. I'd have lots and lots of money.

Mom died of liver disease six months after I'd moved out at age eighteen. And that was that.

Although, it wasn't.

It wasn't over because now *I* was the alcoholic. *I* was drifting, living in a run-down shack with limited funds and an uncertain future. *I* was now the pathetic single thirty-something.

Choking back a sob, I tucked the picture away, then looked around the room to take in the dirt, the grime, the dilapidated house in the middle of nowhere.

Thunder rumbled in the distance, sounding exactly as it did that night. I felt like I was back in my mother's shitty house, in a hillbilly town, with nothing.

With a guttural scream, I hurled the plastic box against

the wall, pictures exploding into the air and then fluttering back down as I pushed off the floor, sucking back the tears.

I wanted a drink.

Grinding my teeth, I stalked to the kitchen. I paced back and forth, my eyes locked on my new laundry basket. In it, beneath my dirty laundry, I'd hidden the two bottles of red wine I had left.

Pacing like a rabid animal, I clenched my hands into fists, a headache brewing between my temples.

"God *damn* it, Mom."

I whirled around, the thoughts in my head like static on television. I yanked the hammer from the counter, stalked back to the bedroom, pushed my way into the closet, and released my pain against the drywall. One hole, two holes, dust and drywall exploding around me, tears running down my face.

Dropping to my knees, I began sifting through the mess, praying to find another letter. Praying to find someone else as messed up as I was. Someone, something, to make me feel better.

And I did. Tucked between the slats was another envelope.

I exhaled relief, as an addict might when the needle pierces their arm.

Make me feel better, you crazy person. Make me feel better.

I blew the dust off the envelope, then carried it into the kitchen where the light was brighter. With a deep breath, I slowly opened it and removed the letter, handwritten in the same shaky cursive as the first.

Swallowing deeply, I began reading.

16

Letter #2

I cut myself today. I don't know why.

I didn't think about the scars, but I am now. Mom and Dad will kill me if they see I've been cutting myself. They'll probably add more pills that I won't take anyway.

Mom's scared of me now. I can see it when she looks at me, in the distance she keeps between us. You know what's kind of fucked up? I think I like that she's scared of me.

I've decided that I kind of like being different. I like having little secrets that no one knows, but everyone wonders what they are. But they're my secrets.

I've heard of people cutting themselves. I've seen it in a few movies. I know I'm supposed to cut down the blue line, the vein, if I'm trying to kill myself. But I wasn't really trying to do that. I didn't feel like dying. Something like that should be prepared for. If I ever commit suicide, I'm going out in a fucking blaze of glory. Something where people will remember my name.

You might be wondering why I did it. Well, it started with a damn stray cat. We've got a few of them around here. I was so fucking bored, I decided to try to catch one. Make it my pet for the summer, I guess. But the fucker scratched the hell out of me when I tried to pin it down. I let it go, although what I really wanted to do was snap its neck. Didn't it realize I was trying not to hurt it? That I just wanted to be its friend? I would have fed it, given it water, a warm place to sleep. Fucking idiot.

The scratches bled, so I went into the kitchen to clean up. I found myself watching the blood. I smeared it along my skin, making a design, and decided I needed a bit more red. I grabbed a knife and traced the tip along the scratches, and one thing led to another. I ran one cut all the way down my thumb and was going to call it a battle wound.

So that's it. That's the story. No big buildup or planning. No sobbing, shaking my fists to the heavens, wishing I were dead or cursing others. I did it because I was bored and wanted to see what it felt like.

After that, I wrapped my wrist in a towel and went to my secret spot in the woods where I hid the whiskey I'd stolen from the bitch neighbor's house. Alcohol is so much better than the pills, or pot even. It makes me feel like the real me, not the me I can see in everyone's eyes when they look at me.

I've read that for someone with ADHD—that's what I was diagnosed with years ago, although I think it's turned into something more now—it's best to keep them busy. A way to burn their energy. A way to keep their minds from racing.

Racing? Mine never stops.

I wonder what it would be like to hurt Mom. I've seen the stories on the news and read the articles of those kids who just snap one day and murder someone.

I started researching.

You've probably heard of Edmund Kemper. He was a serial killer, rapist, cannibal, and necrophile. He murdered ten people, including his mom and grandparents. For no good reason, apparently. I found this quote:

"I just wanted to see how it felt to shoot Grandma." – Edmund Kemper

That's his most famous quote. One I liked is:

"I remember there was actually a sexual thrill . . . you hear that little pop and pull their heads off and hold their heads up by the hair. Whipping their heads off, their body sitting there. That'd get me off."

I found this one from David Alan Gore. He killed six people.

"All of a sudden I realized that I had just done something that separated me from the human race and it was something that could never be undone. I realized that from that point on I could never be like normal people. I must have stood there in that state for 20 minutes. I have never felt an emptiness of self like I did right then and will never forget that feeling. It was like I crossed over into a realm I could never come back from." – David Alan Gore

Masochism is when someone gets turned on from being hurt. But sadism is when someone gets turned on by causing someone else pain and suffering. They get off on seeing the fear, hearing the screams. The helplessness.

I always thought a sadist was someone who worshipped the devil. I guess not. This made me research further.

There are many theories on why someone gains sexual pleasure from another person's suffering. One is that they have an overactive imagination. I thought that was funny. In that case, half the world are sadists, I'd imagine. Another is that they'd seen it somewhere else, making it less taboo to them. Another is that it links to a psychotic disorder. A brain disease.

I found this theory the most interesting, so I read a lot about it. They talk about compulsive genital stimulation from unnatural things. This happens when you get excited by seeing

someone else tortured, like sadism. As it becomes increasingly violent and sexual, your heart rate, blood pressure, and breathing increase. As the torture increases, the arousal increases until you have to make yourself come.

I found some videos online. I'm pretty sure I could get arrested for watching them.

Anyway, in these cases, they talk about how sex is an expression of dominance and anger. I read that the victim usually represents something the offender hates about themselves and usually has some sort of similarities, like age or appearance. They call them thrill-oriented types of killers. They crave excitement and bizarre experiences, most commonly stemming from boredom.

Guess that loops back to the "keep them busy" comment from earlier, huh? Maybe if people like me weren't cast aside, or given handfuls of pills, or thrown in asylums, we'd find our way back to normal. Learn to control our crazy, racing minds, at least.

No one tries to help me, trust me. Not even Mom and Dad.

I hate people.

I hate it here.

I hate my fucking life.

I hate you.

17

I didn't sleep much that night.

When I opened the letter, the hope was that it would make me feel better. Misery loves company, they say. In a weird way, I guess it did, because I certainly wasn't that messed up. But it also made my skin crawl.

I'd reread the letter a few times, along with the first one, spending the evening inside the mind of a crazy person, the beginnings of what very likely made a serial killer. It was unnerving and unsettling to read the words of someone so confused, so conflicted. Someone needing—no, *craving*—answers, and not knowing where to get them, instead finding darkness on the internet.

What would have happened, in that moment, if someone would have stepped in and provided guidance? At that vulnerable, pivotal moment?

Why didn't the writer's family step in? Offering more than just the pills.

I took a particular interest in the writer's disdain for his or her mother. Was the mother, ultimately, the cause of the insanity?

Was my mother the cause of mine? Of my addiction?

I was rooting for the writer, I realized. Hoping he or she had overcome the dark period in their life, and grown into a normal, productive member of society.

One thought led to another, and then I spent some time contemplating how powerful our minds are.

We're born blank slates. Innocent. We aren't born screwed up, we have to become that way. Life happens, but that's not what makes us crazy. It's our reactions to what happens. Our brain becomes molded by our decisions. Our reactions.

Pretty powerful, isn't it?

And then I thought, if the mind can be so overcome and consumed with evil thoughts, surely the mind is strong enough to find its way back from it. The power that made us stumble into evil, depression, alcoholism, or whatever, was essentially *us*. Therefore, *we* are also strong enough to climb out of the darkness and find the light.

My own decisions, my actions, had driven me to alcoholism. I wasn't born an alcoholic. I allowed it. Therefore, my own decisions and actions could also make me sober.

Right?

Wanting to believe the writer had found peace, I decided not to look for any more letters. Instead, I grabbed my serenity bear and sat cross-legged in the middle of the floor, and closed my eyes.

Fervently, I prayed.

For goodness. For light.

At the ass-crack of dawn, I awoke with half my body on the blow-up mattress, the other half dangling on the cold hardwood floor. One arm was clutched around my bear, the other splayed to the side like a gunshot victim.

A headache split my temples, a pounding between matted eyes and sinuses that felt like they'd exploded behind my face. I'd forgotten to take Etta's allergy pills, a mistake I wouldn't make again.

"Ugh." I groaned, wiping away the drool while trying without success to sniff through the congestion.

Utterly miserable, I rolled over and looked out the window, contemplating how I could uproot or poison every blooming plant, tree, and flower in my yard. *Not good for resale*, I reminded myself, pushing the thought away.

The rain the night before had ushered in a cool gray morning with thick cloud cover. Cassidy warned me that springtime in the South was fickle, but the temperature changes were beginning to give me whiplash.

I stared at the ceiling, focusing on the whine of the rotating fan I'd turned on before falling asleep, the white noise offering a comfort of sorts. The breeze picked up a strand of my hair, blowing it against my forehead, where it stuck.

Frowning, I lifted my hand to my face to discover it was wet with sweat. Not only my forehead, but every inch of my body. "Gross."

After peeling myself off the plastic mattress, I slipped into my flannel robe, eyeing the closet. I took a step toward it, almost automatically, then forced myself to stop, remembering that I'd decided I wasn't going to search for any more letters.

No more of that darkness.

Last night before going to bed, I'd stacked both letters neatly on the fireplace mantel. Out of sight, out of mind. I had more important things to deal with than getting lost in insanity. Like the dinner I'd agreed to with Lucas Covington.

"I'll see you tomorrow at seven o'clock, Miss Dalton."

His voice in my head set off a rash of nerves. And guilt. What the hell was I doing? I wasn't even divorced and was already having dinner with another man.

But was it a date?

No. It was business to discuss buying my house so he could bulldoze it down for his big-dick resort.

Just dinner.

Just business.

Seven o'clock.

Tying my robe around my waist, I wandered to the window. Leaves and twigs littered the backyard from the storm the night before. A deep orange strip tinted the horizon, the sun's attempt to rise above the clouds. The early morning sky was dark and brooding, blocking the dimming stars. There was just enough light to see the fields in the distance.

And I saw him. The cowboy, my cowboy, my neighbor.

Squinting, I leaned forward, my breath fogging up the glass. I turned, tripping over my serenity bear, then scooped it into my arms and crossed the house, running up the staircase to the second floor. The room was colder than the rest of the house, the wooden planks like ice beneath my bare feet as I hurried to the window.

A trio of horses grazed behind the cowboy, an ax gripped firmly in his hand. He was closer than the first time I'd seen him, only a few feet from my property line.

The man was massive in height and weight, with a thick body and broad shoulders. He was wearing a plain gray T-shirt and some sort of khaki worker's pants. He'd left the cowboy hat at home this time, and while I still couldn't see the details of his face, his hair was dark, his skin tanned. He raised the ax and with blinding speed, split a tree limb in half, probably fallen during the storm.

My nose bounced off the window as I'd subconsciously leaned forward, feeling a weird tug. A tug to go to him, to meet him.

Although I made a mental note to pick up a pair of binoculars next time I was in town, I filed away the feeling. The tug.

The man's gaze lifted to my house, pinning me through the window. I knew he couldn't see me, but I took another step back. He stared at the cabin for a few beats, then went back to chopping up the debris that littered his pristine field.

Unable to look away, I slowly tiptoed back to the window, thinking about the efficient, fluid swing of the ax, the power as it sliced through the wood. A wave of heat spread through my body, and I flapped open my robe.

"Jeez." I dramatically ripped it off, suddenly suffocating. "Okay, Cowboy, I see you." I looked at the bear in my arms. "Not bad, eh?"

I watched one more piece of wood explode before tearing myself away and making my way downstairs for a glass of water.

The steady drum of a drip caught my attention as I reached the kitchen. The beat led me to my hands and knees in front of the sink. I set Serenity on the floor, opened the cabinet doors, and leaned inside. Water streamed from a rusted pipe above a growing puddle of water.

"Oh, you've got to be *kidding* me."

I fiddled with the pipe for a minute, shaking and twisting it. No luck. *Shocker.*

I pushed to my hands and knees and searched the

kitchen, settling on a half-empty two-liter of Coke. I poured most in a mug, chugged the rest, then cut the top off and set the makeshift bowl under the leak.

"That'll have to do for now," I told the bear before grabbing my coffee mug of Coke and heading to the bathroom.

I reached into the shower and turned the knob to scorching. As I leaned against the bathroom counter, waiting for the water to heat, I found myself wondering if cowboys knew how to fix leaky faucets.

18

As I stepped out of the shower, the low rumble of a truck pulled my attention to the front door. I quickly coiled my wet hair into a bun at the nape of my neck, slipped into a T-shirt and pair of sweatpants, and jogged across the house.

One glance out the window brought a grin to my face.

I opened the door as Etta climbed out of a rusty old red Chevy truck, its bed overflowing with sharp wooden corners, lampshades, legs of chairs and tables. A rolled rug hung like a flag from the side.

"Mornin', New York."

A carbon copy of the day before, Etta was dressed to impress. Her silver hair was fluffed to perfection, above thick-rimmed glasses and gold necklaces. Instead of orange, today she'd opted for a red tracksuit with white stripes down the sides, with a pair of blinding-white orthopedic shoes to match.

"I'm so glad that name is catching on."

Etta winked as she crossed the driveway. "Saw Tad yesterday. Mentioned you, *New York*." She lifted the platter in her hands. "Blueberry muffins, fresh from the oven. There's sweet tea in the passenger seat. Grab it, will ya?"

When I stepped off the porch, Etta stopped cold, her mouth agape. She pulled a small bottle from her pocket.

"Holy hell. I haven't seen a pair of saddlebags that large since the circus came to town," she said, referring to the bags under my eyes, I assumed. "Jesus, woman, you look like a blowfish. What the hell's going on here?"

"I haven't taken your allergy meds yet."

"Do it. I can't look at that all morning."

I laughed as I took the platter from her hands. "I love you, Etta. That's all there is to it."

"Hold that thought until after you see what I brought you. When you didn't come by yesterday, I decided to go through my shed for you. What I have might not be your style, but you'd be shocked what you can do with a little sanding and a fresh coat of paint."

"Thank you, Etta. Seriously. And I'm sorry I didn't come by. The day kinda—"

"Don't worry about it, child. I can see the weight you've got on your shoulders. Come on. Let's eat first."

"Read my mind."

After retrieving the tea, we stepped onto the porch.

"Storms comin' the next few days," Etta said. "Tornadoes possibly, 'cording to Stan the weatherman."

"I wouldn't know. I'm supposed to get my TV today . . . I think."

"Spring storms in the South are nothing to shrug at, young lady. You got a storm shelter in this place?"

"What's a storm shelter?" I said, joking.

"Don't do that to me."

I grinned. "Just kidding. But no, this palace doesn't come with a shelter."

A hiss came from behind a nearby bush.

Etta huffed. "Damn cats."

"Morning, Moonshine," I said over my shoulder. "Sorry to disturb you. We'll go inside."

"She'll keep breeding, you know," Etta said as we stepped through the door. "Before you know it, you'll have a hundred cats under that porch. Pastor Paul will have to perform an exorcism to get rid of them."

"Might not be a bad idea to do the whole house," I muttered.

"Ah, did the lights flicker on you last night?"

"More than that. I heard giggles."

"Giggles?"

"Yeah, I think."

"Should've brought over my sage. Want me to go back and get it?"

"Etta, do you really believe in evil spirits?"

"Yes, ma'am. Ignorant not to, if you'll forgive me for saying so. There's a lot more going on in this world than what you can see and touch. I'll bring that sage next time. We'll take care of her."

I set the muffins and tea on the counter. "You think it's Bonnie?"

Etta shrugged. "It's someone with unfinished business."

"What would be hers?"

"Don't know. But I'm guessing she's trying to tell you."

I sighed, glancing at the letters hidden on the mantel. Ghosts and disturbing letters. Were they connected?

"Anyway, we'll see if your ghost likes sage and will go from there," Etta said. "Back to the storm shelter—add that to your list. You need one, and soon. Not a cheap one. A good one. It'll cost you a couple thousand, at least, but it's worth it. Tornadoes are serious business."

"I've never been through one. Or in one, whatever."

"I've been through them, in them, outside them, around them. Six tornadoes in my lifetime."

"Wow. Any damage?" I grabbed two paper plates and set them on the counter, along with my one remaining coffee mug. The other one lay shattered in the bottom of my trash can, courtesy of my lovely ghost.

"One uprooted a tree, sent it through my living room and into my kitchen. Destroyed everything. Like walking around a tree house for days."

Etta plated the muffins while I poured her tea, then grabbed a can of Coke for myself from the fridge.

"I would've been dead if the tree had hit eight feet to the right. We built a storm shelter the next day. But don't do like I did. Build yours now."

"Noted."

We bit into our respective blueberry muffins and groaned simultaneously.

"Good, Etta. Really good."

She winked, turned toward the living room, then clapped her hands in excitement. "I can't wait to show you what I brought. I'll be so excited to see my things in here. Getting used. Making someone else's life pretty. Have you decided on a color palette?"

I washed the bite down with a sip of Coke. "Well, the floors and paneled walls are dark wood. I'm going to refinish them, by the way. The stone fireplace is dark too. So I'm going to go with an ivory color palette, with pops of color here and there. Thought the ivory on the sheetrock would go nicely against the dark wood."

"Oh, I love it. Clean, crisp, classy. Will help lighten the space too. Make it brighter, happier. Love it."

We ate in silence a minute, staring into the room. Etta,

imagining all the things she could do with it, and me wondering about the owner before me.

"How long had Bonnie and her husband been married before he cheated on her?" I asked.

"Ken was his name. He was a third-grade math teacher."

"No kidding? God bless him—for teaching math to third graders, not the cheating."

"Tell me about it. Math was the only class I had to take twice in high school."

"I still use touch points, Etta."

"What are touch points?"

"Exactly. Keep going."

"They were married ten years, maybe, before they split. The crazy thing is, Ken was the sweetest man I've ever met. Volunteered at the church on the weekends. They were so in love, him and Bonnie."

Etta reached for another muffin, drawing my gaze to the tattoos on her wrist.

"What happened then?"

"No one really knows. Rumors started that he was cheating on her, and next thing I knew, he was moving out."

"There has to be a reason," I said, then stilled at my own words.

What was the reason William had cheated on me? Because I wasn't domestic enough? Didn't do his damn laundry, cook for him? Maybe I wasn't pretty enough? Dirty enough in the bedroom? Was I too boring? Annoying? Nagging?

And why was I sitting here blaming myself *again*?

"You never know what goes on behind closed doors, dear." Etta led me into the living room. "If these walls could only talk."

My attention shifted to the staircase that led up to the

second floor where I'd heard the giggles, then to the fireplace mantel where the letters sat undisturbed.

A shiver rolled through me.

"Was it only depression, you think? With Bonnie?"

Etta shook her head. "Again, honey, you never know."

"Drugs or alcohol, maybe?"

"Oh, hell no. No. Not Bonnie. In the years I knew her, I never saw the woman drink."

"Some people hide it well."

Etta squinted at me, assessing. "Why do you want to know so much about it?"

"Just curious, I guess."

She stared at me another minute. "You really think you've got a spirit in here, don't you?"

I sighed. "I don't know what I've got here, Etta."

"On that note, let's unload your loot and freshen up the juju in the place."

"Music to my ears."

After another muffin, we began unloading the old red truck.

The woman hadn't lied. Etta had packed an entire shed full of furniture in the back of her truck. Unfortunately for me, though, Etta liked apples, apples as red as her starched tracksuit.

She had apple clocks, apple table placemats, apple napkins, apple curtains, apple lampshades, apple paintings, an apple welcome mat. Even an apple-print accent chair with a matching ottoman.

Yikes.

Hidden among the fruit, I found a food-and-water bowl painted with cats and grabbed it. Figured Moonshine could overlook the cheerful kittens. Blood-sucking bats would suit her personality better.

After unloading boxes filled with locally handmade knickknacks, candles, and the like, we moved on to the big things. Etta was stronger than I gave her credit for, and I wondered if she'd loaded everything on her own. If not, who had helped her? Did she have a man in her life?

An hour later, we stood with our hands on our hips, our brows sweaty, and inspected our work.

The living room was now cluttered with boxes and furniture—floor and table lamps, chairs and end tables, accent cabinets—all of which we agreed to refinish together over oatmeal cookies. The furniture was well-made and well-maintained, and I was beyond grateful. My favorite pieces were a matching antique chest and bookcase painted in a distressed turquoise that would work beautifully with my ivory color palette.

All in all, a victorious morning.

We'd begun strategizing placement when Abe from Abe's Furniture pulled up the driveway to deliver the first load of furniture I'd purchased the day before. I became nonexistent when he saw Etta.

The man jumped out of the delivery van and jogged into Etta's open arms. Old friends, I assumed. I smiled, listening to him and Etta gossip about Abe's grandsons, the weather, and business. I wondered if everyone in Berry Springs knew each other as well as they did, or at the very least, exchanged genuine pleasantries.

So different from the city.

Etta left to "tend to her business" while Abe began to unload the furniture. The first load consisted of the priority items, as I'd labeled them. These included a dark cherry-wood sleigh bed and matching dresser—the rest of the bedroom set would come later, a mattress set, a leather recliner, a television, a washer and dryer, and last but certainly not least, curtain rods.

Abe was a one-man shop, not only delivering my furniture and appliances, but assembling and connecting everything as well. Worth every penny.

Five hours later, my cabin was beginning to feel a little less cold. After tipping Abe in cash and blueberry muffins—I think he preferred the muffins—I slapped on a little makeup, pulled myself together, and drove into town to visit a local store called Affordable Upholstery, which Abe had strongly recommended for window treatments and bedding.

His wife sure was helpful.

After that fifteen-hundred-dollar charge, I made my second stop at Tad's Tool Shop to pick up more hardware, a drill, a new broom, and a step stool—you know, manly things like that. Also, a pricey pair of binoculars to stalk my cowboy neighbor next door.

Another hundred bucks was gone in under five minutes. After another hundred, maybe Tad would quit referring to me as "New York." And maybe he'd offer me a cup of the coffee he kept in a huge coffee urn behind the counter—which he offered to *everyone* else.

Locals, only, apparently.

On the way home, I hit not one, but two brand-new potholes on Rattlesnake Road. From the storm, I guessed, and now knew why Etta drove a truck.

The remainder of the day was spent learning how to use a drill, learning how to find studs in walls—almost losing a fingernail in the process—and hanging my new ivory curtains in each window. This was followed by washing my new ivory bedsheets and matching down comforter, then putting them on the bed. Then I began scrubbing the walls. Floors would come later.

Late in the afternoon, Etta stopped by on her four-wheeler and marveled at the new furniture and progress I'd made on the cleaning front. I took her through the house, room by room.

My closet demolition rendered her speechless. Unacceptable to do myself, she informed me, and wrote down the name of the local carpenter, demanding I call him immediately. Etta left me with a gallon of sweet tea and a promise she'd stop by again soon.

Not that I'd asked.

I'd almost forgotten about my dinner with Lucas until Cassidy texted me a GIF of a shirtless Clark Kent blowing kisses. I texted her back a meme of Judge Judy dramatically rolling her eyes, then hustled to the bathroom.

Forty-five minutes later, I yanked off the seventh dress I'd tried on and tossed it onto the bed. I had no clue what to wear for this business-meeting-slash-date. I also didn't know how dressy I should be. "Tomorrow night at seven o'clock" didn't give me much info for planning.

Lucas Covington was definitely a Marchesa cocktail dress kind of guy. Lavish, luxurious. But Berry Springs wasn't. I stared at myself in the mirror, at my run-down shack in the background, and for the first time wondered, was I?

I decided on a summery off-the-shoulder blue dress with flowy fabric. Not too tight, not too loose. The dress teetered between casual and dressy, but definitely sexy. I left my hair down in subtle waves down my back.

Without thinking, I slipped into my Louboutin heels, then kicked them off, opting for wedges instead. Berry

Springs wasn't a heels kind of town. After an extra dab of lip gloss, I stepped back, checking my reflection in the mirror—and stopped on my left hand, on the engagement ring and eternity band I had yet to take off.

Nerves ping-ponged in my stomach as I lifted the four-carat diamond. Tears threatened, and with a clench of my jaw, I slipped both rings off and shoved them into my dresser drawer.

Fuck you, William.

I took another breath, which came out a bit shaky. Damn, I wanted a drink. Squaring my shoulders, I reminded myself that this wasn't a date.

Lucas Covington wants something from me. It's as simple as that.

"Just business," I whispered into the mirror, but was unable to push the guilt away. My thumb rubbed the bare skin of my ring finger, which now felt naked and raw.

Why didn't it feel like freedom?

Why the hell did I feel so guilty?

I turned at the sound of a car coming up the driveway. I glanced at the clock—6:57 p.m. Of course Lucas was prompt.

I grabbed a clutch and shoved it full of necessities—lip gloss, breath mints, floss, powder—and waited in my bedroom doorway until he knocked. I waited a few more seconds before opening the door.

Lucas took a step back as he shamelessly took me in at the same time as I scrutinized him. The man might as well have stepped straight out of *GQ*. Another expensive suit, another mischievous sparkle in those dark eyes.

"You look stunning."

"Thank you."

He continued to stare at me until I finally looked away.

"Let me grab my keys."

He held the door as I stepped back. "Mind if I . . ."

"Nope, come on in."

I stepped into the kitchen and picked up my keys from the counter, glancing at him from under my eyelashes. His gaze was sweeping the house, every line, every corner, probably thinking how easy it would be to demolish. That damn twinge of insecurity crept up, along with embarrassment. If he'd only seen the penthouse suite I'd lived in before.

I cleared my throat and crossed the room.

"The place has potential," he said.

"This coming from the guy who wants to tear it down."

He grinned. "For my big-dick resort."

"Exactly."

He stepped to the fireplace, tracing his fingertip along the rock wall. He looked as out of place as a diamond in a pigpen.

"Ready?" I asked quickly.

Lucas turned, giving my body another appreciative glance. "Ready."

We stepped outside, and as I locked the door behind me, resisted a shiver. Dusk had arrived, ushering in cool night air that rustled the nearby trees.

Lucas opened the passenger door of his Range Rover for me. I climbed inside, taken aback by the sight of the man in the back seat, hidden in shadows.

"Sorry." Lucas laughed as he leaned in. "Edward, meet Miss Grey Dalton. Grey, this is Edward Schultz."

"Your business partner?"

"That's right. You remember. He's harmless. And won't be joining us for dinner, to be clear." The comment was directed more toward the man in the back than to me.

My door clicked closed, leaving me and the weird guy

alone in the car for three excruciatingly awkward seconds. Edward didn't speak.

A few moments of silence passed as Lucas backed down the driveway.

"Just ignore him. I do," Lucas whispered with a wink.

"Okay . . . so, where are we going?"

"To a Mexican restaurant in Eureka, the next town over."

"You've already made your way through all the restaurants in Berry Springs?"

"Yes. Twice. Donny's is good, don't get me wrong, but you can only eat so much bacon. Isn't that right, Edward?" Without waiting for an answer, Lucas continued our conversation. "I'm visiting the local restaurants while I'm in town to get an idea of what the locals like. This is the last one on the list. It used to be one of my dad's favorites."

"Does your dad live here?"

"Born and raised, but moved to Dallas before I was born. This restaurant we're going to tonight has been there since then. Have you been to Eureka?"

"I haven't been past Main Street."

"You need to venture out. It's a quaint, touristy town. Lots of art shops, music, restaurants. I've been making the rounds."

"Trying to get a feel for what kind of resort you should build, in case I sell out?"

"*When* you sell out."

"Let's suspend reality for a second and say I do sell you my property. I get the vibe the others you need to convince aren't as open to uprooting as I am."

He laughed fondly. "So, you've met Etta. She drives a tough bargain; I will say that. But everyone has their breaking point. You've just got to find it."

"And you plan to find mine this evening?"

"I plan to enjoy the company of a beautiful woman while eating the best tacos in the world."

"That's a lot to live up to."

He glanced at me. "You already have."

"I was talking about the tacos."

He grinned, and with that, we pulled onto the highway, my guilt transforming into something that resembled excitement.

19

Night had fallen by the time we rolled to a stop in front of a newly renovated restaurant with a thatched roof, nestled against a natural rock cliff. A weathered sign that read LA HACIENDA hung above the front door painted with bright colors.

Candles flickered in the windows. Dozens of glittering lights illuminated blooming bushes and a pebbled walkway leading to the front door. A young couple held hands by a small fountain, making a wish.

Something resembling for better or worse, I mused. *A little promise bound to be broken.*

Another couple waited outside to be seated. Visible through the large windows, waiters and waitresses bustled to and from packed tables. Overall, the restaurant was small, charming, and very romantic.

A valet opened my door. He took my hand but addressed Lucas. "Mr. Covington, lovely to see you this evening."

"Thank you, Mario." Lucas handed over his keys.

"Have a wonderful evening, sir."

The valet disappeared behind us.

"I thought you said you've never been here."

"I called ahead."

Of course he did.

Lucas and Weird Edward exchanged a few whispered words before Edward disappeared across the street, which was lined with shops and bars.

"Where is he going?"

"To check out a bar," Lucas said, resting his hand lightly on my lower back as we followed the pathway to the door.

I was proud, I noticed, walking into the restaurant with him. As usual, heads turned, although not in my direction. All eyes were on the stunning Lucas Covington. He had an air about him that made people notice him. Made people want to know him.

The inside of La Hacienda was as charming as the outside with indoor trees to allow privacy between tables covered in white linen and lit with small candles. Candles were everywhere, their shadows dancing on the colorful tile walls.

Undoubtedly romantic.

Lucas and I were whisked through the main room and led out a narrow back door. Outside, under a dozen strings of twinkling bulbs were more candles, more trees, and more flowers. Secluded tables lined the natural cliff wall. A little thatched-roof bar was tucked into the corner.

While the main dining room was at full capacity, the patio was vacant. Not a single person occupied one of the dozen or so tables. We were handed off to a stunning blond waitress, her lips as red as her fitted cocktail dress.

"Mr. Covington, we've got your table ready as requested."

Feeling like a celebrity, I wondered if this was what

Lucas's day-to-day life was like. And how long it would take me to get used to it.

Not very long, I guessed.

We were led to the back corner table, hidden behind a blooming dogwood. An arrangement of fresh flowers was centered on the linen, surrounded by flickering candles.

"Here are your menus. I'll be right back." The waitress took a lingering glance at Lucas before sauntering away.

Lucas had reserved the entire patio for us, or was it for me? *No*. For business.

"As *requested*?" I asked.

The slightest cocky smirk crossed his lips as he picked up the menu. "Beautiful, isn't it?" he said, catching me gawking at the space.

"Yes." I ran my fingertip along the cool rock next to us.

"Mr. Covington, the bottle you requested." The waitress returned, displaying a bottle of red wine with a flourish before setting it on the table, followed by two long-stemmed glasses.

I stared at the wine as my pulse rate kicked up. I hadn't even considered that alcohol would be a part of this dinner, or what I would do in the event it was offered to me.

Heat rose up my neck and my heart pounded, my body's reaction to the temptation in front of me.

Oblivious to my plight, Lucas examined the bottle as one might a new car before signing the papers. The waitress waited with bated breath—much like my own at that moment, but for very different reasons. With a swift dip of his chin, Lucas acknowledged the wine and returned it to her, which pleased her to no end, and she set the bottle on the table.

When the waitress popped the cork and poured two

glasses, the scent of the wine hit my nose like an expensive perfume.

Goose bumps rippled over my body as I inhaled that delicious aroma of tannin, blackberry, and oak. The red potion funneled into the crystal, mesmerizing me, lighting up every nerve ending in my body. My heart hammered as an angel fluttered above my right shoulder, a devil heavy on my left. My hands twisted together in my lap.

Lucas lifted his glass, swirling the red liquid as he examined it, and my tongue darted over my lips. "*Salute*, Miss Dalton."

A second slipped by as I stared at him with his glass raised, waiting for me to toast with him. Then, like a puppet on strings, my hand reached out and my fingertips grasped the stem, and my glass was lifted into the air.

"*Salute*," I said breathlessly.

The angel flew away as I took that first sip and my taste buds burst to life.

My body vibrated with excitement. Adrenaline.

How easy it was to take that first sip.

I swirled the liquid around my tongue, savoring its taste, its coolness, the smooth finish. The way the glass felt in my hand.

The way I felt holding it. Me.

The *old* me. The untormented me. The me that didn't have to fight every second to avoid taking a drink.

The *happy* me.

I exhaled as I set down the glass, staring at it like the Holy Grail, and a small smile came to my face.

I was back. A rush of confidence flew through me.

Me. I was back.

With that, the ten-thousand-pound weight of sobriety lifted from my shoulders. Lucas and I fell into easy conversation, the wine lubricating my flirty wit, loosening the nerves.

We ordered the entire left side of the menu. Three different kinds of dips, a bowl each of pozole, stuffed poblanos, enchiladas, fish tacos with fresh toppings, and a plate overflowing with tamales. I sampled them all, and we ordered another bottle of wine.

We talked mostly about his business, his constant travel, my work in New York—sans my drunken acceptance speech—and his plans for the resort. We talked about the economy, money, a bit about politics. I learned Lucas had gone to Yale and currently owned five homes. One in LA, one in New York, one in DC, one in Florida, and one on the Amalfi Coast, where he spent a month every winter.

He didn't ask probing questions about me, my love life, or what exactly had made me move to Berry Springs. I appreciated this, especially as my buzz began to kick in.

Lucas was polite and charming. Mesmerizing, as evidenced by the waitress, who had forgotten my existence not long after pouring the wine. The blond bombshell spoke to him with little hearts in her eyes and a flush on her cheeks.

He ate it up, I noticed, but made a point to glance at me while they spoke. Lucas knew how to handle multiple women at the same time. He also knew how to make a woman feel like the most important person in the room.

An experienced ladies' man, no doubt about that.

Sometime after my second glass, I decided I liked it. I liked the power he exuded, enjoyed watching others fall to his feet and obey on command. It was sexy as hell.

Reveling in the easy, light conversation we had, I felt like the old me. The one after I was promoted to editor-in-chief, not the one with a broken heart just trying to make it day by day.

It felt good, a little *too* good, sometime after the second round of tacos.

Tequila came with dessert. Lots of dessert. Tres leches, churros, flan, sopapillas.

Lots of tequila. Shots of Patrón, followed by a highball of whatever Brad Pitt and George Clooney had created with their billions of dollars.

Weird Edward joined us sometime later. I forced him to take a shot.

I didn't remember much of the drive home, other than laughing. A lot of laughing.

And a lot of simply not giving a fuck.

20

Lucas held my elbow as we stepped onto the front porch. Merely being a gentleman or steadying me, I wasn't sure which.

I didn't care.

Swaying on bare feet, I fumbled with my purse. I didn't know where my shoes had gone. Finally, I found my keys and pulled them out, but they tumbled to the porch.

"Whoops." I laughed, slowly turning.

Before I knew it, my back was pressed against the front door and Lucas's lips were on mine. As we kissed, he placed my keys back into my hand.

My thoughts momentarily went to Edward still lurking in the car, but then quickly shifted to the tongue sliding between my lips. Lucas tasted like warm tequila and sugar. Like heaven.

His hands pinned my wrists at my sides, the press of his groin against mine subtle, but undeniable. My head spun, every sexual sensor in my body whipping to attention.

Reaching back, I fumbled with the doorknob. "I can't . . ."

"Which key?" he murmured between kisses, pulling the keys back from my hand.

"I can't remember."

With his lips still on me, Lucas found the correct key, miraculously entered it into the slot without looking—a move worthy of a superhero—and turned the knob. The door popped open with a creak. We stumbled inside, me backward, him guiding me while kicking the door shut with his wingtip.

My clutch clattered to the hardwood. His hands found my breasts while mine tugged at his suit jacket. My dress was pulled over my head, a flutter of blue disappearing into the corner. Buttons rattled onto the hardwood as I ripped his dress shirt open like an animal.

Heat ran like fire over my skin, the wetness of my panties telling me I had one thing in mind.

I was backed against the counter that separated the kitchen from the living room, then flipped around. My thong was yanked to my knees, cold air sweeping against skin as hot as fire. Lucas didn't bother removing my bra, instead, he kept one hand on me, keeping me pinned against the counter. I startled at the slap of his belt being ripped off, followed by the *whish* of his zipper.

Hands swept down the curve of my sides, my ass, the small of my back. He pressed, forcing me to bend over the counter.

An empty Coke can toppled over as I pressed my breasts against the ice-cold granite. With a swipe of his hand, Lucas sent the can crashing to the floor, then laid his palm on the counter as his body pressed against me from behind. My gaze locked on a birthmark running down his hand like a snake slithering through the water. It stretched all the way down his thumb, and even had a dot on either side of it, like two eyes watching me.

Like a snake.

My stomach flipped.

I reached forward, gripping the opposite ends of the counter, feeling his erection pressing into my ass. My graze drifted along the kitchen, zeroing in on my serenity bear I'd left in the corner after attempting to fix my leaky faucet. I scowled, looking away from his judging little eyes.

Lips on my back, a tongue down my spine.

My head spinning. Pussy throbbing.

His breath hitched as he spread my cheeks.

"Condom," I choked out.

A second later, I heard the rip of foil behind me. I squeezed my eyes shut as he speared into me without warning.

My hips dug into the edge of the counter with each thrust, the breath knocked from my lungs in quick pants. Feeling the sting of nails raking down my back, I groaned in both pain and ecstasy. My head was yanked back, my hair fisted in his hand, my body pounded against the granite.

I gasped for air.

His breathing increased, the tight grip on my hair causing tears to well behind my eyes. Suddenly, he slid out of me, and the condom hit the floor.

Confused, I glanced down at it as my back was sprayed with warm, sticky gunk.

21

Slowly, I sipped my coffee as the rising sun pushed the stars away. It was a cold morning, although I was numb to it.

I shifted on the porch swing, wincing at the pain in my hip bones from being slammed repeatedly against the sharp edge of the counter. The pain between my legs from being pounded like a blow-up doll was worse than the hangover piercing my skull.

Embarrassment—*no*, complete and utter humiliation—heated my cheeks as my stomach sank with that awful what-did-I-do feeling.

I tucked my legs underneath me, readjusting the flannel blanket that covered me as I stared blankly at the orange glow on the horizon.

I didn't cry that morning. I was too empty to produce tears.

My thoughts swung like a pendulum between regret, guilt, disappointment, and hatred.

Hatred of myself. Disgust.

I was furious at myself for drinking, but also, on the flip

side, mad for beating myself up so badly about it. Everyone had slipups, right? Why did I hate myself for my own? Why was I being so hard on myself? I'd just go back to being sober again. And that was that.

I praised myself for the fact that I hadn't thrown up or passed out in front of Lucas. Maybe that meant I'd done a decent job of controlling my intake. And maybe *that* meant I could start drinking again. Occasionally. Here and there, like a normal person.

Yes, those were my screwed-up thoughts as I sat there on the swing. An alcoholic justifying a slipup. An alcoholic trying to release the guilt.

The *damn* guilt.

I hated myself for having sex with a man I barely knew —a man who reminded me of my husband.

I hated myself for being so irresponsible. A whore.

But the worst part? I hated myself because technically I was still a married woman. I'd fucked another man with the lines from my wedding ring still on my finger. *Fucked*, because in no universe what Lucas and I did could be considered making love. It was a shallow, mindless, drunken fuck.

Nauseated, I brought my hand to my mouth, wiping my lips. Wiping him away, the guilt.

I found myself thinking of my husband, wondering if this was how he felt after his many indiscretions.

Then I thought of my mother. The empty bottles she'd hide under the bed, her many men. Her lack of self-control, and how many lives that weakness had ruined. Her battle with sobriety that ended with death.

Did my mother find love in the men she brought home, if only temporary? Or was it always for pleasure? To forget, maybe?

Did I have sex with Lucas to forget? Or did I want more, and was simply unwilling to admit it? Did I want his money, the life he could give me? Was I still running from my childhood, a past that seemed to become my present yet again?

Who needed love? Were security and stability the key to happiness?

Why *the hell* was I so messed up?

I thought of the letters I'd found in the closet. Of the writer. They would understand me. Whoever wrote those letters would understand what I was going through, what I was feeling.

They would make me feel better.

I pushed off the porch swing and stalked to the bedroom. I needed another letter. Needed to feel better.

As drywall exploded around my head, I decided this must be what rock bottom feels like. *It can only go up from here*, I told myself as I spied the corner of the third letter hidden in the wall.

I was wrong.

22

Letter #3

I killed the cat.

It was a girl. I think that's why I feel bad about it. Not that it makes a difference, but for some reason, I thought the cat was a boy. I'm not sure I would have killed it now. But I did, and I can't change that.

It bothered me that the cat hated me so much. I couldn't sleep. So, in the middle of the night, I made a trap. A box with tuna inside, and a trap door. I set it outside and waited. It didn't take long.

I trapped the cat in the box, then tipped it over into a pillowcase. It started howling and hissing, bouncing all over the damn place, trying to scratch me through the fabric. I panicked and slammed the pillowcase against a tree. That scream was different. My heart started to pound, and I wondered if I'd killed it. Then it moved a little. Slower this time, the hissing less angry and more of a plea.

And then something happened. To me. Adrenaline, I guess. It kind of felt like the first few minutes of watching porn for the first time.

I knew then I was going to kill it.

I felt excited, my mind racing. I needed things, I decided, a plan forming in my head. I slammed it against the tree again, then tied the pillowcase to a branch and ran into the house and went to the junk drawer. Hammer, screwdriver, a few other things that looked sharp, and a lighter.

I got the cat and took her to my hiding spot. By then, it was moving again, but it wasn't howling, more like crying. I didn't know cats could cry.

I do now.

I laid out my tools. My hands were shaking.

I took the hammer to it first.

There was too much blood for the fur to light. So I tied her down and gripped her head, making her watch me as I poured the lighter fluid over her fur. I wanted her to watch me watch her die. To know that I did it. She released one final plea as I lowered the lighter to her body.

Watching the cat burn to death, I pulled down my pants and masturbated, coming the moment she let out her last scream.

23

I didn't feel better. For the next thirty minutes, I vomited into the toilet.

Then I showered and scrubbed every inch of my body, washing away the night before, the dirty whore that I was, the hangover, and the sickening feeling the letter had given me. The last few paragraphs had been faded, as if the writer had smeared their finger over the ink in an attempt to erase them, or maybe fade the memory.

Oh, how I wish I could erase the last twenty-four hours.

I couldn't throw the letter away, though, and I wasn't sure why. It felt like a piece to a puzzle, a puzzle I'd yet to solve. Like the letter had meaning, somehow, in my life. So I stacked it safely with the others on the fireplace mantel.

After twisting my hair into a messy bun, I skipped the makeup and pulled on a faded Rolling Stones hoodie, tattered jean shorts, and flip-flops. An hour passed as I sat on the front porch with a glass of water as the wind blew through the trees. Thinking of the letter, of the writer. Thinking of Lucas, of tequila.

I was overcome with unease, a darkness that spread inside me like a virus. I was sick.

Another hour passed as I tried to coax Moonshine from the bushes with a bowl of water and kibbles. Perhaps trying to erase and replace the horrific memories of the letter. Perhaps trying to prove to Moonshine I was good—unlike the person who wrote the letter. I might live in the same house, but I wasn't crazy.

I got nothing from her, though. Not even a hiss.

The morning faded into another bleak day with thick cloud cover. Rain was coming. My love for springtime in the South was quickly fading.

When I heard the growl of a mail truck hauling ass up my driveway, I perked up. I stood as it skidded to a stop in front of the porch and a short, squatty woman jumped out.

"Mornin', ma'am."

"Morning."

She thrust a large envelope marked priority at me. My stomach dropped to my feet as I noticed the return address that used to be my penthouse suite.

William.

"Need your signature, ma'am."

She handed me a handheld device and a stylus. My heart pounded as I scribbled my name across the screen.

"Thank you."

My automatic thank-you in return caught in my throat as she jogged back to the truck and sped down the driveway. I went inside and hurried into the kitchen.

Taking a deep breath, I opened the envelope and pulled the crisp white papers from inside with the letterhead of Dalton Law and Associates, his father's firm.

The top sheet was labeled PETITION FOR DISSOLUTION OF MARRIAGE.

The papers slipped from my fingertips, floating to the floor.

My jaw dropped. William must have had the papers drawn up the day he found my note. The son of a bitch had mailed the papers after we spoke on the phone.

I didn't know why this pissed me off so much. The divorce was my idea, after all, and I'd expected the papers. But the fact that he didn't even give it a week to simmer cut me like a knife.

My heart pounding, I skimmed the papers. Everything was cut and dry, exactly as we'd discussed. What was his was his, and mine was mine. Nothing to be shared or separated. It would be the easiest divorce to finalize, and the quickest, I had a feeling, thanks to his dear daddy's friendship with the judge.

I grabbed a pen from the counter, slashed my name and date at the bottom, and stuffed the paperwork into the prestamped return envelope William had so kindly provided.

Bastard.

My mood had officially turned from bad to absolutely foul.

Envelope in hand, I grabbed my purse and keys and made my way outside, where I planned to drive straight to the post office and end my marriage for good.

Moonshine darted across the driveway, sending me a hiss before disappearing into the woods.

"Not in the mood, Moonshine. Not in the mood."

I sank into the driver's seat and slammed the door. The moment I turned the ignition, a series of angry beeps came from the dashboard, followed by a thin trail of smoke from under the hood.

"Oh. No *way.*" I banged the steering wheel with my fist. "You have *got* to be *kidding* me."

I yanked the key from the ignition, unlatched the hood, and hovered over the smoking engine like I knew what the hell I was doing. My hands perched on my hips, I examined the engine for a solid minute, willing it to magically fix itself under my glower.

When it didn't, I dropped to my hands and knees and lowered my cheek to the gravel so I could peer under the car. All I was missing was the wrench in my pocket and dip in my lower lip.

A massive, shiny black puddle colored the rocks. I knew enough about cars to know it was oil.

Okay, this didn't feel like a catastrophe. Just get more oil, right?

Right.

One of Moonshine's kittens meowed behind me.

"Ha-ha, very funny, I know." I lifted from the dirt, exhaling as I settled onto my butt. Sighing, I turned to the bush where I knew Moonshine and her kittens were hidden, enjoying the entertainment of the morning.

"You don't happen to know how to fix an engine, do you?"

A little pink nose peeked out from behind a leaf, and I stuck out my palm.

"It's okay, baby." I shifted my gaze to Moonshine's slitted eyes through the leaves. "I've got food and water on the porch. Gourmet kibbles. Nothing but the best for you and the babies. I'll also get a few beds when I'm in town. Use them or don't, whatever, but they're yours if you want them, Mama."

The cat didn't hiss, and I figured that was progress.

I pushed to my feet, wiping my hands on my shorts. "Well, I'll be back. Hopefully."

I slid back behind the driver's seat, turned the engine,

said a Hail Mary, and slowly drove down the driveway. Post office first, auto shop second.

I'd only made it a few yards down the dirt road before the smoke turned black.

"Oh God." My back straightened like a rod, my fingers gripping the wheel.

My phone dinged with a text message.

Braking, I kept one hand on the wheel and fumbled through my purse with the other. I clicked it on.

Lucas: I couldn't sleep.

My brow cocked as I reread the message, shocked that he was texting me. Honestly, I didn't think I'd ever hear from the guy again. I thought about my response, and decided to keep it light.

Me: This surprises me, considering.
Lucas: Considering is exactly why I couldn't sleep. Almost drove back to your house at 2 a.m. for another round.
Me: You mean, had Edward drive you.
Lucas: [Wink emoji] Would you have obliged me?
Me: An earthquake wouldn't have woken me.
Lucas: Is that a challenge?
Me: I'm not sure my kitchen counter can take another challenge from you.
Lucas: I'll build you a new one. With handles. How about lunch?

I looked at the envelope in my passenger seat, then at the smoke seeping out from beneath my hood. Too much. Everything was too much.

Me: Maybe tomorrow. A lot going on today.

Lucas: Understood. Have a good day, Miss Dalton. You'll hear from me again tomorrow.

With a groan, I tossed the phone into the passenger seat, clenched my teeth, and slowly accelerated. Black smoke barreled from the hood, blocking my view.

"*Dammit.* Just dammit, dammit, dammit."

I slammed the brakes, rolled down the windows, hung my head outside, and stared at the dirt road, considering my options.

A gust of wind blew the smoke away. In the distance, a thin beam of sunlight sparkled off the tin roof of the building at the end of the *Y*.

"Oh, please, please, please be an auto shop." With my heartbeat a steady pounding, I slowly pressed the gas. "Please, please, please . . ."

I inched toward the brick building, careful to avoid the massive potholes I'd driven over with abandon the day before. The same blacked-out Chevy truck I'd noticed on my first day in Berry Springs was parked under a shade tree, a beat-up Tahoe next to it.

I pulled into the gravel parking lot under a cloud of smoke.

Coughing, I waved at the air around me as I grabbed my keys and slid out of the car. I paused, glancing around. There was no sign or any indication that the garage was, indeed, a business, but the three open bays filled with old vehicles indicated otherwise.

When the whine of a steel guitar carried on the wind, I decided I was in the right place, because all mechanics listen to classic rock.

24

My plastic flip-flops slapped against the gravel as I hurried to the red metal door at the end of the building. Finding it locked, I followed the blaring music to the front of the garage and stepped into the first bay where a vintage truck sat on lifts, missing all four of its tires. The hood was popped, the driver's door wide open. The scent of fresh coffee mingled with motor oil.

"Hello?"

Other than Bob Seger and the Silver Bullets suggesting I take my business to Main Street, there was no response.

"Hello?" I called out a little louder. Cautiously stepping farther into the garage, I looked around, cringing at the mess.

Dozens of tools, buckets, and dirty rags were discarded on a stained concrete floor. Rusty tools, multiple rolling toolboxes, and random plastic chairs were placed throughout. Oil cans and plastic containers crowded the counters, along with a few grease-stained fast-food bags that sat next to a mound of empty Coke cans, stacked like a Christmas tree.

Wires, electrical cords, and ropes dangled from the brick walls. A tattered American flag hung proudly in the back, centered around dozens of hubcaps that I wasn't sure was some sort of an attempt at decoration, or if they'd been hung simply because there was no room among the trash.

I took a step forward and walked right out of one of my flip-flops, then froze in place. Balancing on one foot, I scowled down at a massive wad of gum that had glued my shoe to the floor.

"Ew, gross." Beyond frustrated now, I turned back to the garage and this time, I yelled. "Hellllo?"

A pair of scuffed tan cowboy boots emerged from underneath the truck. A working man's boot, I noticed, with a square toe and thick sole, worn and stained with miles of wear. In seemingly slow motion, a man emerged—who had all the time in the world, apparently.

Above the boots were a pair of jeans, stained with grease and torn at the knee, hugging a pair of thighs as thick as tree trunks. A wrinkled gray T-shirt slid out next—also stained, although this color suggested ketchup, barbecue sauce, or blood. Or maybe all three. I wouldn't be surprised at this point. Sweat plastered the cotton to a stomach so ripped, I could see his six-pack through the fabric.

Next up, a massive chest that I assumed was as hard as the steel on the toe of his boots. A pair of gloved hands gripped the undercarriage of the truck, revealing ropy muscles down a tanned arm covered in tattoos. A pair of scratched goggles covered half the man's face as he finally revealed himself, this topped by a mess of light-brown hair—with something sticky matted above the left ear.

"Mornin'." His voice was deep and smooth, but with a touch of grit. Unrefined.

The man nimbly pushed himself off the rolling cart and

kicked it out of the way, sending it slamming into a metal toolbox. A tool fell off, clattering onto the floor. He either didn't notice or didn't care. Based on the streaks of grease on his cheeks, I assumed the latter.

Although he kept his distance from me, I could tell he was well above six feet tall.

I lowered my foot to my still-stuck flip-flop, balancing my big toe on the sole. When he simply stared at me, I said, "Um, can you turn that down?"

His head tilted to the side as he considered my request, as if I'd just asked him to detail my car—something I was sure this garage didn't do.

Still wearing the ridiculous goggles, the man took his sweet time as he crossed the floor, letting me know I was in his territory and this was his pace. Slow, steady, and absolutely maddening, he instantly annoyed me.

After turning Bob down a few clicks—just a few—the man lumbered back to his place in front of me. "Better?"

I fought an eye roll. "Sure."

When he slid his goggles onto the top of his head, two ocean-blue eyes pinned me with curiosity and interest. I'll never forget that moment.

I had a visceral reaction when our eyes met—an instant dip in my stomach, a flutter that reached the innermost depths of me, if only for a second. My entire body responded to simply seeing his eyes.

I blinked and turned a cheek, this automatic and seemingly uncontrollable reaction throwing me off. But like a magnet, I was pulled back to a blue so vivid, so bright, it reminded me of an afternoon sky on the brightest spring day. Mesmerizing—and totally out of place.

While his eyes were clear, focused, and flawless, the rest of him was unkempt and sloppy, although I got the vibe it wasn't from lack of means or know-how. It was from lack of giving a shit.

Day-old scruff covered a sharp jawline and thick neck, with a grease stain above the tip of a tattoo peeking out of his collar. His lips were thick and pink, with a small cut in the corner. His nose had a slight bump in the middle, and was a hair crooked. A few fine lines creased his forehead, and a few more ran from the corners of his eyes, from either smiling or habitual inquisition, I wasn't sure which.

I wondered how much older he was than me. Was he forty? Just past? Or maybe he looked older from years of manual labor, based on the calluses on his hands.

He was rough. Rugged. Perfectly imperfect, and oddly enough, extremely attractive. And totally, one hundred percent *not* my type.

I shifted under a gaze that felt like it was cutting through to my soul, dissecting each layer with an ease that seemed to come naturally to him.

He made me uncomfortable. And I didn't like it.

He looked over my shoulder to my BMW in the parking lot, then refocused on me. "You lost?"

Lost? The man had no idea.

"My car is smoking."

The corner of his lip lifted higher. Something about me amused him.

"In that case, let me grab a beer and switch over to Marley."

This time, I didn't fight the eye roll. "I mean, the hood is smoking. Under it, the engine, whatever, and trust me, I'm not laughing about it."

"No, I can see that. What color?"

I impatiently thrust my hand toward the car. "Silver. It's right there."

"I meant what color is the smoke?"

"Oh. Black."

"How long?"

"It just started. Ran fine yesterday, and when I turned the ignition this morning, a little smoke came out."

"Define a little."

"A puff."

"A puff?" he asked with a touch of mocking in his tone.

I shifted my weight impatiently. "When I started driving, it got worse."

"Did you hit anything? Run over anything?"

"Aside from the handful of potholes in this road?"

"Where?"

"The middle."

"Where in the middle of the road?"

"I don't know. About a quarter mile down that way."

"What were you doing down Rattlesnake Road?"

"Driving."

"Ma'am, I can do this all day." He sauntered over to a rolling toolbox and picked up a Coke. Sniffing at it, he scowled and set it aside—but not in the trash can. He picked up another and sniffed with the same result. Then he grabbed a water bottle, opened it, and chugged.

This freaking guy.

I turned to him, fisting my hands on my hips. "Home. I was driving home."

He lowered the water bottle from his lips. It was the first time I saw a flicker of something other than amusement behind his eyes. "You live down Rattlesnake Road?"

"Yep."

"Since when?"

"Since not long ago."

"Alone?"

"I'm not sure that's your business."

"Maybe so, but here's some free advice. Either replace the man, or woman, you're currently living with—assuming you are—with someone who can check the oil in your car, or learn yourself. Or consider buying a truck."

"One, I don't need someone to check my oil for me. Two, I don't do trucks. Or lesbians—not that there's anything wrong with that."

"Of course not. And everyone around here does trucks. Lesbians, I'm not so sure. Maybe—"

Cutting him off, I held up a hand as I closed my eyes and shook my head, muttering, "Oh my God." A hangover, a letter about killing a cat, an envelope filled with divorce papers, and a broken car did not go well with this man. He was the absolute last thing I needed at that moment.

Or so I thought.

"Listen. Can you help me or not? This is a mechanic shop, right?"

He gestured to the dismantled cars and nodded.

"Then why don't you have a sign out front?"

Careful not to bring attention to my foot, I curled my toe around the thong of my flip-flop and tried to lift it from the floor. No luck.

"Don't need one."

"All businesses need signs. People don't realize it's a mechanic shop."

"You did."

"What's your name?"

"Declan. What's yours?"

"Are you a mechanic?"

"Where are you from?"

"What does that matter? You gouge prices on tourists?"

He took another sip of water, eyeing me over the rim. A

thin trail trickled from his chin, wetting his T-shirt. He didn't bother wiping it.

"How do you know I'm not from around here?" I asked, not hiding my attitude.

"Because a local would've already unwedged themselves from the gum that's got you stuck in place."

"This is no ordinary gum."

"You're right. It's watermelon Bubblicious."

"I didn't know six-year-olds worked on cars."

He grinned. "You're a Yankee, aren't you?"

"As much as I'm enjoying this little tit-for-tat, can you help me or not?"

"I don't know." He downed the rest of his water, then tossed the plastic bottle into an overflowing recycle bin in the corner. "Oil leak, yep, I can fix, but it depends on what else I find under that hood."

"Look now."

Declan's eyes narrowed with the first sign of disapproval of my attitude. He picked up a towel and wiped his hands, then grabbed a handful of paper towels from a roll sitting next to a tin cup oozing with something. He strode toward me, his gaze on mine.

The man truly was massive. My instinct was to back up a step, but thanks to the damn gum, I was stuck in place. My stomach tickled as he knelt at my feet. A waft of air enveloped me, scented with that musky scent of man and fresh soap, with a motor oil finish.

That tickle turned to butterflies.

A strong grip slipped my ankle from my shoe, sending a wave of tingles over my skin. After sliding the paper towel under the shoe, Declan pried my flip-flop from the floor, then twisted the gum and rolled it into the paper towel.

As I balanced on one foot, he carried the shoe to one of

the many sinks and dabbed a towel in something that resembled nuclear waste. After a few scrapes of the bottom of my shoe, he returned, kneeling again to grab my ankle and slip my gum-free flip-flop back onto my foot.

I felt like a redneck Cinderella.

Heat mixed with the tingles this time—followed by total humiliation when I remembered I hadn't shaved my legs in a week.

"My, uh, razor's . . . broken."

He pushed to his feet. "I've got a bush hog out back."

My jaw dropped.

He grinned widely as he winked. "All right. Let's have a look-see at this smoking silver car of yours."

"I can't believe you said that."

As he breezed past me, he gave me another wink,. I followed him outside, jogging to keep up with his long strides.

Clearing my throat, I said, "I've been really busy." I should have dropped it, but leg hair that long deserved an explanation.

"Don't worry about it. You've got good feet."

"Good feet?"

"Yeah."

"What about my feet is good?"

"They're just good. Want me to write a poem or something?"

I looked down at my feet, a second before stumbling on the gravel. Never breaking his stride or sparing me a single glance, Declan grabbed my elbow and steadied me.

A jacked-up blue truck pulled into the lot and parked in front of one of the bays. An elderly man in denim coveralls and a cowboy hat stepped out, a cigarette dangling from lips as brown as dirt. He took a draw and blew out the smoke, tilting his head as he zeroed in on me from across the lot.

"Morning, Earl," Declan called out. "Be right with you."

"Mornin'. Brought that camera you wanted. Cheryl cleaned it up real nice for ya."

"Tell her I owe her."

"Already did. Told me to tell you she wants some basil, thyme, and some of that stuff that smells like Pine-Sol."

"It's rosemary, Earl."

"Yeah, that, and two jars of that rosemary honey too. She makes me eat it on my toast in the mornings. Tastes like—"

"Pine Sol?"

"No. Tastes like shit. No offense." Although the man was addressing Declan, he kept his gaze on me.

"None taken," Declan said coolly. "But tell her two jars is gonna cost a bowl of chili."

"You're gonna get a hole in your gut, son."

"Then I'll die happy."

The man watched me a minute longer before dipping his chin and disappearing into the garage.

"So, um, like I said, the smoke just started," I said, returning to the subject, although Declan wasn't listening to me.

He reached inside my car, clicked the latch, and popped the hood.

I continued, although he didn't ask. "The check-engine light came on with it. Do you . . . do you work on BMWs?"

Still ignoring me, he fiddled with something under the hood. "Go get my roller, will you?"

I blinked, looking over my shoulder at whoever he must be addressing. When I saw no one, I turned back to him. "Excuse me?"

"My roller. Slats of woods on wheels. The thing I was on

when you walked in. 'Bout a foot to the right of the gum you stepped on."

"Why?"

"There's a broken beer bottle under your car. Don't have time to get stitched up today."

"Maybe if you disposed of your bottles in the trash can instead of the driveway . . ."

"Then I'd have to empty the trash can."

"Ever thought of recycling?"

"Sure." He lifted a shard of glass from the ground. "Why don't you repurpose this to replace that broken razor of yours."

"You're something, you know that?"

"Roller. Get it. Right of the gum. And bring the light, hanging on the toolbox next to it. Yellow and black."

"Would you like me to make you some coffee to go with that?"

He raised his brows. "Gonna go out on a limb here and guess yours might be a bit too strong for me, sweetheart."

With an eye roll so dramatic I felt it in my headache, I turned and took my time crossing the parking lot, feeling Declan watch my every step. I'd never been so happy to be wearing something as unappealing as a baggy sweatshirt. Although something told me that someone like Declan would find baggy anything as sexy as a lace corset.

Earl also kept his eye on me as I grabbed the requested items and returned to my car. Declan positioned the roller and slid under the hood.

Seconds ticked to minutes.

I put my hands on my hips and looked around, wondering how the garage got any business being as secluded as it was. Despite Declan's obvious disdain for organizing—or marketing, for that matter—the bays were full of cars. Hopefully that meant the man was good at what he did.

Earl had made himself comfortable in a rocking chair, watching us with a cup of coffee in hand.

A grunt pulled my attention back to the car.

"Oil pan is cracked," Declan said as he slid out from under the car.

"Okay," I said slowly, unsure of the magnitude of the issue.

He stood, not bothering to dust off his pants. "Gonna have to replace it."

"Replace it? Can't you patch it up or something?"

"'Fraid I'm all out of super glue."

"And I'm all out of patience. Seriously, you can't patch it or something?"

"I could, but I won't."

"Why not?"

"Because that's not what needs to happen. It needs to be replaced. You're lucky I'm not telling you that you need to replace your engine. You don't have a drop of oil in your reservoir. How long ago did you hit the pothole?"

"The first was two days ago. I think."

"You've been driving dry since then. You didn't notice?"

"I've kinda been preoccupied." And why was it that mechanics always made women feel like such idiots?

"Well, you're lucky."

I snorted.

A moment passed as he stared a hole into my cheek. Reading my soul, I was sure.

"Well, let's get it done." I forced eye contact. "What needs to happen?"

"What's your name?" he asked with that damn penetrating gaze.

"I already told you."

"No, you didn't. I asked but you never answered."

"Grey."

"I'm sorry?"

"*Grey.*"

"Grey?"

"*Yes.* Grey."

"That's an interesting name."

"Thanks."

"There's a story behind it, isn't there?"

"Yeah, it's a bedtime tale entitled 'Grey Needs to Get Her Damn Car Fixed.'"

"Why'd your folks name you Grey?"

"Because I'm pissed off all the time. Why are we talking about this?"

"I don't meet many women named Grey."

"I guess it's your lucky day."

"Grey what?"

"Dalton." I waved a hand toward my car, my patience officially gone. "How long to fix this?"

"'Bout all day."

"Is this an actual measurement of time in the South?"

"I knew you were a Yankee, Grey."

The fact that I couldn't get a rise out of the man annoyed me even more.

"How much does *'bout all day* cost me? Two bowls of chili?"

"Three. With mac."

"What the hell is mac?"

"Chili mac. Chili with elbow macaroni shells. Cheddar cheese, pickles on the side."

"And a bottle of Zantac for dessert?"

"No. Tums. The fruity kind."

"To go with the watermelon Bubblicious, I see. Okay, Paula Dean, what else?"

"Expensive car, expensive part."

"Fine. How much?"

"With the chili?"

"*Yes*," I huffed out, exasperated.

He gave me that grin, laughing at me again—and I officially hated him.

"Couple hundred bucks."

My eyebrows popped up. "Seriously?"

"I can run a tab if you need it."

"No. No . . . I know it's more than that for a BMW. I've had the car worked on before."

"Chili makes up for the rest. If you'd like to take it to someone else, I'll give you the names and numbers for the other local mechanics. Even tow it for you. For free."

"No, no." I exhaled, feeling like a total bitch now. Although I'd been nothing but difficult, he was giving me a huge discount. "Thank you," I said quickly, looking down.

"You can thank me with the chili."

"You seriously might be happier if I just added a tip."

"You don't cook?"

"Not chili."

"Every Southern woman should know how to cook a good pot of chili. You want to fit in, learn."

"Get a truck, check oil, and learn how to make a pot of chili. Noted. Also noted that food is a part of the barter system here in the South. Why is that? Whatever. What time will my car be ready? Sundown?" I asked, this time with a smirk.

"I've got two cars ahead of you, and a thirty-minute conversation about commies and World War Two with Earl before that. Should be ready after lunch."

I wrinkled my nose and looked in the direction of town.

"Got something you need to do?"

"Yeah. I kinda needed to get something to the post office today."

"Earl can take you."

I looked over Declan's shoulder where the old man was spitting into a Styrofoam cup.

"I really don't feel like talking about a political doctrine that promotes communal control."

Declan cocked a brow, and I winked.

"I read it on a Bubblicious wrapper."

He chuckled, a low, smooth, casual laugh that seemed to come as easily to him as breathing.

"Seriously, though, no. I don't want to inconvenience Earl."

"He's got nothing better to do. Trust me. And it'll free up thirty minutes for me so I can get to your car a little quicker."

"Well, from where I'm from, women don't take rides from strange men."

Just then, the office door flung open. I turned to see the spitting image of Cher—pre-plastic surgery—step out into the parking lot.

A pair of deeply hooded black eyes pinned me like lasers the moment she saw Declan and me together. Long straight hair, as dark as a raven's wing, blew across a face with high cheekbones and a full, round mouth. She wore a faded black T-shirt, tattered on the edges. Below that, a pair of baggy boyfriend jeans and sandals. Like Declan, a rainbow of tattoos colored her thin arms. *Badass bitch* was my first thought, and the intensity of her gaze on me told me she felt the same about me—minus the badass part.

I squared my shoulders as she beelined it to me with an

aggressive, unfeminine stride that reminded me of the videos I'd seen of Bigfoot. Something I was sure lived in these woods, by the way.

"Shoulda called me, Declan." Although she addressed the mechanic, her hostile gaze stayed on me.

Declan ignored Southern Cher and spoke to me. "You don't want Earl to take you. Fine. Kai'll take you."

"Take her where?" Kai asked, now inches from my side.

"Miss Dalton needs a ride to the post office."

"Didn't realize we ran a taxi service here."

Declan cocked a brow, and her jaw twitched.

In that brief interaction between them, I gathered two things. One, Declan was her boss. And two, she was madly in love with him.

Declan refocused on me. "Kai'll take you to the post office, and wherever else you need to go, then take you back home. I'll call you when your car's ready."

I took another glance at the woman I didn't know, who undoubtedly despised me, then back to the man I also didn't know. But for some reason, I trusted him. I also didn't have any other option at the moment.

"Okay. Fine."

"Great. Glad that's settled. Kai, go get your car."

As Kai sliced me one more look of hatred before obeying her boss's orders, I couldn't help but wonder how he paid her.

I took a step toward the office to fill out whatever paperwork I needed to, but Declan didn't move. Instead, he pulled a cell phone from his pocket.

"What's your number, Grey Dalton?"

I turned, frowning at his phone.

"Work phone," he said to clarify, as if that made it less personal.

I rattled off my number.

"I sent you a text. Lock in my number."

"Thanks, but I don't plan on hitting any more potholes."

"Not for the car. The chili—and the house. That thing's one gust of wind away from falling apart. Let me know if you need anything."

"How do you know exactly where I live?"

"Not many houses down Rattlesnake Road."

"And you know which is mine?"

"Everyone knows that house. Here's Kai."

25

"So, where are you from?" I asked Kai from the passenger seat. Not that I cared, but to simply try to break the wall of tension between us.

The woman was definitely in love. Definitely banging the boss.

"Here," she replied, annoyed.

"Cool." I rolled my eyes and looked out the window as the trees zoomed past.

Not surprisingly, Cool Kid Cher drove a cherry-red 1969 Corvette convertible with red leather interior to match. The car was immaculate, as if it had been driven straight out of a muscle car magazine. A baby-blue rabbit foot hung from her key ring, next to a bottle of pepper spray. The dashboard was made of gleaming wood, not a speck of dirt. The woman liked—respected—her cars, and I wondered if she was a mechanic, like Declan. She certainly had the attitude and tattoos to match.

And the walk, for that matter.

She'd taken the top down. Although my hair was going to look like it had gone through a blender, I was grateful for the white noise of the wind whipping through the inside of the car. It helped with the awkwardness.

The sun had buried itself behind a wall of thick gray clouds, making the breeze cool enough to cut through even the heartiest vintage sweatshirt. Shivering, I wrapped my arms around myself. She didn't notice, or didn't care.

Perhaps it was my mood from having the worst morning ever, but it bothered me that Kai didn't like me. I wanted to change that. For some reason, I cared.

"Were you born and raised here?" I asked.

"Yep."

Well, that was it. That was all I was going to get from Cool Kid Cher.

Resigning myself to that fact, I pulled my phone from my purse to give me something to do. I had four text messages from Cassidy.

Cassidy: How was dinner with Sir Lucas Covington? Tell me everything.
Cassidy: Unless he's laying naked next to you right now.
Cassidy: In which case, why the hell is a phone in your hand instead of [eggplant emoji]?

Two minutes later . . .

Cassidy: I'm dying. Tell me.

I smirked, typing a response.

Me: Sorry. Ran into some car trouble.
Cassidy: Please tell me car trouble is code for morning sex.
Me: I wish.
Cassidy: Everything okay?

Me: Yes. Just leaking oil. Getting fixed now.
Cassidy: I thought BMWs fixed themselves. [winking emoji] TELL ME ABOUT LAST NIGHT.

I'd had enough close girlfriends to know that sex on a first date was worthy of calling an emergency lunch filled with margaritas and two hours of dissecting every second of the experience. But telling Cassidy about getting nailed over my kitchen counter wasn't something I was in the mood for at that moment.

Or proud of, based on the nerves and regret suddenly flooding my stomach. And I certainly didn't want to go into the whole "falling off the wagon" thing. So I kept it light.

Me: He took me to dinner. Good conversation, good food, definitely good view.
Cassidy: [Eggplant emoji]?

I stared at my phone, then lied.

Me: He was the perfect gentleman. I was the perfect lady.
Cassidy: Boooooring. I want to hear about it anyway. Let's meet up soon. Have to work tonight. Tomorrow maybe. I'll text. Sure you don't need a ride anywhere?
Me: I'm good, thanks.
Cassidy: Talk soon.
Me: Sounds good.
Cassidy: [Kiss emoji]

Taking a deep breath, I shoved the phone back into my purse and forced myself to enjoy the view of the budding nature around me. But I couldn't. There was something about my driver that put me more on edge than I already was. Fidgeting, I reached forward to wipe away the thin layer of dust that was gathering on the glovebox.

Her head snapped toward me, her hateful expression warning me not to touch, or open, her glovebox. As if I were going to steal something from it. It was the first time she'd graced me with a glance the entire drive.

I snapped. "Listen, Kai. I might be from New York, but I haven't picked anyone's pockets in at least two months."

"If that's the kind of humor they have up north, I understand the suicide rate."

"Is there something about me that bothers you?"

She didn't respond.

"Seriously."

"Why do you ask?"

"Oh, something about the attitude you've had since the moment you saw me, and the pistol you've got shoved between your seat and the console makes me a little curious."

Her eyes narrowed, but her gaze stayed on the road.

"Is it loaded?"

The corner of Kai's lip curled in amusement. Why the hell was I so funny to these people?

"If by loaded, you're asking if I have bullets in the magazine, then yes. If by loaded, you're asking if I have a bullet in the chamber, then yes."

"Double-action then."

She laughed at this. Loudly.

I found myself grinning at her laugh. It was a deep, throaty, manly laugh. I shouldn't have been surprised.

"That's not what double-action means. It means—" She started to school me but paused, then stopped as if I wasn't worth the effort.

We paused at the stop sign, a cloud of dust settling into

the air around us. Then pulled onto the winding road that led to Main Street.

"You got someone else to drive you around while we get your wheels fixed?" she asked.

We.

"Nope."

"In that case, you'd really probably be better off taking your BMW to Frankie's."

There was an attitude in her voice when she said *BMW.* I didn't care for it. I also didn't care for the fact she was trying to get rid of me.

"One, who's Frankie? Two, is there a reason your boss can't fix my car?"

"One, Frankie is the name of the dude who owns Frankie's Auto. Didn't think that needed explanation. Two, Declan can fix a KORKUT if he needed to."

"What's a KORKUT?"

"A self-propelled anti-aircraft gun."

I looked over, tilting my head to the side. "Were you in the military?"

She ignored the question. "I'm just saying, if you need a car to get around while yours is out, you should take your repair to Frankie. He's got a spare car he lets his customers drive around. We don't."

"I think I'll stay with Declan."

Her jaw twitched. She flicked on her turn signal and swerved into the post office about five miles an hour faster than she needed to.

Nerve hit.

Intended, I realized.

26

I arrived home—correction: was dropped off—to find a platter of oatmeal cookies and jug of sweet tea on my doorstep with a note.

Don't forget to take the allergy meds.

– Etta

After devouring four—cookies, not pills—I spent the rest of the morning busying myself and my mind by scrubbing the kitchen to upbeat hip-hop music.

The sun had made its debut sometime around lunch, right about the time I got a text from a number I didn't recognize, indicating my car was ready and that Kai would be at my house in exactly five minutes to take me to the garage.

Four minutes later, the cherry-red Corvette roared up the driveway. Kai wasn't happy about the assist, and appeared even more annoyed than earlier that morning.

I wondered if she was more than only banging the boss. Declan's girlfriend, maybe? Or wife? She fit him, I decided, and realized at the same time how much I didn't.

Cool Kid Cher and I were polar opposites.

I didn't see Declan when we arrived at the garage to pick up my car. When I pulled out my wallet to pay, Kai shook her head with a scowl and walked away.

"But the bill," I asked to her back.

"Taken care of," she bit back over her shoulder.

The chili.

I tried one more time to pay, but Kai tossed me the keys and stomped back to the office.

My car had not only been fixed, but washed and detailed. When I slipped behind the steering wheel, the faintest scent of *him* lingered—soap, motor oil, and man.

The late-afternoon light was beginning to fade with my energy level as I wrestled with the bookcase Etta had given me. The bastard weighed a hundred pounds, at least.

I dropped to the floor, wiping sweat from my brow, and glowered at the mess of furniture that cluttered the living room.

I *hated* the clutter. The mess. And I wanted the damn bookcase out of the damn living room and in the second-floor mystery room.

I needed help. That was the only way around it.

After dragging myself off the floor, I studied the staircase, wondering if I could create some sort of pulley system to get furniture upstairs.

My quads burned as I took the narrow steps.

Hands on my hips, I scanned the room, the A-frame ceiling, the back of the chimney, the mismatched hardwood floors. I walked over to the window, opened it, and stuck my head out, inhaling the fresh air like a dog. The air smelled like lavender.

I took in the view, the tall, thin cedar trees that led to the cliff, the rock painted orange by the setting sun. The blurred background of mountains behind it. My gaze shifted to the fields where I'd seen my cowboy twice before, and my wheels started to turn.

Cowboys know how to move furniture, right?

Then Etta's words came back to me. *"Love your neighbor as you love yourself."*

Maybe it was time to become a good neighbor.

With that thought, I jogged downstairs, leaving the bookcase crooked at the bottom of the staircase in the den. I checked my reflection in a mirror leaning haphazardly against the wall—and cringed.

My long dark hair resembled a rat's nest, thanks to the joy ride with Kai earlier. My Rolling Stones sweatshirt was speckled with dust bunnies from a day filled with cleaning. My skin was sallow from the tequila the night before, and my eyes shadowed from the guilt. I couldn't help but noticed how different my Berry Springs reflection was from my New York reflection.

A twinge of nerves at that fact made me turn away.

I switched out the sweatshirt for a plain white T-shirt. Brushed the tangles from my hair, and wrapped it into a loose bun on top of my head. Pulled a few strands around my face to give it that subtle sexy look. Then added a swipe of tinted under-eye cream to conceal the circles, and a dab of lip gloss to add some shimmer. It was important to look decent while introducing myself to my neighbors. I could almost hear Etta's voice guiding me.

Gearing myself up to meet a wife—a cowgirl for the cowboy—and a gaggle of kids, I prepared a little welcome speech as I slipped into my running shoes, then pulled a flannel shirt over my T-shirt. Southerners liked flannel.

I replated Etta's cookies to make it look like four of them hadn't been eaten, and covered the plate in plastic wrap. Then I grabbed my Louis Vuitton backpack, carefully slid the jug of sweet tea into it, and shrugged it on.

Although I wasn't exactly sure where the cowboy's house was, I knew the general direction. It was time to get to know my land, anyway.

I searched for Moonshine, surprised when I was disappointed that I didn't see her. The temperamental cat was slowly becoming like a roommate to me. A disgruntled, weird roommate, but one that made you feel not so alone at the end of the day.

I stepped off the porch, hung a left, and entered the woods—my woods. The little patch of earth that I owned. An unexpected pride gripped me.

My land.

A breeze rustled the budding branches above. Birds dipped from branch to branch, feeding their chirping young ones. Patches of vibrant green grass thrived in the dapples of late-afternoon sunlight cutting through the treetops.

A few yards into the hike, the underbrush became thicker, overgrown with bushes and snarls of twigs and dead leaves. I imagined how beautiful it would be if the underbrush were cleared. Like my own little park. I envisioned a picnic table, a hammock, a cat hotel for Moonshine and all her kittens. Grinning, I added all that to my mental to-do list.

Sharp boulders speared up from the ground as I neared the ravine that sliced through the property just below the cliff. If memory served me correctly, the ravine marked the property line between the cowboy's land and mine.

I stepped to the edge, peered down, and decided it was too steep to climb. So I skirted the edge, figuring the ravine had to ease up at some point. No luck. Eventually, I came to a thick, moss-covered tree trunk that had fallen across the ravine, connecting both sides.

Eyeing it, I stopped, realizing I could no longer see my house through the trees.

Option One: Hike back and drive to Cowboy's house.

Option Two: Climb down, then back up the ravine—otherwise known as "hell no."

Option Three: Cross the nature-made bridge.

Considering I'd spent the first half of my life metaphorically walking a tightrope, I accepted the challenge. I shifted my backpack, doubled my grip on Etta's cookies, and took the first step.

My heart rate picked up. I breathed steadily through the next step, and the next, each step a bit faster than the one before. As I neared the other side, I grinned.

Victory.

I pressed on through the woods, noticing the stark difference between the cowboy's property and mine. No underbrush, no shrubs, no fallen limbs. While the woods on my property resembled the set of the latest M. Night Shyamalan movie, his resembled a walk through Central Park.

How much time and effort did it take to maintain such a large area? The idea seemed so daunting to me, along with everything that needed to be done on the house. Maybe I needed a cowboy of my own.

As the land sloped downward, my sneakers slid on loose rocks, and I took it a little slower. Finally, I came to a wooden fence, new and sturdy, cutting through the landscape. Beyond it, the fields.

I looked up over my shoulder and spotted the tip of my cliff through the trees. And barely visible, the window to the second-floor room.

He could see me—my house, at least.

I walked along the fence line for what seemed like ten minutes until the woods began to thin, revealing a one-lane dirt road to my right. A few minutes later, I came to a mailbox, newly painted with 1316 rattlesnake road. The driveway past it resembled mine with trees lining the way, except again, this yard resembled a park.

At the top of the driveway was a log cabin, much newer than mine, nestled between soaring pines. Shadows from the setting sun stretched along an immaculate yard with healthy, vibrant grass.

Shiny, thick log walls supported a red roof with a stone chimney on the side. Two sweeping windows flanked a bright red door. Rocking chairs, as green as the budding grass, sat on a front porch enclosed with a railing of criss-crossed slim logs.

The home was neither too big nor too small. It was perfect for Little Red Riding Hood and her platter of regifted cookies.

A pebbled walkway led to a matching garage with a red door. A shop, almost as large, had been built behind it.

The home was beautiful, unlike my own. Well-kept, well-maintained.

As I drew closer, I noticed a trio of empty longnecks on the porch next to one of the rocking chairs.

I glanced over my shoulder, noting my path back, before stepping onto the porch. The front windows were open, and the scent of fresh coffee drifted through the air. This seemed odd, considering it was early evening.

I paused to peer into the darkened room, noticing more windows at the end of a hallway. A house of windows. No kids' toys, I noticed. No bikes, slingshots, BB guns, as I assumed most Southern kids were accustomed to. And it was quiet. Much too quiet for a family.

Cookies in hand and tea strapped to my back, I took a deep breath, preparing myself for dreaded small talk and a barrage of questions I wouldn't want to answer.

I knocked, but there was no response.

I peered in the windows again, straining to listen for any sounds inside the house, but there were none. No murmur of a television, no country music from a radio. Nothing.

I knocked again.

Waited.

Contemplating my options, I looked down at the cookies. I didn't think to bring a card, in the event no one would be home, so leaving them seemed silly.

As I raised my hand to knock one last time, the front door swung open.

I blinked quickly, my brain suddenly muddled by the sight of the half-naked man in front of me.

I recognized him instantly.

27

"Uh . . ."

That single syllable was all I could manage as I gawked at Declan the Mechanic, wearing nothing but a towel around his waist.

His hair was wet from a shower, darkened strands dripping down a sculpted chest and a six-pack so defined, I could chip a tooth on it. A droplet of water fascinated me as it slid down to soak into the towel, which was secured loosely above a perfect, veiny *V* above a generous bulge.

A *V* that could make even the smartest woman make bad decisions.

My gaze drifted to the tattoos that covered his arms, ending in an intricate design snaking around his shoulders.

"Miss Dalton . . . everything all right?"

The concern in Declan's voice yanked me back to the present. My eyes snapped to his—as blue as the shower he'd obviously just stepped out of.

His brows pulled together with concern as he looked over my shoulder, then back to me. "Are you okay?" he asked again.

"No. Yes. I mean, yes, everything's fine."

"Where's your car?"

"At home."

He frowned. "Everything okay with it?"

"Yes."

I was totally thrown off my game. Between his lack of clothing—and the realization that the man I'd been a stuck-up bitch to hours earlier was my freaking neighbor—I was totally tongue-tied.

"Sorry," I managed to say. "My car's running perfectly. Thank you."

"How'd you get here then?"

"I walked." I kicked out my sneaker.

His brow arched. Apparently, this surprised him.

"Why?" he asked.

I shrugged. "Beautiful evening."

"Okay. Why here?"

"I wanted to meet my neighbor. But I didn't realize that neighbor was . . . you."

"No, you wouldn't have," he said, that amused twinkle returning to his eye.

"What do you mean?"

"It means you didn't ask many questions. Don't usually, if I had to guess."

"Meaning I'm self-absorbed?"

His shoulder slightly lifted.

"When are you talking about? At the shop?"

"That's right." He leaned against the door frame, settling in for a discussion.

Again, the man seemed to have all the time in the world, and was in no hurry to make me feel comfortable standing on his doorstep. The towel stretched against his waist, and I had to fight from taking another peek at his bulge.

I cocked my hip. "So, you're telling me to make more of an effort. Okay. But do most of your customers ask for a genetic report when they drop off their car?"

"Sometimes."

"I doubt that."

"You haven't been around here long enough. I could give you the first and last name of every one of Earl's first, second, and third cousins. And he could tell you what size boxer briefs I wear."

"Gross."

Declan grinned. "He and his wife own the local laundromat. She does my laundry sometimes."

"Oh. Well, I apologize that I didn't reciprocate the Spanish inquisition you gave me. I guess 'getting to know your neighbor' isn't natural for us Yankees."

"Then I'll let it pass." He looked down at the plate in my hands, making me remember the cookies I'd somehow forgotten.

I raised the plate, pasting a sugary-sweet smile on my face, and in my best Southern accent, said, "Well, hello there, neighbor. My name is Grey Dalton. I'm your new neighbor. And in a show of hospitality, I baked you cookies. I'd like to get to know everything about you during this brief visit, including your age, underwear, and shoe size, as is apparently expected in this neck of the woods."

"Age forty-one, underwear size large, and shoe size fourteen."

I gulped.

"What kind of cookies?" he asked, this suddenly taking precedence above all else.

"Oatmeal."

"Seriously?"

"Seriously."

"Oatmeal's my favorite."

"Yeah?"

"Oh yeah."

"Along with chili, right? See? I know a few things about you. Chili is your favorite food."

"That's right." He regarded me coolly. "Favorite food, and also payment for services rendered on your fancy BMW. What's in the backpack?"

"Tea. Sweet," I quickly added as if that sealed the deal. "Consider this my first payment for services rendered."

"Oh, no, ma'am. We agreed on a full chili dinner. No way around it." He took the plate from my hands. "But this makes up for your behavior at the shop."

Declan turned, leaving the door open, and disappeared into the cabin. I watched the towel hug each perfectly round ass cheek with his stride, praying it would drop to the floor.

"Come on in, New York," he hollered over his shoulder.

I stepped inside, dodging two pairs of muddy boots abandoned near the door, and paused while Declan disappeared down the hall. His home was a fusion of rich mahogany, lush fabrics, dark colors, a flood of natural light. Gorgeous—and a total bachelor pad.

The entire front half of the house was a large living space—like a massive sunroom—separated by a Navajo-style runner that led down a hallway. The walls were stacked logs, same as the outside. To the right, large plush leather couches were arranged in front of the biggest flat-screen TV I'd ever seen. And more windows.

It was absolutely gorgeous, aside from the mess that reminded me of his garage. Empty beer bottles, plates, and coffee cups littered the end tables. Books and magazines were stacked on the floor.

I wrinkled my nose.

To the left was a sitting area with a love seat and recliner in front of a stone fireplace that reminded me of my own. More windows and a packed bookcase in the corner. This room had less clutter.

I followed the noise down the hallway that opened up to a large kitchen. My stride broke as I zeroed in on the potted plant centered on a dining table in a breakfast nook enclosed by beveled-glass windows.

"Is that lavender?"

Declan set the cookies on the counter. "You know your herbs."

I opened my mouth, but the words caught in my throat as I stared at the tiny purple petals, sparkling in a single beam of slanted sunlight. The plant looked exactly like mine, like Violet.

It was beautiful.

"Want it?" Declan asked.

I tore my gaze away and found him staring. "No. Thanks. It's beautiful."

I looked back at the table, where shriveled purple petals dotted its surface next to dirty dishes, coffee cups, more magazines, a pair of scissors, a dusty pair of gloves, and at least a dozen empty jars. Empty cardboard boxes and crates were stacked in the corners of the kitchen.

My pulse rate kicked up as I took in the clutter. How could someone live in such disarray? Good thing the man was hot.

Extremely hot.

My focus drifted over the second half of the house. More wood logs, more light. Copper cookware hung from the ceiling of a newly remodeled kitchen, which would be beautiful if it weren't for the mess in the sink and smudges on the windows. More empty jars lined the counters, plus a few funnels, towels, and tools, reminding me of a mad scientist's kitchen.

What the hell was this dude into?

At the opposite end was a door. The laundry room, I guessed, with heaps of size-large boxer briefs. Unlike my distaste of the kitchen, that image gave me an entirely different reaction, deep in my loins.

To the left, the fresh scent of bath soap drifted out of a door, opened a crack. The bedroom—one bedroom, I noted, then quickly glanced around, looking for any sign of a woman. There was none. I caught the faint sound of a radio, maybe from the bathroom, and thought I heard the low sound of Elvis crooning.

"Take the plant," Declan said. "I've got plenty out back."

My gaze lifted from the trail of cat food leading out the back door to the open bag of kibble in the corner.

"You do?"

"Yep. Stuff'll overrun a garden if you're not careful." He grabbed two glasses from the cupboard.

"You garden?"

"You surprised?"

"Yes."

He turned fully toward me—still in the damn towel—and flashed that damn grin. "Why's that?"

"You just . . ." I glanced at his tattoos. "Don't look like the gardening type."

"Never judge a book by its cover, Miss Dalton. Figured a street-wise Yankee would have better sense than that."

A vision of my reckless night with Lucas Covington flashed before my eyes, and embarrassment heated my cheeks. I cleared my throat, desperate to regain control of the conversation. Of myself.

"Anyway. Thanks again for fixing my car."

"Was Kai nice to you when she picked you up?"

"Of course. She's a stubborn one. As you are, I assume. She wouldn't accept my credit card."

"You really don't want to make this chili, do you?"

"I told you. I don't cook."

"Only cookies?"

Whoops. "Yes, aside from cookies, I mean."

He nodded to the backpack I was still wearing.

"Oh. Sorry." I shrugged out of the pack, pulled out the jug of tea, and set it on the counter. The scent of lavender filled my nose.

Declan filled two glasses with ice, then set them next to the tea. I resisted the urge to pick one up to examine it and make sure it was clean.

"There's fresh coffee, if you'd rather."

"I don't drink coffee past six a.m."

He let out a grunt, then breezed past me. "Be right back. Make yourself at home."

I watched him disappear into the dark bedroom, wanting to see more. Of the room *and* him, I admitted. Instead, I followed orders and looked around the house again. Definitely a bachelor pad, but that didn't mean there wasn't a woman in his life.

And why do I care?

I looked for any sign of Kai—a tube of red lipstick, a switchblade, maybe—but came up short.

Again, why did I care? Declan and his carefree attitude and aversion to organization made us about as compatible as tequila and good decisions. I knew this from experience.

Declan returned a moment later, wearing a white undershirt above a pair of faded Levi's. No shoes. There was something about a man with no shoes.

His eyes laser-locked on mine—as they always seemed to—as he crossed the room.

"Should we heat them up?" he asked.

I paused. Did Etta warm up her cookies? "No," I guessed, and followed him to the counter. "They're fine as is."

"Well, I like mine warm."

Declan reached into the cupboard behind me, our shoulders grazing, and pulled down two mismatched plates. I took a step to the left. He mounded four cookies onto his plate, then shoved them into the microwave. He watched me as it hummed, and I put a cookie on the other plate.

"So," I said, trying to break the tension I wasn't sure how to label. "I'm sorry about earlier."

"About what, exactly?"

"Just . . . you know."

"Being rude and self-absorbed?"

My brows shot up.

He winked. "No worries. Not my first."

"Well, I'd like to think I'm not normally such a bitch. Just so you know."

"That's good to hear."

The microwave dinged. He pulled out the plate and set it in front of me. We faced each other, Declan hitching his hip on the counter, me as rigid as stone.

"Try them warm." He pushed the plate to me.

"I'm okay."

"Try them warm," he said again as he poured tea into my glass, then his.

"Fine." I grabbed a warm cookie from his plate.

Pleased now, he picked up one and took half the thing in one bite, then chewed, assessed, and swallowed. "Nice work, New York."

"Don't call me that."

A crumble tumbled off his chin as he gave me a once-over. "You seemed . . . disheveled at the shop earlier."

"Tends to happen when smoke barrels out of your hood." I took a feminine nibble of my cookie.

"What was so important you had to get in the mail today?"

The guy had a memory like an elephant. *Noted.*

"Paperwork," I grumbled, giving in and taking a man-sized bite out of the cookie. He was right. They were better warm.

"What kind of paperwork?"

"The kind that ends things."

He glanced down at my bare ring finger, then back up to my eyes.

A beat passed.

"What brought you to Berry Springs?"

"Seriously, is this how living in this town is going to be? Everyone knowing everyone's business?"

"'Fraid so." He devoured another cookie, letting the question slide. "How's the house coming along?"

"Slowly. The more time I spend with it, the more work it needs, it seems."

"Like most things."

I shifted, then sipped at my tea.

"Your turn," he said.

"My turn what?"

"To ask me a question. Get to know me. Show you care to get to know your neighbor."

"Oh Lord. The pressure of a probing question . . ." I took another sip of my tea, considering. "Okay. You ready?"

"More than you know."

"Where are the wife and kids?"

"Because everyone in the South is married and breeding

before age twenty? There you go making assumptions again."

"Am I wrong?"

He laughed. "Not really. And no wife, no kids."

"Why?"

He tilted his head, regarding me. Or taking a second to gather his thoughts? Thrown off his game, maybe?

"Did I go too far?" I grinned, biting into another cookie. "Have I crossed the line now?"

"I have no lines, that I can promise you. No wife, no kids, because I haven't found a woman that knew her way around a pot of chili."

"God, the pressure."

"Can you handle it?"

"I think so." It was my turn to look him up and down. "So, you're forty-one years old, never married, no kids. You're like a Southern unicorn."

"Displaced horn." He winked.

I grinned, then nodded at the top of the fridge. "What's with the pistol above your freezer?"

"Protection."

"Kai carries a gun in her car."

"Everyone around here carries guns."

"Really?"

"Yeah. Usually more than one."

"You have more than one gun?"

"This interests you. Why?"

"Protection, I guess."

"Protection is needed out here in the sticks. I'll give you one of mine. Teach you how to shoot."

"Guns make me uneasy."

"Uneasy is waking alone in the middle of the night and

finding yourself face-to-face with an intruder twice your size, and you with no protection."

I thought of the ghost in my house and wondered what protection I needed against it. "Where do you keep your other guns?"

"Depends."

"On what?"

"What I'm doing. Where I'm at. I almost always have one in my truck. Sometimes I carry in my boot, sometimes on my belt."

"Are you carrying now?"

"Wanna check?" He wiggled his eyebrows, and I rolled my eyes. "Learn to shoot, then you'll get one. My turn."

"Go," I said, beginning to enjoy the back-and-forth.

"What brought you to my house? Because I know it wasn't to be a hospitable neighbor, or to apologize for your behavior."

"Are you always so direct?"

"It's one of my many charms—along with the horn."

"I'm sure." My gaze dropped to his pants, then refocused on him. "Truth?"

"No other way, Miss Dalton. Not in this house." He shoved the last cookie into his mouth.

"Call me Grey."

"Grey then," he mumbled around the bite.

"I need help moving furniture."

"Did Abe not help when he delivered everything?"

"How do you know I bought furniture from Abe?"

"Everyone knows *New York* bought furniture from Abe."

"I really hate that name." I sighed. "Yes, he did his job, and more. My living room looks like a flea market. I'm needing help with a bookcase, specifically."

"When?"

"Now. And maybe a few more times over the next few weeks. Until I get settled."

Declan glanced at the clock.

Where did he need to be? Dinner? A date?

Again, *why do I care?*

He wiped his hands on his jeans. "Let's move."

I set down my tea.

He left me in the kitchen and returned in a pair of brown leather combat boots.

"Your shoes are untied."

"Powder."

What?

I frowned as he breezed past me and disappeared into the laundry room. Curious, I followed and found him sitting on the floor in a haze of Gold Bond.

I waved the white cloud of powder from my face. "What are you doing?"

"Powder," he said again.

"I see that, but why are you powdering your laundry room?"

"I'm powdering my feet. I get the fungus."

I shuddered. "Gross."

He slipped back into one boot, and while powdering the other, nodded to my sneakers. "Stick around here a few summers, and you'll be powdering more than just your feet."

"Seriously—*gross,* Declan."

He laughed.

"Okay." He tugged on the other boot and jumped to his feet. "Powdered and ready to take on the world."

I shook my head. "Let's start with a bookcase."

28

Declan fell into step behind me as I led him through his house, keenly aware of his gaze on my ass. "Mind if we drive?"

"Nope."

"You sure? I'd hate for you to miss your steps."

I stopped and spun to glare at him. "Are you insinuating I count my steps every day in an effort to lose weight?"

"Don't most women?"

"Most women would slap a man across the face for implying they needed to lose weight."

The corners of his lips pulled up, the sexual tension now at an all-time high.

"You're not fat, Grey."

"Well, thanks." I rolled my eyes and turned back, striding through the mess of his living room. "Anyway, seriously, thank you for doing this."

"Don't thank me yet. I haven't seen the size of your bookcase."

We stepped outside. He didn't bother locking up.

The sun had set, the last of the day's light merely a glow

through the trees. The woods were busy with bugs chirping, squirrels jumping from branch to branch, nature's inhabitants making their final rounds before nightfall.

We stepped around the side of his cabin and were crossing the pebbled path to the garage when I stopped cold.

"Is that a garden?"

My eyes rounded at the rows of raised beds colored with vibrant greens, reds, yellows, and oranges, enclosed in beautiful log fencing.

Declan stopped. "It is. I told you I garden."

"I thought you meant a few herbs in the windowsill. This is an operation."

His brows pulled together, his hands fisted on his hips as he scrutinized what undoubtedly took hours each day to maintain. He nodded. "Sure feels like that most days."

"It's incredible. Did you build it yourself?" Without waiting for a response, I made a beeline for it.

"I did." He followed. "Not many gardens in the city?"

"Not natural. Not like this."

I followed the sharp scent of lavender as we rounded the back of the cabin. Rows and rows of blooming lavender lined the entire left side of the garden. Lilac bushes crowded the deck on the back of the house.

"Oh my God." I closed my eyes, inhaling deeply.

"For someone who says they don't garden, you sure seem impressed."

"I love lavender." I opened my eyes. "And it's just . . . such a feat, you know? I can't imagine how much work this takes. And then the pride you must feel when everything blooms and ripens, and you get to enjoy it at the end."

I noticed then that unlike the disarray of his home, his garden was meticulously built and cared for, each row spaced the exact distance apart. It was perfectly pruned, not a single weed to be seen, not a dead leaf anywhere.

"You like to create things?" he asked.

I thought of my childhood inventions, all the hobbies that included creating something with your own two hands, and of the online magazine that I'd built from the ground up in adulthood.

I nodded, taking another deep breath. "That *lavender.* God, you're so lucky."

"You can have some. Please. Take half."

"Seriously?"

"Absolutely. I've got more than I can manage. And it's prime time to plant."

"Thank you." I looked at him. "Seriously—thank you. I would love some."

He dipped his chin. "Want a tour?"

"Please."

Declan opened the ornate wooden gate. When he saw me inspecting the tall metal enclosure attached above the wood, barely visible, he said, "It's to keep the deer out. You wouldn't believe how many times I've had to replace this fence."

"Crafty little devils?"

"They're the bane of my existence."

I laughed, then stepped inside the garden. "Wow."

"So, the left side is herbs. Basil, parsley, sage, dill, cilantro, rosemary, oregano, thyme, mint. Mint's another beast. It'll take over if you're not careful. Want some of that too?"

Considering my affinity for mojitos, I was about to decline when he said, "It's great in brewed tea."

I smiled. "In that case, yes. I'd love some."

"We'll need to build you a fence. If you garden, you'll

become very popular with the woodland creatures, trust me."

My brow cocked. "I'm surprised they remember how to get back to your place after visiting that far corner."

Declan followed my gaze, then laughed out loud. "That's cassava, not pot."

"Dammit." I winked. "What's cassava?"

"Hell if I know, really. I got it for free from a local farmer. People harvest the roots or something. I planted it and then just kind of forgot about it—ironically. Funny story, though, you're not the first to think it's pot. The sheriff and I are buds. He came over once and started getting a bit jumpy. Thought I had my own illegal operation going on."

I laughed. "But you didn't."

"Nope. Not since high school . . . well, my twenties, I guess. Hit thirty and decided I should drop the stuff. You?"

"Nope." I shook my head. "Been told plenty of times I should try it, though."

"Let me guess, to make you relax?"

"Bingo."

"You're bit high-strung, aren't you?"

"That's putting it mildly."

"Not a bad thing to be, as long as you know how to manage it."

Manage it. There were so many things I had to manage at that moment.

A minute passed as I looked over at Declan. What would it be like to be so easygoing? So carefree? And for the first time, instead of finding it annoying in him, I envied it.

"Anyway," Declan said, "to the right are the veggies. Tomatoes, peppers, jalapeños, carrots, snap peas, cucumbers, corn."

"No fruit?"

He gestured outside the fence. "I've got an apple and a pear tree over there, but the damn deer. I've been thinking about replanting them behind the fence but haven't gotten around to it. Also thought about adding a lemon tree."

"To go with the tea."

"Exactly." He winked.

I knelt to sniff the mint and smiled, then stood and took it all in again. "What's that?" I pointed to a large white structure in the far corner of his yard.

"Brood box."

"Sounds depressing."

He laughed. I liked his laugh, I decided.

"It's a beehive box."

"You're kidding."

"Nope."

"You have bees?"

"About a million."

"You make honey?"

"They make the honey."

"You know what I mean."

"Yes, I harvest their honey. Herb honey is kind of my thing."

The jars, funnels, and boxes in the kitchen suddenly made sense, and I remembered Earl from the auto shop asking about rosemary honey. I had no idea Declan made it himself.

I stared at him a minute, wondering why the discovery of his garden made him even sexier. I pictured him working with his hands in the dirt, shoveling, harvesting, building fences. While all these "manly things" were undoubtedly sexy, it was the fact that the work also required patience, care, a steady hand, skill, effort.

Yeah. *Very sexy.*

"Do you have the white hazmat-looking suit?" I asked with a grin.

"Oh yeah. Suit, gloves, hat, and mask. And even then, I get stung at least five times. I'm numb to it now."

"I want to see how you do it."

"You're in luck. I'm planning the first harvest of the year within the next few weeks. Not quite ready yet."

"How many times a year do you harvest?"

"Two or three. It's seasonal. Only June through September-ish."

"That's so cool."

He regarded me with a squint, as if trying to figure me out. A moment passed between us, his blue eyes sparkling in the growing darkness. The scent of lavender hung in the air as we looked at each other.

I tore my gaze away first and focused on the purple blooms. Inhaling again, I realized I didn't want to leave.

"What is it about lavender that you like so much?"

I sighed. "It has a special place in my heart."

I sensed his stare on me, and a moment passed. He didn't probe further.

"Lots you can do with lavender," he said. "Although I'm not really the guy to ask."

"You don't harvest it?"

"Not really. I like the smell. My mom used to have it in the house. Like I said, it's just kind of taken over. Don't really know what to do with it."

I thought of how the scent of lavender made me happy, then wondered if I could bottle it, spray it on my pillows, diffuse the oil. Where to begin?

I was about to ask his advice when he took a step toward the gate.

"Let's deal with this bookcase problem you've got."

"Okay."

Again, I wondered where he needed to be as I followed him out of the garden. Unlike the door to his home, he locked this gate, which was telling.

We were headed toward the garage as he asked, "You said you walked here, right?"

"Right. You know, counting all those steps."

He grinned. "Through the woods?" When I nodded, he asked, "How'd you cross the ravine?"

"Smooth like Swayze."

His brows arched. "You used the fallen tree?"

I nodded, smiling with the pride of accomplishment.

"Nice footwork. Crossed that bridge many times myself."

"Before or after I moved in?"

"Both." He wiggled his eyebrows.

"Are you spying on me?"

"Your windows are too dirty." He grinned, then quickly changed the subject. "I don't like the idea of you crossing that tree, especially alone. It's too dangerous. There's a few spots you should avoid."

"Show me."

"As much as I'd love to reenact the *Dirty Dancing* log scene right now, I don't have time."

My jaw dropped. "You've seen *Dirty Dancing*?"

"I've seen all of Swayze's movies."

"Nice deflection." I kept poking. "*Dirty Dancing* is a girl movie, Mr. Big Bad Southern Auto Mechanic."

"Okay, fine. Yes, I have seen the movie, but only because it came on after *Roadhouse*. Swayze marathon."

"But you made it all the way to the log scene."

"Truth?"

"Oh, I'm on pins and needles."

"I like to dance."

"Bullshit."

"I also like that tongue you've got on you, Grey."

"Got it from my mom, among other charming characteristics."

"Ah. Where is she?"

"Dead."

He stopped, sobering as he turned to me. "Sorry to hear that."

"Thanks." I dipped my chin, then changed the subject. "You really like to dance?"

"I like music. Music makes me dance."

"You like old-school music."

"I like good music. And I believe they call it classic, just so you know."

"Where did you learn to dance?"

"You don't have to learn to dance. You simply feel the music. Move. The key is not to give a shit about other people watching."

"Giving a shit is my entire life."

"Then give less of a shit, Grey."

I glanced down, a rush of insecurity washing over me. What was it about this guy that could strip me like no one else?

He opened the door to the garage for me.

"Wow." I breathed out the word as I stepped inside, noticing the Harley sitting next to the blacked-out Chevy I'd seen outside his mechanic shop. "That's a nice bike."

He stepped around me. "I'm going to go out on a limb here and assume you've never ridden."

"You'd be right."

"Shame." Declan shook his head, plucking a pair of keys from a corkboard. Organized, ironically. His vehicles and his garden seemed to be the only two things Declan took seriously.

He grabbed a helmet, handed it to me, then walked over to a shiny black four-wheeler I hadn't noticed. *What a shame*, I thought as he cleared off the back seat. I wanted to ride that Harley.

"Have you ever been on a four-wheeler?"

"Nope."

He crossed back over and pulled the helmet from my hands as I struggled with the straps.

"Does everyone around here have one?" I asked.

"Yep."

Closing the few inches between us, Declan secured the helmet to my head, bringing a wave of fresh soap and that same musky scent with him that I'd noticed in my car. My stomach danced. Once the helmet was strapped, he smirked.

"Oh, come on, do I look that bad?"

Tingles erupted over my skin as he ran his fingertip down the line of my jaw, winked, then stepped back.

I swallowed the knot in my throat. Even my toes were tingling. "Where's your helmet?"

"You're in it."

"You don't have another one?"

"Nope."

"Then I'm not wearing it. I—"

"You're wearing it, Grey. Hop on."

"Fine. Can I drive?"

"Not today."

When? was my immediate thought, but I bit my tongue.

The garage door lifted as we mounted the four-wheeler. He let me on first, then climbed in front of me and scooted back. With my thighs spread wide around him, it felt strangely intimate.

As he fired up the engine, he said, "Hold on to me."

I hesitated, already having gripped the guard on the back.

"Hold on to me, I said." Declan reached back, yanked my arms forward, and secured them around his waist.

There was something about Declan that was all man. Strong. Alpha.

Did I mention sexy?

The engine growled between my legs as we took off down the driveway and pulled onto the narrow dirt road. Overtaken by the woods behind us, it was now a dead end, but looked as though it used to be longer.

I leaned forward. "Only you and I live on Rattlesnake Road?"

"Only me before you."

29

Two minutes later, we were at my front door.

Declan slid off the four-wheeler, grabbed my hand, and helped me off. "So, how was your first ATV experience?" He unfastened and removed my helmet, the growing darkness of the evening shadowing his face.

"Fun," I said as I smoothed my windblown hair, and meant it.

"You should think about getting one. It'll make maintaining your twenty-nine acres easier."

"How do you know how many acres I bought?"

"I've lived down this road most of my life. I know the property lines like I know the back of my hand. It's my land."

There was something in the way he said *my land* that caught my attention. Something possessive, something defensive.

I thought of Lucas Covington and how he wanted that land, but bit my tongue. Stammering through questions about Lucas's offer that somehow ended with me bent over the kitchen counter was the last thing I wanted to talk about. Especially with Declan, and this surprised me.

Why did I care what my mechanic thought of me?

I was sure Lucas had already approached Declan about selling his property to make room for the "Big Dick" Resort. The thought of Declan's possible reaction to the offer—and to Lucas himself—amused me.

The men might have been around the same age, but that's where their similarities ended. They were polar opposites, almost comically so. Blue collar versus white collar, and I got the feeling Declan's closet didn't have much white in it. Not because he couldn't wear the color, but because he simply didn't care to. While Lucas was the type to own a boardroom, Declan was the type to own a barroom.

Despite Declan's devil-may-care attitude, I imagined him as a fierce protector of what was his. And that turned me on, which made me wonder what Lucas had up his sleeve to deal with that roadblock—aside from tequila and kitchen counters.

I spotted Moonshine's golden eyes twinkling from behind her bush, noticing that she didn't hiss at this newcomer.

Declan took a step past me, surveying the house. "Porch needs a lot of work."

I laughed. "Oh, hold that thought."

We climbed the porch steps, and with a deep breath, I unlocked and pushed open the front door. Declan paused in the doorway as I stepped into the living room, cluttered with mismatched furniture. I flicked on the lights, then turned, bracing myself for an onslaught.

"Wow."

Cringing, I said, "I know."

"No, I mean it's a nice place." He knocked on the wall. "Good, solid framework."

"Oh." I studied the arched door frames.

"Nice stuff." He was surveying my furniture now.

I blinked. "Oh. Thanks. Yeah." I ran my fingertip along an antique chest of drawers. "I guess so."

"A few of these pieces are worth some money."

"Trust me, I'm aware."

"Not the new stuff you bought from Abe. The old stuff."

I looked around at the clutter, and instead of regarding it all as merely a mismatched mess, I considered the potential—and realized it was the first time I'd done that. Leave it to Declan to find the glass half full.

"Some pieces are from a flea market I stopped by the other day. The rest are from a woman named Etta."

"Etta May?"

The tone of his voice surprised me. "You know her?"

"Everyone knows her."

"Ah, that's right. I forget that everyone knows their neighbors around here."

He glanced out the window, in the direction of her house.

"Why do I feel like you're not saying something?"

"I'm sure Etta will fill the silence."

My brow arched. "You don't like her?"

"Never said that. Etta says a lot. Means well." He looked at the pieces again as if searching for the ones that were hers, then back to the windows. He changed the subject with a frown. "Your windows need to be addressed first."

Offended, I shoved my hands on my hips. "I spent the entire morning scrubbing these bastards clean."

Declan smirked. He might not approve of my dirty windows, but he certainly approved of my dirty mouth.

"Not the second-floor windows," he said with a wink.

I narrowed my eyes. "I should have you arrested on Peeping Tom charges."

"Go ahead. I know the sheriff, remember?" He refocused on the windows and clarified. "It's tornado season. Those cracks won't hold. One limb would take out your entire wall of windows, and then you'd have a real mess on your hands. The trees outside need to be trimmed too. You've got at least three widow-makers."

"Widow-makers?"

"Trees with loose limbs."

"Why widow-maker?"

"Your husband's just going about his day, raking leaves, then *bam,* a big limb falls on him and kills him. Widow-makers."

"That's morbid."

"So is a death that could have easily been prevented."

"Fine. Trim trees. Got it." I groaned, scrubbing my hand over my mouth. "I had no idea how much work this place was going to be when I bought it."

"Nothing worth having ever comes easily."

"Let's hope it comes with a few extra zeros at the end of this. I'm thinking about flipping it."

"You're not staying around?" His gaze was now focused solely on me.

"To be honest, I don't know."

He stared at me a moment with a look I didn't quite understand. I expected him to launch into all the reasons why Berry Springs was a good place to live, and why I should stay, blah, blah, blah. Try to convince me to stay. But he didn't.

"This house and land needs someone to commit to it," he said instead. "The foundation is solid. Strong. It just needs a little TLC. The land is thriving, it just needs to be maintained."

"Agreed." I squinted, knowing he was going somewhere else with the comment, other than renovation.

"It's a good place to start over." He eyed me. "Not to sell out."

And there it was.

"I've already been approached."

"By who?" His eyes flashed, reminding me of Moonshine's.

I lifted a shoulder with a casual shrug. "Can't remember the name," I lied.

"Lucas Covington." Declan spat out the name like poison. "The man is committed to building his resort. I hope your resolve is stronger."

The air in the room had totally shifted with the mention of Lucas. I nodded because I couldn't find my words, or another lie, more accurately. How heated had their exchange become when Declan turned down Lucas's offer to buy his property?

Declan looked away. After a quick exhale that I wouldn't have noticed if I weren't staring at him, he dropped Lucas and returned to the subject. "Have you had the house checked for mold?"

"*Mold*?" I jerked back my head in horror, as if the man had suggested I replace my Louboutins with Crocs. "As in—nasty, furry, deadly *mold*?"

"You're on a hillside, and the house was built on a flat spot. When it rains, water comes downhill and settles on the flat. Ten bucks says it floods at the change of seasons."

"How do I check for something like that? For mold?" My eyes widened as I scanned the floorboards.

"I'll send someone out."

"Who?"

"A buddy."

"Who's a buddy?"

"A buddy."

"What happens if I have mold?"

"Well, if it's inside the walls, we'll have to have it professionally cleaned, or replace everything."

My mouth fell open.

"Then we'll have to fix the source. If there's flooding in the back, you'll need to level the ground. Add drainage."

My jaw unhinged.

Ignoring my shock, Declan began pacing the room, looking at the ceiling and in the corners, checking for things I undoubtedly had no clue to look for. He knew his stuff, I could tell. I wondered if he'd renovated his house himself.

I knelt next to a crack in the window, just now noticing that it didn't shut all the way. How had I missed that?

"That's one hell of a fireplace," he said, and I surged to my feet, remembering the envelopes that were stacked on the end of the mantel.

The instant panic that bubbled up surprised me. A possessiveness, a protectiveness, suddenly gripped me. The letters were mine. The mystery was mine. I didn't want anyone other than me to read the letters. It felt like a gross invasion of the writer's privacy.

I held my breath as his gaze swept over them, then past them. Relieved, I exhaled.

"Holy *sh—*" He cut himself off as he stepped into the master bedroom and flicked on the lights. "What *the hell* did you do here?"

I walked in to find him gaping at the closets. Flashing him a smile, I shrugged. "Renovating the closets."

He blinked at me, then shook his head. "I'd tell you not

to touch another thing in this room and let the professionals do it, but I'm getting the vibe you're not the kind of gal to take orders well."

"Guilty."

"And that you like to handle things yourself."

"Very guilty."

"And that you're stubborn."

"Pot calling the kettle black, if I had to guess."

"You've got to at least have checkpoints, Grey. Someone to come in and check your work as you blow your way through this house. *Jesus.*" He looked back at the demolition, still shaking his head.

It wasn't a bad idea—and one that I hadn't thought of.

"Fine. I'll find a construction worker."

He blew out a breath. "Contractor, Grey. It's called a contractor," he muttered with pained dismay.

I grinned.

Declan took a deep breath, shook off my ineptness, then surveyed the bathroom. "Nice tub. My buddy'll check around the plumbing too. For mold, specifically."

"Oh *shit.*" I ran a hand over the top of my head, fisting a clump of my hair. "I do have a leak. I almost forgot. Under the sink. Does that mean I definitely have mold?"

"Where?"

"In the kitchen."

Declan turned and strode out of the bedroom to the kitchen. I followed, stopping as he dropped to his knees at the sink and opened the cabinet doors.

"Towel."

I jogged to the laundry room and grabbed a towel. When I returned, Declan was on his back, his head under the sink, fresh streaks of grime on his side. I felt terrible. I set the towel on his stomach, then took a second to admire the tanned skin peeking above his waistband.

God, I was obsessed with that *V*.

"I'm kind of afraid to ask this," he muttered from beneath the sink, "but do you have a wrench?" He pulled the towel inside.

"Yes." I jogged into my bedroom and grabbed the sack of tools I'd purchased from Tad's Tool Shop. I searched through it, then shoved the tool under the sink.

"That's a socket wrench." He thrust it back out.

"It won't work?"

"Not unless your sink is built on a chassis."

"What's a chassis?"

"The frame of a car."

"Why would my sink be built on the frame of a car?"

His movement suddenly stopped. I imagined his face pulled in the same horror as when I'd muttered the words "construction worker." He scooted out and addressed me slowly, as one might a distracted toddler with ADHD.

"Grey. A socket wrench is for changing tires. I'm currently not changing a tire. I need a wrench. Look for something with claw-like grippers on the end of a long handle."

"Are you familiar with mansplaining?" I muttered as I searched the bag.

"I'm familiar with tools."

"The sales tag on that socket thing said wrench, just so you know."

"Yes, I'm sure it did. Because it is a wrench. Just not the one I need."

I dumped the tools on the floor, knowing he was grinning at me, and turned quickly before he caught the blush creeping up my neck. After another fumble through the sack, I chose the "claw-like" one and thrust it at him.

"Nice work."

A few bangs and squeaks later, Declan shimmied out from under the cabinet. "You're all set. And I didn't see any mold."

"All set? Like, you fixed the leak?"

"Yes, ma'am." He wiped his hands on the towel.

"Oh, wow. What a relief. Here."

I took the towel from his hands and ran it under the water as Declan stood from the floor. I dabbed at the grime on his white T-shirt, my fingertips bouncing off of rock-hard abs. The blush crept back to my cheeks—for a very different reason.

"Sorry," I whispered. "I ruined your shirt."

"It's Hanes," he whispered back. "Came in a five-pack. I can get more."

"I'll add it to the chili," I said softly, my fingertips still gripping his shirt.

"Please don't."

I grinned. "I meant, I'll get you another five-pack. Add it to the list of things I already owe you."

"Why are we whispering?"

"I don't know."

I took a step back, the cool air sweeping the heat from between us.

He glanced at the wall clock I had sitting on the counter, then back at me. "Where's this bookcase you need moved?"

"Follow me."

I led him into the den where I'd left the bookcase at the base of the staircase. "I need this gaudy monstrosity," I gestured, "up there."

He rocked it back and forth, testing its weight. "Please tell me you didn't attempt to drag it up the stairs alone."

"Okay, I won't."

"Grey . . ." He pulled in a breath, biting his tongue. "Okay. You're going to pull and guide, and I'm going to push it up the stairs."

"I'll push, you guide."

Exasperated, he dropped his hands from the bookcase, daring me to challenge him again. "You guide and pull, I'll push, Grey."

"Fine."

"Hop up." He impatiently motioned to the stairs. He was late for something, and I really wanted to know what that thing was.

"All right, we'll rock it up the stairs one step at a time. One side, then the next, then the next. Make sense?"

"Got it, boss." I positioned myself on the stairs above him, gripping both sides of the bookcase.

"Okay, here we go. Nice and easy."

"Nice and easy," I repeated, biting my lip as the weight grew heavier in my hands. He rocked the left side onto the first step.

"Lift."

Then the right side onto the second step. By the fourth step, we'd established a rhythm. Sweat was beaded on my forehead by the time we reached the top of the stairs.

With one final shove, the bookcase slid onto the floor, and Declan squeezed into the room. I doubled over, stretching my back and taking a breath. Declan wasn't even flushed.

"Thank you."

He dipped his chin, his gaze landing on the window

where I'd spied on him in his fields a few times. Our eyes met.

"Where do you want it?" he asked.

I blinked. "Oh. Ah. I think this wall for now. I can scoot it later, if I change my mind."

"No scooting. You'll scuff up the floors. Beautiful floors. Lift on three." He grabbed one side, and I grabbed the other. "One, two, three."

Releasing a masculine grunt that I wasn't necessarily proud of, I lifted the case as he guided it against the wall.

"What are you going to do with this room?" he asked once we had the bookcase settled.

"I don't know. Haven't decided."

"It would make a good office."

"Office," I said, considering it for the first time. But office for what?

"Need anything else?"

"Not right now. Thanks again. I know you've got to get going."

He didn't argue, so I led him downstairs and to the kitchen where I pulled two twenties from my wallet—all the cash I had—and shoved it to him. "Thank you. Really. Please."

Frowning, he accepted the twenties, took my wallet and shoved the bills back inside, then clicked it closed and set it on the counter.

"No, Declan, please take it. You took time out of your day and ruined your Hanes."

"Chili tomorrow?"

"Uh . . ."

"Chili tomorrow."

"Okay," I said reluctantly. "Six o'clock?"

"See you then, New York."

Declan strode through my house, taking the energy with him. He opened the front door and paused, turning back.

"And, Grey?" A smirk tugged at his lips. "Thank Etta for those cookies."

Dammit.

30

After an hour of scrubbing windows, or to be honest, hoping to see Declan—washed in moonlight, in the fields below—my stomach reminded me that it was dinnertime.

I padded to the fridge, pulled it open, and tilted my head to the side. Lunch meat, a block of cheese, half of a tomato, and one Diet Coke left in a ring that had held six. That was it. My gaze lifted to the small liquor cabinet above the freezer, which was empty. I inhaled through my nose, exhaled, and refocused on my pathetically empty fridge.

The thought of making chili for a man who loved it seemed more daunting than the lack of booze in the house. Thinking of everything I'd need to make the dinner, I decided now was as good a time as any for a quick grocery run.

The night was dark and cool as I slipped into my car, clicking on my headlights before heading down the dirt road. Lights twinkled through the trees as I came up on the *Y*.

Declan's garage was fully lit with two cars in the parking

lot and all three bays open, classic rock blaring from inside. I slowed, my nose nearly pressed to my side window as I passed. I recognized his combat boots peeking out from under a rusty Oldsmobile.

A man sat outside the garage under a light, reading the newspaper and puffing on a cigar. I looked at my dash clock —8:44 p.m.

Declan didn't have a date or a poker night with the boys to get to. No, he had appointments to take care of. He had to work. And for the first time, I wondered if money was an issue for him.

Coming to a complete stop, I considered pulling in and asking if he'd like me to pick up dinner for him while I was in town.

Just then, Kai stepped out of the office with a stack of empty Coke cans in her arms. She zeroed in on my vehicle, then scowled. Eyeing me with disdain, Cool Kid Cher crossed the grass to the recycle bin.

I forced a crooked smile, waved, and accelerated on by, watching in the rearview mirror as she glared at me until I faded out of sight.

31

The next morning was warm and surprisingly humid, the last day before the beginning of a rainy week packed with thunderstorms. This, according to Stan, the local weatherman, who enjoyed fishing, biking, and walking his dog named Spot, as he seemed to mention during every forecast.

God, I was lonely.

With a mug of coffee in one hand and my serenity bear tucked under the other arm, I allowed myself extra time on the deck, watching the sun rise and the woods lighten. A little celebratory moment for twenty-four hours of sobriety. A new day.

I'd gone more than twenty-four hours already once, and I could do it again. More, this time, I promised myself. The thought of "forever" felt too daunting, so I stuck with "more."

More withdrawals, I worried, but pushed the thought away. I'd lived through it once, and I could do it again.

The courage to change the things I can . . .

I thought of William and wondered what he would do

when he received my signed divorce papers later that day. Would he call? My stomach tightened painfully at the thought.

Would we ever speak again?

I thought of Lucas, my devastatingly handsome mistake, and wondered when I'd hear from him again. I knew I would. I knew his type.

Finally, my thoughts drifted to my neighbor, Declan, and that grin, the twinkle in those baby-blue eyes, that *V*. That insouciant attitude that made me want to walk into oncoming traffic. The chili I'd committed to make for him that evening.

It was a lot.

Everything felt like a lot.

At eight in the morning, I received my first visitor of the day. Etta stood on my doorstep, her signature platter of baked goods in one hand and a large antique mirror gripped in the other. She was wearing her loudest tracksuit yet, this one neon green. Her shoelaces were bright pink, and her glasses red-rimmed.

"Rain's comin'," she said as I opened the door.

"Did the mirror tell you that?"

"Always nice weather before the rain. Supposed to be eighty degrees and sunny today, the wrath of God tomorrow. You need to get that storm shelter, young lady."

Ignoring the warning, I took the mirror from her hand and gawked at it.

"Whattaya think?" she asked eagerly.

"It's gorgeous." My eyes lit up as I looked at her. "Mine?"

"Of course, dear. It's why I brought it over. How're the allergies?" Etta stepped inside behind me and closed the door.

"Better with whatever pills you're feeding me." I lifted

the mirror, imagining it on the wall. "God, it's beautiful, Etta. The turquoise frame matches that end table perfectly. I think I'll put it in my bedroom."

"That's what I was thinking."

Making herself at home, she set the cookies on the counter. I appreciated the comfortable routine we'd established.

"I found it buried back in the shed," she said.

"A hidden treasure indeed." I leaned the mirror against the wall and refocused on my guest. "What's got you out and about so early?"

Etta scoffed, her nose wrinkling in disgust. "That cocky city boy, Lucas Covington, came knocking again."

My stomach dropped. An interesting immediate reaction to his name, I noted.

"Did he come by your place too?"

"No," I said, but frowned at the memory of hearing the hum of an engine as I had my morning coffee on the back deck. A weird unease joined the swooping feeling in my stomach.

"Has he come here at all? Offering to buy your place?"

"Yes." I avoided eye contact, breezing into the kitchen for a pair of paper plates. "Don't worry. I didn't sell out."

Other than my body.

"Keep your wits about you, Grey Dalton. He's a smooth one. I can see it in those eyes. Black as coal, they are. Unsettling."

I cleared my throat. "Did he have his partner with him? An angry-looking older man?"

Etta nodded. "Lurch didn't say a single word."

I laughed. "Lurch. Fitting." My laughter faded. "He is weird, isn't he?"

"They're all weird. City folk. Different breed. No offense."

"None taken. So, what do you think?" I gestured to the kitchen cabinets I'd stained the day before, eager to change the subject.

"Looks damn good." Etta perched her hands on her hips and surveyed the kitchen and living room. "You've done a lot. Abe delivered a lot."

I nodded, blowing out a breath.

"Well, take a break for breakfast. Zucchini muffins this morning."

"Ah, music to my hips. I'm not sure how much more of your cookies this ass can handle."

"You could use a few pounds. Eat up. You got coffee?"

"Old. I'll make a fresh pot."

"Get the butter too. Zucchini needs a little fat."

"Yes, ma'am."

I poured the dregs from the pot, filled the water tank, scooped in fresh grounds, and started the brew.

"So, what's on the agenda today?" she asked.

"Abe's delivering the second round of furniture. And I might meet up with my cousin at some point today."

"Who's your cousin?"

"Cassidy Schaefer."

"Bob and Donna Schaefer's girl?"

"One and the same, although Bob and Donna moved to Florida last year. Cassidy stayed here."

"I didn't realize they were your kin. Good people. I don't know the daughter personally, but I know her folks. She's from good stock."

"Glad you approve." I winked, setting the butter on a plate next to a knife.

"You can take me at my word. I've been around these

parts for longer than that peeling wallpaper you've got in the bathroom."

"It is terrible, isn't it?"

"Makes me itch—and no woman wants to itch in the bathroom."

"Ain't that the truth."

"Ah." Etta clapped her hands with glee. "Another *ain't*. I'm so proud of you."

"Next up, cowboy boots and tracksuits." I grinned.

"Hey, this might not be a fancy designer suit, but it's made of a poly blend you can't get locally."

"I don't doubt it." I winked again and Etta laughed.

"All right. What else? After lunch, with the cousin?"

"I think I'm going to start on the yard before the rain comes. Start a plan, anyway. A garden, maybe. I thought about visiting the farmers' market this morning. Then later, maybe begin painting the inside after the rain starts."

"A garden, huh? I like it. You need to go to the nursery before it rains then. Buy some plants, shrubs, bushes, maybe a few of those Japanese maples to add some color to the front. Plant it all before it rains."

"Not a bad idea. I'm assuming you know a place?"

"I'll write down directions before I leave."

Etta unwrapped the muffins as the coffee pot dinged. "Are you still thinking ivory paint for the walls?" she asked around a bite of zucchini.

I nodded, swallowing my own bite. "I think it will pop against the mahogany window frames and log walls. Pick up the light."

"Yes." Etta tilted her head to the side, plotting furniture placement. "Where's the bookcase?"

"In the spare room, upstairs."

"How'd you manage that?"

"I had help."

She lifted a brow. "Who?"

"I met my other neighbor yesterday."

"Old man Ericsson?"

"No, a man named Declan. Owns that mechanic shop down—"

"Declan *Montgomery*?"

"Yeah, I guess." My voice lifted with curiosity at the disdain in her voice.

She dropped her fork and pointed a finger at me. "You need to stay away from that boy."

My brows drew together. There was no way we were talking about the same man who repaired my car for free, fixed my faucet, and helped me move my furniture.

"Why?"

Etta picked up her fork and aggressively stabbed a piece of muffin. "Troublemaker, that boy is."

"Are you sure we're talking about the same Declan Montgomery? He's over forty years old."

"Age doesn't cure his kind."

I set down my coffee, now hanging on her every word as she continued.

"The kid grew up on the wrong side of the tracks. His parents were bad eggs, you might say, and he grew up to be exactly like them. Getting in trouble all the time, fighting, drinking. Always the ringleader. In and out of the county jail when he got old enough. If anything happened in this town that caused a headache, Declan's name was attached to it."

"So he was a rebel in his youth. So what?"

She gave me a pointed look. "Declan's got a temper on him like a rattlesnake, Grey."

"No."

"Yes, ma'am. He's notorious. Everyone knows he's got a short fuse. Stay away from him."

I blinked, still questioning the fact that we were speaking of the same easygoing, carefree guy.

"Just like his daddy," Etta grumbled.

"What do you mean, like his daddy?"

"Declan Senior—same name—was banned from every bar within a sixty-mile radius for fighting. Rumor is his temper didn't stop there."

"What do you mean? He abused his wife?"

Etta lifted her coffee. "Not only the wife."

My brows rose. I couldn't picture Declan being a victim of abuse. Maybe it was his height and weight, both so intimidating that I couldn't imagine anyone raising a hand to him, or maybe it was his breezy attitude and that twinkle in his eye. Someone that innately happy couldn't have been abused as a child. But then I remembered my own childhood, and the ways I'd hidden the effects of it.

Etta set down her fork and took a sip of coffee, and I knew she wasn't done. Yes, Etta liked to talk. Declan was right.

"You know that pond on Declan's land?"

"Yeah. I can see it from my second-floor window."

"Well, a few years after I moved into my house—so, 'bout thirty years ago—a young girl name of Anna Hopkins, so sweet, eight years old, lived in a house on the other side of the mountain. One day, she was playing around the pond. The pond," Etta gave me a knowing look, "on *Declan's* land. That night, the girl never returned home. The cops were called and a search team went out. I actually helped on the search. A few hours in, we heard someone yelling from across the field. Old man Ericsson followed the shouts, just in time to see Declan—only eleven years old at the time—pulling the girl's body from the pond. Dead."

My mouth dropped open. The hair on the back of my neck prickled as my thoughts suddenly centered around the faint giggles I kept hearing in my house. A girl. An eight-year-old girl.

"That's right," Etta said. "Anna was dead as a doornail. Her parents were devastated. So devastated, in fact, they moved six months later to get away."

"She drowned?"

Etta's eyes narrowed, suggesting she believed there was more to the story.

I narrowed mine in return. "Etta. You think Declan did it? Declan drowned the girl?"

Etta shrugged and picked up her fork again. Popped a bite into her mouth.

Yes, Etta loved her gossip.

"But he was only eleven years old at the time, you said."

"Plenty old enough to hold a girl's head underwater."

"*Etta.*"

"What?"

"That is some *serious* gossip."

"Not all gossip is false, honey. Remember that. That's around the age Declan started getting pulled out of school for fistfights. For being violent. I always say, where there's smoke, there's fire."

"Was he interviewed as a suspect? Can an eleven-year-old even be a suspect?"

"Of course, and yes. But you know how that goes."

"No. Enlighten me."

"The cops spent a day on it, then was on to the next crime in town."

"What about Declan's folks? The bad eggs, as you call them. Were they interviewed?"

"Neither of his parents were home around the time the medical examiner guessed Anna died."

"Okay, assuming her death wasn't innocent—*if* Declan did it—why the hell would he pull her body from the pond for everyone to find?"

"Maybe he knew someone was gonna find her eventually, what with the search team and all."

A moment passed in silence as I poked at my zucchini muffin.

"You know . . ." Etta lowered her voice. "Between Anna's untimely death and Declan's abusive father, they say Rattlesnake Road is cursed."

I dropped my fork, sending it clattering on the plate. "Well, that's just freakin' great, Etta. I moved to the armpit of the South, bought a dilapidated house that may—or may not—be riddled with mold and filled with ghosts on a pitted dirt road rumored to be cursed. Fan-freaking-tastic."

Etta lifted her plate, a crooked smile on her face. "At least you get fresh muffins and everything."

I forced a smile. "That counts for something." I shook my head, looking out the windows toward Declan's property. "Declan. I just don't see it, Etta."

I thought of the chili dinner I had planned with the man in less than eight hours. An appointment I decided not to share with Etta.

"Well, keep your eyes open," she said.

I pressed a hand to my stomach for a second, feeling like a concrete ball had settled there. Standing, I gathered our plates and set them next to the sink. Etta followed suit, bringing the coffee cups.

"Paper and pen?"

I frowned.

"Directions to the nursery. To get this garden of yours going."

"Ah. Yes." I rummaged through a box, and found a pen and something to write on.

Etta scribbled on a notepad. "Tell Ginny I sent you. That'll be good for a few free bags of soil, at least."

"Will do. Thanks, Etta."

"Call me if you need anything." Etta crossed the living room and pulled open the front door. "And, Grey, stay away from that Montgomery boy."

32

Later that afternoon, I slipped on a puddle of spilled water in my kitchen, sending one of my flip-flops flying into the air, along with two cans of beans, three ripe tomatoes, and four jalapeños.

My ass hit the floor with a thud, matching the beat of the Top Dance radio station I'd turned up to ease the anxiety of preparing a meal I'd never cooked before. For a man I barely knew. The edge of a metal can bounced off my temple, another slamming onto my shin while a tomato exploded next to me on the tile.

"Son of a . . ." Wiping the slimy pulp from my face, I examined my fingers, not sure if the red liquid smeared on them was tomato juice or blood.

"Holy *shit*. Are you okay?"

I squealed like a pig, whipping my head in the direction of the deep voice that came out of nowhere. Scaring the hell out of me, Declan dropped to a squat beside me.

Nearly hyperventilating, I said, "How the . . . how the hell did you—"

"Are you okay?" He cut me off, shouting over the blaring music while he frantically checked me over.

"You *scared* me. I didn't even hear you come in." My voice was pitched with stress and the pain of an aching tailbone.

"Not surprised." He nodded to the speaker on the counter. "I could hear the bass from the bottom of the driveway. An entire herd of buffalo could have blown through your front door, and you wouldn't have heard them. You okay?"

"Yeah." Wincing, I shifted my weight. "Sorry, I—"

I started to stand, but Declan grabbed my shoulder, holding me in place.

"Stay. I've got it."

The room went silent as the music was muted, replaced by the pounding of my pulse. I didn't know you could feel a heartbeat in your temple.

"You sure you're okay?" Declan squatted back down beside me, a beam of afternoon sunlight slicing through the room, twinkling on azure-blue eyes as clear as the ocean. He was wearing a gray T-shirt under an unbuttoned plaid shirt, khaki tactical pants, and boots.

A warm breeze blew in from the open window above the sink. My senses perked up as I inhaled the scent of fresh soap on his skin—the scent of Declan. He tucked a wayward strand of hair behind my ear, and I noticed the way his T-shirt stretched over his pecs.

"You really okay?" he asked, pulling my attention back to him.

"Yeah. I slipped. The can hit me."

He ran his finger across my forehead, then stuck it into his mouth and sucked. I gasped in horrified disgust.

He smacked his lips. "It's tomato juice, not blood. You're good."

"That's *disgusting*."

"No, blood would have been disgusting. Come on. Let's get some ice on that bump."

I wobbled as he pulled me to my feet, one arm wrapped around my shoulders and the other hand with a tight grip on my wrist. My guts churned as I was eased into a folding chair I'd set up in the breakfast nook.

"You good?"

"Other than my pride? Yes."

"Hang tight."

A moment later, a pint of Ben and Jerry's was pressed to my forehead. I jerked at the cold against my skin.

"Cherry Garcia," he said. "I'm impressed."

"It was on sale."

"It's my favorite. Whole cherries, chunks of dark chocolate, all mixed together in vanilla-bean ice cream. Hold it there."

I did as I was told. "You know, they say only old people like fruit in their ice cream."

"So I shouldn't tell you that one of my favorite snacks is sliced peaches smothered in cottage cheese?"

I laughed, then winced.

"Keep it there. It will help with the swelling."

"This is blasphemy."

"Relax. We'll put it back in the freezer before it melts. You sure you're okay? Your ankle, your back?" He bit back a grin. "I came in on the tail end of that karate kick."

I rolled my eyes. "How did you even get in?" I nodded to the doorway, and that's when I saw the pop of vivid purple on my countertop. "What's that?"

"Lavender. I told you I'd bring you some. Got a lot more in the back of my truck."

Smiling, I said, "It's beautiful."

"We'll plant it this evening before the rain comes. And to answer your question, I came in through the front door."

I frowned. "It was locked."

"No, ma'am. You need to lock your doors, hear me? While you're at home and away."

"I swear to God I locked it."

"Well, someone unlocked it then. Anyway, I knocked. Twice, I promise. But Sean Paul was mid-scat."

I snorted. "That's not scat."

"Kinda sounds like it."

"Not really." I looked at the clock. "You're an hour and a half early."

"Based on what I just witnessed, I'm right on time."

I glanced down at my clothes, suddenly aware of the train wreck of my appearance.

My plan was to dress minutes before dinner, to ensure I looked my best, which meant no chili stains. I'd laid out a casual-but-sexy jersey dress for my chili dinner with Declan. Bright yellow, to match the glorious spring day and my mood every time I thought of him. I'd even shaved.

Instead, Declan was getting a banjo-playing cartoon bear sketched on a white T-shirt that I'd gotten for free with the purchase of a soy candle at the farmers' market that morning. This was worn over a pair of yoga shorts, and now, only one flip-flop. My hair was pulled up into a tangled knot on the top of my head, and whatever was left of the makeup I'd applied that morning had been erased by the tomato pulp.

My eyes rounded in horror as I realized I wasn't even wearing a bra. "Uh . . ."

"Take your time." His gaze dropped for a second to my peaked nipples.

Heat rose up my neck. Keeping the pint of ice cream

pressed to my forehead, I wrapped the other hand around myself and staggered to my feet. "I'll, uh, be right back."

Declan's lips twisted in the worst attempt ever to hide a smile. "Got more tomatoes?" he asked as I hustled out of the kitchen.

Pausing, I turned. "Like thirty. Maybe more. I didn't know how many I'd need, so I bought a whole box at the farmers' market."

"Fresh and local, attagirl. Bet Herbert appreciated that." Another glance at my chest.

"Be right back."

I darted into my bedroom. In a flurry of clothes, makeup, and perfume, I pulled myself together the best I could in under five minutes, a feat worthy of a gold medal.

When I returned to the kitchen, Declan had removed his button-up and was waist-deep in my fridge, his arms loaded. My "scat" dance music had been replaced with the smooth beats of "Suspicious Minds."

"What's this?"

"The birth of rock and roll."

"I didn't take you as an Elvis fan."

He scoffed into the fridge as if this offended him, and I grinned.

"What are you doing?" I walked over, ice cream in hand.

"Teaching." He looked over his shoulder at me, then immediately straightened, hitting his head on the top of the fridge and dropping a pepper on the floor. His eyes met mine, a flare of heat behind the blue.

"Nice dress."

"Thanks. I'm all covered now."

"A shame."

I grinned, and he grinned back.

"Okay." I cleared my throat. "What are you teaching?"

After tearing his focus away from me—to my dismay—Declan emptied his load onto the counter, then rummaged through a drawer until he found a spoon. He pulled the ice cream from my hands, removed the lid, stuck the spoon into the ice cream, and handed it back.

"I'm teaching you."

I licked the spoon. "Teaching me what, exactly?"

"Well," he said as he began moving around my kitchen, easily making himself at home. "Something tells me you've never made chili mac before." He glanced over his shoulder, one brow cocked.

"This is correct."

"Thought so." He refocused on gathering ingredients. "Here's my problem, Grey. I've had all these women try to make me chili mac, each missing the mark by at least three jalapeños, leaving me with an evening on the toilet and a disappointed woman in my bedroom."

"Thanks for the visual."

"Better than the foot fungus?"

"Marginally."

He winked. "Anyway, a lot of women have been deleted from my contacts list due to their lack of chili competency."

"Chili competency?"

"It's in the dictionary."

"Redneck dictionary?"

"Is there any other kind?"

I shook my head. "Continue."

"Thanks. So it hit me today, after moving your bookcase. Everyone who's ever been great at something has been taught, right? I was taught how to make chili by my grandma at six years old. *Six.* So in an effort to mix things up a bit and not be disappointed, I decided to come over and teach a man to fish, so to speak. If you're going to make it in this town, you've got to know your way around the kitchen. I figure it's my civic duty to teach a Yankee how to make a solid pot of chili."

"I have to learn how to cook to be respected around here? A woman in an apron equals respect? That's extremely antiquated."

"Don't twist my words. Not what I said. You eat, right?"

I shoved a spoonful of ice cream in my mouth and nodded, my eyes narrowed.

"Southerners bond over food. It's as simple as that. Family dinners. Sunday dinners. This is very important. Cooking helps you bond. So, learn."

"Well, I don't like that you assumed I was going to miss the mark without any help."

Without a word, Declan gestured to the busted tomatoes he'd mopped from the floor and tossed in the sink.

"Okay, fine. But no mansplaining."

"Deal—but learning requires detailed instructions. You can't go into this with pre-judgment, or already feeling defensive. Remove your pride from it, Grey. Accept the help openheartedly."

"You sure take this seriously."

He blew out a breath. "Grey—"

"It's important, I know. Okay, okay, I get it. Fine, I'm a blank canvas, Montgomery. Paint me."

His gaze swept over my body, leaving a trail of metaphorical paint—or fire, maybe. Our eyes met, lingering a moment too long.

I spooned another cherry into my mouth.

He smirked. I smirked back. With that, two hands gripped my waist and hoisted me into the air before plopping my ass onto the counter.

"We'll paint later. Sit, eat your ice cream, and watch and learn, Grey."

Declan skillfully chopped with quick, precise movements, explaining the importance of each vegetable to the chili. He'd brought a handful of his own spices and herbs from his garden. I liked that.

A colorful mix of peppers, jalapeños, onions, and garlic were tossed into a large Dutch oven, heated with olive oil. Next, enough beef to feed a football team. This was followed by sausage that I'd grabbed at the last minute with a solo Sunday brunch in mind.

Oh well. The man liked his meat.

Declan walked me through each ingredient, each step, providing detailed instructions as he'd promised—without mansplaining. He was a good teacher, I decided, finishing the pint of Cherry Garcia while Declan "toasted," as he'd called it, the chili powder over the beef, emphasizing this very important part of the process.

The house smelled heavenly, rich with warm scents. Homey. I liked hearing our voices and his laughter mingle with the smooth oldies playing from the radio. Life replacing the loneliness of the walls.

I liked the easy energy Declan brought with him. I was relaxed, having fun. He never asked a single thing of me, other than my attention, which was easy to provide.

Another pot was added to the stove, this one filled with water. Once it came to a rolling boil, elbow macaroni was poured in, along with precise instructions on cooking time. Apparently, overcooking pasta for chili mac was detrimental to the dish, as it was important that the noodles soak up the juices from the chili once combined. Finally, Declan added the tomatoes and beans to the Dutch oven, topped off with another exact mix of seasonings.

Wiping his hands on a towel, he turned to me. "Now, usually, this should simmer for at least an hour. Two at the most. So if you're counting, you should've started the chili at four this afternoon. But for now, we'll let it simmer for only thirty minutes because I've worked up an appetite."

I hopped off the counter. "Sit. I'll clean."

"Deal." Declan tossed the towel he'd used to cook into the laundry room, then paused with his back to me. "Any reason you've got two bottles of expensive red wine in your hamper?"

The measuring cup slipped from my hands, clattering into the sink. He'd found my hidden stash. My security blanket. The bottles keeping me from fully letting go.

Declan walked back into the kitchen, bottle in hand, reading the label. "Would've opted for beer with chili, but red'll do."

"Oh. I . . ."

I was frozen in place, my mind racing as my stomach tied itself into knots. I didn't want a repeat of my night with Lucas. Didn't want to fall off the wagon again. More than that, I didn't want a repeat of letting myself down and hating myself.

The blood drained from my face as I tried to come up with an excuse for why we shouldn't drink it.

Declan stared at me, my mouth opening and closing like an idiot. A flicker of awareness sparked in his eyes. He gave me a slight nod, returned the bottle to its place in the hamper, then stepped back into the kitchen.

"Tea then," he said easily—not a question.

I released a relieved breath.

"Tea. Yes," I said quickly. "I've got tea. Yes, that's what I'd like. Tea."

He nodded, still eyeing me. *Seeing me.* Then he winked,

pulled a jug of tea I'd brewed earlier from the fridge, and that was that.

It was done. I did it. I was strong. I'd won that battle.

Feeling the lightest I'd felt on my feet in a while, I cleaned the kitchen as he poured the tea. I took a sip, pleased with it. With myself.

"Let's see." I checked the time. "We've got exactly twenty-three minutes until the chili is ready. Want to go outside? The sun's going down."

"You read my mind." Declan picked up his tea and followed me out the back door.

The early evening was humid ahead of impending storms, the scent of budding flowers thick in the air. It was a glorious seventy-eight degrees.

The back deck groaned as we stepped across the rotted planks. I cringed when I noticed a portion of the railing was completely gone. Rotted and fallen off, or maybe busted out for whatever reason. We stepped over a hole the size of a fist.

"The outside needs as much work as the inside," I said.

"I've got some leftover lumber from my deck. You can have it."

"Really?" I turned.

"Really."

"Listen. At this point, I'm not going to be polite anymore, or proud. I'll freaking take it. I'll take whatever you can give me. Not kidding."

Grinning, he closed the inches between us and tucked a strand of hair behind my ear. It was the second time he'd done it, and both times felt like lightning against my skin.

"Truth always, and direct," he said.

I nodded. "Truth and direct. Direct, I can definitely do."

"Deal."

"Deal."

A swarm of butterflies took flight in my belly as he looked down at me. A breeze as smooth as silk swept between us.

I took a step back and turned away to hide the flush that burned on my cheeks. Declan and I might be polar opposites in personality, but chemistry definitely wasn't an issue.

He followed me down the porch steps.

"I'm going to level the back, as you suggested, to avoid flooding and mold in the future. I'm also going to landscape it." I crossed the small yard, gesturing as I spoke. "And I'm thinking about a garden. Maybe a pebbled walkway with little decorative stones right here, leading into the woods. Maybe light the sides with solar garden lights."

When I didn't hear him behind me, I turned. Declan had made his way to the far corner of the yard, his back to the tree line, his hands on his hips as he stared at my house. He seemed to be concentrating, a million miles away.

"What do you see?" I asked as I joined him.

"Flower beds here. Shrubs there. Window boxes on all the windows—after you get new windows, of course. Lavender bushes to line that pebbled walkway you're thinking about. Mulch the trees, add a circle of lavender around their bases."

I pictured it as he spoke. Something deep inside me warmed.

"Your garden here." He turned and motioned to a flat, sunny spot next to us. "A big garden. You know, for all those fruits and veggies you're going to use for your Sunday dinners."

I laughed. "Jalapeños, tomatoes, beans. Check."

"Not only for chili. More than that. I see corn, squash, lettuce, carrots, cucumbers, sweet peppers—God, I love those—and herbs. Lots of herbs."

"Is this garden for me or for you?"

He wiggled his eyebrows with that twinkle in his eye, then continued. "You could take what you don't eat to the farmers' market on the weekends. Great way to get to know the locals."

I released a huff, imagining me, Grey Dalton, kneeling in the dirt wearing pink-flowered gardening gloves, a wide-brimmed sun hat, and a chartreuse button-up.

From Louboutins to knee pads.

"We're a little later in the season to start than I'd like, but you could plant most everything now. Give it lots of attention. It'll grow."

"You'll help me?"

"I'll help."

I smiled. "Come on. You haven't seen the best part."

Tea in hand, I led him down what would soon be a pebbled walkway. The trees thinned, the view of a mountainside in the distance beginning to take shape past the ravine between.

We stepped to the cliff's edge and stopped.

"Wow."

"Yeah."

"I've seen this cliff from my land, but the view from here is even more beautiful than I imagined."

We stared at the sky, the setting sun a blazing yellow and orange fading into deep indigo. Big, fluffy clouds dipped in gold floated around it.

I led him to the edge of the cliff. "This is where I sit when I come out."

Lowering myself to the ground, I sat cross-legged. He sat next to me, pulled his knees up, and leaned back on his elbows, tilting his head to the sky.

"Ever slept out here?" he asked after a beat.

"I'd end up at the bottom of the ravine."

"A tent then. Add that to your list. One with a net top so you can see the stars. And cuffs. The furry ones."

"Cuffs?" My brow cocked.

"You know, to keep you in place. So you don't roll off."

"Ah, I see. And the fur?"

"More comfortable." He winked.

I loved that wink. Grinning, I watched him for a minute, then followed his gaze to the sky.

He could turn it off so easily, I realized, the worries of life. He could relax. Breathe. There was a calming side to Declan that was so different from anyone I'd ever been around. So different from myself.

Different from the man Etta had warned me about. But I pushed that aside.

I closed my eyes and took a deep breath. *Turn off,* I demanded of my mind. *Relax.*

A few minutes passed comfortably between us. The breeze picked up, and I inhaled.

"Smell that?" I asked. "I can smell the chili."

"Me too. Hear that?"

"What?"

"My stomach."

I laughed because mine growled too.

I started to push up, but Declan laid his hand over mine. "We've got a few more minutes. Let it simmer."

Relax, he meant.

I leaned back on my elbows, mirroring his position.

"You never told me what brought you here," he said, but I didn't respond. "Truth and direct, Grey. That's our deal."

"Well, it's not pretty, Declan. There's your warning."

"Most escapes aren't."

"How do you know I'm escaping from something?"

"It's written all over your face."

Exhaling, I nodded. "Okay. What brought me here? A cheating bastard and two back-to-back losses."

"Sounds like a triple whammy."

His lack of shock, pity, or the obligatory *I'm so sorry* response eased me. No drama. As was his way, I was realizing.

"You left him?" he asked.

"Yeah. It was the third time."

"Ouch."

"Yeah, ouch."

"You two were married?"

"Yes. For ten years. None of which he was faithful."

"Were you?"

The question caught me off guard. Direct—also his way.

"Yes. All ten of them. Although if you ask him, he might have a different story to tell."

"How so?"

"He'd say I cheated on him with my job."

"Nothing wrong with hard work. Even better if you love it. What job?"

"I was the editor-in-chief of a fashion magazine. Built it from the ground up, you could say. I pitched the idea, got it running, then ran it. Made it my bitch. It became one of the top online fashion magazines in the country."

His brows arched. "A glamour girl."

"Is that not obvious?" I shimmied my shoulders, flashing him a winning smile.

He chuckled. "From the moment I met you, yes."

"Was it the BMW?"

"No. The alligator-skin purse the size of an Altoids tin in the passenger seat."

"Faux."

"Faux what?"

"It's not real alligator skin."

"That's a relief." He looked at me. "You like shiny things, Grey."

Lowering my gaze, I frowned, a twinge of defensiveness creeping up. Was he judging me?

I thought of the decrepit house behind me, my sleepless nights on the floor next to the toilet. The layer of dust I'd been covered in the last few days.

Did I like shiny things anymore? Was I already losing that part of me? Or maybe the more disturbing question was . . . Was it ever the *real* me?

"You said *was*," he said, drawing me from my thoughts. "You said you *were* the editor. I'm assuming you're no longer editor-in-chief of this fashion magazine."

"No." I swallowed the lump in my throat. "That's one of the losses."

"Sorry to hear that. Resign or fired?"

"Fired," I said, daring him to judge me.

He nodded. "I've been fired from a few jobs myself."

"I fell off a stage during a speech in front of the entire company."

"Those fancy shoes."

I snorted and looked away. A moment passed.

"The way I look at it is, I figure I wasn't meant to have the jobs I lost." Declan tilted his face up at the sky. "It's the path. Loss makes us stronger, makes us see things we might not have otherwise. Sometimes loss leads us to what we really need."

I took a second to chew on the words that seemed to be spoken just for me. "Here's to hoping."

"So, what are you going to do now? For work?"

"Well, you mentioned the farmers' market." I flashed him a hopeless, crooked smile.

He laughed. "Okay, but you've got a bit of grow-time before that weekly fifty dollars comes in."

I groaned.

"You have no job, do you? Nothing lined up?"

"Nope."

"You can clean the gum off my shop's floor. Full-time job, guaranteed."

"Hope it comes with health insurance."

"That's a negative."

I laughed. "Thanks, but I don't know if I could handle Kai all day."

"She's harmless."

"She's possessive of you."

If Declan was surprised, he didn't show it. When he didn't respond or elaborate, I became more certain than ever the two had more than a professional relationship.

"You could do something from home," he said. "Remotely. Maybe even in fashion, if you wanted to stay in that industry. That second-floor room . . ."

"Makes a good office, you said." I lifted my chin thoughtfully to the sky. "Yeah, it does."

"You got enough money to make it for a while? While you figure stuff out?"

I looked at him, and he shrugged.

"Direct, remember?"

"Yes, for a while, but not much longer than that. I need to figure out something soon. For my sanity, if nothing else."

"Very important."

"How long have you worked at the garage?"

"Twenty-one years."

"Wow. You own it?"

He nodded. "Twenty-one years."

"So you started your own business at, what, twenty?"

Another nod. "I always liked working on cars. Fixing things. Liked going at my own pace too, so I started a business where I could combine all three."

"Good for you."

"Good for the sanity."

"Very important," I said, playfully mocking him with a smile. "Your folks must be proud."

He turned his head, his expression hardening.

If the gossip Etta had shared over zucchini muffins earlier about Declan's abusive father was true, I wanted him to tell me about it—which was crazy because we were strangers. I also wanted to know about the girl in the pond, but didn't know how to work that bomb into the conversation.

But I wanted him to open up to me about his dad, his family, his childhood. I wanted to hear that he was, or had been, as screwed up as I was.

Fucked up, I know. Desperate, maybe.

Declan didn't deliver.

"So," he said, avoiding the comment, "you took off in your fancy BMW, and of all the places in the country, you came to little ol' Berry Springs. Why?"

"I have a cousin here."

"Who?"

"Cassidy Schaefer."

"No kidding?"

"You know her?"

"I do."

"Oh God, tell me it has nothing to do with your long line of women who didn't deliver on the chili."

He laughed. "No. She's quite a bit younger than I am. How old are you, Grey?"

"Thirty-one."

"I'd have guessed twenty-one."

"It's the retinol."

"Retin-what?"

I grinned. "Skin care. For wrinkles."

"Fancy."

"Not really. You can get it at Walmart, which, by the way, how have I lived my entire life without visiting one of those?"

He laughed.

"Seriously, I could furnish my entire house, fill my fridge, build my garden, get my annual eye exam, my hair done, and my oil changed, all for a third of the price of anywhere else—and all at the same time. It's heaven on earth."

"This is true. Are there no Walmarts in New York?"

"A few, but they're not big like the ones down here."

"Come to think of it, I think Cassidy worked at the local one a while back. Customer service."

"Is that how you know her?"

"I don't know her, really. Not since we were kids, anyway. Before my folks moved out here, we lived in town, a few doors down from Cassidy's grandmother, where she and her family would visit a few times a year. We, and the other kids on the block, would meet up and play soccer on the street. I met her older sister a few times too."

"Brianna." My stomach dropped.

"Right." His tone of voice suggested he knew about her death. It was probably the hot gossip when Cassidy and her family moved to Berry Springs.

I panicked for a moment, wondering if he—or anyone in

Berry Springs—knew about my mother's drunk-driving accident, then dismissed the thought. If Etta had known that detail, she would have addressed it immediately. If the Queen of Gossip didn't know, it was safe to assume no one else did. After all, my aunt didn't speak of my mother after the incident, and hadn't moved to Berry Springs until years later.

"And when Cassidy and her family officially moved here," he said, "I was all grown up. We didn't exactly run in the same circles."

"What circles did you run in?"

"Fast ones."

"A bad boy then." I nodded to the tattoos that covered his skin.

"Believe it or not, I didn't get my first tattoo until I was thirty."

I leaned over, admiring the lines and colors, and pointed to his forearm. "What does this one mean? The numbers 171613."

"My inmate number."

My brows popped.

He chuckled. "Just joking. It's First Corinthians, chapter sixteen, verse thirteen. One and seven, for the seventh book in the New Testament, then sixteen and thirteen."

"A godly man?" My voice hitched with shock.

"This surprises you?"

"I guess so. Although I don't know why. Do you go to church?"

"Used to, when I was little. My grandma would take me."

"It's been a long time since you've been little."

"I do church in my own way."

I nodded, looking back at the tattoo. "First Corinthians sixteen, verse thirteen. What verse is that?"

"It reminds me to be on my guard, walk in faith. Be courageous. Strong."

"I know that one . . . saw it spray painted in the subway once. When did you get it?"

"This was one of my first."

"What were you on your guard from? Others? Negative people in your life? Things that led you down the wrong path?"

"Exactly, all that. But maybe more so—from myself."

The words hit me like a wrecking ball.

Myself.

On guard from myself.

I thought of my drinking, my inability to control. Be on guard from *myself.* Be courageous, be strong.

Stronger, Grey, a voice said inside my head. *Stronger.*

"You left out the end of the verse," I told him. "'Do all things in love.'"

"Missed that part, I guess."

I cocked my head. "That's telling, Declan."

"Is it?"

"You're forty-one, have never been married, and have no kids."

"Are you suggesting that by me leaving out the part of the verse about love, means that I subconsciously don't make love a priority?"

"If the shoe fits . . ."

He focused on a bluebird fluttering at the edge of the cliff. "Cliff-side confessions."

I smiled.

"And you owe me one more," he said.

"Shoot."

"We've talked about one loss, your job. You said two. A

cheating bastard and two losses made you escape. What's the second loss?"

"Miscarriage." I blurted the admission, the single word escaping my lips with the grace of a nuclear bomb.

He was quiet for a few minutes, considering it, letting me have a moment to myself. When he finally spoke, his voice was soft. "Maybe it's like the job."

When Declan didn't explain, I thought about it, and his words replayed in my head. *It's the path.*

His thumb found my lower back and gently pressed against it. I leaned into it, his touch—only the touch—being exactly what I needed.

"Chili's probably ready," I whispered, because a whisper was all I could muster at the moment.

"Probably," he whispered back.

I shifted to stand.

"Hey, Grey?"

"Yeah?"

"Are you still married?"

I stared at him a moment. "Technically, yes."

He dipped his chin, then pushed to his feet and held out his hand. "Let me know when that changes."

33

The evening that followed was one of those whose impact lingers well after the sun rises the next day.

Declan and I arranged folding chairs around a makeshift dining table we'd created from an end table, where we settled in to sip iced tea and eat the chili mac. Which, I had to admit, was incredibly good. He added about a half pound of shredded cheddar to his, while I opted against it, saving calories for my daily visits with Etta and her baked goods.

It was light and casual. Carefree, like Declan.

We talked about the house, everything that needed to be done, and things that I wanted to do to it. Smooth, easy conversation. Then, with full bellies, we retreated outdoors where we planted the first of many lavender bushes.

He didn't stay after, and I had to admit this disappointed me.

Instead, he left a handwritten chili mac recipe with the words *Practice makes perfect* scribbled on the top. We bid our farewells, and I watched him drive down the driveway. At the end of it, his headlights turned right, not left to his house. To work, I assumed.

~

To my utter shock, I fell asleep easily that night and without much torment—for the first time in my new house. When I woke up, I had visions of tattoos, elbow macaroni, and lavender dancing in my head.

Unable to get Declan off my mind, I took my coffee outside to tend to my newly planted lavender bushes. The morning was dark, the sun hiding under heavy, brooding cloud cover. Rain was coming.

I wasn't sure exactly what it was about the man that consumed me. His looks were enough to make any woman fall to her knees, but it was more than that. It was the electricity between us, the heat that lingered long after our touch. It was the way he made me smile and laugh.

It was also the way he made me feel insecure. Not good enough for him. The way he could look into my eyes and make me feel like he was reading my soul. The way he knocked me off my game. I didn't like that. It made me uncomfortable.

I couldn't understand why a man who was so opposite from anyone I'd dated in the past could consume me so much. I'd lose my mind if I had to live in Declan's pigsty.

The man somehow made me want to both rip his pants off *and* slap him in the face—and not in a good way. In a *you're so damn frustrating* way.

Yep, there was something about Declan that made me feel like I was losing my mind. Or giving it to him, maybe. Because that morning, I literally couldn't think of anything else.

While tending to my new bushes, I noted how relaxing the scent was. Calming. Happy. I found myself wondering, again, how I could bottle the scent and use it in my house. This led to an entire morning of googling how to make essential oils. After only five minutes of research, I learned there are roughly a million different ways to do so.

As with anything I do, I decided to go all in and buy a distillation kit, which, according to the advice column I'd read, produces the purest form of oil. Not cheap, by the way.

Funnily enough, my oil wanderings had taken me to the second-floor mystery room to research and ponder ideas. Ironic, I know that now.

Although I'd opted for overnight delivery of the kit, I was too excited to wait twenty-four hours, so I drove to the local Walmart, thankful the rain was holding off.

I brought home a Crock-Pot and about thirty other things I didn't really need, and then for the next two hours fumbled my way through a DIY recipe that included distilled water and half of one of my new lavender bushes. According to the recipe, I'd have my essential oil in twenty-four hours.

After setting the Crock-Pot to boil, I refocused my creative energy on the house but found myself unable to concentrate, returning to my laptop every few minutes to research more about essential oils. Writing down tips and ideas, I was particularly drawn to homemade lavender-oil body butter. I couldn't imagine how relaxed I'd be if my entire body carried that scent.

I organized my notes into a folder. Created a plan.

All of this was done in the second-floor room, with a few breaks that might or might not have included looking out the window, searching for my Chili Mac Cowboy.

No luck.

I spent the rest of the day cleaning, organizing, unpacking, and dancing to new radio stations I was discovering hourly. I avoided the creepy mystery letters, still safely tucked on the fireplace mantel, and also the closet. I wasn't sure why, other than that I didn't want to darken my abnormally light, creative mood.

I also hadn't heard from Lucas. I wasn't sure why that was, either.

At sunset, Cassidy texted me, demanding a girls' night out. With Declan's advice that I needed to get out and meet the locals ringing in my head, I obliged.

Be a good neighbor.

Make connections.

Maybe find a damn job.

34

The rain came fast and hard, as promised by the weatherman.

With a deep breath, I yanked up my hood and jogged down the steps, the glow from my porch light illuminating the way. A chorus of meows sounded from the shadows past the tree line.

I stopped, squinting into the rain. "Hey there, Moonshine. You okay?"

Another meow, from one of her babies, I was sure.

Ignoring the fact that I was already running late to meet Cassidy, I turned and jogged back up the steps. A minute later, I was strategically dropping a trail of kibbles from the porch steps to four cans of tuna and a bowl of water. I tossed a few more kibbles on the ground, stepped back, and waited, watching the rain sparkle in the porch light.

Finally, a pair of golden eyes emerged from the shadows, followed by another and another. I smiled as Moonshine and all three of her babies slowly crossed the lawn, lifting each paw with a flourish to avoid the puddles and mud.

I stifled a laugh.

There was a leader of the kittens, an alpha, I realized, as they fell in line. Each piece of kibble was devoured, leading the pack closer and closer to the steps.

Mama hesitated.

"There's fresh tuuuuna over here," I sang in a creepy, overly happy tone, luring them like a sex offender on Halloween.

One paw on the step, then another and another.

My heart leaped.

"You can do it. Come on, little babies."

Slowly, I edged closer until I was inches from their furry little bodies. I was overcome with excitement as if approaching a lion in the desert. It felt like a victory. Moonshine was finally beginning to trust me.

Slow and steady. I focused on those words for a moment, thinking of my sobriety. Good things came from being slow and steady. Perseverance.

Moonshine hung back to allow her kittens all the tuna they desired. *A good mama*. After watching them a few minutes, I took my chance and reached out to lightly pet the alpha kitten. Moonshine froze, watching me with an intensity that reminded me of Declan.

"It's okay, Mama. It's okay."

After a few seconds, she hissed, letting me know it was enough.

"Okay, okay." I scooted back.

A fierce protector, I thought as I watched them finish the tuna.

I wanted that. I wanted that kind of love. Basically, I wanted children.

Men? That was another story, full of doubt and fear, but kids? Those I wanted. I was one hundred percent sure of that.

My spirits fell at the thought of my miscarriage, and I wondered if kids would ever happen for me.

"You're a good mom, Moonshine." My voice cracked, and I cleared my throat. "Your babies are safe here. I promise you that."

I sat back on my heels, watching the family, listening to the drumming of rain around us. Finally, Moonshine and her pack slinked back into the growing darkness. Calmer now, and satisfied.

It made my night.

After cleaning up the plates, I hurriedly locked up again, then darted to my car, avoiding the growing puddles of rain.

A smile came to my face as I passed Declan's garage, fully lit, the bays open, his truck parked in the usual spot between two pines. Seven thirty in the evening, and he was still at work.

The man worked constantly. I admired that.

Using the directions I'd scribbled on notebook paper from Cassidy's text message hours earlier, I navigated the narrow roads, slick with rain. Cassidy didn't give the name of the place, only the directions. For all I knew, I was meeting her at the local indoor rodeo stadium for the demolition derby I'd heard about while exploring the farmers' market earlier.

My stomach knotted with nerves as I turned into a small gravel parking lot packed with trucks, SUVs, and two big rigs in the back. My fancy BMW stuck out like a sore thumb.

All the parking spots were taken, so I created my own under an oak tree. As I put the car into park, my phone dinged from the passenger seat.

Cassidy: Where the hell are you? Lost?

Me: Just pulled in.

Cassidy: [Dancing woman emoji] I'm in the back right corner. Place is packed. I'll be carrying a red rose.

I grinned.

Me: Be right there.

I grabbed my faux alligator clutch—otherwise known as my Altoids box, yanked up my hood, and stepped out of the car.

Due to the weather, I'd chosen to wear jeans and a simple black tank under a raincoat. Simple, not flashy—aside from the heels. Because why not? Girls' night always involved heels, right? I'd curled my long, dark hair and carefully applied makeup, including a smoky eye and a glossy lip. I felt good, and was confident I looked good.

With one hand gripping my hood and the other my purse, I nimbly jogged across the parking lot, but stopped cold when my eyes locked on the flashing neon sign that read FRANK'S BAR.

It was a bar? *Shit.*

I took a deep breath. *Okay, I can do this.* Just because I was sober didn't mean I couldn't enjoy good company at a bar.

I can do this. Be strong.

The whine of a steel guitar floated through the air as I resumed my jog through the lot.

The bar had once been a log cabin, recently renovated and added onto, I guessed, when I noticed a large patio peeking out from around back. Strings of lights ran from the tree limbs above, and I so wished the rain would stop long enough for Cassidy and me to relocate outside. Easier to avoid booze outside, rather than inside while surrounded by it.

Right?

A few catcalls came from a couple cowboys loitering under the awning in the shadows, puffing on cigars. I gripped the large copper handle on the door with a sweaty palm. As I opened the door, a gust of stale air perfumed with barbecue and beer swept my hair over my shoulder.

Cassidy wasn't joking. The place was packed.

Dozens of Berry Springs' finest were dressed in cowboy hats, Wranglers, and boots. They mingled, whispered, and laughed around mahogany tables that matched the log walls, which were covered in old road signs, beer signs, and deer heads. Red vinyl booths, all packed, lined the left side of the room, and a long bar lined the right. The music was loud, and I thought of Declan, as he would have definitely approved the classic country carrying through the large room. The lighting was dim, shadowed faces turning my way as I closed the door behind me.

It was a real Southern honkytonk bar. I stuck out almost as much as my car in the parking lot.

"Girl!" A hand shot up from the end of the bar, waving wildly.

I maneuvered through the crowd, drawing more catcalls and whistles. Under normal circumstances, I'd pretend to be offended while secretly loving the attention. That night, though, I was more focused on keeping my distance from the mirrored wall lined with hundreds of liquor and wine bottles.

"How do you look so pretty in this rain? Here. Sit." Cassidy pulled her black Prado bag from the bar stool next to her. Not Prada, Prado.

"Is the entire town here?" I asked.

I squeezed past a trucker with the sleeves cut off from his button-up. A naked pinup girl colored an arm as thick as a tree trunk, a swollen hand wrapped around a pint glass of beer. Secured in his other hand was a Styrofoam cup filled with brown sticky liquid.

"It's karaoke night." Cassidy gestured to the small stage in the back. "Otherwise known as singles' night here in Berry Springs. So, yeah, it's always packed, and always a blast. Trust me, you'll love it." She leaned in to lower her voice. "Sorry about Tobacco Trucker Guy. This was the last seat."

The bartender walked up, wiping his hands on his apron. "Another one, Cassie?"

"Please. Grey, this is Frank. He owns the place. Former BSPD. Frank, this is my cousin, Grey Dalton. First time in your lovely establishment."

Pushing fifty, the owner of Frank's Bar sported a mop of shaggy brown hair threaded with gray. His eyes were dark, his skin marked with the onset of deep wrinkles from years of hard living, I guessed. Despite his edge, he was a handsome man, with a ruggedness that reminded me of Declan.

"Pleasure to meet you, ma'am. Sorry for all the commotion. Karaoke nights bring out the best of 'em. What can I get ya?"

My stomach clenched, and I froze. "Tea," I said quickly, with a sharpness that didn't fit the casual mood around me.

"Sweet or unsweet?"

"You're the first person to ask me that question since I've been in Berry Springs."

He laughed. "My daughter's diabetic. No sugar for me."

I nodded. "Unsweet."

"You got it." He winked.

Cassidy tilted her head to the side, studying me as he walked away. "You feelin' okay?"

"Yeah. Just drank too much last night, you know," I lied, waving a hand dismissively in the air.

A small smile came to my face.

I did it. I was proud of myself.

And with that little victory, I relaxed.

Cassidy and I fell into conversation, coming up for air only to take quick sips of our drinks.

As expected, she pelted me with questions about my dinner with Lucas Covington, to which I responded with a carefully crafted story I'd rehearsed in the shower, a story that did *not* include too many drinks or counter sex.

Once satisfied with that topic, Cassidy moved on and we talked about the house, her last bad date, and the most recent town gossip, including recent rare sightings of an aggressively large mystery fish in Otter Lake that the locals had dubbed the Southern Loch Ness Monster. They'd named him Ozzy. There was already talk of creating an annual festival around the monster.

The barroom lights dimmed as a spotlight clicked on. I followed the light, smoke snaking through the bright yellow beam pooling onto the stage in the back.

Cassidy rubbed her palms together excitedly. "Karaoke. Here we go."

We shifted in our seats to get a better look at the two scantily clad cowgirls in pleather minis and red boots stumbling onto the stage.

Thank you, I whispered to the man above, grinning from ear to ear while settling in for the show that was going to undoubtedly make my evening.

A pair of knuckles rapping on the bar top pulled our

attention as horns blasted the beginning beats of "Respect" by Aretha Franklin. *Shocker.*

Frank nodded to the two shot glasses in front of us. One shot was dressed with only one lime. The other—two limes.

Tequila with *two* limes. Only one man in town knew I took my tequila with two limes.

"From the man at the end of the bar." Frank nodded, then turned to the next patron.

I looked over my shoulder as the crowd parted long enough for me to see Lucas Covington, a cocky smirk on his devilishly handsome lips. Instead of his usual flawless suit, Lucas had gone casual to mingle with the country folk, in a short-sleeved golf shirt and gray khakis. Definitely couture, based on the way the clothes molded perfectly to his body.

"Oh my." Cassidy's jaw dropped, much like it did when she saw Lucas for the first time at the diner. "Big-dick resort guy bought us drinks."

My heart dropped I turned back to the shots he'd sent over. *Oh shit.*

"Girl." Cassidy's eyes glittered as she picked up her shot glass. "Your man bought us Patrón. That date must've been better than you're letting on."

"He's not my man, and it wasn't a date."

"Who cares? Here's to free shots." Cassidy lifted her shot glass, nodding to mine.

I looked over my shoulder again, but Lucas was gone.

"*Girl.*" She nodded impatiently to my shot glass.

Saliva pooled in my mouth as my fingertips wrapped around the icy glass. My heart roared in my chest.

A hand rested on my back. I didn't have to turn around to know it was Lucas. Cassidy's hypnotic ogle was enough.

Frank handed Lucas a shot, then disappeared.

Lucas lifted his shot, his gaze on me, and Cassidy lifted hers.

Feeling that I had no other choice, I lifted mine. "*Salute*."

I tossed back my shot, goose bumps forming on my skin as the burn slid down my throat. Lucas said something to me, and then Cassidy said something to him, although I didn't hear either comment. Every sensor in my body came to life.

I inhaled deeply, inwardly cringing at the tingle on my tongue. Guilt—that godawful guilt—gripped me, and then it made me mad. I was so sick of the guilt.

Everyone in the bar was drinking, having a good time. Why the hell was I so hard on myself?

"You've been a tough gal to get ahold of." Lucas's voice slowly penetrated the internal battle raging in my head.

I forced a smile. "You've seen my house."

"True. Time-consuming, indeed. Well, I'm glad you make time to escape."

"You too, although I'm guessing this is just as much for work as for pleasure."

"Always." Lucas winked.

"Well, to save you some time here, you should know that I've decided I'm not selling out."

His dark brow arched. "Not even an extra fifteen thousand dollars can change your mind?"

"Nope. I'm settling here, for a while at least."

"You know what you want."

"More like I know what I don't want."

"Well, I guess if your decision is made, then this visit is for pleasure."

Lucas reached over my head, taking three more shots from Frank, who apparently had been ordered to keep them coming. He handed one to Cassidy, and one with two limes to me.

He raised his own. "To an evening of fun."

I swallowed the knot in my throat.

Fun.

Hell, yes.

~

Three shots later, five if you were counting—and I certainly wasn't—Lucas's arm had found its way around my shoulders. Tobacco Trucker Guy had vacated his seat, which now served as a purse holder while Lucas leaned against the bar top.

Karaoke night was in full swing. Tables had been moved —pitchers spilling in the process—to allow for dancing in front of the stage.

The tequila had done its trick. I felt like a million bucks. Happy and carefree, exactly what I'd been searching for, I realized.

Who cares that I'm in the middle of a divorce? I'd bet half the people in the bar were divorcees, based on the amount of alcohol being served in the bar.

Who cares that I got fired? Screw them. Screw them all.

And who cares that I had a miscarriage? Many women had miscarriages, and some women, multiples. *It's life. Fuck it.*

Fuck it all.

I'd land on my feet like I always did. Berry Springs was growing on me, and so was the bar.

Lucas was growing on me as well, as was the air of confidence he wore like his expensive cologne. The proverbial scent of money and power. I wasn't the only woman who'd taken notice. Our end of the bar had received almost as many winks as empty PBR cans.

Lucas leaned into my ear, whispering something I couldn't hear over the music. Grinning, although I wasn't sure why, I scanned the crowd as he nibbled my ear.

Until my gaze stopped cold on a narrowed pair of ice-blue eyes burning into mine. My stomach dropped to my feet.

Declan.

I'll never, *ever* forget the way I felt at that moment.

Embarrassed. Cheap.

Worthless.

35

*S**hit,* was all I could think.

Then *why*? Why did I feel like I'd just been "caught"?

Caught drinking. Caught flirting with another man.

And why did it matter?

The thought was ridiculous because Declan wasn't my boyfriend. The dinner he and I had shared wasn't a date. It was payment for services rendered on my BMW. That was it.

What was it about him that made me question myself so much?

Asshole.

I grabbed my alligator Altoids box from the stool next to Lucas and Cassidy, who were deep in conversation about the stock market, or maybe Lucas's uncanny ability to pull out before even the slightest saturation—as I knew from experience.

"I'm going to the restroom. Be right back."

They weren't listening.

I stumbled as I spun off the bar stool. No one noticed.

Pushing my way through the crowd, I made my way to the corner where Declan had been watching me.

Scowling, I scanned the room. He was nowhere in sight.

I nodded to a glass on a windowsill "What is that?" I asked its owner, a man I didn't know.

"Coke," he said, frowning.

"Diet?"

"Nope. Straight-up Coke."

"Good." I grabbed it and chugged, willing the caffeine to erase the buzz from the tequila.

After slamming the glass down on a nearby table, I stomped away—and got *really* mad. Mad at Declan. Mad at him for ruining my night.

I pushed my way back through the crowd, looking for the stupid blue Henley he'd been wearing that made his eyes glow.

A duo of drunk cowgirls stumbled into me. I shoved one off, sending her stammering into a table.

That was the first time a faint little warning bell went off in my brain. The same little warning bell that went off the night I tumbled off the stage during my awards acceptance speech. The night I let Lucas bend me over the counter. The night Brianna and I got into the car with my drunk mother.

"Hey!"

"Bitch!"

My heart rate spiked. *Keep walking.*

Keeping my head down, I increased the distance between me and the two drunk girls.

How long had Declan been watching me? *Spying* on me?

Who was he here with? Another woman? A date? Kai and her AK-47? Who, I imagined, was probably arm wrestling Tobacco Guy in a booth somewhere.

I wanted to know. All of it.

A sputtering neon light caught my attention through the commotion:

BATHROOMS HERE

I pivoted and ducked into the ladies room.

The wooden door slapped shut behind me as I stumbled to the mirror. I dropped my purse in the sink and braced my palms against the porcelain to stare at my reflection.

And saw my mother.

Disgust made my stomach burn like acid.

I smoothed my hair, clumsily reapplied the lip gloss that had been transferred from my lips to the rims of five shot glasses.

I need to get the hell out of here.

The speakers were blaring, lights flashing, as I hurried out of the bathroom. A crowd had gathered around the stage where five girls were singing about "Friends in Low Places."

I felt suffocated, like I was about to have a panic attack. I had to get the hell out.

Now.

I turned, spying an exit sign past the bathrooms. Throwing myself out the back door, I gasped for air as it slammed shut behind me.

Rain pelted my shoulders as a hand gripped my elbow. I spun around, purse up, ready to fight.

Through the haze of rain, Declan emerged from the shadows. His hair was wet, his shirt soaked.

"You scared me."

He offered me a disapproving scowl.

I tried to yank my arm away, but the grip around my elbow tightened.

"What are you doing?" His voice was sharp. Menacing.

"Having fun," I snapped back.

Rain slid down my face and arms, cooling heated skin.

"Is this your idea of fun?"

"Yes." I squared my shoulders and stood strong, fighting the sway from the buzz that was now full-blown drunkenness.

"Is he your boyfriend?"

"Who?"

"Lucas Covington."

"Who's—"

"Don't patronize me. Is he your boyfriend?"

"No. And what the hell does it matter anyway?"

"You let strange men in bars nibble your ear then?" Darkness from the moonless night hid much of Declan's face, but there was no mistaking the anger. The possessiveness.

I thought of Etta and the temper she warned me about. *Boy's not right . . .*

"So what if he is my boyfriend?" I taunted, despite my better judgment.

"You're better than that, Grey." But even as Declan said it, he looked me up and down in a way that was intended to let me know that he knew that I was drunk. And that this displeased him.

"Thanks for your assessment."

"You almost got your ass kicked back there, do you know that?"

"What? No, I didn't."

"That girl you pushed, the one you *pushed* into a table. She's been arrested for fighting before."

"So she's Kai's sister then?" I mocked.

"You think that's funny?" Declan snapped, leaning

inches from my face. His fresh scent, ripe with the rain, tickled my nose. "You were two seconds from getting your nose broken before I pulled her away, Grey. Didn't see that, did you? She was coming after you."

My stomach clenched with fear. The thought of getting into a physical altercation made me sick.

Jutting out my chin like a defiant child, I changed the subject. "How do you know Lucas?"

"I don't."

"Then why are you judging him?"

"Because I know his dad." Declan's eyes flashed with anger. Hatred.

"How?"

His jaw twitched, his hand tightening around my elbow.

"How?" I repeated. When he didn't answer, I clenched my teeth and attempted to pull out of his grip again. "*Dammit,* Declan, if you don't—"

"My dad and his dad went into business together, until his dad fucked him over. Pulled out of a deal, left us bankrupt. Ruined my family and then left town."

I blinked.

"Four days ago, the motherfucker had the balls to come to my house, offering me the same deal to sell out as I'm assuming he offered you. Although," Declan's sharp gaze cut through me, "based on what I saw tonight, his offer to you includes much more than just money."

My jaw dropped. "How *dare* you . . ."

"He's a snake, Grey. Like his dad. He'll do anything to get what he wants."

"Well, he doesn't *get* me," I lied. "And we didn't come here together."

"You were together in the bar."

"No, we weren't."

"His tongue was in your ear."

"What the hell is your problem? It's my business. Not yours."

"How are you getting home?"

"I—I'm . . ." I stuttered. *Shit.*

"You're not driving. Let's go."

I yanked my arm away. "Get off me. You can't tell me what to do. Get the hell away from me, Declan."

Tears burned as I yanked the back door open. My heart was racing, my stomach churning. I spotted the door to the kitchen and pushed through it.

Confused faces turned my way as I stumbled through a wall of grease, and by sheer luck, found another exit. After ripping off my heels, I took off running like a drunk deer through the parking lot, rain pounding my head, tears streaming down my cheeks.

Tripping over rocks, I stumbled onto my car, yanked open the door, and slammed it closed as Declan emerged from the front.

Go, go, go . . .

He searched the lot. A duo of pickup trucks fired up next to me. I took a chance and drove between them, exiting the lot under their cover.

Declan was still searching for me as I pulled onto the road.

Tears filled my eyes as my fingers curled around the steering wheel. My thoughts crystallized on one goal as I navigated the slick roads.

Just make it home.

A drive that should have taken five minutes took fifteen. When I finally pulled into my driveway, the rain was coming down in a steady deluge, blurring my house as I topped the hill and parked.

Headlights reflected in my rearview mirror.

Declan.

Bracing for a fight, I climbed out of my car, not caring about the rain, and slammed the door. Only it wasn't Declan —because Declan didn't drive a Porsche.

The headlights cut off, and the shiny Porsche purred to a stop at my feet.

Lucas slinked out of the driver's side. "Where did you go?"

My gaze shifted over his shoulder to where another pair of headlights sparkled through the trees in the distance. *That* was Declan—I knew it in every cell of my tequila-soaked body.

Lucas didn't notice my shift in attention as he walked toward me.

Lights came up the driveway . . .

"I was worried—"

Cutting Lucas off, I wrapped my arms around his neck and crushed my lips to his.

Bright headlights lit the back of my eyelids as my mouth slid messily over Lucas's. My heart pounded wildly, but this time not from lust. I cracked open an eye as Lucas wrapped his arms around me, and stared into the headlights that were now stopped in the middle of my driveway.

That's right, Declan, I'm making out with Lucas. I'm drunk, messy, and a whore. How do you feel about that, Mr. Fucking Perfect?

Lucas slid his hands to my ass, totally unaware of the truck coming up behind him. The truck stopped, and my pulse roared in my ears.

Finally, I heard the grind of the reverse gear clicking into place. Declan slammed the gas, sending rocks and gravel flying into the air.

Lucas jerked away and turned around as Declan's truck backed quickly down the driveway. "Who the hell is that?"

"Some lost redneck," I mumbled, wiping the rain from my forehead.

Amused, Lucas snorted, watching the truck fishtail onto the road and peel out again.

"Dime a dozen around here," he muttered, then turned back to me. He grabbed my waist and yanked me back to him. "Now. Where were we?"

My stomach churned as his lips pressed to mine. Suddenly, I hated the rain.

As bile crawled up my throat, I pulled back. "I'm actually tired. I think I'm going to call it a night."

"What? No way." He slammed his lips on mine, sliding his fingertips under my tank top.

I was going to vomit. Right there, in my driveway, in the rain, on his thousand-dollar wingtips.

I slid my hands between us and pushed him away. "Good night, Lucas."

Breathing hard, he cocked his head. "Really?"

I nodded, took another step back. "I'm leaving soon, you know."

"I know. I'll call you tomorrow."

"I'll look forward to it."

I stumbled up the porch steps as Lucas backed out the driveway. Bastard didn't even walk me to the door.

It took three tries to get my key into the keyhole.

Once inside, I slammed the door behind me, and with a guttural scream, threw my clutch across the room, sending it slamming against the window.

Break, you son of a bitch. Add another thing to my damn to-do list.

I paced the entryway like an enraged tiger, back and

forth, back and forth, a hurricane of emotions flooding me. Anger, regret, guilt.

Screw it.

I stalked to the laundry room and plucked one of the wine bottles from the hamper. It wasn't full, so yanked out the cork with my teeth and chugged. I'd already starting drinking, so what difference did it make at this point?

I *hated* Declan.

Seething with misplaced anger, I grabbed the pot of chili from the fridge, stomped across the kitchen, flung open the back door, and hurled it over the side of the porch. It hit the mud with an explosion of tomatoes and beans.

Screw you, Declan. I wanted nothing to do with him anymore. Him and all his judgment.

I wanted to forget. I wanted to get fucked.

As I found my way back inside, the wine began to kick in.

I stumbled across the house with laser focus—only one thing in mind. I was drunk, and I was going to make the damn most of this night.

When I snatched my cell phone from the counter, it slipped from my clumsy hands and tumbled to the floor. Gripping the counter for support, I swooped down and picked it up just as a door creaked on its hinges.

My head snapped toward the noise. I stumbled into the den, flicked the lights on, and walked to the staircase. The door to the second floor—that I always kept shut—was open.

"Leave me alone, ghost. Anna, Bonnie, whoever. Go find somewhere else to live."

I returned to my bad judgment in the kitchen. Swaying and squinting, I typed a text.

Me: Come back.
Lucas: I thought you said you were tired.
Me: Turns out I just needed more wine [three wine emojis].
Lucas: On my way.

I tossed my phone across the counter, took another swig from the wine bottle, then hurried to the bathroom for a whore's bath—wipe, perfume, and lotion. While pulling off my tank and pants, I fell to the floor, an absolute mess.

Buck naked, I rifled through my new dresser drawers, tossing clothes into the air before realizing I hadn't packed my negligees. Didn't think I'd need them.

My head popped up at the sound of tires on the driveway. My hazy focus landed on the red sole of a pair of black patent Louboutins with a six-inch heel. Grinning and still naked, I snatched them up and stuffed my feet into the sky-high heels.

A knock sounded at the door.

I took a few breaths, then pushed myself off of the bed. Holding on to the wall for support, I laughed, wobbling in my heels, while guiding myself through the house.

My crooked grin widened as I pulled open the door.

"Oh . . . my." Lucas's jaw dropped.

"Hi there," I said in a voice meant to be deep and sultry, but actually sounded more like Clint Eastwood in *Gran Torino*.

Lucas's greeting was less subtle than the one before. He lunged forward, jerking me to him, his mouth crashing onto mine while he kicked the door shut behind him.

The taste of tequila mixed with the metallic tang of blood as he bit my lower lip.

"Suck me, Grey. Suck my dick. Please. Suck my dick."

He desperately pulled at my waist. I obliged, bent my

knees, crumpling unsteadily to the floor as he pulled himself from his khakis with an ease and speed that suggested he'd done it more than a few times. He gripped my hair, yanking my head forward.

My eyes teared as I took him into my mouth, his hands forcefully guiding each stroke. My hair bounced on my shoulders, my jaw popping with each thrust.

When I gagged, he laughed and made me take him deeper.

My head started to spin.

I was lifted into the air and taken into the bedroom I didn't remember showing him before. My body bounced like a rag doll when he tossed me onto the bed.

"Touch yourself," he commanded me. The sound of clothes hitting the floor told me he was undressing.

I locked onto his voice, looking for anything to steady the room spinning around me.

"Touch yourself, I said."

Obeying, I pulled my knees up and spread them wide, then inserted a finger that I couldn't even feel. Groans carried through the dimly lit room, followed by deep breathing.

I couldn't look at him.

"Turn over," Lucas demanded, stepping to the bed.

Awareness sent a split second of sobriety to my hazed brain—but I shook it off.

Fun, I reminded myself. *Fun. Get fucked. Forget. This is what people do.*

I rolled over and pushed up onto all fours like an animal. Two hands gripped my waist, and the room spun around me. When I felt his weight climb onto the bed, I closed my eyes.

Without warning, he speared into me, knocking the breath from my lungs, and I scrunched my face in pain.

Forget, forget, forget . . .

As he raked his fingernails painfully down my back, I buried the top of my head in a pillow. My eyes locked on the Louboutin dangling from my toe at the edge of the bed.

You whore.

Silently, I wept as Lucas fucked me from behind.

Again.

36

Moments later, Lucas's heavy footfalls crossed the living room, followed by the sound of a doorknob turning and then the squeak of the front door closing behind him.

Staring up at the stained, chipped ceiling, I lay naked on the bed, tears streaming down my face, remorse stronger than the booze sloshing in my stomach.

I wanted to have fun. To forget.

Instead, I felt hollow. Dirty. Empty.

Deplorable.

Rolling onto my side, I pulled my knees to my chest, concealing my body from the room around it. Hating my body. And myself.

The ring of my cell phone began to register over the shame consuming my head. I frowned, remembering hearing it ring during the entire six minutes Lucas had his way with me.

Was it Declan?

I wanted it to be Declan.

Swiping the snot from my nose, I poured myself out of

bed, stumbling, this time not from the booze, but from the raw pain between my legs. I straightened, cringing at the stinging pain on my back, vaguely remembering Lucas's nails scoring it.

My knees felt weak, my muscles like jelly, as I maneuvered through the mess of the living room to the kitchen and picked up my cell phone.

Eight missed calls, all from Cassidy. I bit back my disappointment.

I couldn't make much out of the voice mails, other than Cassidy's giggling voice and something about girls just wanting to have fun. Each voice mail was followed by a text pleading for me to come back to the bar. Apparently, Lucas had told Cassidy he was going to escort me home, and not to worry.

I looked at the clock—11:47 p.m.—then over my shoulder to the bedroom where Lucas had fucked me like a back-alley whore. I knew I wasn't going to sleep, especially not in that bed.

I didn't want to be alone. Didn't want to have to face the decisions I'd made, and I knew that's exactly what I'd do if I stayed home. Sitting in silence, I cried, berating myself.

With that acknowledgment, I sucked back the tears, stalked to my room, and pulled on the first pair of pants I saw—a pair of baggy gray sweatpants with paint stains on them—followed by a tee, and then I slipped into flip-flops. I didn't even bother looking in the mirror.

I spun around, looking for my purse, and found it in the same place it landed when I threw it across the room. It was on the floor next to the living room windows, inches from the button-up Declan had left behind after our chili dinner.

I grabbed the purse and pulled on the shirt.

Bypassing the lights, I grabbed the wine bottle from

the counter, and in sweatpants, a plaid shirt five sizes too big, and mismatched flip-flops, I stumbled out the front door.

The sound of heavy rain whooshed in my ears. The night was as black as coal.

Moonshine meowed from a nearby bush, a hint of desperation in her cry, again and again. It wasn't a hiss, more of a whine, as if begging me not to go. Or warning me, maybe.

The porch steps swayed under each foot as I made my way down them, squinting to focus on each step.

My car keys fell from my hands. Once, twice. A sign—I knew that now.

Soaking wet, I collapsed into the driver's seat and slammed the door. My hand shook as I started the engine. Not even then did I reconsider this decision.

Stupid.

I shoved the car into reverse and carved a U-turn out of my front lawn. Midway down the driveway, I remembered to turn on my lights.

Visions of my mother flashed before me, as vivid as if she were a ghost floating in front of the hood of my car. This was followed by visions of Brianna, lying broken on the side of the road.

You shouldn't be driving.

You shouldn't be driving.

You shouldn't be driving.

I hate you, Mom.

My heart pounding with adrenaline, I pressed the gas, blasting through the visions, the warnings, the guilt.

One more drink. That's all I wanted. One more damn drink.

Fuck you, Mom.

My tires spun around a curve. Starting to feel sick, I rolled down the windows.

Faster, faster, my heart racing, the blood not reaching my brain.

My phone dinged from the passenger seat. I reached over, checking a text from Cassidy, but I couldn't read the blurred words.

I looked up the moment the curve passed me.

Screaming, I slammed on the brakes.

But it was too late.

37

"Grey . . . *Grey*!"

The distant voice above me slowly began to register.

I was wet.

Was I underwater? Dreaming?

A hand was on my face, another shaking my arm.

Say it again, I thought, begging the voice to speak again. *Pull me out of this.*

"That's it. That's it, baby. Come on. You're okay. Wake up."

My eyes fluttered as I tried to make sense of the world around me. A man, silhouetted with blinding backlight, loomed over me with raindrops falling like diamonds around him.

I was on the ground. I remember being so thankful for that. For the strong ground, holding me. Supporting me. Being there for me.

With my hand that wasn't being held by the man, I ran my fingertips over the mud and gripped a rock, felt the cool wetness of it in my palm. I was alive.

Slowly, my senses began to awaken.

Sight—*him.*

Smell—*him.*

Touch—*him.*

Declan.

"That's it. Stay with me, Grey."

I blinked again, objects coming into focus.

My eyes locked with a crystal-clear sapphire blue against the backdrop of the black night. A light penetrating darkness. *Him.*

"Oh my God," I murmured weakly, trying to sit up.

"No, hang on." Declan gently pinned me down. "Take it easy."

I turned my head, and the underbelly of my BMW filled my vision. The *ding, ding, ding* of the open door rang out in the night.

"Oh my God!" I lifted my torso from the dirt. "My car."

The headlights from Declan's truck illuminated the wreckage. Smoke rolled from the hood of my car—which was wrapped around a tree trunk. Crinkled like an accordion.

Panic ripped through me. I fought like a wild animal, swatting against him, frantically trying to push myself off the ground.

"Is everyone okay?" I shrieked, desperately scanning the interior of the car. "Is anyone hurt? Oh my God—"

"No, Grey. You were alone. No one was with you. No one is hurt."

Wide-eyed, I looked at him, my chest heaving. Horrified. Defenseless.

Then I doubled over and puked all over his cowboy boots.

I wasn't sure how long I threw up, but when I came to, I was sitting on the ground, my head between my knees, a few feet away from my car. It had stopped raining, with only a few drops slipping from the canopy of trees above.

The smell was atrocious.

My head bowed in humiliation, I scooted away from Declan. Vomiting had cleared my head a bit. I felt more stable, off of the boat being tossed around in the ocean, but now in the middle of an emotional hurricane.

He moved closer.

"No," I said quickly. "Please. It stinks. It's so . . . gross. Please," I whispered, shame turning my face away from him.

Tears filled my eyes. The shame and embarrassment I felt in my stomach was crushing. Devastating. Life changing.

"My mom," I said softly as they fell. "I'm my mother."

Weeping, I fell over, directly into Declan's arms as he emerged at my side.

"My mom." I sobbed, my body shaking. "I'm my mom. I hate myself, Declan. I *hate* myself."

"Shhh, don't say that. We'll figure this out." He stroked my hair. "Everything is going to be okay, Grey. Everything is going to be all right."

I clung to each word. To his voice. An anchor in the storm.

"Come here," he whispered, pulling me closer. "Everything is going to be okay."

Wanting desperately to believe him, I nestled into his chest, inhaling the scent of Declan. Soap, dryer sheets, a hint of motor oil—that distinctive scent of male.

A few minutes passed, each one settling a little easier than the one before. Easier in his arms, I decided.

I sighed. "I threw up on your shoes." I pulled away and looked up at him.

"On yours too." He smiled, continuing to stroke my hair.

"Yeah, but yours." I groaned and shook my head, looking down.

"Grey, I have a buddy in the military. This isn't the first time I've had vomit on my shoes."

I tried to smile. But it dropped.

"*God,* Declan." I pressed my palms to my eyes, undoubtedly smearing the mascara that was already smudged.

"I know . . . I know."

He held me tighter. Another minute passed.

"Let's get out of here," he said softly. "How does that sound?"

Straightening, I nodded. "Am I hurt?"

Declan shook his head. "I checked you over pretty good while you were out. No blood, cuts, or bumps. Currently, anyway."

"I'm drunk. I was drunk, Declan," I shamefully muttered, as if in a confessional.

"I know." He nodded. "I also know the routine of hiding liquor bottles throughout the house. The hamper is a common hiding place, by the way. I knew the look in your eyes when you saw me find them. I know a struggling alcoholic when I see one."

He nodded to the car, the neck of the wine bottle peeking out from behind the tire. "And it looks like you found your way to the bottom of the bottle tonight."

Rock bottom.

I cringed at the hood, totally destroyed. "My car."

"Don't worry about it, Grey. I'll take care of it."

I shook my head, looking away.

Declan took my hand. "I fix things, Grey. It's what I do."

Tears came again. Desperate, I grabbed his arm.

"Declan," I whispered, unable to hold back the flood. "I need to be fixed."

38

I was taken to his house, not mine. I didn't ask why, because I didn't care.

Declan carried me over the threshold like a new bride—or maybe a mental patient on the run.

I was carried into his den, lowered onto a soft leather chair, and covered with a wool blanket. It smelled like him. A wall of windows faced me. Declan's manicured yard sparkled with lingering raindrops under a glow of landscape lighting, chasing the darkness away.

"I'll be right back."

I stared blankly outside as Declan quietly stepped out of the room, my thoughts as vacant and hollow as I felt inside. I was all cried out at that moment.

The scents of coffee and warm bread filled the air, piquing my senses.

I looked toward the arched entryway as Declan walked in, carrying a tray. He pulled a small table across the floor and placed it next to me. On top, he set a cup of coffee. Steam curled into the air as he placed a small loaf of French bread next to it, warmed, with blocks of butter softening to the side. The final touches were a bottle of water and a medicine cup of aspirin.

When he added a spoonful of honey and creamer to my coffee, I asked, "How do you know how I take my coffee?"

"I pay attention." He winked, then frowned as he stroked my head. "How are you feeling?"

"Better." My gaze shifted to his feet, where he'd changed out of his vomit-covered boots.

A fingertip lifted my chin. "I told you, don't worry about it."

Mortified, I squeezed my eyes shut.

"Stop, Grey. I've been there too. We all have. Stop."

I nodded in concession.

"Good. Now eat. Soak up the rest of that booze. Then water and meds."

"Oh, Declan," I said on a sigh. "Thank you."

"Eat." He smiled and set the plate in my lap. "*Eat.*"

He smoothed a dollop of warm butter on the tip of the bread and lifted it to my lips. I took a bite. It was delicious, warm and flaky with a hint of sugar.

"Good girl. Butter makes the difference. Trust me."

He waited until I took another bite, then dragged the second armchair around to face me, but far enough away to give me space. He sat and settled back, leaning his head against the back of the chair as he looked out the window. A million miles away.

We sat in silence as I ate, realizing I was absolutely ravenous. Sometime after I had most of the bread and a full cup of coffee in me, I began to feel human again.

"Better?"

"Yes."

"You've got color back in your cheeks."

"That's a start."

"You're telling me. You looked like a slab of drywall."

"How's the makeup?"

"You've got a little Ozzy going on under the eyes, but nothing that won't scrub off."

I snorted, leaning my head back. "*Dammit,* Declan. I . . . I just . . ."

"Got drunk. I know. That's the story." His voice sharpened. With pain, I thought. "That's what happened."

My eyes met his. "Exactly. That's what happened," I whispered. "That's what happened."

He dipped his chin, and that was that.

I knew he knew. He saw me kiss Lucas, saw Lucas's hands on my ass. And I knew he knew I'd let Lucas have sex with me. He knew I was a struggling alcoholic . . . and there was an unexpected comfort in that.

No more hiding or pretending. No more fighting it. I'd been metaphorically stripped naked, revealing the good, the bad, and the ugly right there in Declan's leather chair. Staring at him, I silently begged for acceptance, nothing more than a lost little girl, broken, vulnerable, and helpless.

We stared at each other, the weight of a thousand unsaid words between us. Tears filled my eyes, and he slowly shook his head.

I sniffed them away and nodded, blinking hard until my eyes cleared.

Declan nodded to the bread. "Finish."

I picked up what remained of the loaf and nibbled, variations of *what now* flooding my brain.

"I'll tow your car to my shop in the morning and get started on it right away. Parts will need to be ordered, but I know a guy. He'll get them as quickly as he can, but you'll be without a car for a few days, at least."

"I could probably use a few days—at least—of not leaving the house."

"Do you have anything you need to get done in town?"

I thought of the divorce papers I'd already signed and sent off. "I don't think so. Not right away, anyway."

"If you do, I'll take you. If for some reason I can't, Kai will take you."

"Thank you."

"You're welcome."

I took a sip of coffee. "The day we met, you asked me how I got my name. You asked the meaning behind Grey."

"I remember."

"You ready for the story?"

"I'm ready for everything."

"I was named after Grey Goose, Declan. My mother and father named me after fucking vodka."

His expression didn't waver. He didn't move, simply let me speak. Let me release.

"My mother was an extreme alcoholic. I don't know my dad. He left when I was a baby. Mom had a lot of men in and out of the house after that. That's the kind of life I was brought up in."

I stared at him a minute, and he nodded in understanding. Of what I meant, but also of my actions.

"She drank and smoked—a few different things—while she was pregnant with me. She admitted this to me, can you believe that? When I was only nine years old. I remember it like it was yesterday. You see, when I was little, I got sick all the time. I'd catch everything that was going around school, although I'd get it a million times worse than the other kids. I had life-restricting asthma and terrible allergies—a shitty immune system overall. I know now it was because my mom smoked two packs a day while she was pregnant. She also drank and smoked weed occasionally."

Taking a breath, I went on. "Anyway, my illnesses would usually turn into pneumonia, and I'd be in the hospital for days, sometimes weeks at a time. One day, she was sitting there next to me, trying to get me to eat applesauce, and she laughed and casually said that maybe she shouldn't have smoked and drank while I was in her belly. I'll never, ever forget that moment. How casually she'd said it. Like it was no big deal."

"That must have made you feel pretty insignificant."

"Exactly. You'd think a mother would be riddled with guilt, but not mine. She said it, then turned her attention back to the television that she kept on some daytime soap opera. She never even thought to let me watch cartoons or something lighthearted while I was in the hospital. It was always what she wanted to watch. Like she was bored with it all."

"Did her drinking last your entire childhood?"

"Until she went to jail."

"For the accident?"

I blinked. "You know about that?"

"I don't, really. Just that Cassidy's sister died before they moved here. Gossip like that doesn't get swept under the rug in small towns like this. The word was that she got into an accident with her aunt—I'm assuming your mom—and never fully recovered."

"I can't believe you know about that. I didn't . . . I didn't think people knew about the accident. Oh my *God,* people are going to hate me before they even get to know me."

"One, I don't think anyone has put together that the driver was your mom. They likely never will. Hell, around here, people have five aunts and the same number of uncles.

Who's to say it was *your* mom driving the car? Two, let's get something straight here. You are not your mother. We are not our parents. Three, do you know how many skeletons people have tucked in their closets in this town?"

I thought of the letters I'd found in my closet.

"Everyone has their secrets, Grey, their demons. If people do link you to the accident, it will be gossip for a week, then forgotten. Trust me. And," he shrugged, "it might not be a bad thing. Unearthing it might make it go away—for you."

I thought on that a moment. "You might be right. I haven't talked about it since that day. My husband, ex-husband—God, I don't even know what to call him—doesn't even know about it. I've kept it locked away, deep inside me."

"Except it's not locked away, Grey. It's defining you. Don't be a victim. You're stronger than that."

A minute passed between us until I met his gaze again. "Want to know the whole story?"

"Yes."

I inhaled deeply, then told him everything that happened that day, from me seeing Brianna's body next to the front tire, to my mom getting hauled to jail, to the dissolution of our relationship after, and the guilt I still carry from allowing her to drive.

He blew out a breath. "Parents have an uncanny way of screwing kids up."

"Direct?"

"Direct."

"Etta implied that you had a rough childhood too."

"I thought you were going to be direct."

"Fine. She said your father was physically abusive to you."

"She was correct."

"I'm so sorry, Declan."

He let out a humorless laugh. "Me too."

"She also told me about the girl in the pond. Anna."

Something flickered behind his eyes as they met mine. If I wouldn't have been watching for a reaction, I would have missed it.

"Etta had a lot to say."

"She did."

"Did she tell you I killed Anna?"

"No."

"Did she imply it?"

"Yes."

He nodded, a muscle twitching in his jaw. "That day is my 'Brianna' day."

"Tell me."

"Not much to tell, despite what Etta had to say. I'd heard Anna had gone missing, and in an effort to help in the search, I went walking our land. I came to the pond."

A glaze slid over his eyes, his focus fading into the past.

"I remember that day so well. It was fall. The leaves had started changing. The afternoon was cool, mid-fifties. I remember it was the first day of the season that I wore a hoodie."

He shook his head. "Silly. Anyway. There was a strong breeze that day. The water rippled on the pond, like snakes over the black water. And then something . . . materialized, just below the surface. A figure. Her face, body, arms, distorted under the ripples. Her hair, snaking out of her head."

His voice cracked. "At first, I thought I was seeing things, like a horror movie, but then it was like the wind completely stopped. The water stilled, and I saw her, Anna, sinking back down into the pond. Her hand outstretched, as if she were grabbing for me . . . and I screamed. And the rest is history."

"Did you know her?"

"No. I didn't play with the other kids nearby. I wasn't exactly social. Anyway, the gossip mill started churning like crazy, and from that day forward, I was forever known as the guy that 'might' have killed Anna Hopkins."

"Did you kill her, Declan?"

"No. Do you believe me, Grey?"

"Yes."

"Good."

"Want to hear something crazy?" I asked.

"Bring it."

"I think she haunts my house."

"You think you have a ghost in your house?"

"I think I have *her* in my house."

"Who? Anna, specifically?"

"I think so."

"What makes you say that?"

"Weird things happen. Doors opening and closing, things being knocked off the countertops. And . . . there's giggles. Like a young girl's giggles."

Rolling his eyes, he said, "Giggles?"

I clucked my tongue. "I'm being serious here, Declan."

"Okay, okay. So, Anna Hopkins haunts your house."

"I think so, yes. You know how they say that ghosts are people with unfinished business here on earth?"

"I've heard."

"I think maybe she was drowned. Not by you, but by someone else. And she's hanging around until she gets justice."

"Until her murderer is caught?"

"Exactly."

"That was thirty years ago, Grey. *Thirty*."

"Not like she has a lot to do."

"Good point."

"Also," I said as I shifted in my seat, "I found some letters."

"Letters?"

"Yeah. Old ones. Between the walls."

Declan sat up, giving me his full attention now. "What kind of letters?"

"Creepy ones. Someone's journal, or a diary or something."

"Whose?"

I shrugged. "I don't know."

"What do they say?"

"The person, the writer, is going through some personal struggles."

"That's what diaries are for, I guess. You think it's Anna's or something? Is that where you're going with this?"

"No, I don't think they're hers." I paused, clamming up.

Where was I going with this? Did I think it was somehow connected? Did I want to go into all that? I didn't even know the exact time frame that the letters were written.

"Do you know who lived in my house during that time? That Anna drowned?" I asked, diverting from diving into the content of the letters.

"Oh." Declan squinted in deep thought. "A woman, I think. Not married. I can't remember the name."

"Bonnie?"

"That sounds right. Maybe. Or maybe she and her husband came not long after. Ask Etta. She was around then."

"I did. She can't remember."

"Makes two of us then. Like I said, I didn't really get to know my neighbors. People kind of stayed away from us."

"Because of your dad?"

Declan nodded.

"Do you think more people than Etta knew your dad was abusive?"

"I think so, but not to the extent. And no one knew how bad it got after the Anna incident. The beatings got worse. Everything seemed to get worse."

"Is this why you got into so much trouble as a kid?"

"Etta told you that too, huh?"

I nodded.

"Yes. That's why I started getting into fights at school. Dad would beat me every night, after his evening whiskey, and I'd retreat to my hiding spot under the bed, where I'd attempt to sleep. I literally had a bed under my bed. That's where I slept every night, with a pillow, a blanket, and a kitchen knife. My safe space, away from him. When I woke up each day, I had so much rage in my body, I couldn't control it. I didn't know how."

Declan pulled in a deep breath, his gaze unfocused. "So, I'd get myself ready for school, and then fight the first asshole I'd come across. Had nobody to teach me how to control my emotions. Things need to be taught. I've learned that. We're born with certain survival instincts but beyond that, it's on us—and those around us—to educate. To become the best humans we can be. I've always said teachers are the most important people on the planet."

"That's why you came over to teach me how to make chili. You've got a passion for teaching others, leading others, doing what should have been done for you. You like to teach."

"I guess so."

"You think your life could have been different if someone had taken you under their wing."

"I guess so."

"Like you're doing with me." I smiled, and he smiled back. "Where was your mom during all this?"

"Quiet. She faded into a shell of a person, like most abused women, I've learned. Like a robot, going through the motions day by day. It was her survival instinct."

"That's so sad. She never tried to step in while he hit you?"

"Once." His jaw clenched. "And she never did it again."

Understanding, I nodded. His gaze shifted to the windows. A moment passed between us.

"Dad hit me until I was fifteen years old. *Fifteen.* That's something, huh?"

I shook my head, my heart breaking.

"I hated him, and in the most ironic twist in the world, I then became him. Kind of like the way you felt tonight, with your mom. I used my fists, like he did, started drinking at age fourteen, like he did. Drank every day of my life until the day I turned thirty and turned my life around."

"Do you drink now?"

"Occasionally, yes, but not at first. I quit cold turkey. And then I realized it wasn't the booze that I needed to quit, it was the deep-seated anger inside me—the catalyst for the drinking. Once I let that go—the anger, the past, how I was victimizing myself—it was like I suddenly had a clean slate to work with. My soul was open to whatever I wanted to fill it with, so I filled it with work. I got this tattoo the day I quit drinking. Be on guard for myself, my demons, others wanting to wreck my progress. Be courageous. Be strong."

"But no love."

His head tilted to the side. "You've really latched onto that, haven't you?"

"Yes, I have. And I'm not entirely sure why."

"Well, I guess watching your dad beat your mom kinda messes with your perception of love. Want to know the catalyst for my dad becoming a raging alcoholic? When things got *really* bad?"

"Yes."

"The bankruptcy our family went through because of Lucas Covington's father's dirty business deal."

I sucked in a breath. That was the reason for the disdain he had for Lucas. It was personal. And it was deep.

"I'm so sorry. What was the deal?"

"Lucas's dad was born and raised around here. Once he started getting into real estate, he, my dad, and two of Lucas's dad's buddies bought a subdivision of apartments off Main Street to renovate. A big deal. Dad emptied our savings account and took out a loan to be a part of it. Spent the loan on materials—my dad was in construction. Six months in, Lucas's dad backed out, so the other two did as well. My dad was left with four half-renovated apartment buildings and no money and or collateral to get another loan to complete the project."

"Did he take him to court?"

"Tried, but Covington had so many damn lawyers, Dad just gave up. Shriveled away. Became an angry drunk until the day he died of a heart attack—two months after my mom died of breast cancer."

"I'm so, so sorry, Declan."

His eyes narrowed in warning. "That's the stock Lucas Covington comes from, Grey."

Message received.

A long moment passed before Declan said softly, "I like your shirt."

His soft, deep voice pulled me from my thoughts. I'd forgotten I was still wearing the shirt he'd left at my house.

I smiled, fingering one of the buttons. "Me too."

Declan pushed off the chair and closed the few feet between us. He put his hands on the armrests on either side of me and leaned down. "You scared me tonight, Grey."

"I scared myself," I whispered back, feeling that sting of tears again.

"Let's get ahold of it, okay?"

I took a deep breath. "Okay."

The ease with which he said it made it seem more attainable than if he'd launched into a twelve-step program.

Let's just get ahold of it.

Simple as that. Don't overcomplicate, don't overthink. Just get ahold of it.

I could do that.

"Good." Declan nodded to punctuate the decision that had just been made. He took the plate from my lap, set it aside, then grasped my hand. "Come on."

"Oh, but this chair is so comfortable."

"I know. Come on."

He pulled me up slowly, waiting while I found my footing.

I didn't protest or ask questions as I was led down the hall to his bedroom. I was too physically and mentally exhausted.

A dim lamp glowed from the nightstand, and a jar candle flickered on top of his dresser. A down comforter as white as snow glowed against dark hardwood floors and the posters of a king-size bed. A red wool blanket was folded on the end. The comforter had been pulled back, revealing sheets as white and soft as clouds. The shades were drawn.

"Beautiful room," I murmured. "Simple."

"I'm a simple man."

Our fingertips danced together as he led me to the bed and lowered me to a seated position. He knelt at my feet. One flip-flop was removed and the other, then my legs were lifted and tucked under the covers.

My body went limp as I fell back against the pillow. It was the most comfortable bed I'd ever laid on in my life.

And it smelled like him.

"I know I should be telling you not to go to all this trouble, that I should go home and take care of myself, or at the very least insist I sleep on the couch. But I don't want to leave right now." I reached out from the bed. "I don't want you to leave me, Declan."

His hand clasped mine. "I was never going to, Grey. Try to sleep."

He crossed the room and settled into an armchair in the corner. A moment passed as we stared at each other, saying everything with no words at all.

And with his watchful gaze on me, I fell fast asleep.

39

The next morning, I awoke to the smell of fresh coffee and sizzling bacon—and to a headache the size of a nuclear blast.

I pulled my knees up to my chest, cringing at the dull, stinging pain down my lower back. Frowning, I reached back and ran my fingertips over the deep scratches on my lower back that Lucas had left the night before, which had already scabbed over. He'd left his mark.

Hopefully, the scars were only skin deep.

Lucas had texted me five times after he'd left my house, while I was busy wrapping my car around a tree and being saved by Declan. One was a trio of flame emojis, indicating that he thought our six-minute rendezvous had been "hot." One asked if I was still awake. Another what I was doing the next day, and the last informed me that he'd stop by again soon.

His messages set off a little warning bell inside me. They felt a bit possessive and a bit clingy. I didn't answer a single one, and as I tried to calm my churning stomach, I knew I'd never answer another text from Lucas Covington.

Groaning, I squeezed my eyes shut and buried my head into Declan's pillow until the *whomp, whomp, whomp* of my pulse began to ease.

"Morning."

A pair of calloused fingertips smoothed my hair from my forehead. I rolled onto my back, wrinkling my nose with a pained expression.

Declan chuckled. "It'll pass. I've got more aspirin and a hearty breakfast to start."

"I'm not sure I can eat."

"Yes, you can. And you will. Now, do you want to lay here a bit longer—or do you want to go ahead and face this day?"

My heart swelled, a smile cracking my face. "Face the day."

"That's my girl. Come on, Lindsay. Up."

"*Not* funny."

"Sorry. I've got a bad habit of humor in the morning."

"Bad humor, you mean. Nothing about Lindsay Lohan is funny—to be clear."

"Noted. No Lindsay."

With my hands in his, I lifted my head from the pillow, sat on the edge of the bed, and then slowly stood.

"You okay?"

I nodded, swallowing a wave of nausea.

He slowly guided me into the kitchen, where a spread worthy of a five-star restaurant was laid out on his round dining table.

"Declan, you shouldn't—"

"Hush. Sit."

I sat, my gaze shifting to the misty morning outside. Rain streaked the windows against a backdrop of muted colors and shades of gray.

"Beautiful day." Declan scooped eggs and breakfast

potatoes onto my plate, followed by three slices of bacon and two slices of toast, pre-smeared with butter and jelly. Grape—exactly as I would have chosen.

"You seem like a sunny-day kind of guy. Not a rainy one."

"I like the rain. We usually need it in this neck of the woods. I'm sure your new lavender bushes are loving it."

My breath hitched with a spark of excitement. "My distillery is supposed to be delivered today."

He frowned, freezing in mid-scoop. "Call me crazy, but doesn't an in-home distillery kind of goes against our sobriety conversation last night?"

I laughed. "No, not for booze. For essential oil. I'm extracting from the plants."

His brows lifted as he settled into the seat across from me, his plate overflowing with protein. "No kidding. What are you planning to use it for?"

I shrugged as I added an extra squeeze of honey to my coffee before stirring it. "Not sure yet. I've got to get the process down first. But I've got some ideas."

"I can show you how to infuse too."

"I'd like that, Mr. Montgomery."

He winked. "It's a plan. For now, eat."

I forced the first few bites in my mouth, and to my utter shock, inhaled the rest, making me wonder exactly how much I'd thrown up the night before.

Once I'd cleaned my plate, I sat back with my hand on my stomach. "I have a confession."

"Shoot," he said, biting into his fourth piece of bacon.

"I threw out the chili."

His brow cocked. "This does not please me, Grey."

"I know." I grimaced. "I'm sorry."

He shrugged. "Guess you'll have to make another pot."

"I will. Promise. Aren't you going to ask me why?"

Lowering his fork, he focused on me. "No. You weren't thinking clearly last night. We've already covered that."

"It was because I was mad at you," I said, even though he didn't push. "And your ability to see right through me. You make me feel vulnerable, Declan."

"I know the feeling," he said, eyeing me over the rim of his cup.

It was a thinly veiled confession of whatever was happening between us. Something I was far from ready to label, but something I couldn't ignore. Something neither of us could.

I thought of Lucas inside me, and my gut twisted with guilt. I set down my toast.

"How are you feeling now?" Declan asked. "After eating."

"Better."

"Good. Because we've got somewhere to be."

"Wh—what?"

"Yep. And although I love the way you look in my shirt, the fact that you're in it will get the rumor mill going overtime. I don't mind much, but you don't need that right now."

"We're going into town? In *public*? You're wanting to take me into public *today*?" I swept a hand over the mess of my appearance. "You're wanting to take *all this* into town today?"

"That's right." He stood and began gathering the plates. "In an hour, exactly."

"Where?"

"The doctor."

"What? No. No way. You told me last night I wasn't hurt. I'm not hurt."

"Not a body doctor."

I frowned, pushing up from the chair.

"A head doctor." He turned on the faucet and began rinsing the plates.

"*What?* No. *Way.*" I crossed the kitchen with a burst of energy. "You are *not* taking me to a therapist."

"A psychologist. And yes I am." His defiant gaze met mine.

"No." I crossed my arms over my chest.

He dropped the silverware in the sink and turned fully to me. "You told me you were ready to face the day. *This* day."

"I am, and I meant it. But . . . a *psychologist,* Declan?"

"You told me you need to be fixed. I don't take that lightly. Grey, I fix things. I told you that last night. This is part of your fixing. I'll be with you. By your side, if you want. You will not be alone. You're going to try this—openminded, openhearted. If you hate it, we won't go back."

I groaned, scrubbing my hands over my face. "Where's my car?"

"Towed already. Kai took care of it."

"What time is it?"

"Eight thirty."

"You seriously made an appointment for me for today already?"

"I know the doctor's husband. I texted him."

"You know her hus—" I stopped because it didn't matter. I began pacing, my thoughts racing. "Have you ever been to a psychologist, Declan?" I snapped out.

"No. Have you?" He loaded the plates in the dishwasher, unfazed by my childish freak-out.

"No. And tell me, why haven't you?"

"I don't know. Doesn't really feel comfortable spilling my guts to a total stranger."

I threw my hands into the air. "Exactly!"

"Yeah, but girls are better about that kind of stuff than guys. Talking about emotions and stuff." He clicked on the dishwasher and turned to me.

"Are you seriously going there right now? You chauvinistic son of a—"

"Look, I'm just saying when something needs to be fixed, I peel it back layer by layer, ripping apart the engine, if you will. Then I examine the pieces, see what needs to be fixed, replaced, assessed. I put in the work, then put everything back together, and ten times out of ten, it runs better than ever."

Listening, I stopped pacing.

"If there's anything I learned from my dad, it's that there's always something deeper than the obvious issue. A catalyst behind the drinking that needs to be addressed. For him, it was the failure of letting his family down, losing everything. He blamed himself. For you, I'm guessing it's your mom and this whole Brianna thing. It simply needs to be examined deeper instead of covered with a Band-Aid. That's what this psychologist will help with."

I groaned again.

"Stop, Grey. Take the emotions out of it, the fear. Everything you want is on the other side of fear. Don't let it rule you. You've gone to the doctor for viruses, a stomachache, your sinuses maybe, right?"

I nodded.

"Just think of this as going to the doctor for a checkup of the biggest muscle in your body—your brain. It's as simple as that, and only as complicated or dramatic as you make it."

It made too much sense to ignore.

I began pacing again. "*Shit,* Dec. Can I call you Dec? I'm calling you Dec. *Shit,* Dec." I spun around, facing him.

"Okay. I have to say this. Don't overstep lines. I don't like it when people overstep their lines with me. Okay?"

"Maybe you need it."

I rolled my eyes.

"Did I overstep a line with you this morning, Grey?"

Groaning again, I turned away. "No. No, you didn't. Fine. *Shit.* Okay. I need to shower. *Shit*, Dec."

"Now where's your Northern accent when you need one?"

"Not the time for jokes. *Shit, Dick.*"

He chuckled. "Go to the bathroom for whatever women do in the mornings. I'll meet you outside in five minutes. We'll go to your house, you'll shower, then we'll go."

"I hate you."

"No, you don't."

Sprinkles of rain dotted the windshield as we rolled to a stop next to a sign that read ROSE FLOWER CENTER FOR COUNSELING.

"Rose *Flower?*" I gave him the side-eye.

"Chick's as smart as a whip. Trust me. She worked for one of the biggest clinics in the area, Harold and Associates, before starting her own business. Ran an insanely popular psych podcast before that."

"Seems like you know her well."

He laughed. "Not like that. Like I said, she's married to a buddy of mine, Phoenix Steele. He and his brothers own a private security firm in the middle of the mountains."

"Steele Shadows Security. I've heard of it."

"Everyone has. They're known worldwide. Good people. And so is she. I trust him, and I trust her with you. Oh, and

FYI, Phoenix says she can be pretty blunt in sessions, doesn't sugarcoat things, but I figured that was okay because it sure sounds like someone else I know." He smirked.

"Blunt's good. *Heyyy.*" A mischievous smile crossed my lips. "Speaking of . . ."

"*No.* Pot is not part of the recovery process. Trust me."

I laughed, and it felt good.

"I like your laugh."

"I like you making me laugh."

"Enjoy it while it lasts. My humor's usually tapped out by lunchtime."

I clasped the handle on the passenger door. "Let's do this thing."

As we stepped out of the truck and into a blast of chilly air, Declan said, "Storm's coming."

I looked at the brooding sky above. "Looks like it's already here."

"Rain today, storms tomorrow."

Rain today.

I stopped at the sidewalk, staring at the front door of the clinic as an inmate might the moment they saw the cuffs on the table.

Declan slid his hand into mine. "One step at a time, Grey."

"One step at a time," I repeated.

I took a deep breath, squared my shoulders, and with Declan by my side, took that first step.

40

The rain had turned into a steady deluge by the time my hour was up with Rose Steele.

Five minutes in, I'd decided her name was ironic. As Declan had warned, there was nothing delicate about the therapist named Rose. She was a no-small-talk, no-bullshit kind of gal. In fact, Rose was a confident, smart, direct, and extremely competent type of woman.

I liked her instantly.

The session wasn't a "tell me how you feel about that" type of environment. Instead, Rose took a teaching approach by explaining the body's response to stress and emotional assaults, and how this can have long-term effects on the body. She broke it all down in bite-sized pieces so it was easy to understand.

Rose interjected scientific facts and figures into her therapy—proof, if you will. Much like Declan, the woman made too much sense to ignore.

She kept me on topic, steering me back when I strayed or got nervous. She exposed me, stripped me raw, much like

Declan had, but explained to me that the feelings I was having were all part of the process. All part of healing.

After suggesting that we meet three times a week for three months, then reassess, she and I said our farewells. On shaky legs, I stepped into the lobby where Declan was waiting for me with a smile on his face and a gift in his hand.

I wasn't alone.

I smiled. "Whatcha got?"

His eyes twinkled. "A little something I picked up next door."

"Yeah?"

"Yeah."

"Well . . . can I see it?"

He handed the gift to me.

I turned it over in my hands, cocking my head as I eyed him. "Wow, Declan, you're a really good gift wrapper."

"You think a mechanic can't wrap gifts?"

"I think those sausage fingers of yours can't make a fancy bow like this to save your life."

He lifted his hands and wiggled his fingers. "Making fancy bows aren't the only thing these fingers can do."

I cocked my brow and smirked. "Noted."

"Open it."

Standing in the middle of Rose's lobby, with my pride somewhere on the floor, I pulled apart a beautiful pink bow and carefully unwrapped the white and gold foil paper—and laughed so hard, it echoed off the walls.

"You like?" Declan's boyish grin stretched from ear to ear.

"Uh . . ." I wiped tears from my eyes, blinking at the half-naked cowboy on the cover of a calendar titled *Studs-N-Spurs*. "I love it."

"Joanna, the gift shop owner, helped me pick it out."

I snorted. "I'll bet she did."

"Confession. She also wrapped it."

"I knew you didn't wrap it." I flipped quickly through the pages. "Okay, explain, cowboy."

"Well, I was thinking it could be a calendar to mark your progress. Each day without a drink, you mark the day. Celebrate it. That way your success doesn't get lost in the daily shuffle—it's right there in front of you." He tilted my chin up. "To remind you how fucking badass you are, Grey Dalton."

Smiling, I sighed. "That's actually extremely thoughtful."

"Thanks. I had to stretch after."

I laughed again and refocused on the half-naked cowboys. "But wouldn't a calendar of cute little puppies or rainbows go with my kitchen better than nipples and happy trails? Not that I'm complaining."

"I wanted something that would catch your eye every day. Joanna promised this'll do it."

"Mission accomplished." I nodded, chuckling. "Good job, Dec. Thank you."

"Use it."

"I will."

"Ready to go?"

"Ready."

With one hand gripped around the photo of a shirtless cowboy and the other secured in Declan's palm, I walked with him out of the clinic.

Declan didn't press me on the drive back. He knew the last thing I needed at that moment was more talking. I needed silence.

As we drove through the rain, my thoughts fixed on

Rose's comment that success in sobriety is much more likely —and happens much more quickly—if I have a solid support network. Friends or family who I'm honest with, who I admit to that I have a problem—unlike I did with Cassidy at the bar, Rose pointed out. Instead of trying to convince myself I was strong enough to go to a bar and not have a drink, I should have admitted to Cassidy that I'm an alcoholic and can't be around others who drink. Better yet, I shouldn't have gone at all.

Rose suggested I remove the emotions from the admission, when I chose to make it. Keep it short and sweet. An informative statement rather than one that felt like defeat or weakness. She suggested I simply tell people my issue in two short sentences, as unemotionally as if we were talking about the weather, and then move on.

"They'll only make as big a deal of it as you do," she said. "You'll lose ninety percent of your friends and family, but the ten percent who stick with you will be by your side until the end. Ride or die."

Ride or die, I thought as I waved from the front porch while Declan's truck disappeared into a blur of rain as he backed down my driveway. He had work that he couldn't shuffle, but promised to be back soon.

After checking on my lavender bushes, I made my way inside, closed the door, and leaned my weight against the cool wood. Inhaling deeply, I breathed in the silence. The hangover was fading, and I had no doubt it had something to do with the amount of food Declan forced me to eat for breakfast. I was thankful.

When I opened my eyes, my bedroom door was in my line of sight, and the momentary peace I'd felt suddenly shattered. A bad vibe gripped me.

Bad juju.

I pushed off the door, walking with purpose to the bedroom where not twelve hours earlier, Lucas had bent me over my bed.

A bad, bad vibe.

I yanked the damn brand-new comforter from the bed, ripped off the sheets and pillowcases, and wadded them up. Tripping on the trail of fabric, I stomped outside and shoved them into the trash can. With that task done, I inhaled deeply, wiping my palms together.

Good riddance.

Feeling a burst of positivity—of hopefulness—I turned on some up-tempo dance music and surveyed the mess of the living room.

Rose's voice echoed in my head. *"Stay busy, stay focused. Projects are good."*

My phone beeped from the countertop. The smile from thinking the new text was from Declan quickly faded when I saw Lucas's name.

Lucas: I want to see you.
Lucas: I'm leaving town soon.
Lucas: Need my fix before I leave. [Wink emoji, Flame emoji]
Lucas: Maybe I can stop by?
Lucas: I'll make it worth your while. [Wink/kiss emoji]

My stomach flipped while I read the flurry of texts. Not in a good way, in an uneasy way. A red-flag kind of way.

As rain pelted the windows next to me, I stared at my phone, trying to decide my next move. A voice in my head told me to tell him I want nothing to do with him anymore. Another voice told me to ignore him, and I went with the latter.

I should have gone with the former. I know that now.

A knock sounded at the door.

I jumped, spinning around toward it. I checked my phone, expecting to see an *I'm outside your door* text from Lucas, and was relieved when there was none.

I slid the phone on the counter and silently crossed the room to peek out the window. A tall, muscular man with boxes stacked in his hands shifted impatiently on the welcome mat. His salt-and-pepper hair curled above the collar of his brown uniform.

Pulling in a breath, I opened the door. "Hey, there."

"Packages for a Miss Dalton."

A smile spread across my face as I took the boxes from the deliveryman's hands. My essential-oil distillery kit.

"Thank you."

"Ma'am." He tipped his head and jogged back to his delivery van with speed and agility that gave me no question where his trim figure came from.

I kicked the door closed behind me and hurried to the kitchen counter. Like a kid on Christmas morning, I ripped open the boxes, Styrofoam popcorn and packaging pillows raining down around me.

I marveled at the contents as one might a newborn baby. It was beautiful, glowing copper—with about a million different parts that included tubes, pipes, and many, many small pieces.

I blew out a breath. It would be the largest, most intricate puzzle I would ever put together.

Projects are good.

"Okay then, Miss Rose Flower." I rubbed my palms together. "Here's my project of the day. Let's do this."

~

It took me three hours to put the thing together, using a folding table that I'd set up in the corner of the kitchen as ground zero.

Once I was sure everything was assembled and placed, I dug in, spending an hour reading the manual and learning how to use the distiller, and then another hour writing down ideas and dozens of different recipes for body butter as they came to me. I needed to go to the store for supplies, but without a car, my options were limited.

Needing something to do, I checked on the oil I'd started in the Crock-Pot the day before. As expected for a first attempt, the quality was poor. Regardless, it gave me something to experiment with. I was on to something. I felt it in my bones.

I avoided my bedroom. Not only because of the bad vibes lingering from what I'd done with Lucas there, but because I was fighting an urge to search for more letters. Fighting the urge to slip back into that darkness that somehow brought out the worst in me.

I'd have to completely renovate the room, I decided. Rearrange furniture. More windows, more light.

Maybe use some of that sage Etta had talked about.

It was just past one in the afternoon by the time I pulled myself away from my "mad scientist lab," as I'd dubbed the entire left side of my kitchen, and decided to take a coffee break.

I glanced outside, pleased to see a momentary break in the rain. The clouds had separated, allowing blinding beams of sunlight to shoot through the trees. The leaves glittered with raindrops.

After pouring my coffee in a travel mug, I grabbed a jacket, pulled on my rain boots—muck boots, according to Declan—and went outside. The temperature had lifted with the sun, its golden rays like a warm blanket. I tossed my jacket over the deck railing and left it there, wanting to feel the heat on my skin.

Moonshine and Company met me as I stepped off the back porch. We'd made major strides in the last few days.

"Hey, Mama."

Her fur was matted with rain, her paws dipped in mud. Her babies were much the same. They were such a hot mess, they made me laugh.

I squatted down and reached out my hand. Instead of her usual "hiss and dart" reaction, Moonshine froze, and her babies followed suit.

Smiling, I waited, then dropped my hand when she didn't approach.

"Progress." I stood. "Wanna go for a walk?"

She blinked.

"It's really pretty outside. I love the smell of the lingering rain. I'm going through the woods for a bit. Come on, take a walk with me."

Moonshine angled her head, a queen assessing her servant.

I laughed. "All right, fine. Grace me with your presence, or don't. Totally up to you."

Coffee in hand, I walked through the yard, avoiding the puddles before chancing a glance behind me. Four balls of black fur followed from a safe distance.

My heart swelled. Definitely progress.

I took a deep breath, inhaling the fresh scent of a rainy forest in springtime.

Birds had made their way out from cover, singing loudly

and swooping through the trees, looking for worms that had risen through the mud. A pair of squirrels zipped up a pine tree next to me. I took another deep breath, imagining the fresh air cleansing my lungs, my body, my heart.

Reflective, I slowly strolled through the woods, taking the same path I'd chosen when I'd taken cookies and tea to my neighbor, not realizing that neighbor was Declan. How things had changed since then.

As I strolled along the ravine, I noticed a new small stream running along the bottom. A breeze blew raindrops down from the trees onto my shoulders.

I looked over my shoulder at Moonshine and her kittens, playing in the leaves. When I turned back, I gasped.

My jaw dropped at the newly constructed swing bridge swaying in the breeze—less than a foot from the fallen tree I'd used to cross onto Declan's land.

"Not sure I like you dancing across that tree. Long way down."

Declan's voice echoed through my head along with a flutter in my stomach. Nerves—*happy* nerves. Excited nerves. Something that felt a hell of a lot like feelings.

If I had to guess, Declan had built the bridge the very next day.

"Moonshine, look." I beamed like a schoolgirl. "He built me a bridge."

The cat blinked at the structure, surprised at the intrusion in her woods.

"Come on."

Light on my feet, I jogged along the ravine, grinning like a total idiot. Like a lovestruck pre-teen.

My phone beeped, alerting me to a new text message.

Declan: Sun's out. Take a break. Go for a walk.

Me: If only I had a bridge to dance on.
Declan: Found it, huh?

I clicked over to my camera and took a beaming-smile selfie with the bridge in the background. I looked like crap, but I didn't care. It was me—whoever that was now. Me—raw and exposed, for better or worse.

Declan: Beautiful. Didn't have that much sparkle when I built it.
Me: I can't believe you built a bridge.
Declan: Confession, I can fix anything but broken bones. I told you I didn't like you crossing that tree.
Me: That's the only reason you built it, huh? [Wink emoji]
Declan: That, and I really do like you bringing me cookies—maybe yours instead of Etta's next time. [Wink emoji]
Me: Oh, the pressure.
Declan: Practice makes perfect. Master the chili first, then the cookies. How are you feeling?
Me: Great.
Declan: I thought we always promised to be direct?
Me: Fine. I'm decent—that's an honest answer. Staying on top of the aspirin and staying busy.
Declan: Busy is good. Get that fresh air. Meditate or something.
Me: You don't even know what meditation is.
Declan: I saw it on a poster in Rose's waiting room.
Me: Next to a Studs and Spurs calendar?
Declan: No, that was in the gift shop. This was next to a Kate Upton calendar.
Me: You like Kate Upton, huh?
Declan: Wouldn't kick her out of bed.
Me: So that's your type?
Declan: You mean big boobs, big ass, modern-day Marilyn Monroe?

Me: Exactly.
Declan: Not really. I kind of have a thing for recovering alcoholics who look like Shania Twain. Know any?
Me: Note to self: Buy cowboy hat and leopard-print body suit. STAT.
Declan: And boots. Red ones. And matching tassels—placement optional.

Blushing, I smiled.

Me: How's my car?
Declan: Working on it. Stop worrying about it.

I looked at the bridge.

Me: Thank you, Declan.
Declan: Breathe, New York. You've got this.

I inhaled deeply, held it, and exhaled.

Declan: Talk soon.
Me: [Heart emoji]

I shoved the phone into my pocket and secured my coffee mug between the snarled roots of a tree.

"You first or me?" I asked the crew behind me.

Four pairs of eyes stared at me in horror.

"Okay, fine," I said with a laugh. "Me first."

I wrapped my fingers around the corded metal handrail, damp with rain, cool to the touch. Then I placed my foot on the first wood slat, strong, thick, without a single nick, knot, or crack on it. Holding my breath, I released my weight and took another step.

Grinning like a Cheshire cat, I crossed the bridge, imagining I was a fairy princess with glorious wings to fly on the wind. Back and forth I went, losing myself in imagination. In nature.

Moonshine and the gang became bored with my immature whimsy and sauntered away sometime after the fourth crossing. I crossed the bridge eight times that day, my smile never once wavering.

41

The next few days passed quickly.

When I wasn't immersed in my essential oil project, I was cleaning, organizing, and decorating, only coming up for air when Etta or Cassidy would swing by to gossip, or when Declan would come by to check on me.

His unannounced visits were, by far, my favorite. Two mornings, two evenings, and one lunch after taking me to my second appointment at the Rose Flower Center for Counseling. Each day, we'd mark the calendar, celebrating another day of sobriety—together.

Whatever was happening between Declan and me was building, electrifying, with each visit. I'd begun to dream of him not only at night, but during my daytime strolls through the woods.

I had a crush. A big, hairy, monster of a crush.

So, what did I do? I stayed busy. I occupied my thoughts by occupying my hands, every second of the day.

If I stopped and found myself drifting, spiraling, I knew to replay the visits with the therapist in my head—what she said, what I said, what I should have said, etc. Because if I didn't, I'd worry.

I'd worry about my sobriety, or my car. I'd dissect my mistakes, thinking of Lucas, the letters in the walls, my failed marriage, my uncertain future. Finally, I'd begin counting the moments until Declan wised up and realized what a total train wreck I was, and then walked out of my life for good. That was possibly my biggest worry.

So, I was a machine, going full speed from dusk until dawn, pushing everything else aside other than being productive.

Lucas had sent me a text every day, none of which I'd responded to. The man was committed. To what, though, I wasn't sure. I was just thankful he hadn't stopped by. According to the texts, he'd be leaving soon. Honestly, that departure couldn't come quick enough.

I'd slept on the couch the last two nights, avoiding the bedroom, where I'd yet to replace the sheets and comforter that I'd thrown out after Lucas had sex with me in it.

It had rained on and off, the temperatures rising and falling with each storm. Volatile weather, but beautiful all the same.

I'd just checked my latest invention, a yet-to-be-named organic lavender-infused body butter, when my stomach growled, reminding me I'd skipped lunch.

I ate lunch on the deck, watching the next round of storms roll in. After tending to my distillery, I found myself looking for what to do next. I needed a break from the cleaning, organizing, and decorating.

Rose's words echoed in my ear. "*Plan for the future.*"

The future.

I made another cup of coffee, then gathered notebook paper, a few cardboard boxes, pens, markers, tape, and a handful of magazines. Slowly climbing the stairs, I headed to the mystery room upstairs, balancing my speaker and cell phone on top of everything.

Once I'd unloaded everything in the middle of the room, I kicked out of my sneakers and lowered myself to the floor, crisscrossing my legs.

I didn't know much about vision boards, but Rose had suggested I make one. She advised me not to get too caught up on what it should be, and simply go with inspiration. If something caught my eye, add it, she'd said. Its meaning would most likely reveal itself later.

With dance music on full blast and caffeine pumping through my veins, I got started.

I cut up the cardboard boxes and made a large board by taping together the pieces. Then I flipped through the magazines, cutting, pasting, thinking, dreaming. Cutting letters, creating words, thoughts, headlines, pasting each on the cardboard.

Slowly, the board transformed from a drab brown to an explosion of color from landscape scenery, plants, and flowers. I'd pieced together the word strong. Next to that, a cash symbol, a cartoon diamond, and a sports car—stability and success, I assumed was where I was going with that montage. In the center, I glued a curious mix of images that included lavender, oils in little jars, a baby in a diaper, a rattle.

Purple, purple, purple.

Ideas rapidly formed in my head, and I grabbed a pen and paper and began scribbling.

Chewing on my bottom lip, I studied the heart I'd glued

in a corner. Next to it was a cabin, and then an image of a heart in the palm of a hand. Each image was glued above the page number of the magazine I'd cut it from—171. Below that, a hand-drawn picture of a dove and part of an article dated 6/13.

171
613
171613

I blinked and pulled back, my breath catching in my throat. *Declan's tattoo—First Corinthians, sixteen, thirteen.* Below those images, I'd pasted a single word—faith.

A little tingle filled my heart as I stared, shocked at the message I'd unknowingly created.

Just then, a repetition of loud knocks came from downstairs.

I looked over my shoulder, glanced back down at the board, then pushed myself off the floor and jogged down the steps. I was expecting Etta. Declan would be a welcome surprise.

But I didn't get either.

"Suit up, New York. Class starts in twenty."

Kai stood on the other side of the door, dressed in head-to-toe black spandex. Her black hair was swept into a bun on top of her head. The tattoos I'd noticed before on her arms ran up her shoulders and onto her back.

I gave her a once-over. "You look like Maleficent and Travis Barker had a kid."

"You look like Meghan Markle and Courtney Love had a kid."

"Pre- or post-princess?"

"Post. Definitely. You've still got that snooty city-girl

about you, but you look like hell. Seriously, I've got a jug of latex paint in my trunk I can smear over those circles under your eyes."

"Thanks."

"Come on. We're late." She impatiently checked her black wristwatch. "Go get dressed in your designer matching Pilates leotard, or whatever."

"Late? For what?"

"Zumba."

"Oh, *hell* no. I don't Zumba."

"You're Zumba-ing, whether you like it or not."

"With who?"

She opened her arms.

I blinked at her. "You want to Zumba with me?"

"Not really. But Declan does."

"I'm not following here, Kai. What's going on?"

"Listen. Declan's track record with women is about as successful as your ability to take a sharp curve. No offense."

"None taken. That tree came out of nowhere. So you're saying you're vetting me, making sure I'm good enough for your boss. That, or Declan asked you to come check on me."

Kai innocently shrugged. "Hey, I'm just getting to know the new girl in town."

"I have a feeling your typical greeting involves a paint gun."

She laughed at this. "Come on. I don't like to be late. Seriously."

"I feel like shit, Kai."

"Exercise helps. Let's go."

"I can't believe you're here."

"Neither can I."

"I'll make a deal with you."

"I don't do deals."

"I highly doubt that. I'll go to stupid Zumba, if you take me to the market after."

"Why?"

"I need a few things."

"For what?"

"Something."

Her black eyes narrowed. "Something what?"

"A project."

"I'll take you if you tell me what this project is."

"God, you're stubborn."

"And in good company, according to Declan."

"Fine. I'm making aromatherapy products."

Frowning, she jerked her head back, as if I'd just advocated for tighter gun restrictions. "That's weird."

"Thanks for your support."

"How do you make aromatherapy products?"

"With essential oils."

"Just use the oil from your forehead. Seriously, why are you so sweaty?"

Annoyed, I started to close the door, but Kai thwarted the attempt with the toe of her shoe.

"Fine. I'll take you to the market for your aromatherapy shit. Let's go. Go change."

"Come in. Try not to rub your tattoos on anything."

She *really* laughed at that one.

Five minutes later, I slid into the passenger side of Kai's vintage Corvette. "Seriously, did Declan ask you to do this?"

"Seriously, no." Kai started down the driveway.

"So you're vetting me. Did he tell you everything?"

"No." She gave me the side eye. "And that was the final red flag, so to speak."

"Flag?"

"Yeah. The first red flag was when he asked me to shuffle around some appointments so he could fix some Yankee's fancy BMW. Declan doesn't shuffle appointments. He sets them and keeps his word. The second was when he told me not to bill you. Declan doesn't do anything for free. The third was when he texted me at one in the morning, asking me to get my ass out of bed and tow a fancy BMW to the shop—not so fancy anymore. The fourth was when he informed me he'd be late to work that day. Declan never misses work. The final red flag was when he stuttered like a freaking schoolboy when I asked him what was going on between you two. Dec doesn't lie to me."

"Kai," I deadpanned as we pulled onto the main road. "I'm a raging alcoholic whore who's recently decided to turn her life around."

Kai looked over at me. The corner of her lip curled up. "I like you, New York. Fix your shit and don't hurt my boy. That's it. That's all I want from you. He's a good man and has taken a liking to you—for reasons beyond me. No offense."

"None taken, trust me.

"More than that, though, I think. More than liking, I think. Fix you, fix him. Just don't hurt him. You understand me?"

Don't hurt him.

I sighed. "Why is it that being sober sometimes feels more daunting than the mistakes I make when drunk?"

"Drinking makes you forget things. Sober makes you address them." Kai flicked on her turn signal and pulled into a small parking lot on the side of a beautiful plantation-style home. "Exercise helps the addressing."

"This it?"

"Yep. The instructor is a retired teacher. Does classes all day long in her guest house. But don't let the teacher thing fool you—the woman is the devil herself disguised in self-tanner and double-Ds. I've literally seen her whip someone."

Trying to dredge up a comeback, I stared out the windshield. A dozen women made their way to a small building behind the magnificent home. They were smiling, laughing. Beautiful, skinny women. Happy, carefree. All friends, I assumed.

My stomach flip-flopped.

"I don't Zumba, Kai."

"You'll learn. And maybe make some friends while you're at it. Ready?"

Nodding, I blew out a breath. "*Dammit*. Ready."

42

Declan's truck was parked in my driveway when Kai and I returned from seventy-five minutes of hell, otherwise known as Zumba, followed by a trip to the market to gather more supplies for my essential oil project. The rain had started up again, a cool drizzle against a darkening afternoon.

His tailgate was down. A toolbox teetered on the edge, with dozens of shiny tools scattered on the truck's bed and on the ground. A shiny black four-wheeler was parked on the side.

Kai shook her head. Sweaty strands of hair stuck to the sides of her cheeks where her eyeliner had melted off. I liked her even more that she didn't care.

"Yeah, more than like, I think," she muttered, rolling her eyes.

My heart fluttered as Declan emerged from the side of the house after hearing us pull up. A smile spread across his face. His usual gray T-shirt was saturated with rain, tucked into a tool belt around his waist. Dirty jeans and combat boots completed the sexy-carpenter look.

Sexy. As. Hell.

"Wednesday at four, next class." Kai shoved the car into reverse, waiting for me to get out.

"I'll be there with bells on."

Kai grinned at Declan through the windshield before backing down the drive.

His smile widened as he closed the few feet between us.

Normally, I'd shield myself from the rain, or dart under the porch to keep from getting wet. Instead, I welcomed the cool drops against my heated skin. Besides, I literally couldn't look worse.

"How was it?" he asked.

I swept a hand up and down my body, the cotton tank I'd worn sticking to me like glue. "Hot."

"Couldn't have said it better myself." His eyes sparkled as they focused on my nipples, perky from the cool breeze.

"You knew what Kai was up to?"

"I had a suspicion."

"Give a gal a heads-up next time, will ya?"

"And ruin a surprise? No way."

"Speaking of surprises . . . what are you doing here?"

"Stuff."

"What kind of stuff?"

"Manly stuff."

"Eating chips in bed and using your neck hole to pull off your T-shirt?"

He laughed. "I totally do that."

"Not surprised. No wonder you buy undershirts in bulk." My focus dropped to his waistband. "You look kinda hot in a tool belt."

"You look kinda hot in spandex." He playfully flicked my ear, sending tingles down my neck. "Kai treat you okay?"

"About as good as a junkyard dog."

"So, not good?"

"No, fine. I'm joking. I actually like her. She's very protective of you, though."

"Always has been. She's that type. Kai has few people in her life that she trusts, and she guards those relationships with an iron fist."

"I'm beginning to understand that type of mentality."

"It's not a bad thing to clean out your social closet every now and again."

"You sound like Rose."

"I'll take that as a compliment."

"Who else is here?" I nodded to the four-wheeler.

"That's your ride until I get your car done."

Brows raised, I walked over to the black beast and ran my fingertip along the wet seat. "She's a beaut, but I don't need her. Really. I plan to stay home."

"Just in case. I filled it up too, cleaned it up—and the rain is getting what I missed. Only the best for Grey."

"Can it make it to town?"

"Technically, yes. But I don't want you driving it on the highway. It can make it to my house or the shop, and I'll take you to town if you need it. Come on. I want to show you something before the rain picks up."

"A surprise?" I asked as we fell into step together.

"It's not jewelry. I can promise you that. You'll see. So, how you doing? Really?"

"Good. Really. I organized, cleaned, put together my oil kit, and I danced on a bridge." I winked. "I also started a vision board."

"What's a vision board?"

"Something to keep me focused on my goals, per Rose. Or maybe show me ones I didn't know I had."

"I'd like to see it."

"Yeah?"

"Yeah."

"Well, I'd like to see what you're doing on the backside of my house."

My eyes widened as we rounded the corner to the back of my home. Where was once a row of smudged, cracked windows was now new windows, as clear as a mirror, reflecting the dark clouds moving swiftly overhead. A ladder leaned against the side of the house, more tools scattered below it.

"Declan." Blinking in shock, I gaped at the sight.

"Storms are coming. Bad ones. I told you the windows you had weren't safe, especially with these untrimmed trees. These are. Come here."

Still gawking at the house, I stepped next to him. A rumble of thunder sounded in the distance.

"These are fiberglass windows," he said. "They're strong, durable, better insulation for energy and noise control. You know, for all those parties you plan to throw for your new friends. They'll last up to fifty years. I still have to paint the trim, but they'll get you through this round of storms. Oh, and they also flip down so you can clean the outside easily."

"I can't believe you did this."

"It needed to get done, so it's done."

"That simple, huh?"

"I wouldn't say simple."

"You did all this in three hours?"

"Not my first time switching out windows."

"How much do I owe you?"

"I already had some of the materials, left over from when I renovated my house years ago."

"How much do I owe you?" I repeated.

"Ten therapy sessions."

"Huh?"

"You, continuing therapy with Rose for ten more sessions. That's how you can pay me."

I sighed. "Declan, you don't have to do all this. I can do it. I can manage."

He turned fully toward me as huge raindrops began to splat on our shoulders. "I want to." Stepping closer, he tipped up my chin and whispered, "God's honest truth."

Butterflies flapped wildly in my stomach. My throat tightened as we stared at each other.

Kiss me, I begged silently under the raindrops. *Kiss me.*

His gaze dropped to my lips, and my heart kick-started with anticipation. But instead of kissing me, he dropped his hand from my face and took a step back with a hint of torture behind his eyes.

Why? Why was he holding back?

I was left breathless, unstable with the realization of how badly I wanted Declan to kiss me.

The bottom fell out of the clouds above us, pouring buckets of water onto our heads. Declan grabbed my hand, breaking the moment, and we jogged through the sheets of rain and into the house.

Laughing, I wiped the rain from my skin as Declan tossed me a towel I kept on the windowsill for moments like this. Many, over the last week—minus the almost-kiss.

As Declan wiped his boots, I beelined it to look out of my brand-new windows.

"They're so beautiful." I ran my finger along the trim.

"I'm hungry," Declan blurted from the entryway. "You?"

I looked over my shoulder to find him staring at me. "Starved, actually."

"Zumba."

I nodded. "Zumba."

"Good. Be right back."

Declan turned and disappeared out the front door. Confused, I watched him jog across the driveway. He quickly pulled something from his truck, then hurried back.

"What's . . ." I pulled in a breath, enveloped in the scent of cheese, Italian spices, and warm bread. "Pizza."

"Hope you like pepperoni."

"I love pepperoni."

"Good. It's still warm. Marge gave me one of those travel thermal sleeves. Where do you want it?"

"In my mouth."

He wiggled his eyebrows at this, and I laughed.

Like a starving dog, I followed him to the kitchen. "You can put it on the counter. Tea?"

"Sure. Sugar."

"How much?"

"Tablespoon."

Declan grabbed two plates and a roll of paper towels, and we settled onto the bar stools Abe had delivered earlier that day.

Rain pounded the windows and the roof above, a calming background noise as we talked about our day, about Zumba, and about my oil distillery kit. Much like our chili dinner, the pizza was enjoyed over smooth, casual, light conversation.

Darkness had fallen by the time we finished.

"I want to see that vision board."

"Really?" To my surprise, my stomach clenched. There was something intimate—very private—about the board.

"Really."

"Okay."

Why not? Declan had already seen the worst of me.

"Come on." I stood from the stool and put the plates in

the sink. "It's makeshift, nothing fancy. It's, like, kind of silly."

"I'll be the judge of that."

"Really. It's not professional or anything."

"Professional?"

"Yeah. People go all out with vision boards. Glitter, streamers, frames, the whole shebang. It's a big thing for some people." We started up the stairs. "I made mine out of used cardboard boxes."

As we stepped into the second-floor room, Declan studied the mess in the center of the floor.

"Wow."

I put my hands on my hips, surveying my work. "Yeah, this was about two hours."

"I woulda guessed four."

I picked up the board from the floor and set it in the window frame. We observed it as one might a Picasso.

"Gardening," he said, looking at the flowers and plants I'd included.

"Yeah, I noticed that."

"It might be a secret calling of yours. Did you go to the nursery?"

"Not yet. It's on my to-do list, after the car gets fixed."

"We need to go soon. Tomorrow. Now's the time to plant. You're gonna miss the sweet spot."

I nodded. A minute passed.

"That's a nice baby."

I cringed at the image I'd cut out of a magazine and glued in the center of the board. I'd almost ripped it off ten separate times. Bad memories, uncomfortable. Still heavy, I realized.

Turning to him, I jutted out my chin and squared my shoulders. "I don't know if I can have kids, Declan."

"Because of one miscarriage?"

"That's right."

"That's crazy."

"What?"

"I'm assuming you went to the doctor and were examined, right? Did the doctor tell you that you wouldn't be able to have kids in the future?"

My mouth opened, closed, opened again. "No."

"Then you'll try again."

I blinked, shifting my focus to the pudgy little thing on the board as I thought about what he'd said. "What if I have another miscarriage?"

"What if you never try again?"

I swallowed hard, the words hitting me hard.

"Don't let fear, or those little what-ifs run your life, Grey."

You'll try again.

Declan kept his gaze on the board, but swept his hand down the back of my hair, softly, sweetly. Then he did exactly what I wanted him to do. He changed the subject.

"You included lots of lavender and different oils. Is that a tub of body lotion?"

"Yeah. Ah—that reminds me." I grabbed the notebook from the center of the floor. "I had some ideas. Jotted them down."

"Ideas for what?"

"Well, I don't know, really. A business, I guess." I looked up at him, tilting my head. "What if I started making essential-oil lotions and body butters. I've done a lot of research . . ."

A burst of excitement had me flipping through the pages.

"Lavender has a lot of benefits for the skin. It can soothe

eczema and dry skin. It conditions, detoxifies, and can help heal wounds—it has antiseptic properties. It's an anti-inflammatory, and can even help with acne and wrinkles. It's like God's little miracle, right there out your window. I'm really interested in it. There's a business here. Somewhere."

He gestured to the room. "Well, you've got your office space."

"Exactly." I flipped to another page. "I've already written down things like furniture and office stuff that I need to buy for the room."

"I like it." He smiled, a hint of pride in his eyes.

"Thanks. The ideas are scattered, at best, but they're there. Tugging at me."

"Can't ignore that tug."

"Nope."

"Maybe you could glam up the products."

"Did you just use the phrase *glam up*?"

"Impressed?"

I glanced at the tool belt around his waist, the mud on his boots. "Intrigued. What do you mean?"

"Well, you could use that fancy fashion background that I know you miss so much. Maybe in the packaging, the marketing. Target stay-at-home moms who don't get to pamper themselves often. Package it in a way that makes them feel like they're bringing 'New York spas' to them. Fancy, but accessible."

"Stay-at-home moms," I said slowly, nodding as my mind raced with ideas. "Purple. That could be the brand color. I would play up the organic side of it. Clean, free of chemicals . . ."

"Gréyce, you could call it, with one of those fancy accents above the first *e*. It would read like the word Grace. G-r-e-y-c-e—a mix of your name and grace. Lavender represents grace, peace, tranquility. A fancy name, classy, with an upscale feel to it."

"Gréyce." My eyes rounded in excitement. "I like it. Definitely better than Grey Goose."

He winked. *Oh my God, that wink.*

"You could even sponsor girls' nights out—or 'in,' maybe."

"You're pretty smart, Declan Montgomery."

"I pay attention."

We shifted our attention back to the board, my mind racing with ideas for logos.

Declan stilled next to me. He was staring at the corner of the board, at the heart, the word *faith*, and the combined numbers of 171613. I knew he put it all together, as I had.

A moment passed, the air suddenly charged with electricity between us. I was a bit embarrassed and on pins and needles for what he might say. Instead, he simply looked at me, smiled, and winked again.

As was Declan—that was that.

Looking back, that was the moment I fell in love with Declan Montgomery.

He turned fully to me and took my hand. "Tired?"

"Beyond."

"Thought so. Let's get you to bed."

"But it's seven o'clock."

"So?"

"So I'm not eighty years old."

"Tell that to your liver, Lindsay."

"Not. *Funny*."

"Remember, I told you, the humor drops off after lunch. Come on."

My hand in his, I was led downstairs, through the living room and into the kitchen. Rain slid down windows darkened with a gloomy dusk. A rumble of thunder rolled in the distance.

Declan grabbed a pot, filled it with water, and set it to boil. Next, he pulled out a box of chamomile tea, and honey that I'd picked up from the store.

"Milk's good in it. Yes?"

"Yes."

I sank into the folding chair in the corner, my body as limp as a wet washcloth. Between the lingering emotional toll of two visits with the therapist, seventy-five minutes of Zumba, sleeping on the couch the last few nights, and a full day of working on the house, I was exhausted. Emotionally and physically. The last few days were taking their toll. And Declan had noticed, not to my surprise.

I zoned out while he puttered around the kitchen, waiting for the water to boil. A few minutes later, he handed me a mug of warm, calming tea. Then he took my other hand and pulled me to my feet.

"Take a warm bath and drink that."

"And then I'll be cured?"

"According to my grandmother and her friend at the nursing home, yes."

I smirked.

He smiled, then reached out to touch my face. "I've got to do something real quick. I'll be right back."

"In this weather?"

"It's not even lightning. I'll be back. Go take that bath."

43

After what felt like three hours later—although it was probably only about twenty minutes—I lifted my head from the back of the porcelain tub at the sound of a truck door slamming outside.

Pouring myself out of the most relaxing bubble bath I'd ever taken, I quickly dried off and slipped into my robe. My muscles were languid, my headache curbed. The tea, plus the Epsom salts I'd added to my bath, had done the trick.

As I walked out of the bathroom, Declan stepped into the bedroom with a massive, tangled ball of fabric wrapped in his arms. His shoulders were speckled with rain, his hair wet.

My lips parted as I stared at the sheets and fluffy comforter in his arms.

His comforter—*his* bedding.

I looked at my bed—stripped bare—then back to Declan. My stomach sank. I tried to think of an excuse as to why I'd stripped my bed, other than that it was the last place Lucas had been inside me.

Wide-eyed, I stammered. "I . . . I . . ."

"I know."

The sharpness of his gaze told me that he did, in fact, know.

Staring at him, I took a deep breath, waiting for the onslaught of questions, or the lecture, or the guilt. Instead, he pushed aside his emotions and began making the bed.

"I didn't realize you'd been sleeping on the couch until I poked my head in here today."

I nodded but didn't say anything. Together, we smoothed the sheets onto the mattress.

"Thank you," I whispered.

He dipped his chin, crossing to the far side of the bed.

"Hey." He stopped cold, staring at the serenity bear I kept next to my lavender plant on the nightstand. "Where'd you get that?"

"Brianna gave it to me, actually. Years ago—a few months before the accident." When he frowned, I said, "What?

"I gave that to her." He blinked. "That bear. That's my bear."

Confused, I looked at the bear and then back at him. "What?"

"Yeah." He scratched his head. "Wow, I can't believe you have it."

"Wait. How . . ."

"I told you, when they'd come to Berry Springs to visit their grandma, we'd play together. My grandma gave me that bear, and for some reason, Brianna loved it. I thought it was kind of girly, so I gave it to her."

My mouth dropped open, and we stared at each other in shock. In a way, our paths had crossed decades ago.

"Serenity . . ."

He nodded. "Yeah. Grandma was very religious."

"That bear . . ." Tears filled my eyes. "It was with me when I felt the most alone I'd ever been. During my miscarriage, when I left my husband . . . through it all, that bear has been my strength." A tear slid down my cheek.

Declan crossed the room but I looked away, the emotions too heavy, the realization of the weight of the moment so great.

I was never alone. Declan had always been with me.

"Grey. Don't cry," he whispered, turning my face toward him. "It's a lot, I know."

"I feel . . . tired."

"You've been going full speed for two days. Adrenaline. But maybe things are starting to hit, and that's okay. It's all part of the process. You are going to make it through this, Grey Dalton."

I wrapped my fingers around his wrists, staring into twinkling blue diamonds, then I cupped his cheeks. Another tear rolled down mine, and I pressed my lips to his.

His body froze for a second. Then he wrapped me up, pulled me to him, and opened his mouth to mine.

We kissed in a frenzy, a release of the emotions and sexual tension that had been building between us since the second we laid eyes on each other. My heart pounded as desire swept through me, setting off every nerve ending in my body.

We fell onto the bed, him over me, frantic arms and legs trying to touch and connect with every part of each other.

But the moment my fingertips slid up his shirt, he pulled away, leaving me breathless, my chest heaving, my body tangled in the sheets. Declan pushed off the bed and stood, breathing heavy too.

Our eyes locked, both of us acknowledging the moment we'd just experienced. Everything had just changed.

A muscle in his jaw twitched, that torment back in his eyes. In a voice quiet but loaded with conviction, he said, "I don't sleep with married women, Grey."

"You wouldn't be you if you did," I whispered back.

And *that's* the moment I fell in love with Declan Montgomery.

44

A crack of thunder awoke me with a jerk.

Blinking, I rolled over as a flash of lightning lit the room. It was early morning, the woods beginning to lighten as a storm built. I watched the rain streak down my new windows—the ones Declan had installed—as the events of the day before slowly came back to me.

The *kiss.*

I ran my fingertips over my lips, where Declan's had been hours earlier. Butterflies fluttered in my stomach, and I smiled.

I'd heard people describe their first kiss with someone special as resembling fireworks. Nope. The kiss Declan and I had shared was beyond colorful explosions in the sky. Instead, it was as if the entire world had stopped around us, all its energy funneling into that one kiss. A sweeping swirl of light, sound, and motion wrapping around us as we merged into one. We were all that existed at that moment —*us.* Not him, not me. *Us.* It was all-consuming.

Life changing, I know now.

As I sat up, I noticed a folded blanket on the chaise

lounge in the corner of the room. Declan had slept next to me all night. He'd stayed with me to make sure I was okay.

I grabbed my phone from the nightstand and tapped the screen, shocked to see it was eight thirty.

Eight thirty.

I'd slept like a rock for thirteen hours.

"Declan?" I called out, my voice as smooth as a chain-smoking trucker's.

When there was no response, I called out again. But nothing.

Fear settled like lead in my stomach.

He'd left.

Was it because he'd finally realized I wasn't worth it? That life with me would very likely be a few good days, followed by a few bad? Did he regret helping me? Getting involved with a neurotic alcoholic who was in the middle of a divorce, and oh, by the way, might never be able to have his children?

We'd shared an amazing kiss, yes, but did that moment outweigh everything else?

I looked around the room, taking in my suitcases on the floor, the demolished closet, the new windows. I watched the rain, nerves slowly building as I wondered what the day would bring.

Sobriety.

More headaches? Mood swings?

Was I going to go to therapy? Had Declan made another appointment? Shit, had I? I couldn't remember.

My heart beat faster, and the walls felt like they were beginning to close in on me.

Why had Declan left?

A knock at the front door pulled me from my impending panic attack.

I pulled on my robe and quickly stepped into my slippers. As I straightened, I groaned, my muscles tight from Zumba. Silently, I padded into the living room and peeked through the curtains. Utter relief had me yanking open the door with gusto—followed by a wave of embarrassment at my eagerness.

He was wearing a crisp baby-blue dress shirt as bright as his eyes, an ill-fitting navy tie that made me grin, a pair of pressed khakis, and shined loafers that hadn't seen dirt in years.

Declan—*I think*—flashed me a crooked smile. He was nervous, I realized immediately, noticing the stiff shoulders, the barely contained energy.

I cocked my head. "Late for your wedding?"

"Church." The single word came out like a bullet, almost as daunting as a ball and chain.

My brows popped. I couldn't remember the last time I'd been inside a church. Years? A decade?

Not giving me time to think, he continued. "It's Sunday. How about church?" he asked nervously, as if asking himself the question too.

"Uh . . ."

We stared at each other, the cartoonish fear on his face probably matching my own. I couldn't help but smirk. He did too.

"Listen," he said. "I'll be as uncomfortable as you. Trust me on this. And I can also promise that I'll get just as many, if not more, looks than you'll get."

"Therapy, then church." I blew out a breath. "It's a lot, Declan. Why?"

He lifted a shoulder. "Felt a tug."

I slowly nodded, remembering the tug I felt when I'd

first seen him in the fields below my house. "Can't ignore the tugging."

"No, ma'am."

I nodded. "Okay. Give me ten minutes."

"You've got longer. Take your time. Figured you'd want to fancy up. There's a nine thirty service." He checked his wristwatch, wiped clean for the occasion. "An hour from now. There's also an eleven thirty service. Although, truth be told, I'm hoping we'll make it to the nine thirty. I've got to put in some time at the garage today."

"Nine thirty it is. Start the coffee?"

"Hell yeah."

I winced. "I don't think we're supposed to cuss if we're in church mode."

"Hell isn't a cuss word." He paused, then blinked. "No cussing? Wow. The stress."

"Yeah. Welcome to my last seventy-two hours."

"Give it to God?" he asked, tilting his head as if trying to recall the saying.

"Yeah, something like that. Or lay your troubles at his feet, I think."

"Hope he has big feet."

Turning, I laughed, then stopped to turn back. "Wait. What religion are we attending today?"

"Christian." He frowned, confused by the question. "You know . . . Christian."

"I know *that.* I mean which . . . like, Baptist, Methodist, Catholic?"

"Oh. Sorry. Baptist. But the cool kind, though. The pastor's around my age. Real chill, and funny too. Kai dragged me there once. They've got really good music. A whole band. And there's no yelling. Or snakes."

"Phew. Okay. I can do that. What do I wear?"

"A bathing suit. Go. Don't overthink this. Wait, no. A thong—one of those thong bikinis."

"Maybe later." I winked. "Coffee. Go."

~

I stilled at the voices coming from the kitchen as I stepped out of the shower. Clutching a towel around my wet body, I peeked around the bathroom door.

"No, son. Good Lord in heaven, were you born in a damn barn? Now listen to me. It's right *there*. You gotta—"

"Ms. Etta, do I need to remind you again that I fix things for a living?"

My mouth widened into an awestruck smile as I watched Declan, on his hands and knees under a vanity. Attached to the top was a round mirror encircled with bulbs. Scattered around the vanity were three new pieces of furniture, presumably also from Etta's shed.

"It's got new bulbs, Declan," Etta yelled at Declan from her stance above the vanity, three octaves louder than needed. "I put the damned things in this morning. I promise. It lights up, I'm telling you—"

"Screwdriver, please, Ms. Etta." Declan's voice was calm but loaded with irritation.

I grinned and slinked behind the door, peering through the crack as Etta hurried to the kitchen and grabbed a tool from the junk drawer.

A minute later, the room lit up in a warm yellow glow.

Etta clapped her hands, jumping up and down. "Ah, there it is. See? I told you it works. She's going to love it."

Declan pushed off the floor, trying to dust off his formerly freshly pressed church slacks, now dirty and wrinkled.

"Thank you, son. Sorry for snapping. Now, are you sure you don't mind fetching the other things from my truck?"

"Not at all."

I stepped into the doorway. "Morning, Etta."

"Surprise!"

"I *love* it."

I tried to ignore Declan's eyes scanning my almost-naked body as I stepped into the room, the electricity between us so palpable, I could almost reach out and touch it.

I wanted to touch it. *Him.*

"I didn't realize you had company." Etta's brow arched with curiosity. "I was about to turn around when Declan stepped outside and offered to help carry the load."

"That was sure nice of him, wasn't it, Etta?"

"It was." She eyed me with a slight smirk. "He's grown up a lot since I saw him last. At least three inches." She winked, then turned back to the vanity. "Anyway, it's for all your fancy New York makeup and stuff. I got it at a garage sale yesterday and cleaned it up. Thought you could put it next to the window in your bedroom." She pretended to notice the towel for the first time. "Where are y'all going?"

"Church."

Etta's eyes widened as she glanced between Declan and me. A proud smile brightened her wrinkled face. "Well then, I certainly won't stand in your way."

She turned to Declan and paused, as if trying to figure him out. Or seeing him in a new light, maybe.

"Come on, son. Let's get the last bit of stuff I brought over, and then y'all head on out."

"Yes, ma'am."

I grinned as they left through the living room, Etta asking Declan's advice about a rattle in her engine. Declan glanced over his shoulder as they stepped onto the front porch, and winked at me.

~

Thirty minutes later, Declan drove us slowly through a sea of people and cars at the church, then pulled into the last parking spot available.

"Holy shit." I slapped my hand over my mouth. "Whoops."

I looked out at the hordes of people, all moving in one direction. The rain had momentarily stopped, a few drips falling from the trees here and there in the parking lot. "Look at all those people."

"I know." Declan peered out the streaked windshield. "The whole town goes to church. Berry Springs has almost as many churches as meth labs."

"This does not please God."

"Probably not. Which is why there's two new churches currently under construction on the south side of town."

"Seriously, *everyone* goes to church?"

He nodded. "Wednesday nights too."

"What?"

"I know. Welcome to the Bible Belt."

I sighed. "I wonder how many of these people got drunk and wrapped their car around a tree this week."

Declan grabbed my hand. "More than you think. Everyone has their problems. All those people over there? They're not perfect just because they go to church every Sunday morning—and Wednesday night. Hell, they probably go *because* of their imperfections. Their struggles, their sins. I think it's all about becoming a better person."

I smiled. "You said hell."

"You said shit. Yours was worse."

"I guess we need to repent."

"I guess so."

I stared out the window at the families huddled under colorful umbrellas. Kids in their Sunday best, splashing in the puddles. Mothers in conservative low heels and cotton dresses, wagging their fingers. Husbands, greeting each other with a handshake. A line of well-meaning citizens funneling through double doors underneath a wooden cross.

Church. Family.

"You look nice. Did I tell you that already?"

I smiled. "You already told me."

"I'll probably tell you a few more times."

I blushed, smoothing the outfit that had taken me fifteen minutes to put together. I went with a white silk blouse tucked into a simple beige pencil skirt that ended at mid-calf. Conservative two-inch heels to complete the look. I'd pulled my hair into a messy bun, mainly because that was all I could do with the wavy bedhead.

Note to self: Never go to sleep with wet hair before church.

"We're going to have to sit in the front row if we stay here any longer," Declan said, acknowledging that neither of us were moving.

"Dear God, no."

"My thoughts exactly. Stay here, though. Hang on."

Declan hopped out of the truck and jogged around the hood. I smiled as he opened my door and held out his palm.

"Such a gentleman."

"God's watching."

I laughed and slid my hand into his. "Okay. Here we go. No cussing."

He nodded. "No cussing."

"Grey!"

I turned to see Cassidy jogging across the parking lot, a few of her girlfriends watching from a distance.

"Girl, what are you doing here? Why didn't you call?" Her gaze flicked to Declan, then landed on mine with the subtlety of a Mike Tyson punch.

"You know Declan, right?"

"Uh, yeah. Used to, anyway. Good to see you."

They shook hands, her what-the-hell-is-going-on expression locked on me.

"We're neighbors," I said.

"Neighbors who church. Okay." Although her tone was loaded, she let the topic slide, but I knew I'd get a text in under five minutes.

"Hey, Cassie." I cleared my throat. "Can I talk to you real quick?"

"Of course."

Declan smiled at me and dipped his chin—*do it,* his eyes urged—then stepped back to give us privacy.

With an inhale, I turned fully to my cousin. "Cassidy, I'm an alcoholic. And I'm trying to become sober."

A brutal moment passed, then she blinked and shook her head. "Well, hell. I would be too after all you've been through."

The air expelled from my lungs with a rush of relief at her casual response.

It's only as big a deal as you make it.

"Are you okay?" She gripped my arm.

"Yeah. I just need to quit."

Cassidy nodded. "You know . . . I've actually thought about laying off the booze for a while too. I'm in."

"Really?"

"Really."

I smiled. "Okay then."

She wrapped her arms around me. I glanced at Declan, and when he smiled proudly, I smiled back.

"Cassie, come on!"

Cassidy pulled back. "I'm in the choir, believe it or not, so I gotta go. Don't leave without saying good-bye, and let's meet up real soon to talk about that tall drink of water you're with. Jesus, Mary, and Joseph—he's *hot.*" She winked.

"Coffee or tea okay?"

"Yes. Promise."

"Thanks."

"Talk soon, girl. Glad you're here."

I grabbed for Declan's hand before he was even next to me. For an anchor. *My* anchor.

Our palms slid together the moment my name was yelled yet again.

"Hey, Grey!"

I looked over my shoulder, searching for the other person that must be named Grey—because I didn't know anyone else in Berry Springs. Did I?

I blinked, recognizing two women from Zumba the day before, beelining it over to me.

"Hey, there." I squeezed Declan's hand as they approached. He gave me two quick squeezes of support back.

"I didn't know you came here. It's Grey, right?"

"It's my first time. Emma, right? From Zumba?"

I remembered her because she was the only other woman who'd struggled her way through class as I had. We'd acknowledged each other with smiles a few times, laughing at our lack of coordination. I'd also noticed her because she was also the only other woman without a fancy matching Zumba outfit.

For church, Emma had chosen a yellow sundress that practically glowed in the cloudy, overcast morning. Her long blond hair was swept back in a simple ponytail. No fuss.

"Emma is right. You got it. Good job—I'm terrible with names." She gestured to her friend, who was gawking at Declan.

Unlike Emma, the pixie-cut redhead had chosen jeans and a T-shirt for the occasion. I decided I liked her instantly for that.

"Carol here had to remind me of yours when we walked up."

"Declan Montgomery. I'll. Be. *Damned*," Carol drawled in a thick Southern accent. "*You're* coming to church?"

"Appears so."

Emma slapped her friend's arm. They were younger than Declan, probably around my age, which meant they likely only knew him by reputation.

Carol looked at me, back at Declan, then smiled. "Well, stranger things have happened. Good for you for coming. Welcome."

"Thanks," Declan said, and this time he squeezed my hand for support.

Emma checked the time. "Come on. We're late. Y'all can sit with us. Hank and Mary aren't coming today. Sick, flu, something, who knows." We fell into step together. "You coming to Zumba tomorrow?"

"That's the plan."

I guessed it was. The new plan.

"You?" I asked.

Emma groaned. "If I can manage. I could barely get out of bed this morning."

I laughed. "Same here. You should try some lavender-oil rub."

"Yeah?"

"Yeah. Supposed to be anti-inflammatory and relaxing."

"I'd take anything right about now. Are you talking, like, essential oils?"

"Exactly."

"Fancy. Where would I get that?"

"I can get you some, if you want. I make it, actually. And I'm thinking about making a salve for post-workouts, along with a few other products."

"Really?"

"Yeah. Kind of a weird hobby that I've picked up."

"My niece is about to have her first baby—she married a rich dude and has already bought everything under the sun for the kid. I've been racking my brain trying to figure out something unique to get her. You know, something she can really use, not a stupid stuffed animal or a monogrammed rattle. Something that helps her out, and I think she could use something relaxing, for sure. Do you make anything for babies?"

"Yeah, actually. I have a few ideas for diaper-rash cream and soothing baby wipes."

"Organic?"

I nodded. "Made right here in good ol' Berry Springs."

"Awesome. I'll take some. Two bottles of the rash cream and a box of wipes. And I also want some of that post-workout stuff."

"Really?"

"Yeah. Put in an order for me."

"You'd be my first order ever." A zing of excitement ran through me. An order—*a job*. A source of income. A focus.

"I'm honored." Emma shimmied her shoulders as if being my first client was something special.

It *was* special, I decided. It was the beginning of something. It felt like the beginning of a lot of new things.

I looked up at Declan and smiled. He looked at me, smiling back.

And with simultaneous deep breaths, we stepped under the wooden cross.

45

"First rule of baking . . . take a damn deep breath, my dear. You're stressing me the hell out."

I released an exasperated groan.

"Tighten your apron." Etta's tone reminded me of my eighth-grade math teacher, Mrs. Heinkleschmidt. "Pull on your big-girl panties and straighten your shoulders."

Gritting my teeth, I yanked at the ties of the apron Etta had brought over ten minutes after I'd called for help. It read OH CRÊPE.

"And that's not the tablespoon, Grey. Does that look like a tablespoon?"

Frowning, I looked down at the measuring cup in my hand labeled *1/4 cup*. Etta yanked the cup from my hand and replaced it with the appropriate tool.

"Now," she said. "Because we're baking these cookies for a man, we're going to add raisins and walnuts. Make it nice and hearty for him. Does Declan have a nut allergy?"

"Uh . . . I don't know."

"Second rule of baking . . . know all allergies of the man you're trying to impress."

"Got it."

She cocked a brow, waiting for my response.

I chewed my lower lip, contemplating. "Add them. I feel like he's a nut kind of guy."

"I've got an EpiPen at the house if he needs it. I'll be on standby."

"Thank you."

She winked. "Okay. Now set the oven to three fifty. You know how to do that?"

"Red Baron pizzas are my weakness."

"Red Barons aren't pizza. They're flavored cardboard."

Once I'd clicked on the oven, I returned to my place on the battlefield—a counter full of pots, pans, baking sheets, something called parchment paper, and measuring cups. Then there were the ingredients, which included butter, brown and white sugar, eggs, vanilla, salt, cinnamon, baking soda, something called molasses, flour, oats, raisins, and nuts. To the side were powdered sugar and milk for making icing.

The icing had been my idea, as I remembered Declan telling me how much he liked icing.

Lastly were two mugs of steaming coffee, front and center. Both large, because Etta warned it was going to be a long two hours.

"Butter is the base of any cookie recipe," she said. "Real butter—not that fake bullshit. I don't ever want to see that stuff in this house. Got it? And it should always be room temperature before you bake. Luckily, I had some sitting out before you called, so we're good there. After we mix everything, it's going to have to chill for thirty minutes before it bakes. Ideally sixty, but we'll settle for thirty. How long is he working this afternoon?"

"I get the vibe he'll be there a while. I think he's behind."

"Good. While the dough is chilling, we'll clean up the mess, and you'll tell me all about your relationship with Declan Montgomery."

"There's no relationship," I lied, my tone not very convincing.

"A woman doesn't surprise a man with homemade cookies if she doesn't have feelings for him. Especially when that woman normally uses her oven to store fashion magazines. Don't think I didn't see you take them out. And by the way—that's an extreme fire hazard."

"I'll keep the magazines somewhere else. Why don't you like him, Etta?"

She sighed, rearranging a few things on the counter to her liking. "Men with tempers, Grey, are to be steered clear of. Trust me on this."

"Have you seen his temper? Personally?"

"No, but that's the thing. Sometimes they just snap. They'll have it under control, and then one day, *bam,* it's like a bomb exploding. Honey, his daddy was no good. I told you. Declan Montgomery is not from good stock."

"My mama had her faults too, Etta. And you still like me."

"There've been a lot of rumors about the Montgomery family over the years. And the fact that the boy just kinda keeps to himself, well, he's done nothing to quiet the rumors."

"He didn't kill that girl, Etta. He didn't. I know he didn't. And anyway, it sure seemed like you were enjoying bossing him around when I got out of the shower."

"He was eager to help. I'll give him that."

"Is he going to fix that rattle you were griping about in your truck?"

"He offered, yes."

"Let him. Get to know him. He's a good man, Etta, despite his father. Or in spite of him, maybe."

She regarded me closely, then nodded. "Well, it wouldn't be the first time someone surprised me. I wish the truth would come out about little Anna."

"Me too. For his sake. But it's not too likely now, thirty years later. Can you imagine living every day knowing that people think you killed a little girl?"

Etta looked out the window, lost in thought.

Continuing, I said, "I wish everyone could see the side of him that I've seen."

"Well, it must be a darn good side because you're so desperate to please him that you're baking for him. And you even asked for help—something I know you don't do often. All signs point to relationship."

"I know." I sighed. "God, Etta, I'm not even divorced yet."

She handed me a measuring cup. "Pour a half cup of sugar in the mixer, followed by the butter. Just because a judge hasn't signed on the bottom line doesn't mean you're incapable of feeling something for someone else, Grey."

"Brown or white sugar?"

"White."

"He . . . just came out of nowhere," I said as I slowly poured the ingredients.

"The best things come out of nowhere, that I can promise you. Thing is, most people don't see them."

"Kinda like you with Declan, with him helping you today. Isn't that right?"

"Touché, my dear. Touché."

"I don't have to see it, Etta. I *feel* it. The moment I first saw the guy, my entire body seemed to respond to him. A little tug to go to him."

Etta smiled as she mixed. "That's how it was with

Stanley—my late husband. That's your womanly instinct telling you something is there. Listen to it, Grey. The most powerful messages are the ones we hear in our heart. Second most powerful? The ones I'm about to tell you about getting this dough right. Enough about boys; you're on the right path. Let's get to these cookies so you stay on it."

With that, Etta walked me through how to make my first batch of oatmeal cookies—the first thing I'd ever baked for a man.

~

It was almost three in the afternoon by the time the cookies were baked, cooled, and iced—with little white hearts. I learned two things over the course of those four hours.

One, baking is utterly exhausting.

Two, I could drink my weight in molasses.

Etta left me with a "grade B" for my efforts, along with the recipe and advice to hide it from Declan. Our plan was to let him think I baked the cookies all on my own, with a recipe and without Etta. Although, something told me he'd suspect otherwise, regardless.

That was okay. It was the effort that mattered, right?

Per Etta's final suggestion, I took time to fix my makeup and hair, and spent an embarrassing amount of time putting together an outfit that struck a delicate balance between sexy and *I don't give a shit.*

I opted for my favorite pair of skinny jeans and a tank top low enough to see a hint of cleavage. Flip-flops, because he likes my feet. Lastly, a rain jacket to cover it all because it was still wet outside, and the pitch-black clouds rolling in suggested much more were on the way.

Nerves mixed with excitement as I crossed the driveway, cookie platter covered in plastic wrap in hand and a giddy grin on my face. As terrible as it sounds, I'd never gone to such efforts to surprise—or please, as Etta would call it—a man. It was both thrilling and terrifying. And very telling.

Had I ever been in love?

Was I in love?

A light mist as thin as fog hung in the air. Despite the thick cloud cover, the temperature hovered around a very humid seventy degrees, a heat wave ahead of the storms, according to the weatherman.

I yanked up my hood and approached my ride—Declan's ink-black four-wheeler. My makeup would be sweated off and my hair a ball of frizz by the time I got to the garage, but I didn't care. I was getting these cookies to Declan, come hell or high water.

Carefully balancing the platter on my lap, I started the engine and slowly inched down the driveway and onto the dirt road.

A gust of wind drew my attention to the angry clouds building in the distance. There was an electricity in the air, so compelling I could almost feel it buzz on my skin. Like a little warning of something to come.

Nerves started getting the best of me as I drove closer to the garage, Declan's approval of my hard work suddenly meaning more than anything else.

Another blast of wind sent my hair spinning around my face as I pulled into the parking lot. Only a single light was on in the garage, over the bay where Declan was working—on *my* car. No customers, no Kai, no music. Sundays were supposed to be for relaxing, not work.

Well, not for Declan.

I noticed movement inside as my four-wheeler rumbled

to a stop next to the office. I quickly hid the platter on the rack behind me.

"Well, well, well . . ." Declan stepped out of the bay, wiping his hands on a towel.

He was wearing jeans, boots, and a thin T-shirt covered in oil and sweat. Oil streaked the side of his face and his arms. He smiled, although it didn't reach his puffy, shaded eyes. His skin was sallow, his movements slow, his vibe the opposite from his usual chipper self. This was likely due to sleeping in a chair all night next to me. To make sure I was okay.

I felt terrible, wishing I'd done more than bake him cookies.

"You look beautiful. How are you doing?" he unselfishly asked me, despite his own weary appearance.

"I'm fine. How are *you*?" I frowned, looking him over.

"Fine," he lied as he extended his palm and helped me off the four-wheeler.

"I'm calling bullshit."

"You know I like that dirty mouth." Declan playfully flicked the corner of the hood I'd pulled tightly around my face.

"I believe that's called deflecting. What happened to our truce of directness? What's wrong?"

"Fine. I'm just a bit . . . I've got a lot of work to do." He rubbed the back of his neck.

Just then, an old, dented black Chevy pulled into the lot. A burnt orange stripe ran down the side, and a trailer, carrying a horse, towed behind it.

Declan groaned. "Hang on. That's my three o'clock."

"You fix horses now?"

The truck rumbled to a stop. A muscular man, almost as tall as Declan, unfolded himself from the cab. Wearing a faded T-shirt, ripped jeans, and combat boots, the man emanated a subtle back-the-hell-off vibe. Tanned skin and inky black hair with brooding eyes to match completed the bad-boy look.

"Who is that?"

"Name's Christian Locke."

"Never heard of him."

"Most haven't. Lives down Redemption Road in the old John Stafford Manor. Rarely leaves his house. He's a loner—former military or something. And not the type to wait on anyone. Be right back."

Few words were spoken between the men. After pulling his Chevy to the bay, the man climbed onto his horse and disappeared into the mist.

Declan hurriedly crossed the lot, back to me.

"You're behind on work," I said.

"Yeah."

"Well." I smiled—beamed, more like. "Do you have a quick second for a break? You deserve a break, and I have a surprise for you."

Declan spotted the platter I'd balanced on the back of the four-wheeler. "Does it involve oatmeal?"

"And raisins and walnuts."

"Healthy oatmeal then."

"And icing."

"Ah, there's my girl."

When he started to step past me, I spun around and grabbed the platter. "Oh no, sir. I'll serve you."

"*Sir.*" The corners of his mouth curved up. "Good thing you didn't call me that last night."

"Noted." I winked, feeling a blush creep up at the thought of that kiss. "Can you take a break?"

"For oatmeal cookies? You bet." He glanced up at the sky.

"Looks like the rain's going to hold off for a bit longer. Come on."

Declan led me to a picnic table nestled under a pine.

"Hang on. Don't sit down."

He sprinted into the office and returned three seconds later with a towel and two Cokes. After wiping the rain from my seat, I slipped off my rain jacket, and we settled at the picnic table.

I couldn't believe how nervous I was for him to try the cookies.

"You ready?" I asked.

"Very."

Grinning, I carefully pulled the plastic wrap away from the platter and dramatically unveiled the plate with a flourish. "Ta-da!"

"That's the second prettiest thing I've seen today."

"Don't get too excited." I picked up the gooiest one, wiggling my eyebrows. "I'd serve you, but no plates."

"Give it to me." He leaned forward.

My stomach danced as he took a bite from the cookie in my hand.

"Holy smokes," he mumbled, a walnut tumbling down his chin. "These are really good."

My smile reached epic proportions. "Guess what?"

"What?" He grabbed another and demolished half of it in one bite.

"I made them."

His brows popped. "Really?"

More crumbles fell down his chin. I'd never been happier in my life.

"Yep. Really."

"Kinda like you made the first ones?"

"No. I really made these." I lifted my palms. "With these two little hands."

"And I thought you were in demand before."

Although the comment was said in a lighthearted tone, the implication was anything but. He was referring to Lucas's persistent interest in me. And it was then that I noticed something more than just fatigue in him.

I nibbled on a cookie, watching him chug his Coke, then devour another cookie. I wondered if he'd had a single thing to eat since leaving my house that morning. I also wondered what else was going on with him. I looked around again for Kai, waiting for that other shoe to drop, but I was certain she wasn't there.

Each bay was filled with cars, two more parked to the side.

"You really are behind with your appointments, aren't you?"

He shrugged, chewing feverishly.

"And you didn't sleep last night."

"I slept a little."

"Dec, I know you stayed at my house last night, and that chair isn't comfortable. Trust me, I've tried to sleep on it myself. I can see it on your face, the way you dragged yourself over here."

"I think they call that swagger." He winked, but there was no sparkle in his eyes.

"They call that burning the candle at both ends. I know you're behind on work because of me. Dec, you can't do all this for me."

"Why not?"

"Because you've got your own life to take care of. And because, despite what you've seen since you've met me, I am a capable adult. I can take care of myself. I've been taking care of myself since I was six years old."

"Your car needs repair. I'm a mechanic. It's what I do."

"That's not what I'm talking about. I'm—"

"What are you talking about then?" he said with a sudden sharpness to his tone that I'd never heard from him before.

Sitting up a little straighter, I said slowly, "I don't want you to go out of your way so much for me."

He scowled at me. "You wrapped your car around a tree in the middle of the night. Someone's obviously got to."

My eyes narrowed at the below-the-belt punch, and I leaned back. "Listen. I'm sorry. Yeah, I know I've been a mess. But I never asked you to put your life on hold for me. I didn't call you after the accident. I didn't want this."

"Well, *fuck*, Grey." He laughed, although there was no humor to it.

A little tingle formed at the base of my spine as I watched a switch flip in him. The switch Etta had warned me about?

Declan pushed off the picnic table, stood, and opened his arms while giving me an asshole grin. "What the hell am I doing then?"

Staring up at him, I blinked, taking in this new side of him. The easygoing, carefree Declan was gone, replaced by an emotional, seemingly volatile man.

Careful to keep my tone even, I said, "I'm trying to release some of the obligation that I think you feel."

"Obligation?"

I tilted my head to the side. "Am I missing something here, Declan?"

His jaw clenched. He jabbed his fingers through his hair

and began pacing. He was cagey. Overtired, overworked, whatever, but I didn't know this man, and I didn't like it.

"What's going on, Declan?"

He waved a hand in the air, giving me that asshole laugh again rather than respond.

"Don't dismiss my question. Something's up. Talk, Dec. Direct, remember?"

"All right. You're right. I am behind on work, and I lost a client this morning because of it. A client that's been coming to me since I opened shop over twenty years ago. I'd pushed his appointment back and he couldn't wait, so he took his business elsewhere. And no, I didn't sleep last night. Not a goddamn wink."

"I told you, you didn't have to stay."

"I know, Grey," he snapped. "I know."

"Why did you then?"

He stopped pacing and stared at the woods for a moment, then turned fully to me. "Are you even staying here, Grey?"

Then it hit me. Declan wasn't only uptight because of work and lack of sleep. He was struggling with the same emotions as me about whatever was happening between us.

"Answer the question, Grey. Once you renovate your cabin, are you gone? Are you leaving Berry Springs?"

I shook my head, struggling for words. "I don't . . . I can't answer that question right this second, Declan."

"Will you go back to New York? To him?"

"No. No way."

He snorted. "You're not even divorced. What the hell am I thinking?"

"I will be," I said quickly, embarrassed at the desperation in my voice. "I will be."

His jaw twitched as he looked away, and a moment passed.

"That kiss," he finally said in a voice so low, I almost missed it.

I stood, closing the inches between us. I wasn't sure why, but my eyes filled with tears. "I felt it too, you know," I whispered back as I reached for his arm.

He jerked away, and the rejection felt like a slap in the face.

I took a step back. "Okay. I'm sorry. I'm sorry for everything. And I've obviously come at a bad time. You need to work; I get it. I just wanted to bring you cookies as a thank-you. That's it. I'll leave you alone."

A bolt of anger swept through me, probably amplified by the rejection. I turned and clumsily grabbed the platter, causing half the cookies to tumble to the ground.

"Shit." Tears burned my eyes as I dropped to my knees, gathering the cookies I'd worked so hard on for the man who was regretting meeting me in the first place.

"What. The *fuck*. Is that?"

That tingle at the base of my spine? It shot up to my neck. Warning bells roared in my head.

"Grey." Declan's voice was so hard, so sharp, it could have cut glass. "What *the fuck* happened to your back?"

I froze. Images of Lucas bending me over my bed, scratching his nails down my back, flashed behind my eyes. The scabs had fallen off and the marks had faded, but were still visible, apparently.

Oh my God, oh my God, oh my God . . .

I yanked down the back of my top that had crept up when I bent over, then shot to my feet and turned around. My blood turned to ice at the look in Declan's eyes. He was absolutely terrifying.

"It's nothing," I said quickly, my voice shaking.

"Bullshit," he bellowed. "Did he hurt you?"

"Who?"

"Don't you patronize me, Grey. Did Lucas hurt you when he fucked you the other night?"

"How *dare* you talk to me like that."

"Turn around," he demanded, a fiery flush coloring his neck and cheeks.

"No."

He grabbed my arm, and I snatched it back. Took another step back.

"I fell down," I lied, trying to say anything to defuse the situation.

"Bullshit. I know scratches when I see them, trust me. I saw the same on my mother after my father would *rape* her. Turn *the hell* around, Grey."

Our attention was pulled to the sound of a car coming down the dirt road.

A bolt of lightning pierced the sky, followed by sprinkles of rain as Lucas's cherry-red Porsche came into view.

Oh shit.

"That him? That's him, isn't it?" Declan's voice pitched low with fury, and his eyes bulged with rage. "He's coming to see you today? To fuck you again? Hurt you again?"

The next few seconds were a blur.

Declan didn't wait for my answer. I tried to block him, but he lunged around me, shoving me to the side. Something was yelled through the rain.

Brakes squealed and gravel crunched.

My heart stopped as I watched Declan pull Lucas from his car by his hair.

"*No*!" I screamed, sprinting across the lot.

The clouds broke loose, pouring rain on my head and shoulders, and thunder boomed in the distance.

I screamed and screamed as Declan threw Lucas to the ground and began hitting him, the beating so vicious, so raw, that my stomach rolled in fear. I'd never forget the terrifying sight of Declan's face contorted with rage. Or his voice as he told Lucas that if he ever hurt me again, he'd kill him.

Blood spattered on my shirt as my name spat out of Declan's mouth. I stumbled back, tears streaming down my face.

It was no contest. Lucas was no match for Declan's rage. Declan had him pinned on the ground, pounding his fist into Lucas's face, over and over until his skin matched the color of his sports car.

I couldn't stand there. Couldn't watch it. So I ran.

I darted to the four-wheeler, wanting to get as far away from there—from *them*—as possible. Gravel spun as I peeled out, squeezing my eyes shut for a second while I zoomed past the bloodbath in the rain.

46

Sobbing uncontrollably, I stumbled up the steps to my porch, my hands trembling and knees shaking.

With clumsy fingers, I swiped the strands of hair from my face, droplets of water slinging against the blue-and-white priority envelope that was leaning against the front door. A flash of lightning behind me illuminated the neatly typed letters on the return address, DALTON LAW AND ASSOCIATES.

"Oh my God."

My breath hitched as I stared down at the envelope that likely held my final divorce papers—countersigned by William and his team of lawyers.

My marriage was done.

William's father had pulled strings, rushed through the paperwork, and gotten his son the fastest divorce in history.

It was done.

My stomach dropped to my feet with a wave of nausea that made saliva pool in my mouth. With the evidence of my failed marriage in one hand and spatters of blood on the other, I fumbled with the lock. When it finally turned, I staggered inside and fell to my knees. Dropping my face in my hands, I let go and heaved out tears, gasping for breath in the mother of all panic attacks.

I was done. My mind, body, and spirit—done.

Curling into a wet ball on the floor, I clutched my knees to my chest and screwed my eyes shut, feeling such despair and hopelessness that I wanted to fade away into the nothingness within me.

Outside, the storm raged. Rumbles of thunder filled my ears, and flashes of lightning burst behind my closed eyes.

I'd lost track of space, time, everything, when suddenly, there was a knock at the door. I was so physically exhausted from the panic attack that the sound didn't even startle me.

Sniffling, I slowly pulled myself up to a seated position, careful to remain unseen behind the door. I noticed the storm seemed less angry outside, and wondered how long I'd been lying there.

Holding my breath, I waited for the next knock.

"Grey." Declan's gruff voice called out from the other side, followed by another knock.

A light breath escaped me. I was so grateful that it was him, and not Lucas. And grateful that he was alive.

But I didn't move. My gaze dropped to the divorce papers on my lap.

"Grey, open up."

Tears filled my eyes again.

"Grey. Please." His voice was broken, desperate, as soft as the thud against the door that I imagined was his forehead. "Please."

A minute passed, then a few more knocks came. I listened to each footfall as Declan paced the wooden planks of my front porch, waiting for me to open the door, but I didn't.

More pacing followed.

After at least five minutes, heavy footfalls thudded down the porch steps and into the rain. I waited another ten minutes before peeling myself off the floor and peeking through the curtains.

He was gone.

You want to know the most screwed-up thing at that moment?

I was disappointed that he'd left. Given up.

While I hated the man I saw that afternoon and knew the image of his face covered in blood would haunt me for the rest of my life, I still wanted Declan to be by my side. I wanted him to be close, to hold me. To give me as much time as I needed before opening the door.

But he'd left.

Mad at him, mad at myself, mad at Lucas, mad at William, my failed marriage, this damn house, this damn town, I turned and stalked to the kitchen.

I wanted alcohol. I wanted wine. Vodka. Tequila. Moonshine, a bottle of mouthwash to chug, a bottle of rubbing alcohol. I wanted it all.

I stomped into the laundry room and fished the remaining bottle of red wine from the dirty clothes hamper, where I'd kept them hidden since moving in.

My hands shook as I grabbed a coffee cup from the cabinet. I shoved the corkscrew into the top of the wine. After yanking out the cork, I poured the wine, spilling as much onto the countertop as in the cup. I would have bathed in it if I could.

I slammed down the bottle and lifted the cup, emotions whirling in my body like a tornado.

I inhaled the sweet, smoky scent. My lip trembled as the cool ceramic touched it.

"Dammit!"

With a guttural scream, I hurled the cup against the wall, watching it shatter into a million pieces. I picked up the bottle and did the same with it. Red wine splattered everywhere in the kitchen as tears of anger streamed down my face.

"God, God, God." I chanted like a crazy woman, pacing back and forth, back and forth. I was going nuts. I could feel it.

I thought of the letters. Of the writer of the letters, the only person in this world more screwed up than I was. Someone who would understand me.

I grabbed the hammer from the junk drawer, ran into the bedroom, and slammed the head of it against what was left of the closet wall.

Again and again, each blow I took released some of the rage swirling inside me. Splinters flew past my head, tears dripped onto my shirt. I destroyed what was left of the wall, looking for that hint of white against the grime.

But there were no more letters.

47

The crack sounded like a shotgun going off, followed by a frightening thump that I could feel through the floor.

I ran to the window to see angry slashes of lightning illuminating a large dead tree that had just fallen in my backyard. My heart pounded like a drum. Carried by the wind, leaves and twigs pummeled the windows, and I thanked God that Declan had replaced the cracked ones that would have surely broken under the barrage of the current storm raging through the mountains.

It had been two hours since I'd destroyed my closet, looking for more letters. The first storm had calmed, the world momentarily silent except for the light pitter-patter of rain—but not for long. A second round of storms rolled in shortly afterward, angrier, more powerful, packing energy from the heat of the day.

There was no dusk that day. The muted gray daylight had faded into an evening as black as coal.

I was scared. Terrified, more like, and wished I would have listened to Etta when she'd told me to get a storm shelter installed ASAP. I realized quickly that there's nothing you can do in a tornado other than shelter in place and hope for the best. It's either going to hit you, or not, and there's not a damn thing you can do about it.

Images of homes leveled and lives lost flashed through my head as I clicked on the television and turned to the local news channel.

". . . I repeat, our storm chasers have reported a tornado on the ground east of Westville, heading toward Berry Springs. If you have not already taken shelter, do so immediately . . ."

I jumped back as a branch crashed into the window. Shaking, I grabbed the blanket from the couch and then ran into the bedroom to pull Declan's comforter from my bed.

"Stay away from windows, bring your pets inside if you can . . ."

I froze.

Moonshine.

"Oh no, *no, no, no, no . . .*"

I dropped the load in my hands and ran to the front door. When I yanked it open, leaves and twigs spun madly on the front porch, the rain coming down sideways in sheets. Lightning lit the yard as bright as day as I stepped onto the porch.

"Moonshine!" I cupped my hands over my mouth and yelled. "Moonshine, come! Kitties! Here, kitty, kitty, kitty," I sang.

I hurried from one end of the porch to the other, my hair whipping into my face, the T-shirt I'd thrown on to replace my wet clothes flapping in the wind. I thought I heard a faint meow, but I couldn't pin its location.

A crash of thunder sounded so near, it made me jump.

"Kitties!" I yelled into the wind. "*Dammit.* Dammit, dammit, dammit. Come on, Moonshine. *Come on*!"

My instinct was screaming at me to get into the house. I yelled a few more times, then darted back inside, closed the door, and peered out the beveled glass, waiting for those two little golden eyes to emerge from the storm. When they didn't, I gathered my blankets, my phone, and ran to the bathroom, remembering watching a movie once where people huddled in a bathtub during a storm.

My heart pounding, I crawled inside my tub as three booms echoed from the living room. I stilled, my eyes rounding.

"Grey!"

Declan.

More frantic knocks came as I leaped out of the tub. I swung the door open, my gaze dropping to the four cats wrapped in Declan's arms.

"Oh my God." I hurried backward, opening the door wider. "Come in, come in."

Hail had started, tiny bullets of ice bouncing off the ground, slowly becoming a dull roar as they pummeled the roof.

Declan's hair and clothes were soaked, his boots covered in mud. A leaf stuck to the side of his face where spots of purple bruising colored a swollen jaw and split lip. Moonshine jumped out of his arms with a hiss. He lowered the kittens to the floor.

"They were huddled next to the door. Mama's got some bite to her."

"Oh, Declan." I grabbed his face. "You're here. Are you okay? I *hate* you. Why did you do that?" Tears ran down my face as the words vomited out. "Are you okay? Your face. Declan, I—"

"I'm fine, but we've got no time for this now, Grey. Do you have flashlights and a radio?"

"Ah, one flashlight, I think. I have a few candles in boxes over there. And I have a radio. But the TV is working—"

"It won't for long. Get the candles." He hurriedly stepped past me. "Get all the blankets in the house and put them in the laundry room."

I had to jog to keep up with his strides into the bedroom. "I've got everything in the tub."

"No—always go to the smallest, most central spot of the house with no windows." Declan yanked the blankets from the tub. "Grey, get those candles. Now."

The calmness in his voice sent a chill up my spine. This storm was serious.

I jogged to the living room, tossing things out of boxes until I found a few old Yankee candles—French Vanilla, my favorite scent.

"Is a tornado coming? Here?" I met Declan in the kitchen and handed him the candles and the radio.

"None had touched down in our area when I left my house three minutes ago, but that doesn't mean they won't. The center of the storm is coming right this way. Get a few bottles of water."

I grabbed the bottles as he continued.

"We've got a few more rounds after this one too. We're in for a hell of a night."

"Oh my God."

"Let's make it through this one first. Welcome to springtime in the South."

The electricity flickered but stayed on as we stepped into the laundry room.

"Stand back."

Declan yanked the electrical cords from the socket, pulled the washer away from the wall, and dragged it across the small room, allowing a small space between the dryer and the floor-to-ceiling cabinetry. He angled the washer in front of the space, closing us in almost completely.

A large crack of a branch sounded somewhere in the distance. Our eyes met.

"Crawl in. Now."

"The cats—"

"Are fine. They're under the bed." Declan checked the batteries and clicked on the radio, dialing into the local station. "They're smarter than you think. They'll be fine."

I dropped to my hands and knees and crawled into the tiny space, and Declan followed suit. Sitting on the floor, I pulled my knees up to my chest and scooted as far as I could into the corner. Declan angled himself in front of me, pressing his back against the washing machine. My entire body was enclosed—to my left, a thick wood cabinet, to my right, Declan and the dryer, and in front of us, the washing machine.

I glanced up at the cabinets on the wall. If they fell, they'd fall onto the tops of the machines, sparing our lives. Declan had built us a little shelter.

I was safe.

I looked at him, looking at me. We stared at each other a moment, the world going to hell around us.

He opened his arms, and I didn't hesitate. I turned my body, scooted backward, and leaned my back against his chest, the back of my head on his shoulder. Two thick, strong arms wrapped around me like a security blanket.

We sat together in silence, peering at the thin slit of light between the dryer and washer, waiting out the first round of storms. The radio faded in and out with warnings to take cover.

For a girl raised in the North, where tornados are few

and far between, the word *terrifying* doesn't even cover what we went through that night.

Once the winds lessened to tropical-storm levels, Declan gave my arm two quick squeezes. "I think we're good for now."

"That was it?"

"Yeah. The worst of a storm like that usually lasts under five minutes."

"There's more coming?"

"Yes."

"When?"

"Soon. Let's get out of here and check the radar."

The next two hours, we hunkered down in the laundry room during the worst of the storms, and spent every second otherwise placing buckets throughout the house to catch the countless leaks from the roof. *Get new roof,* was immediately pushed to the top of my to-do list.

Moonshine and her kittens remained huddled together under the bed, sparing us hisses as we passed. Despite her badass demeanor, I think she was scared too.

I'd never seen anything like it.

Limbs as large as kayaks had been tossed from trees, and leaves and twigs beat repeatedly against the windows before spiraling to the ground. Wind pummeled the four walls of the cabin, whistling through the thinnest cracks with eerie, ghostly sounds. The door to the second floor slammed shut a few times, planks of hardwood groaning against the relentless wind outside.

The last storm struck after midnight, a fury of wind and hail as large as golf balls. I cringed to think what Declan's truck looked like. The first flash of lightning took out the electricity, leaving the house as black as ink.

Never in my life had I been so grateful to not be alone.

Safe in the laundry room, Declan and I waited out the storm, undoubtedly the worse one yet. Finally, we emerged, hand in hand, and ventured into the kitchen.

The drop in temperature had me turning on the heater, only to discover it wasn't working. Another thing to add to the list.

Declan clicked on his flashlight and scanned the room. We walked to the windows, and when he shone the light outside, I gasped at the mess in the darkness. If not a tornado, surely a hurricane had blown through.

The yard was littered with branches and leaves. A rake lay cracked in half, a shovel next to it, neither of which belonged to me. A plastic bag fluttered in the wind from its perch high in a tree. And stretched across the length of the yard was the dead tree that had fallen with the first storm.

It was a mess.

I opened the back door, took a few steps back, and watched as Moonshine and her babies emerged from the bedroom and darted outside.

"Do you need to check your house?" I asked Declan as I closed the door.

"No. It's fine. Like this, I'm sure."

"Minus the leaks," I grumbled.

"We'll get it fixed. I can patch the spots until you're in a place where buying a new roof is manageable. They're not cheap. Light the candles. I'll empty the buckets, then I'm going to check the outside."

The radio had switched back to its regularly scheduled program—*Late-Night Lounge with Kandy Cane*. The house smelled like warm vanilla from the candles, with a hint of rain wafting in from outside.

I was setting the last candle on the fireplace mantel when Declan walked inside, clumps of mud falling off his boots, specks of raindrops in his hair.

"Everything okay?"

He nodded, wiping his boots on the welcome mat. "Aside from limbs and that tree that'll need to be taken care of, everything's in one piece. We're lucky."

"How's your truck?" I wrinkled my nose.

His grunt confirmed my suspicions that the hail had turned it into Swiss cheese.

Declan crossed the room and gathered the logs that he —thankfully—had the foresight to bring inside the day before, probably while I was sleeping. I knelt beside him as he stacked them in the fireplace, then handed him the lighter.

We sat in silence as the fire caught, the tension in the air thicker than the smoke snaking up the chimney.

"This fire will last you until morning."

The implication felt like a brick in my stomach. Was he leaving?

I wanted to ask him to stay, but the words stuck in my throat. Truth was, I didn't know what to say at that moment. About the fight, and *our* fight. About the new, aggressive, angry side I'd seen of him. The side I never, ever wanted to see again.

Declan stood and took a step back, his expression stoic. "I'm sorry."

With that, he turned and walked to the door.

"Wait." I surged off the floor.

He froze, his hand on the knob, but didn't turn.

"Declan, I don't know what happened tonight, but it's

something I know I never want to see again. I also know that I don't want you to leave."

"Are you asking me to stay, Grey?" His voice was low, spent.

I could imagine what getting into a physical fight did to your energy level, not to mention hunkering down for hours anticipating a tornado that never came.

"Yes. I want you to stay. Please stay."

His hand dropped from the knob. He turned toward me, his body concealed in shadows, the low hum of the radio in the background the only sound in the room.

"I have a temper, Grey. I do. I've got it under control, but it's there. And I'm sorry you had to see it tonight. I truly am. But if Lucas hurts you again, or if any man causes you harm —ever—you *will* see it again. Do you understand?"

"Yes." My voice came out in a whisper.

"And if you allow Lucas to touch you again, in any way, I'm gone."

"Okay," I whispered. "Declan, come here."

He stared at me for a lifetime, my heart beating faster and faster with each passing second.

Finally, Declan took the first step, then the next.

48

"Why him, Grey?" Declan asked as he met me in front of the fireplace.

"He made me forget."

"And me?"

"You make me address."

"Forgetting is easier than addressing."

"Maybe, but trying to forget is what got me into this mess in the first place. Addressing is what I need."

"I can never give you the things he can, Grey."

"I don't want the things he can give me. I'm going to pick myself up and do it *my* way. I'm going to make my own money. Again. And if that poor little girl from upstate New York still holds a light inside me, I'm going to make a boatload of it. *My. Way.*"

Declan scrubbed his hand over his mouth, squinting into the fire as if carefully choosing his next words.

"When I saw those scratches, Grey . . . the emotions—rage, I guess—that overcame me was nothing I'd ever experienced before. And that's saying a lot. But it was more than that. Something snapped in me more than anger. A protectiveness, a primal need to protect what was mine—only you aren't mine. And that made me even angrier."

Questions gathered on the tip of my tongue but I bit them back, knowing Declan didn't open up like this often. I wanted to hear it all.

"You're right," he said. "Something was wrong with me when you pulled up with the cookies."

He scrubbed his hand over his mouth and groaned with frustration as if it physically pained him to talk about his feelings.

"Listen, Grey, I'm used to running the show. I live by myself. I have no kids. I run my own business, where I spend over ten hours a day, seven days a week. I've created a decent life for myself doing what I want, when I want. I've had plenty of women in my life, wouldn't call them girlfriends, but the truth is—I'm not good when things start to get heavy. I like my pace, my life, and so I keep it that way."

"In case you turn out to be like your father," I said softly, venturing a guess. "In case you find yourself in another marriage like you witnessed while growing up. Declan, look at me." When he didn't, I put my hand on his arm. "You're living in a bubble, not letting anyone in. Out of fear."

"Says the woman who left everything and bought a house in the middle of nowhere."

"It's different. You know that. You haven't let a woman into your life because you're scared to. You've seen how messed up relationships can be. How they can screw up someone's life."

"Exactly. I'm a walking example of that, what with my temper and my lack of a family. But, Grey, what I'm trying to say here is that I started seeing it all with you. My future—with you in it—a family. Children. Everything." He shook his head as if the idea was unbelievable to him. "I can see it all with you, with no basis whatsoever."

"Well, thanks a lot." I smiled.

"I don't mean it like that. I mean, why are you different from any other woman that's walked into my garage?"

"I don't have tattoos."

"You will."

The ghost of a smile crossed his face before quickly falling away again. The fire hissed and popped in front of us.

"Last night," he said, "I watched you sleep and thought about this the entire time. Why you? Why do you have me throwing off my routine, bending over backward to help you? Why you? Why the hell am I suddenly questioning my retirement plan, trying to figure out how I could make more money, and having visions of playing catch with my son in the backyard? And then it hit me. The tug."

"The tug?"

"You've heard people say, 'when you know, you just know'? I always thought that was for weak, naive idiots who were searching for anything other than the monotony of their own boring lives. People who were trying to justify something."

"Do you still believe that?"

"Not since I met you. *You.* You're the reason why I've lost my mind. You're the reason I imagine a future with family and children. It's simply *you.*" He sighed, took my hand, and pulled me to him. "But, Grey, the thought of you leaving town after you renovate this house . . . The knife in my gut that happens every time I think about that is enough for me to end whatever is starting between us."

"Run from it, you mean." I squeezed his hand. "Declan, you've been with me since the moment Brianna gave me that serenity bear, decades ago. The path was already mapped out. Think about it. Why here? Of all the places I could've run to, why here? The tug."

Glancing down for a moment, I chose my words carefully.

"I'm scared too. Declan, I'm scared that I'm not strong enough to make the changes I need to be a better person for you. I'm scared I'm going to start drinking again. I'm scared I'm going to be sober for ten years, then all of a sudden fall off the wagon. Would you leave me? I'm scared of you hurting me. I'm scared of your temper. I'm scared of you leaving me if the going gets rough. I'm scared of you cheating on me."

Tears swam in my eyes.

"I'm scared that my body might not be capable of having children. I'm scared to be alone for the rest of my life . . . But then I remember what you told me—everything you want is on the other side of fear."

In the background, Kandy Cane introduced the next song in her lineup, followed by the slow beats of Elvis's "Can't Help Falling in Love."

"Declan," I said softly as he wiped the tear from my cheek. "If I fuck up, will you stand by me?"

"Grey, if I fuck up, will you stand by me?"

"Yes."

"Yes."

"If I can't have your children, will you stay with me?"

He tucked a strand of hair behind my ear, his gaze dropping to my lips. "Yes," he whispered.

"If I—"

"Grey. Dance with me."

He wrapped one arm around my waist and lifted my hand in his. Our bodies molded together, swaying with the beat of one of the greatest love songs of all time.

Declan leaned into my ear, warm breath against heated skin. "Shall I stay," he whispered the lyrics in my ear. "Would it be a sin? If I can't help falling in love with you . . ."

Goose bumps ran over my skin as we swayed together, a warm tingle settling in my heart.

"Declan." I looked up at him, tears swimming in my eyes. "Take me to bed."

49

Devouring each other, we stumbled into the bedroom, leaving a trail of clothes in our wake.

Declan clumsily set the candle he'd grabbed from the fireplace mantel on the dresser, leaving it dangerously close to the edge. A golden glow of flames danced on the ceiling as we fell onto the bed, kissing, kissing, kissing.

In nothing but my bra and panties now, I wrapped my legs around his bare waist, his undone jeans barely hanging onto his hips.

I thrust my hips against him, needing to be closer. Needing to all but crawl inside him. His fingers threaded through my hair as mine tiptoed down his back.

Kissing, kissing, kissing.

His lips left mine as he pulled back, his chest heaving. Dread—despair—pulled at his face.

"What?" I asked, breathless.

"I can't." He pulled further away from me.

"No. Yes, you can. Please. Yes, yes, you can."

I had no clue what he was talking about, but I didn't care. At that moment, the man could have blurted a murder confession, and I wouldn't have asked questions. I wanted him inside me. Right then, nothing else mattered.

"I'm not . . ." With a groan, Declan shook his head and pushed off of me to stand at the side of the bed. "I can't, Grey."

And then it hit me.

"Oh, Declan." I breathed out, lifting onto my elbows. I nodded to the signed divorce papers on the dresser. "It's done. Today. I just received the papers. I'm not married anymore."

His brows lifted. He snatched the papers from the dresser and scanned them in the candlelight. My heart pounded as he skimmed the words, then looked at me with a spark hotter than the flame dancing behind him.

"It's done." His voice was low, husky.

"Yes." I smiled. "I'm a single woman."

The papers were tossed into the air, raining down around him as he crossed to the bed, his gaze fixed on mine.

"No, you're not." He crawled on top of me, pinning me with an intensity that froze me in place. "You're mine," he whispered.

Lips met mine again, feverishly now, demanding, as if to prove to me how much I was now his. To show me how he treated what was his.

His.

Fingertips walked down the side of my rib cage, gripping the straps of my thong and pulling it down. I flicked the thong off the tip of my toe as Declan slid a hand around my back, deftly undoing my bra. The silk tickled against my peaked nipples as he pulled it away. The air around me was ice cold compared to the heat between us.

A thick arm wrapped around my back and with a smooth yank, he pulled me farther up the bed, my heels dragging along the soft sheets until he placed me where he saw fit. I was like a rag doll under him. Submissive. Willing.

His.

Shadows from the candlelight flickered on the walls as he took my nipple into his mouth, one hand cupping the back of my head. My hair was caught, fisted between his fingers, as the other hand trailed down my stomach. I was pinned in the most glorious way.

Lips made their way down my stomach, past my navel, settling onto the inner crease of my thigh. The scruff from his jaw against my skin made me squirm on the sheets.

Declan lifted my knees and pushed my legs open, exposing my most private place to him. I squeezed my eyes shut in both exhilaration and with a touch of embarrassment. The man had seen my soul, and now he was seeing my body.

His face disappeared between my legs, a puff of warm breath against my inner lips sending my pulse hammering.

Then he kissed me there. A warm, slick wetness slid over my already tingling skin, lightly, teasing a moment before he devoured me with the same hunger as his kisses. Frenzied, starving.

"Oh my God . . ." I fisted the sheets in my hands, searching for an anchor as his tongue penetrated me.

As if separate from my body, my knees sank open, widening for him, opening every inch of me to him.

With his tongue licking my folds, his fingers danced inside me, his thumb pressing against my clit as soft, warm, wet pressure circled over the swollen nub.

Every sensor in my body came to life in a drum-like throb between my legs.

"Declan," I whispered again, fighting the orgasm. But it was too late.

I screamed out as the sensation ripped through me, wave after wave, under his mouth. He drank me in, sucking me with each thrust of my hips.

When I finally opened my eyes, he was watching me, the rise and fall of my chest, the slightest move of my fingers, in awe, as one might when they uncovered the Holy Grail.

A soft smile crossed my face.

"We're not done," he told me.

"Yes, sir."

His lips quirked.

Not bothering to close my legs, I watched him lift off the bed, slashes of golden flames across his bare chest as he slid off his jeans, then his boxer briefs. His erection sprang out of the boxers, long, thick, and hard. Intimidating.

My breath caught.

"Come here." The words were spoken before even filtering through my head.

Declan closed the few feet between us, his tall, thick body shadowing the room. I leaned up, grabbing at him as he crawled onto the bed. Lifting onto my knees, I wrapped my hands around his neck, kissing, feeling a fresh rush of wetness below.

He pressed my shoulders in an attempt to lay me down again.

"No." I shifted, pressing his shoulders in return. "Your turn."

He blinked, then smirked as I lowered him onto his back, my fingertips sweeping over the ripples of his six-pack.

With my eyes on him, I took him into my mouth in long, slow strokes, watching the fire ignite as he watched me back. Hands gently gripped my head, his fingers sifting through my hair.

Yes, I'm his.

He guided me softly back and forth, as he wanted. Although I literally had him by the balls, the control he still demanded turned me on like nothing else.

I began to throb. Declan was all man. Alpha in every way.

Mine.

I pulled away and crawled on top of him, hovering over his erection, positioning the tip at my opening. Looking down on him, a queen above her servant, I inserted a finger between my legs, then smoothed the wetness from my orgasm over my inner lips and onto the tip of his head.

He groaned loudly and gripped my breasts, squirming beneath me.

"You ready?" I asked.

"Yes."

I lowered onto him, closing around him like a sheath.

"*Fuck,* Grey." His grip shifted to my hips.

I exhaled, my face squeezing with a twinge of pain as he stretched me farther than I'd ever gone.

"Are you okay?"

Biting my lip, I nodded, but was held in place with his grip on my hips. He lifted me and then very slowly lowered me, lifted again, then slowly lowered a bit farther, easing me into it. My weight released in his hands as he guided me again.

I couldn't speak, my breath taken as he filled every inch of my body, the sensation sending tingles rippling over my skin.

Then the pain flittered away.

Gripping his chest, I moved with him, sinking into it, the gentle curve of his erection sliding against my G-spot. And that was it—an animalistic rush of need overtook me. I rode him in long, smooth strokes, goose bumps spreading over my body. He moved under me, meeting each thrust, his springy hair tickling my clit with each wave of motion.

Faster, we rode together, faster, my breasts bouncing, my breath hitching.

"Oh fuck, Grey."

He released a hand from my waist and pressed his thumb against my clit. Lightning shot through me.

"Declan . . ."

Our eyes met.

My heart thundered. Tears filled my eyes.

I screamed his name as we shattered together.

50

I awoke naked, in Declan's arms, with a beam of sunlight warming my face.

The scent of the fireplace lingered in the chilly air around us as Declan's fingertips slowly drifted down my thigh. A smile came to my face. My body was languid, sated, beautifully sore in all the right places. From him.

Declan.

My man.

My *everything.*

"Good morning." His voice was gravelly against my ear, sending a shot of heat between my legs.

"Morning."

I felt his smile against the back of my head.

"How are you?"

"Couldn't be better."

"Yeah?" He wrapped an arm around me and squeezed.

"Yeah. Except I might need to learn how to form a pair of crutches out of two branches."

Declan burst out laughing, then began massaging my very sore hips. "How about coffee first?"

"No, *that*," I said, referring to the massage that was already beginning to turn me on. "A few more minutes of *that*."

The hip massage turned into kissing, then turned into a seven a.m. simultaneous orgasm.

Afterward, I said, "Now I'm ready for coffee."

"That makes two of us. Stay." Declan kissed my temple. "Take your time. I'll get it going."

I washed up quickly in the shower, a little ice cold to bring me back to life and out of my euphoric daze. When I stepped out of the bedroom, the smell of sizzling bacon made my mouth water. Nothing like an evening of multiple orgasms to increase the appetite, apparently.

In nothing but a pair of boxer briefs, Declan danced to Lionel Richie's "Easy Like Sunday Morning" while flipping a pair of eggs in the skillet—sunny-side up, of course. Two pieces of bread popped up from the toaster as I wrapped my arms around the back of him.

Declan turned and kissed my forehead. "Sit."

"Yes, sir."

He wiggled his eyebrows—*he likes that*—then refocused on the gourmet breakfast he was whipping up in my kitchen.

I sat at the table, gazing out at the woods. No storm that morning. A crystal-clear sapphire-blue sky stretched for miles without a cloud. Beams of sunlight shot through the trees, dappling the dewy grass. Despite the litter from the storm, it was gorgeous. Declan had opened a window, allowing a fresh, warm breeze to drift though the kitchen.

A beautiful spring morning to start a beautiful day.

Or so I thought.

I was served coffee, and minutes later, enough food to feed an army of kittens. Declan settled in comfortably across from me and dug into his breakfast without preamble.

I was relieved we weren't going to talk about "us," and what happened between us last night. It was too early for heavy conversation like that.

There was something about Declan's easygoing nature, the way he innately avoided drama or making something bigger than it should be, that eased every nerve in my body. It set the tone for the day. And I realized, as I sat there watching him eat, I could very easily get used to that.

Declan Montgomery was like a drug. The smoothest, sweetest, most calming drug.

"So," I said, biting into a piece of warm toast slathered with butter. "What's on the agenda today?"

"I'm going to get up on your roof and check those leaks—"

"*After* work."

He eyed me over a forkful of eggs. "Fine. Yes, ma'am. After work then. So, work, work on your car—should be done soon—then you. All you. That's the agenda. Let's plan yours."

I glanced over my shoulder at the *Studs-N-Spurs* calendar hanging on the wall. "I don't think I have an appointment to rip my guts out today, so I think I'll work on the house in the morning, then on my oil project this afternoon. Then," a seductive smirk crossed my lips, "work on you. All you."

"Solid plan. I'll get a few quotes on a new roof," he said, already on to the next step. "A buddy of mine can do it cheap. You should meet his wife. She could definitely use some of that relaxing lavender oil."

We fell into our usual easy conversation while we sat at

the makeshift dining table, eating breakfast together. It felt good. Comfortable. Natural.

But most of all, it felt right.

After breakfast, Declan insisted on another walk-through of my property to inventory the damage in the early morning light. I cleared the kitchen while watching him from the window—and decided now was the time.

After wiping my hands on a dish towel, I grabbed Violet, my lavender bush from my nightstand, and carried her outside.

"I didn't realize you potted one inside."

"This is mine. I brought it from New York."

He tilted his head, sensing a story. "Yeah?"

"Yeah. I . . ." My words caught, and I swallowed deeply. "I'd like to plant her outside."

He nodded, his eyes squinting, but he didn't push. That was the thing about Declan. He knew when to press, and when to let it go.

"Good time to do that," he said evenly.

"Yeah, that's what I thought. I . . . simply got a tugging to do it now. *Right* now."

Smiling, he nodded. "Garden tools?"

"In a box, under the deck."

He disapproved of this, I could tell, but didn't say anything. Seconds later, we were knee-deep in mud, securing my lavender plant into the ground at the top of what soon would be a pebbled walkway that led to the cliff.

I stepped back, tears burning my eyes, a smile on my face as I looked at Violet, no longer confined in a tube of plastic. Now she was a part of nature, where she would thrive, prosper, and become one with the earth.

It was the first time I felt closure from my miscarriage.

After a long kiss—and some extremely inappropriate

groping—I waved from the driveway as I saw Declan off to work.

~

I spent the morning engrossed in Gréyce, the new official name of my essential oil project. But my focus repeatedly wandered to Emma's niece's pending baby, and what I could offer a new mommy.

Baby products. I couldn't get them off my mind.

Although a bit disconcerting, I went with it, researching, scribbling, creating. Losing myself in a hobby that was undoubtedly turning into a business.

By lunchtime, I'd solidified the recipe for baby balm and soothing wipes, and got started on making the oils. One pleasant side effect of having an essential oil distillery in your kitchen is that your entire house smells like lavender. Fresh, clean, energizing.

I'd refrained from texting Declan, in an effort not to distract him from the work he had to do. I hoped he'd spend the entire day catching up on everything he'd let go while taking care of me. When he hadn't texted me either, I assumed he was doing exactly that. It made me happy. Normal routines beginning to take shape.

I felt carefree, relaxed, light on my feet, and decided now was as good a time as ever to refocus on the master bedroom that I'd been avoiding since Lucas scored my bare back with his fingernails.

After checking the lavender that was boiling away in the distillery, I took a deep breath and walked into the bedroom. My gaze landed on the closet, and the bad vibes I'd felt the day before returned in an instant.

Maybe if I just cleaned up a bit . . .

After plucking the broom from where it was leaning against the wall, I stepped into the half-demolished closet and began sweeping, sifting through the mess I'd made during my many emotional breakdowns since arriving in Berry Springs.

I was midway through my sweeping when a spider dropped in front of my face. Squealing like a pig, I stumbled backward, my back bouncing off the bare studs of the closet.

I waved the broom wildly in the air until I was sure the spider was wrapped in the bristles. Then I assessed, examining the swath of spiderwebs in the upper corner, dozens of the nasty things that I hadn't noticed before.

Frowning, I poked at them with the broom, then froze when I spotted a dingy flash of whiteness against the dark.

An envelope.

Another letter.

My stomach dipped, and something deep inside told me to leave it alone. To not touch it.

To run away.

I didn't.

But I should have.

51

The Final Letter

I killed her.

I actually fucking killed someone.

I can't go back, I've realized. That single decision has changed my life. I crossed a line, crossed over to a dark place that only few have walked.

Edmund Kemper.

David Alan Gore.

I'm now one of them.

It wasn't hard. You hear about all these stories of people murdering someone, and it sounds so crazy. But the thing is, it isn't hard. You just do it.

It was different from the cat. I didn't have time to work on her. People are definitely smarter than animals and have a much stronger will to survive.

I only wanted to kiss her. That's all. But she laughed at me like the snobby bitch she is. Was, I should say.

I snapped. Different from the other times.

I grabbed her, and she jerked away. Then I hit her, hard, across the face.

And that's when I saw that first flash of fear in her eyes, like the cat. I think that was the first time she'd ever been hit. I liked that I did it.

From that moment on, everything kind of became a blur.

I lunged for her, wrapping my arms around her. She started screaming, and I panicked. There was no going back then. She'd tell her stupid dad that I hit her and he'd tell mine, and I wasn't going to face that bullshit again.

And then it just happened.

I got her on the ground. Wrapping my hands around her neck, I strangled her until her eyes bulged from her head and her legs quit kicking under me. It was so fast. Too fast. Too easy. Not as fun as the cat.

I need to do better. Plan better.

My first instinct was to run. Maybe steal a car and cross over to Mexico. Buy a new identity. But I'm too young for that. People would notice and ask questions. So my other option was to cover it up, knowing I have a secret that no one else will discover. A secret that maybe one day I'll share with the world, but not today.

I chose to cover it up.

I left her hidden in the woods while I put together a plan. I found a cinderblock and rope in the barn, and tied the block to her ankles. I waited until dusk to drag her body through the woods and dump her in a nearby pond. I figured the water will wash any evidence away, if her body is ever found.

You want to know the crazy thing? I kind of don't care if she's found. If I get caught, they'll send me away to juvie or put me in a padded room. I don't care. It's not like I love my life anyway.

There was a snake swimming along the shoreline as I pushed her off the dock. He looked at me as he passed. We stared at each other, a quiet acknowledgment of the secret between us.

Eat her, *I thought as he dipped under the water. I imagined it, the snake slowly eating away her skin.*

I masturbated right there on the dock, shooting my load into the water as a final fucking good-bye.

A kiss would have been easier, wouldn't it, bitch?

It's thrilling to know she's there. To know I did it.

I burned myself after. I lit a cigarette that I stole from my dad, took a few hits, then dotted the burning tip down the scar on my hand, like a snake slithering down my thumb, like the snake in the water. I dotted an eye on either side of the burn.

A snake to remember the day.

The day I fucking did it.

The day I killed Anna Hopkins.

52

The letter fell from my hands.

Like a snake slithering down my thumb.

I gasped, the birthmark on Lucas's hand flashing vividly behind my eyes. The snake I'd noticed when he'd bent me over my kitchen counter our first night together.

Only it wasn't a birthmark, was it?

Suddenly everything coalesced, like jagged puzzle pieces clicking together.

One: The snake on Lucas's thumb wasn't a birthmark—it was cigarette burns. I closed my eyes, picturing it in my head as clear as day. The skin was a pale pink, raised in certain spots. Not a damn birthmark—a burn mark. How could I have been so stupid?

Two: I recalled the way Lucas seemed to know his way around my cabin during his subsequent visit. He'd been here before.

Three: I remembered Declan's story about Lucas's father and his, and that Lucas's father did business in the area. This meant that at some point, surely Lucas had been in

Berry Springs too. In *this* house. With Bonnie? But why? How? What was the connection?

My stomach rolled as I pictured Lucas in my house.

He'd only been a boy when he killed Anna. Had there been more?

Gripping the side of the closet for support, I picked up the letter from the floor and read it once more, my brain struggling to understand the weight of the paper in my hand.

A murder confession.

In my hands, I held a murder confession.

Lucas Covington was the writer of the letters hidden in my house.

Lucas Covington murdered Anna Hopkins thirty years ago.

A gust of air swept up the back of my neck, icy fingertips tapping up my spine.

Letter in hand, I turned toward the doorway where no human stood, but a spirit drifted under the arched trim, staring directly at me. I couldn't see her—I could *feel* her. As sure as my next breath, I knew I was not alone in that room. And I knew I was with Anna Hopkins.

Anna Hopkins was the spirit with unfinished business who haunted my home.

I wasn't afraid.

I was simply told what to do.

Stepping out of the closet, I gripped the letter in my hand with sweaty fingertips. I stared at the entryway for a moment, then nodded.

"Fly away," I whispered. "I've got it from here, little Anna. You can finally rest. Fly away."

My eyes drifted closed and I inhaled, goose bumps

rippling over my skin. When I opened my eyes again, she was gone. I knew it.

The air was thin. Vacant. Calm.

Anna was gone.

Tears filled my eyes. "Yes, I've got it from here," I whispered.

After gathering the other letters from the fireplace mantel, I strode through the living room, plucked my phone from the counter, and with trembling hands, dialed the number.

"Berry Springs Police Department. How can I help you?"

"This is Grey Dalton." My voice shook, the rattled tone of it in the silence spiking my pulse. "I live at 1314 Rattlesnake Road. I . . ." I paused, struggling with how to begin. "I have kind of a weird story I need to speak an officer about."

"Are you in any kind of danger at the moment, Miss Dalton?"

"No."

"Are you alone?"

I looked out the windows, the late afternoon sun hidden behind clouds. "Yes."

"Okay. Let me see if I can get someone on the line for you."

"No. No . . . I think it's best if you send someone out here."

"Ma'am, I'm going to need a bit more from you here. What exactly is going on?"

"I think I know who murdered Anna Hopkins thirty years ago."

After a pause on the other end of the line, the dispatcher said, "Just a minute, ma'am."

Seconds later, a man named Detective Darby was on the

line. Although his voice was young and eager, there was an edge to it, a control that suggested he'd seen more than his age suggested.

Gripping the letter, I stumbled through the story of the letters, and of my history with Lucas, trying to keep it together.

Trying to keep from crumpling to the floor.

53

As I waited, I paced the front porch, the scent of rain thick in the air. Rivers of thick gray clouds moved swiftly across the sky, promising another storm.

One more storm.

My heart raced, my palms sweaty as I paced back and forth, my gaze locked on the bend in my driveway that continued down the hill.

Come on, Detective.

Twice, I'd called Declan with no answer. On the third try, I left him a rambling voice mail that cut off midway through the crazy story that, in all honesty, I wasn't sure he'd believe in the first place.

She's drinking again, I assumed he'd think.

He knew I'd found letters in the closet, but now I told him the whole story, and of the last one that confessed that the man whose father destroyed Declan's family was also the boy who'd killed Anna Hopkins—a murder that had been linked to Declan for three decades, leaving a dark cloud over the Montgomery name. Lucas Covington, the same man who Declan knew I'd allowed to have the most sacred part of me. *Twice.*

I imagined Declan's head metaphorically exploding as he listened to the voice mail. But it had to be done. It was all out now.

There was no turning back.

I startled at the sound of tires on gravel and turned with a sigh of relief—although it wasn't the police, and it wasn't Declan.

My heart pounded as Lucas's red Porsche sped up the drive.

Did he know?

No, it had only been five minutes since I'd hung up with the detective. There was no way Lucas knew.

On legs as weak as twigs, I mechanically began making my way to the middle of the porch as the car door opened.

He doesn't know, he doesn't know, he doesn't know. Be cool.

I almost didn't recognize him as he stepped out of the car. His left eye was black and swollen shut, the perfect lines of his jaw marred with purple bruises. A nasty gash split the corner of his mouth. Visions of Declan's fist pummeling into Lucas's face flashed behind my eyes.

Instead of his usual designer duds, he was wearing a faded T-shirt, jeans, and running shoes.

The passenger seat of his car was empty. No Edward. Lucas was alone.

My heart hammered, my thoughts colliding with accusations, questions, and finally doubt.

What if I was wrong?

Had I done the right thing?

"I'm leaving town in an hour." His voice was hoarse. The car door slammed, echoing in the silence of the woods. "I came by to say I was sorry."

I took a silent inhale. *Be cool.*

"Sorry for what?" I asked, my voice wavering, riddled with nerves. I swallowed to clear my throat, my gaze flickering over his shoulder.

Come on, Detective.

"For everything," Lucas said. "For making you uncomfortable. For yelling at Declan. Everything."

I inched backward, closer to the front door as he walked up the porch steps.

"Can I come in for a minute?"

I looked over his shoulder again, then back at a pair of irises as black as tar.

"No." I shook my head. "I think it's best for both of us if we keep our distance."

Something flashed behind his eyes. Something that made my skin prickle.

I only wanted to kiss her . . .

I took another step closer to the door.

"It's been a long time since I've been here," he said quietly, as if lost in memories.

This wasn't the Lucas I'd met. This Lucas was off. Something was off.

My heart hammered against my rib cage as I focused on his every move, every twitch, every breath, ready to react to whatever was about to come.

His eyes found mine again, and in the eeriest, most emotionless tone, he said, "I want the letters, Grey."

My heart stopped, and I swallowed hard. "What letters?"

"The letters I saw on your fireplace mantel the first day I met you."

Air escaped me, the scorching heat of panic zinging up my spine.

All I could think was *run. Get inside, lock the door. Run.* I knew then, at that moment, that every second counted.

"Grey." Lucas took a step forward, his eyes burning with intensity. "Give me the letters."

My gaze frantically darted over his shoulder again, my ears searching for the sound of the vehicle that wasn't coming. I had to think of something.

"Why? Why do you want them?" I played dumb, hoping he didn't realize that I'd put the pieces of the puzzle together.

He squinted at me, assessing my bluff. "They belong to me."

My chest began heaving, despite my effort to remain calm.

"Okay." I nodded. "Let me go get them."

I edged back, my fingertips searching for the doorknob behind me.

He stepped forward.

"No," I said quickly—much too quickly. "I'll be right back."

Finally, my hand gripped the cold brass of the knob. The door popped open as he lunged forward.

I stumbled back, dropping to the floor and out of his grasp. I flipped over and spun out on the welcome mat, desperately grasping at anything to propel me forward. I found my footing and lunged ahead. My pulse roared as I scaled the back of the couch, landing seconds before he tackled me.

I fought. Like a wild animal, I fought, even when I noticed the switchblade in his hand.

Focus on his wounds, a voice whispered in my ear.

I pulled my knee up, slamming it into his rib cage. The

brief moment of his shock allowed me to shove the palm of my hand into his swollen eye.

Lucas howled like a wounded dog.

I scrambled across the floor, stumbled, then took off across the den. Gasping for breath, I took the steps to the second floor two at a time. When I reached the landing, I slammed the door behind me and locked it.

Heavy footfalls ascended the staircase as I darted to the window.

Terrifying, incoherent screams and shouts vibrated through the thin walls while the door bounced on its hinges. My hands trembled as I wrestled with the window latch.

The door bowed against the rage pummeling it from the other side.

I had seconds.

My fingernail ripped as the latch gave, and with a grunt, I shoved up the window, kicked out the screen, and watched it tumble twenty-eight feet to the ground below.

Gripping the sides of the window, I pulled in a deep breath as I climbed over the windowsill—

"Grey!"

I froze at the voice from somewhere downstairs. *Declan.*

The banging on the door stopped. The screams stopped. The world fell silent.

I held my breath.

Heavy footfalls sounded from downstairs, followed by Lucas's footsteps thumping down the staircase.

Oh shit.

I looked down at the ground, almost thirty feet below, then back at the door, now cracked down the middle. "Shit!"

I pivoted, jumped to the floor, and sprinted across the room as the shouting downstairs began.

Don't kill him, Declan! The single thought suddenly outweighed all else. *Don't kill him, don't kill him, don't kill him . . .*

I flew down the staircase, landing in the den with a stumble just as the blur of two bodies flew out the front door.

"No!" I screamed, sprinting out of the room.

Everything stopped. Absolutely everything.

I froze at my front door, gripping the door frame, staring at Declan pointing a pistol at Lucas's head.

"No," I croaked. "No, Declan."

His finger flexed, beginning to squeeze the trigger.

"No!"

I turned and buried my face in my hands as the gunshot echoed through the trees.

54

Six months later...

A smile crossed my lips as I navigated my BMW up the hill to my driveway. The sun was about to set in a soft band of orange resting on the mountains in the distance. Behind me, a deep indigo sky with pale stars beginning to twinkle.

It was my first autumn in the South, and the colors did not disappointment.

My gaze locked on the blazing red maples as they came into view. Behind them, a forest of bright oranges and yellows that seemed to reflect the setting sun. The nights were turning cooler, the air crisp and fresh.

Autumn was my favorite season here, hands down.

The cabin was lit, a warm golden glow illuminating the windows. My smile widened when I saw Declan's truck parked in its usual spot under the pine.

I rolled the car to a stop, in front of the garage that was

almost finished, and stared at the house a moment, thinking of how much my life had changed in the last six months.

After Declan had fired a warning shot at Lucas, he held him at gunpoint until BSPD arrived on scene. Lucas Covington was arrested and charged with the murder of eight-year-old Anna Hopkins. The story made national news, not only because Lucas was the heir to the Covington hotel fortune, but because of the cutting-edge forensics that were used in the case.

Each letter had been analyzed down to the type of ink that was used, to the brand and batch of paper, to determine the dates that they were written. A forensic handwriting analysis expert had been brought in to link the letters with Lucas's handwriting now to his fifteen-year-old self, using old schoolwork they'd dug up from his private school.

Pandora's box had been ripped open, revealing not only Lucas's struggle with borderline personality disorder, but his mother's as well.

When Lucas had been officially diagnosed as a child, his father, Douglas, didn't handle this well. Some speculated that Douglas didn't want his son's struggles to taint the empire he was rapidly building at that time. Lucas was sheltered, homeschooled, kept out of the public eye, and placed on a cocktail of drugs that he remained on into his adult years.

Not wanting his son out in the world, Douglas pulled him into the family business, but never without a chaperone by his side to ensure he was taking his pills and staying in line. This chaperone was none other than Edward Schultz.

As for the letters—Lucas's father and Bonnie grew up together in Berry Springs, dating off and on until college, when Bonnie left to get her doctorate in psychology. When Douglas was in Berry Springs for business, he would leave

Lucas with Bonnie during the day, as an intense in-home therapy rehab program. This is when Lucas wrote the letters. Bonnie was compensated well—although not well enough to contain the rapidly deteriorating mind of a disturbed fifteen-year-old boy, apparently.

Lucas was currently in a mental hospital, awaiting his trial. Regardless of his conviction, he would very likely remain there for the rest of his life.

Six months had passed, yet some days, it still feels like yesterday.

I wrestled with pulling my luggage in the trunk while my Louboutin heels sank into the earth, throwing off my balance. *Must have rained sometime over the last few days.*

I was surprised Declan didn't meet me at the front door as he usually did after one of my trips. More lately—and more to come now.

Flinging my purse over my shoulder, I dragged my luggage along the driveway, not giving a second thought to dirt. I was tired and exhausted, as I usually was these days after a trip to New York City.

The place drained me every time I went there. Funny how quickly things can change.

The front door was unlocked. The warm scent of fresh bread and something Italian perfumed the air—but the smell wasn't what stopped me in my tracks.

The house was immaculate. Mopped floors gleamed under sparkling windows framing the setting sun in the distance. End tables and counters were dusted, cleaned, organized. Even the wood chips that constantly surrounded the fireplace had been swept away.

Something was up, I immediately decided, considering Declan's definition of cleaning was wiping down the only open space on the counter with a used paper towel.

That's when I noticed the cookie on the floor. An oatmeal cookie, with a little white heart made of icing in the middle, lay in the center of a heart-shaped red napkin. A few feet beyond it was another, then another.

A trail of cookies.

Yep. Something was definitely up.

Grinning like a schoolgirl, I abandoned my luggage and purse at the door, toe-heeled out of my Louboutins, and picked up the first cookie, then the next. Nibbling through grins, I followed the trail into the kitchen where a chai latte in my favorite travel mug sat on the counter—otherwise known as my new favorite "get home from work" drink.

I looked around. The tea was steaming hot, which meant Declan had just made it.

Where was he?

After washing the oatmeal cookie down with a sip of tea—the world's most perfect combination—I continued to follow the trail. It led me through the kitchen, out the back door, over the deck, and onto the lighted pebbled trail Declan had made through the woods months earlier.

A cool breeze swept strands of hair across my face as I maneuvered through the cookies that I wondered how Moonshine and her rapidly growing babies hadn't already discovered. Moonshine and her family had officially become a part of ours. She even let me hold her in my lap now.

A flash of cherry red peeking through the trees caught my eye. More curious than ever, I picked up my pace and stepped onto the cliff.

My jaw dropped.

Beams of the setting sun illuminated the large red tent that had been constructed in the middle of the cliff, surrounded by hundreds of twinkling tea lights.

Nerves and butterflies, or a maybe just a woman's instinct, fought for dominance in my stomach as I passed the last cookie and rounded the tent.

Declan was squatted in front of it, his back to me, his full focus on securing the last strap. Sensing my presence, he stilled and straightened, then stood and turned to me. His eyes twinkled, his smile as magnificent as the setting sun.

My heart pounding, I asked, "What are you up to?"

He didn't answer, simply crossed the rocky ground and swept me into his arms. "Congratulations, baby," he whispered in my ear.

I wrapped my arms around his neck and released a muffled squeal, kicking my feet back as he lifted me into the air. A rush of excitement combined with the scent of Declan gave me an instant shot of energy.

He laughed and spun me around, squeezing hard, then set me down.

"This is so romantic, Declan. Do you remember—"

"Yes. I remember. I suggested sleeping under the stars on this cliff the first time we met. I can't believe we've never done it. But hang on—rewind first. Tell me. Tell me *everything* again."

Smiling, I heaved out a breath, hardly able to believe the last twenty-four hours.

Over the last six months, my hobby project, Gréyce, turned into a full-blown business with its two flagship products, lavender baby balm and soothing lavender baby wipes. Overnight, it seemed, Gréyce became the regional go-to brand for local organic baby products. Southerners were loyal to those in their community, and for that, I'd be forever grateful.

The business skyrocketed when I started a website and began selling nationally. One morning, I awoke to an email from Abby Ross, a former fashion designer turned business mogul, who now owned a wildly successful organic skincare line. She'd seen my brand splashed across social media and ordered my entire catalog of products.

The quality wasn't the only thing that sold her, she said. It was the fact that I had given Abby her first showcase as a struggling designer when I offered her a spotlight feature in my fashion magazine years earlier. She said it was the single thing that launched her career, and it was time to pay it forward.

Abby was interested in buying me out, but I was interested in a partnership.

After several trips to New York to meet with her, then several more to meet with a team of lawyers, Abby and I signed on the dotted line with my commitment to run the essential-oil side of her business.

And the best part was that I could do it all remotely, from my cabin in Berry Springs. I'd have to travel frequently, but I could handle that.

While Declan had been by my side the entire time, he'd let me handle my business, knowing I needed to be in control of it. It was part of my healing, part of my promise to myself as a poor little girl that I would become financially stable someday—on my own.

And I did it.

It's funny how little things, seemingly insignificant at the time, can fall into your path years later.

After I finished giving him the latest updates, Declan

took the tea from my hand, set it down, and hugged me again.

"God, honey, you did it. I am so proud of you."

I lifted my face to the sky, smiling under the waning light.

He set me down. "Ready for the tour?"

"There's more than this?" I motioned to the tent, the candles, the cookies.

Declan took my hand. "Your palace, my queen," he said with gusto, spreading open the flaps of the tent.

"Pizza." I inhaled deeply as the scent wafted out.

"New York-style pizza. Homemade. It's almost as good as my chili."

I lit up from the inside out. "You made me homemade pizza?"

"Figured if you're going to be traveling more, I needed to step up my game. There's nothing New York has to offer that you can't get here."

I dipped my head and stepped inside, soaking it all in. "Oh my God, Declan . . . it's beautiful."

I dropped onto a bed in the center of the massive tent, complete with a thick plaid comforter, sheets, and fluffy white pillows. A covered tray sat to the side, a bottle of alcohol-free champagne chilled on ice, alongside two long-stemmed glasses. Next to that was a warm pizza.

"It's a mattress," I said, beaming as I bounced. "An actual *mattress.* Not a blow-up one."

He winked. "Only the best for my businesswoman."

"Come here."

I threw my arms around his neck as he dropped to his knees. We tumbled onto the mattress. Declan flipped me onto my back and straddled me.

A finger trailed from my forehead, down my face to my cheek, as we stared at each other.

"I love you, Grey. Have since the day I saw you."

"I love you too, Declan. Have since the day I hugged that teddy bear."

He reached into his pocket and pulled out a small red velvet box, and I gasped.

"Marry me, Grey. It's as simple as that. Marry me."

Breathless, speechless, I sat up and pushed him backward, my mouth gaping. Tears filled my eyes.

"Marry me," he said again, his eyes glistening as he swept a strand of hair behind my ear.

He leaned in, his fingertips trailing down my neck.

"Take my hand, Grey," he whispered in my ear. "Take my whole life too. For I can't help falling in love with you."

He opened the box, revealing a princess-cut diamond encircled with glittering purple gemstones.

Lavender.

Tears streamed down my cheeks as he slipped the ring onto my finger. It was a perfect fit.

"Yes," I whispered, my voice trembling. "Yes."

My mouth crushed onto his, wild kisses filled with tears and devotion.

"Make it good," I whispered between kisses. "I'm ovulating."

He chuckled against my lips. "Challenge accepted, Mrs. Montgomery," he whispered back. "Let's make some babies."

I wrapped my arms around my future husband and gazed through the net ceiling at the stars beginning to twinkle in the sky, thinking how lucky I was to have found this man.

The man who accepted me. Accepted all my flaws—and all my independence.

The man who picked me up when I fell.

The man who put me back together and healed my soul.

The man who saved my life.

★ REDEMPTION ROAD ★

Ready for another ride?

Coming Summer 2021...

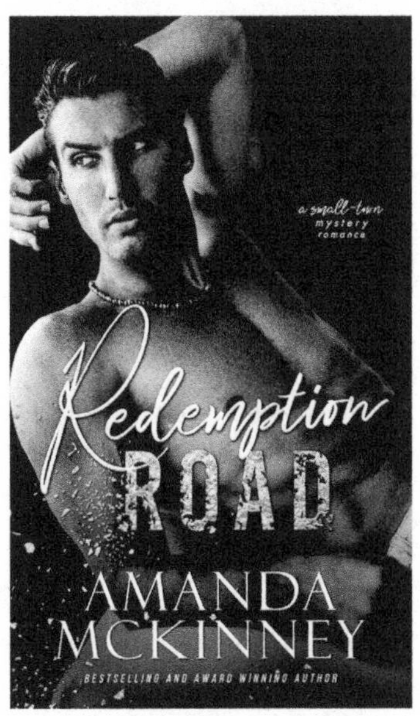

***Redemption:** The act of being saved from sin, error, or evil.*

She waits behind a thicket at the base of the old stone manor. Clutched in her hand is a necklace. A vintage gold locket engraved with secrets, tarnished by guilt, and adorned with three gemstones that link the past to the present, angels to demons—and Rory to her destiny.

They say Christian Locke is a loner, an orphan, a mysterious cowboy the small-town gossips deem an outsider. They tell her to stay away. But Rory can't ignore the connection she feels to the mulish recluse, or the interest he has in the cursed necklace she wears around her neck—gifted by her mother the day she was killed.

Christian says he doesn't believe in fate, but every twist and turn of the locket's story seems to lead her to the same place...

Welcome to Redemption Road.

Your secrets are not safe here.

RESERVE YOUR COPY TODAY

Sign up for my newsletter to be the first to receive details on this emotional and twisted new small-town mystery romance...

♥ *And don't forget to sign up for my exclusive reader group and blogging team!* ♥

📷 *Redemption Road Image Credit:* 📷
Michelle Lancaster
www.michellelancaster.com

STEALS AND DEALS

★LIMITED TIME STEALS AND DEALS★

1. The Creek (A Berry Springs Novel), only **$0.99**
2. Bestselling and award-nominated Cabin 1 (Steele Shadows Security), **FREE**
3. Devil's Gold (A Black Rose Mystery), only **$0.99**

(1) The Creek (A Berry Springs Novel)

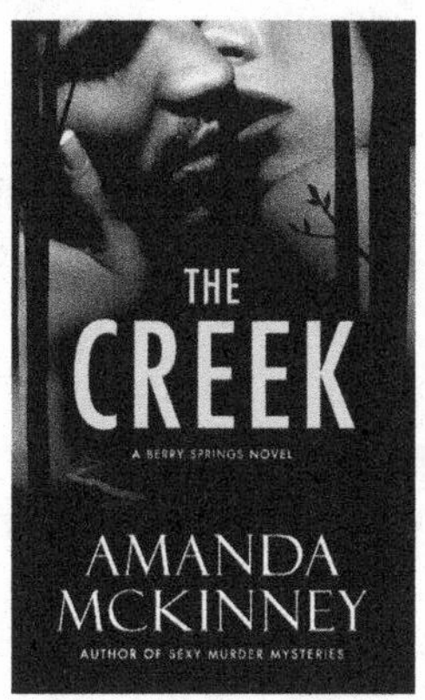

When DNA evidence links Lieutenant Quinn Colson's brother to the scene of a grisly murder, Quinn realizes he'll do anything to keep his brother from returning to prison, even if it costs him his job… and the woman who's stolen his heart.

Get The Creek today for only $0.99

(2) Cabin 1 (Steele Shadows Security)

★2020 National Readers' Choice Award Finalist, 2020 HOLT Medallion Finalist★

Hidden deep in the remote mountains of Berry Springs is a private security firm where some go to escape, and others find exactly what they've been looking for.

Welcome to Cabin 1, Cabin 2, Cabin 3…

Get Cabin 1 for ★FREE★ today

(3) Devil's Gold

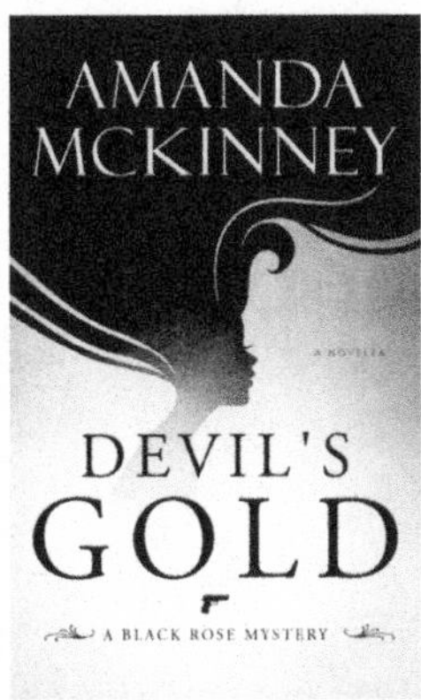

"With fast-paced action, steamy romance, and a good dose of mystery, Devil's Gold is a solid whodunit that will keep you surprised at every turn." -Siobhan Novelties

"...smart, full of energetic thrills and chills, it's one of the best novellas I've read in a very long time." -Booked J

Get Devil's Gold today for only $0.99

Sign up for my Newsletter so you don't miss out on more Steals and Deals! https://www.amandamckinneyauthor.com/contact

ABOUT THE AUTHOR

Amanda McKinney is the bestselling and multi-award-winning author of more than fifteen romantic suspense and mystery novels. She wrote her debut novel, LETHAL LEGACY, after walking away from her career to become a writer and stay-at-home mom. Her books include the BERRY SPRINGS SERIES, STEELE SHADOWS SERIES, and the BLACK ROSE MYSTERY SERIES, with many more to come. Amanda lives in Arkansas with her handsome husband, two beautiful boys, and three obnoxious dogs.

Text **AMANDABOOKS to 66866** to sign up for Amanda's Newsletter and get the latest on new releases, promos, and freebies!

www.amandamckinneyauthor.com

If you enjoyed Rattlesnake Road, please write a review!

THE AWARD-WINNING BERRY SPRINGS SERIES

The Woods (A Berry Springs Novel)

The Lake (A Berry Springs Novel)

The Storm (A Berry Springs Novel)

The Fog (A Berry Springs Novel)

The Creek (A Berry Springs Novel)

The Shadow (A Berry Springs Novel)

The Cave (A Berry Springs Novel)

#1 BESTSELLING STEELE SHADOWS

Cabin 1 (Steele Shadows Security)

Cabin 2 (Steele Shadows Security)

Cabin 3 (Steele Shadows Security)

Phoenix (Steele Shadows Rising)

Jagger (Steele Shadows Investigations)

Ryder (Steele Shadows Investigations)

Rattlesnake Road

★*Redemption Road, Coming Summer 2021*★

Like your sexy murder mysteries with a side of evil witch? Check out THE BLACK ROSE MYSTERY SERIES about three super-rich, independent, badass sisters who run a private investigation company in a creepy, southern town...

Devil's Gold (A Black Rose Mystery, Book 1)
Hatchet Hollow (A Black Rose Mystery, Book 2)
Tomb's Tale (A Black Rose Mystery Book 3)
Evil Eye (A Black Rose Mystery Book 4)
Sinister Secrets (A Black Rose Mystery Book 5)